ABOUT THIS BOOK

Trapped Within a Wish by **Brynn Myers**

For eighteen years, Nathan Wade has searched for answers regarding his father's disappearance. Now, in 1920, he receives a letter from Calla Lily Mircea saying she's in possession of some of his father's belongings in a town called Havenwood Falls. Nathan wonders how a field camera lost on an archeological dig in Egypt could end up in a small town in Colorado, but something draws him in. Nathan takes the leap of faith, only to have his world turned upside down when he finds not only the camera, but a hidden treasure within.

Amani lost everything the day she came of age and her true nature was revealed. Now, having been trapped for eighteen years, her only hope is that someone will save her from the hell she's had to endure. When a handsome stranger inadvertently releases her, the wait is over, and the truth of her imprisonment comes to light.

Nathan and Amani are now bound to one another and determined to piece together the past. Someone wanted her gone, and she and Nathan race to solve the mystery that connects them both before it's too late.

Blood and Damnation by **Belinda Boring**

With the world laid out before him, Marcus St. James enjoyed the many fruits of society, none more so than the women who fell at his feet and lifted their skirts. A few whispered promises and he could have whichever beauty caught his eye. Until the night he led a young gypsy woman into the alleyway, where more than just heated kisses were exchanged.

Knocked unconscious, Marcus awakens to find his companion dead in his arms, her blood screaming for justice. Before he can uncover the truth, her family arrives—hellbent on punishing the person who murdered their kin. Ignoring his pleas of innocence, they curse him to an existence as a blood drinker.

In the wake of death, a new purpose is born, transforming Marcus into a monster. Driven by his thirst for vengeance, he focuses on hunting down the gypsies who destroyed his life. But when an innocent girl finds her way into his fortress, Marcus must decide what the true curse is: a life filled with blood and damnation or one void of love and hope. He'll discover one lasting truth—love can soften even the hardest of hearts. And can also stoke the fires of retribution.

Fated Beginnings by E.J. Fechenda

Ever since he was a young boy, Daniel McCabe and his family have been running to escape his father's past—a past scarred by the cruelty of humans against their kind. Indian reservations, the Japanese internment camps of World War II, and racial segregation only reinforce what he's been taught: humans mistreat those who are different. Fearing the same treatment if his shifter abilities are ever discovered, he keeps to himself and trusts very few. While the war may be over, the 1950s seem to be a time of conformity, and Daniel is anything but a conformist.

After Daniel moves his mom back to Colorado, the only place he has really considered home, a job opportunity brings him to a small town nestled in the Rocky Mountains. Havenwood Falls offers the promise of a new beginning—a chance to help the town grow and to establish a life for himself and for others like him. He even finds his mate.

Colleen Campbell is smart, funny, bold, and beautiful. And human.

Havenwood Falls has everything Daniel has dreamt about, offering a stable future with a woman he could love. But if he can't overcome everything he knows and believes, this fated beginning may already be at its end.

LEGENDS OF HAVENWOOD FALLS VOLUME TWO

A LEGENDS OF HAVENWOOD FALLS COLLECTION

BRYNN MYERS   BELINDA BORING   E.J. FECHENDA

LEGENDS OF HAVENWOOD FALLS BOOKS

Lost in Time by Tish Thawer

Dawn of the Witch Hunters by Morgan Wylie

Redemption's End by Eric R. Asher

Trapped Within a Wish by Brynn Myers

Blood and Damnation by Belinda Boring

Fated Beginnings by E.J. Fechenda

Emeline by Katie M. John

Released From a Curse by Brynn Myers

A Pack of Lies by Kallie Ross

Kiss the Ashes by Desiree Lafawn

Hidden Truths by Colleen Nye

Wrath and Retribution by Belinda Boring

Changing Fate by Char Webster

Also try the signature New Adult/Adult series, Havenwood Falls, and the YA series, Havenwood Falls High

Stay up to date at www.HavenwoodFalls.com

TRAPPED WITHIN A WISH

BRYNN MYERS

~ A Legends of Havenwood Falls Novella ~

Havenwood Falls

Legends

Trapped Within A Wish

BRYNN MYERS

ALSO BY BRYNN MYERS

The Prophecies of The Nine Series
Entasy Book 1
Redemption Book 2

The Jorja Graham Duology
The Life & Death of Jorja Graham
The Echoed Life of Jorja Graham

Falling Out of Focus

Captivated by Crimson

Fairytale Confessions—print only

One Last Con—e-book only

CHAPTER 1

*T*he hallway of New York University bustled with students roaming around—some were on their way to exams, while others were chatting about the upcoming summer break.

In his office on campus, Nathan Wade rifled through term papers, trying to find a student's dissertation on the 42 Laws of Ma'at when the door to his office opened, startling him.

"Is this what you've been waiting for?" Lillian asked as she entered the room.

"I don't know, Ms. Hartman. What is it?" Nathan replied as he continued to shuffle through the stack of papers in his hands.

"Enough with that formal business, young man. There are no students around," Lillian scoffed as she wagged the paper she held in the air. "This came in about an hour and a half ago, but you were teaching, and I didn't think it was important enough to interrupt the class to give it to you," she replied with a sly grin. "And why is he sending telegraphs anyway? Has he forgotten we're in the twentieth century? It is 1920, after all."

Nathan shook his head and chuckled under his breath. "What did Edgar have to say with his antiquated form of communication?"

Lillian reached for the silver chain holding her cheaters and pulled them on to see the words clearer. She read the two words and clicked her tongue in frustration. "Nothing yet."

"Nothing yet, what?"

"That's it. That's all it says." Lillian walked over to her desk and sat down. "I do not know why you continue to pay him to look for your father's satchel—it and the camera are long gone." She shook her head slowly. "I'm sorry. I know that is not what you want to hear, but it's true. It's been eighteen years, son. You have to move past this." Her tone shifted from judgmental to soft as she took off her glasses and let them hang around her neck.

"I can't stop searching and you know why," Nathan said as he stared into the eyes of the woman who'd cared for him after his father's disappearance.

Lillian Hartman was widowed, like his father had been. Before Nathan was born, Lillian and her husband, Charles, had been neighbors and close friends with his parents. When Nathan's mother died of consumption, Lillian became Nathan's surrogate mother. Then, after his father disappeared, she and Charles raised Nathan— gave him a life in lieu of his loss.

When Charles passed away a few years ago, Lillian was in need of a hobby to keep her mind busy. All that unused energy was going to waste, and Nathan was in need of an office assistant, now that he was an associate professor at the university. Lillian was the perfect assistant and the most qualified candidate to manage all of Nathan's pastimes.

"Nathan," Lillian soothed, "the clue to where your father disappeared to is not in that camera. Edgar can search the world over and still conclude what we already know. Sam and the camera are gone."

"I want to know what happened, Lillian. Not knowing is what binds me to this quest."

"But some mysteries will never be unraveled. You simply have to move on."

Nathan bowed his head and whispered, "I know."

"You're better suited spending your energy uncovering the mysteries found in those Egyptian tombs you love so much." She grinned and then threw her hands in the air. "That reminds me. I received notification from Howard Carter's office about an expedition opportunity. I'm not certain how that will work with your current class schedule, though."

Nathan glanced up. "They requested me?"

"Yes," she said, handing him the letter. "Here, read it. It's very complimentary."

"Wow, I didn't expect that," Nathan said as he put on his glasses to read the letter. When he read the last line, he grinned appreciatively. "It is indeed very complimentary, but sadly, I'm going to have to pass on this offer and use my time here to study linguistics in my off time." He sighed. "Maybe they'll ask again, for another dig. I can't imagine there won't be more to come."

"Always wanting to learn more. You always were such a curious boy."

"I received word that new funerary texts have arrived at the Metropolitan Museum of Art. They'll need to be translated, and as you have pointed out, it may do me some good to dive into a distraction."

Lillian picked up a stack of mail from the inbox on the corner of her desk and started to flip through it. As she did, she pulled her glasses back on and examined one envelope with an odd symbol pressed into a wax seal.

"Who uses letter seals anymore?" she mumbled under her breath. "Well, I guess whoever this is from," Lillian said to herself as she reached for her letter opener.

Lillian pulled out the neatly folded letter and read the words, disbelief and shock contorting her face with each word she read.

Dear Mr. Wade,

I'm writing this letter to inform you I am in possession of a camera I believe belongs to you. Inside the top flap of the tattered brown leather case is a tag with this New York address. The inscription reads, Samuel N. Wade. I do hope I've not contacted the wrong person in error and that this field camera indeed belongs to you. When you receive this, please reply to the address listed on the envelope.

Sincerely,

Calla Lily Mircea

"What's wrong, Lillian?" Nathan asked.

"Someone in," she paused to flip over the envelope, "Havenwood Falls has found your father's camera. They even have the bag," Lillian muttered. "I can't believe it."

"Where is Havenwood Falls?"

"According to the postage mark, it's someplace in Colorado."

"Colorado?" Nathan exclaimed. "How in the hell did the camera get there? It has to be a mistake. Egypt to some random place in the middle of nowhere is a bit of a stretch, don't you think?"

Lillian nodded, still trying to comprehend the words she'd just read. Sam's camera had been missing for as long as he had been, and no one, besides Nathan, thought they'd ever see it again. She eyed him over her glasses. "Nathan, I don't want you to get your hopes up."

Nathan took the letter from Lillian and stared at the words on the page for a moment before responding. "It may be nothing, but this is the first lead we've had. I will have to contact this Calla Lily and find out for myself."

"No, you can send Edgar. That is why you hired him, is it not?"

Nathan sighed. "It is, but there is something odd about this letter —this woman's writing. I feel like this is it. This," Nathan paused, "this is my father's camera, Lillian. I have to do this."

"Oh, Nathan," she replied gently.

"Look, it won't hurt anyone. Only another week and classes will be out for summer break. I can go then, and that way nothing will be affected here."

Lillian laid her hand on Nathan's. "This could indeed be a mistake, but I understand what you're saying. I will cover you here. I want you to have peace of mind, and I need you to find closure and put your father's death behind you."

"What if it is his? What if he is alive and has been living in Colorado all this time?"

She pulled him into a hug. "Then I guess that is all the more reason for you to go," she said as she stepped back. "Either way, you'll have an answer."

Nathan nodded. "I don't know, Lillian. I have a feeling I can't shake."

"Well, then let me respond to this Miss Mircea and make the arrangements for you to stay a few days," she said, before she kissed him on the forehead and walked over to her desk.

"This had better not be another dead end," Nathan mumbled under his breath as the gentle clicks of the typewriter sounded in the background.

CHAPTER 2

The week passed by quickly, and Nathan was almost ready to go. Lillian had made all the arrangements with Calla Lily for Nathan to stay at Whisper Falls Inn upon his arrival. She also made sure Nathan's colleagues were aware he'd only be gone a short period of time on a fact-finding mission and would be back before summer's end at the latest.

Lillian thought back to when Samuel disappeared. He'd been working at the excavation site for Hatshepsut's tomb in the Valley of the Kings. Everything was going as expected according to his correspondence, and then one day they received a telegraph stating he'd gone missing—simply vanished, no trace of him found by the other Egyptologists on the dig. The only evidence they had was from a worker who reported seeing him taking a photograph of two young women near the excavation site.

Nathan had convinced himself that his father's satchel was the key to finding out what happened. He'd go on and on about photos, or maybe something Samuel found, and how it could show not only inside information about the tomb, but could also provide clues as to what happened on that day. Either way, Lillian worried about how all of this would affect Nathan in the end. Not knowing left him sad, but hungry for information—a conclusion could leave him broken.

Lillian hoped this trip to Havenwood Falls would confirm the final piece of the puzzle and finally let Nathan accept the truth—Sam met with foul play that fateful day, and the camera and any other belongings were long gone from this world. She typed up the last page for the itinerary and slipped it out of the typewriter wheel with a zing, placing it neatly on her desk. As soon as Nathan returned from afternoon class, she'd let him know the whos, whats, and whens for his departure tomorrow.

The door opened with a click and startled Lillian.

"Finished," Nathan called out as he entered the office. "The only thing left to do is mark the grades and submit them, then it's off to Colorado."

"I've made the final arrangements," she said as she stood. "You'll be taking the train into Montrose, Colorado, and Miss Mircea will meet you there. Apparently, they don't have direct access other than a bus to take you into the town itself, so she's offered to be your means of transportation."

Nathan gave her an odd look.

"Yes, my thoughts exactly, but considering your insistence that you yourself flesh this one out, you will have to abide by the rules set forth by the woman who has the satchel," Lillian said with a slight grin.

"Then I shall take it all at face value," Nathan replied, returning her smile. "Did she say where to meet her?"

"No, only that she'd be there when the train arrived, and she'd be on a bench near the platform."

"Okay then," he sighed.

"Have you finished packing?" Lillian asked as she began to sort the papers Nathan had set on her desk.

"Oh you know, I still have a few things to pack," he replied shyly.

"Nathan Allan Wade. I swear, will you never change?" Lillian laughed out loud. "Go home and get packed this instant."

Nathan grinned, knowing his truth was revealed. He hadn't packed a thing, but he was only going to be gone a few days. Nathan didn't see the point in bringing his dress attire. Instead, he'd settle for his field clothes: a couple of sport shirts, casual trousers, and a pair of suspenders.

"I don't have that much . . ." He relented under Lillian's motherly gaze.

"Nonetheless, off you go," Lillian said, shooing him out the door. "And don't forget to stop by the bank on the way home. You should have plenty of cash with you—enough to last the week at least."

"How about dinner tonight at six at Lombardi's?" Nathan asked as he grabbed his coat and hat.

"That sounds lovely, but only if you've done as I've asked and will be ready to leave in the morning. Your train departs at seven, and you cannot be late," Lillian chided.

"I will not only be ready to leave but will have my bags by the door." Nathan grinned. "I'll pick you up at five thirty," he said as he opened the door to leave.

"Five thirty it is." Lillian waved him out.

Nathan stopped by the bank, as Lillian suggested, and then the library. He needed to grab a book or two to keep his mind occupied on the train. It was, after all, going to take a few days to get to Colorado.

It was five thirty sharp when Nathan knocked on the door of Lillian's apartment. She was always a stickler for being on time, and Nathan knew if he was late, she'd balk over needing to rush to dinner. He adored Lillian and wanted nothing more than to make her happy. They lived in separate apartments, but within the same building. Lillian lived on the floor below his, and as they headed down the stairs, Nathan remembered carrying his father's satchel clumsily down each flight before his dad left for his latest expedition. He'd set it down on the last step and taken Lillian's hand as Samuel told her when he'd be returning. That was the last time he saw his father. It was also the day Lillian became his guardian.

"I want you to order whatever you like tonight, and no scrimping because you're worried about the cost, understand?" Nathan insisted.

"Oh no, you will not," Lillian scolded. "We're going to have a lovely dinner, but it will be on me." Nathan started to protest but stopped when she gave him "the look." "Besides, if you pay, I will assume it is to say goodbye, and I will not be saying goodbye to you, young man. You'll return in a week, and when you do, you can buy dinner then." She winked.

"Deal," Nathan replied as he raised his arm in the air to hail a cab.

"We can walk, Nathan."

"I didn't want you to have to walk all that way," he replied as the car pulled up to the curb. "And you gave no stipulation about a taxi, only dinner."

Nathan opened the door and offered his hand to her.

Lillian clicked her tongue, but didn't argue. Instead, the two rode to the restaurant, enjoyed a lovely meal, and returned home early enough for her to be able to read a chapter in her book before heading to bed. Nathan had left before on excursions, but he always came home. Something about him leaving this time felt different, though. They hugged one another tightly as they said their goodbyes.

"Don't worry. I'll be home in a week," Nathan insisted as he kissed her forehead. "I love you, Lillian."

"I love you too, Nathan. Now be careful. I'll hold the fort down here until you return."

He smiled. "You always do."

Nathan looked back one last time before he headed upstairs.

NATHAN SLEPT for most of his three-day trip. The gentle sway of the train and clatter of the wheels on the track lulled him to sleep. When the train pulled into the station, he gathered his things and headed toward the exit. He was anxious, and not because he hadn't traveled before, but because he was not simply venturing into the unknown, but into his own *personal* unknown. What if he found more than just his father's satchel? Then again, what if it was a fake, a trick of some sort? Nathan quickly dismissed both lines of thinking, because it was pointless. Why would someone in Colorado play a joke on a professor in New York? It made no sense.

As he stepped onto the platform, Nathan glanced around, hoping to find a sign saying Havenwood Falls or a woman sitting on a bench waving her hand in the air, but there was nothing—no reference and no woman.

"Excuse me," Nathan asked the conductor. "Which way to Havenwood Falls?"

The man stared at him with an odd expression. "I have no idea where that is, sir. This is Montrose, Colorado. Maybe you should check with the office," he said, pointing to a window in the main building off the platform.

Nathan was confused, but thanked the man and headed in the direction the conductor pointed. He knew this was Montrose, but assumed Havenwood Falls was a town nearby. Why did the conductor act like he'd never heard of it?

"Mr. Wade?"

Nathan turned to see a young woman offering her hand to him. He gave her an odd look, but shook her hand anyway.

"Let me guess, you expected someone older?" she said.

"Ah! Miss Mircea. Actually, I did. I apologize. I meant no offense."

"None taken. Glad to see you made it here safely," she replied with a slight nod. "And please call me Calla Lily."

"What a beautiful name."

"Thank you." She smiled kindly. "This way, we're right over here." Calla Lily pointed to a Ford Model T that had been retrofitted with tires thicker than the norm, obviously a necessity for dealing with the Colorado terrain.

Nathan deposited his bag in the back and climbed inside, choosing to stick to a generic topic like the weather as a way to pass the time while Calla Lily navigated the mountain pass. He was, of course, bursting at the seams to ask all the questions pooling on the tip of his tongue. How had his father's camera ended up in Colorado? Did she remember who brought it in? Did she perhaps see his father firsthand? But, remembering Lillian's words, he wasn't ready to have his hopes crushed just yet, so he'd wait—wait until he saw it with his own eyes before broaching the sensitive subject.

"So, are all the mountain towns around here this hard to find?" Nathan asked as they rounded yet another bend in the road.

Calla Lily stifled a laugh. "No, probably not. Our little town is . . . special, a hidden gem, and we wouldn't have it any other way.

Nathan arched his brow, but dismissed her comment. Instead, he turned back to the window and glanced up at the snow-tipped mountain caps.

CHAPTER 3

*N*athan saw a large wooden sign atop a solid stone base that read "Havenwood Falls" as they entered the town. It wasn't what he expected, but then again, this was the country, and he was a city boy. It was late afternoon when they rolled up to Whisper Falls Inn—a large Victorian-style manor complete with a wraparound porch, turrets and gingerbread trim. He definitely wasn't in New York anymore. The next few days would be slow, easy country living, and for a brief moment, he allowed himself to take in the calm, cool mountain air.

"You coming?" Calla Lily asked as she stepped onto the porch.

Nathan nodded. "Of course. Sorry. Was just taking in the fresh, clean air. Not something I'm used to, I'm afraid."

"Well, there is plenty for you to enjoy while you're here," Calla Lily said as she stepped inside the doorway.

"Nathan, this is Mihail Petran. He and his wife Irina run the inn," Calla Lily said with a bright smile as they made their way to the front desk.

Nathan nodded and extended his hand. "Mr. Petran, it's a pleasure to meet you."

Mihail gave Calla Lily a quick glance before extending his hand in return. Nathan looked between them and dismissed whatever silent conversation they were having.

"A woman named Lillian Hartman made the reservations for me," he said, pulling a slip of paper from his pocket.

Mihail trailed his finger over the guestbook until he found Nathan's name. "Mr. Wade?"

"See," Calla Lily lilted, "everything is as it should be. They'll get you checked in, and I will be back in a bit with the camera, if that works for you?" she said as she touched Nathan's shoulder. "I know you want answers," Calla Lily said softly. "And soon, you shall have them."

Nathan started to speak, but Calla Lily seemed to be out the door before he could gather the first question he wanted to ask her. He'd waited this long, though, so what were a few more hours in the grand scheme of things?

"I have you all checked in, Mr. Wade," Mihail said with a smile. "Irina will show you to your room, and if you need anything while you are here, please do not hesitate to find one of us."

"Thank you, Mr. Petran."

"Please, call me Mihail."

Nathan nodded, but was confused by the sudden chill he felt as he looked at Mihail's eyes—grey-green with an oddly handsome intrigue behind them.

"This way, Mr. Wade," a woman's voice spoke from over his shoulder.

Nathan turned and came face to face with a woman with the same grey-green eyes as Mihail's. He stared for longer than a man should, before apologizing to her profusely. "I'm so very sorry. I was taken aback by your eyes."

"No need to apologize, Mr. Wade. My name is Irina, and I'll be showing you to your room."

"O-of course," Nathan stuttered as he reached for his bag and glanced back at Mihail, embarrassed for staring at the man's wife. "Thank you. Thank you both."

Mihail grinned slightly at Nathan before the professor moved to follow Irina down the hall. When the two of them arrived at his room, Irina opened and held the door for him.

The room was spacious, larger than any he was used to in New York. People often joked that hotels and apartments were postage-stamp-sized unless you were fortunate enough to be wealthy and could afford a larger space. Either way, Nathan was pleased with this room and happy to have the space to spread out. Maybe he'd view this as a vacation after all.

"If you need anything, Mr. Wade, please feel free to call down. We'll be happy to help. Oh, and while we are working on putting a bathroom in each room, yours does not have one yet. The communal bathroom is down the hall to the right. We only have a few guests staying currently, so this floor should be relatively empty. At least that should give you a little peace and quiet while you're here."

"Thank you, Mrs. Petran."

"Madame Luiza serves dinner in the dining room promptly at six. I'll expect to see you in half an hour," she said with a smile before closing the door.

Nathan grinned and thought of Lillian. She, too, was always concerned with whether or not he was properly fed. His stomach growled as he glanced at his watch. It had been a long trip, and while he'd eaten on the train, that had been hours ago. He opened up his bag and grabbed a few toiletries before heading down the hall to wash up.

Nathan stared at his reflection and sighed. He was only twenty-six, but with the circles darkening under his eyes, he appeared much older. The quest to find the answers surrounding his father's death had taken its toll on him. He knew Lillian had seen it, but she always danced around the topic. Yet now, as he looked at himself, so close to the end of this quest, Nathan realized that no matter what he uncovered, he would have to move beyond this. He needed to put his father's death in the past and move forward with his life. When his mother died of consumption, he was too young to have any memories of her, but with Samuel, he had eight years of laughter and fun. All not easily forgotten. Especially when there were no reasons why.

Nathan washed his face and tamed the wild hairs on his five o'clock shadow before heading back to his room.

The smell wafting down the hall was too tempting, and Nathan decided to arrive a few minutes early. Irina's mouth curved into a smile when she caught his eye, and he gave her an approving nod as he found a seat and put a napkin into his lap. Nathan thought about Lillian when "Regretful Blues" started to play on the Victrola. It had only been a few days, but he missed her and this was one of her favorite songs.

"Good evening, Nathan," a woman with salt-and-pepper hair and elegant features said as she set down a loaf of bread and a few pats of butter. "We have two dishes this evening, if you're hungry," she lilted. "Pot roast with potatoes, carrots, and onions, or meatloaf and mashed potatoes."

Nathan knew immediately. "Pot roast, please, with extra gravy if you have it to spare."

She laughed. "Extra gravy it is."

"Thank you, Madame Luiza," Nathan replied.

"Ah, a perceptive one. How did you know I was Madame Luiza?"

"I just assumed." He grinned as he reached for a piece of bread.

She winked and turned to leave. "Calla Lily will be joining you shortly, if you care to wait."

Nathan pulled back his hand and set them in his lap, confused as to how Madame Luiza knew he was about to grab the bread with her back turned. A moment later, Calla Lily stepped into the foyer. Nathan saw her talking to Mihail and Irina before turning toward the dining hall. He could see underneath the evening cloak she was wearing that she brought the satchel. *Moments from the truth*, Nathan thought, standing as Calla Lily drew near.

"Calla Lily," Nathan said as he pulled out the chair next to his. "Madame Luiza said you'd be arriving shortly. It seems she was correct."

Calla Lily grinned as she moved to sit, setting the bag next to the chair. "She does have a keen sense when it comes to timing."

Madame Luiza walked in, carrying a tray of teacups and a small teapot. "I assumed you'd want your usual green tea, but I added a bit of passion fruit and mango to it."

She removed the items from the tray and placed them in front of Calla Lily.

"That sounds magnificent, Madame Luiza. I cannot wait to try it, and the pot roast smells heavenly. May I have some of that as well?"

Madame Luiza nodded her head gently. "Two pot roast plates, one with extra gravy, coming right up."

As Madame Luiza made her way to the kitchen, Nathan stole a glance at the bag sitting next to Calla Lily.

"I know you are anxious to see this bag, but I'd like to share a meal—talk and get to know one another—first," Calla Lily said as she laid her hand on his. "Will that be okay?"

"I didn't mean to be obvious. It has been a long time of wanting to know the truth."

"You know, when I saw you this morning, you weren't the only one who was expecting someone older. When I sent the letter, I didn't know who the satchel or camera belonged to, but as I sit here before you, I am curious to know why it means so much."

Nathan sat back in his chair and wondered why it felt as though Calla Lily could see parts in him that he desperately tried to keep hidden. Her caring, soulful eyes seemed to almost draw out the words.

"It's a simple story, but nonetheless a painful one," he started. "My father, Samuel Wade, the man whose bag you have there, was an Egyptologist—a great one, in fact. He was on a dig for Hatshepsut's tomb in the Valley of the Kings when he disappeared—he and the camera. No one has seen either since."

"And you've been searching now for how long?"

"Eighteen years."

"Hope you two are hungry," Madame Luiza said, setting their plates in front of them. "I put a little extra for each of you. And save room for dessert."

Nathan and Calla Lily inhaled and let the scent of the roast tease their senses.

"Thank you very much, Madame Luiza. It looks delicious."

"Enjoy. I'll be back around in a bit to check on you."

"By the way, Madame Luiza, the tea is delicious." Calla Lily beamed. "I believe I have a new favorite."

Madame Luiza laughed. "You say that every time."

When she left, Nathan and Calla Lily ate and chatted, but left the conversation about Sam on hold to enjoy their meals. When they were finished, Madame Luiza refreshed their drinks and cleared their plates before leaving them once again to grab two bowls of homemade cobbler—another one of her specialties.

"So, you've been searching eighteen years for answers to why your father went missing, and you're hoping this bag," she said as she lifted it and set it on the table, "will give you those answers, yes?"

"I do," Nathan replied with conviction.

"Then please promise me you'll look at this as an opportunity for peace. I think you've earned it after all this time, have you not?"

He stared at Calla Lily. "You sound like Lillian."

"Just remember, sometimes the answers you seek don't always come the way you hope. You may find something entirely different. Either way, keep your mind open to the possibilities that may be beyond your understanding." She laid her hand on his. "I only hope for your peace, Nathan."

"Thank you, but if you don't mind me asking, why would *you* be concerned with my peace? You don't even know me."

She scooted out her chair to leave, bringing Nathan quickly to his feet to assist her.

"If you should need anything while you are here in Havenwood Falls, my shop is down the street. Mihail, Irina, or Madame Luiza can show you. Otherwise, I wish you well," Calla Lily said, extending her hand.

Nathan was taken aback as to why she didn't reply, but assumed it was because their business was unofficially concluded. "I will make certain before I leave town to find you and let you know what, if anything, I have found. It has been a great pleasure meeting you."

"And you also. Be well."

Nathan watched as Calla Lily retrieved her coat and made her way to the door. When she was out of sight, he sat and stared at the bag. He ran his hands over the supple leather, but flinched when a spark ran up his arm.

"Everything okay?" Madame Luiza asked.

"Yes," Nathan stammered. "I'd like to pay my bill, please."

Madame Luiza shook her head. "No bill. Dinner is served with your stay. If you get hungry later, and are looking for leftovers, we're up late around here. Just come on down, and we'll fix you a plate."

"You're too kind."

"Have a good evening."

"You as well."

Nathan reluctantly reached for the bag but was surprised when it didn't shock him this time. He made his way upstairs, and when he got to his room, he set the satchel on the dresser. All this time, and now he didn't want to open it. *What's another day?* he thought.

CHAPTER 4

*N*athan lay in the bed, staring across the dimly lit room at the satchel. He wanted to open it, but feared the truth, now that it was here within his reach. He rubbed his fingers together, remembering the shock it had given him. Was that part of the reason why his father was missing, or was it the altitude and dry air here in the mountains? *Get up and open it, you idiot. All the answers you seek are right there. But what if . . . what if what?* His internal debate raged until he finally sat up with a renewed determination. Nathan reached over and turned on the lamp on the nightstand, before deciding to settle this once and for all. He stepped over to the dresser and picked up the bag.

With the light beaming on the satchel, Nathan ran his hands over his father's name, and when he didn't feel a shock, he opened it slowly. Inside, it was like a time capsule of Samuel's life. Nathan knew in an instant this was indeed his father's bag. He pulled out a leather-bound journal and set it on the bed, followed by a stack of pictures from the dig, dated in his handwriting days before his disappearance. Nathan removed the elastic band on the stack and flipped through them. They were nothing more than images of artifacts and some of the other Egyptologists posing with their finds.

He then unwrapped the leather strap on the journal and opened it. Tears came to his eyes. There on the first page was the last photograph of him and his father together before Samuel had left for Egypt. Snow covered the ground, and they were sitting on a sled. He remembered the day vividly. They'd had fun going up and down the hills near the cabin they'd been staying at in the Catskills. Nathan was sad but grateful to have it back. Samuel was only supposed to have been away for three months when he'd left. No one could have ever predicted it would've been the last vacation they'd have together.

Nathan flipped through the journal pages, but nothing stood out. There were field notes and scaled drawings, along with slips of paper with hieroglyphics sketched onto them. Everything in there, besides the photograph of him and his father, was related to his work. Nathan flipped to the center, where the binding of the journal was broken and the pages lay flat, exposing a detailed description of a canopic jar unlike anything he'd ever seen.

Notation: Most jars are cylindrical and between five to ten inches tall and range in material based on the wealth of the owner whose remains are inside. This one is different. It appears to be two jars connected as one, while still maintaining its individual shape. It is made of alabaster with ribbons of red and orange running through it and stands nineteen and a half inches tall.

Nathan read his father's notes and wondered, just as he had, why such a jar would exist. When it was found, it was sitting on a ledge with a dozen or so red stones carved like scarabs and a shimmering liquid no one could identify. Nathan ran his fingers over the ancient symbols to the right of the page. They were unlike anything he'd ever seen. He wondered if maybe they were the key to explaining the jars and the mysterious liquid. Nathan scanned the next few pages, hoping they'd provide some insight, but found nothing. He closed the journal and decided he'd research this later, after he returned to New York, where he had the resources to uncover more information.

Nathan reached into the bag again, this time taking great care when lifting the field camera out. It was lighter than he remembered, but then again, he was a boy the last time he'd had his hands on it. He set it on the bed and stared at it a moment before something at the bottom of the bag caught his eye—a stack of aged images scattered across the bottom. Nathan moved to pick them up, but flinched when he got another shock, similar to the jolt he had received when he had picked up the bag the first time. *What the hell?*

He lifted up the satchel and dumped the rest of the contents on the bed. The pictures scattered, leaving a few of them facedown, but two were facing up. A beautiful blond woman with pale eyes was dressed in a simple sheath gown and stood slightly off center, as if there was someone standing next to her just outside of the frame. Nathan poked the corner, and when it didn't shock him, he picked it up. The woman in the image was innocent and childlike, but there was something else about her, something powerful and seductive. He flipped to the next image, but it was nothing but a blur. Nathan reached for the other ones, but they were only shots of canopic jars and some interior shots of the tomb itself—nothing of note. Nathan flipped back through the stack until he was looking at the young woman again. There was something in her eyes, but he couldn't decide whether it was sadness or something else.

Nathan set the stack of photos on the bed and turned his attention back to the camera. He clicked the clamp and watched as the front fell open. He examined it carefully, looking for clues. The lens was intact, the cloth bellows were in working order, and the leather on the outside was barely worn. For all intents and purposes, the camera hadn't aged or changed a bit. It was as if time hadn't touched it in the least. The rack and pinion still moved back and forth to adjust the focus, and the automatic shutter still clicked. The camera was in perfect working order.

But Samuel had two identical cameras. One used film, while the other used glass plates. His father used both mediums, depending on his need. Nathan was unsure of which one this was, but it would be easy enough to identify—not because of the obvious features, but because his favorite camera was engraved with the Eye of Horus. It had been given to his dad as a gift before his first expedition. The eye was considered a sacred symbol, said to protect anything behind it. Samuel would go on and on about its power to keep him safe on his journeys. *A lot of good it did him on his last tour*, Nathan thought.

Nathan flipped over the camera and found what he was searching for. There it was. The "all-seeing eye." Nathan wondered but doubted if there would still be any plates secured in the back. Samuel used to say he preferred to use the plates because of the way they captured the subject, while generally using film for quick shots of artifacts instead. Gingerly, Nathan examined the back and found a plate still in place. As he examined it closer, he noticed something etched onto the glass. He pulled it out and moved it into the light. The girl from the photograph was once again staring back at him—same dress, same look on her face, but instead of the pyramids in the background, there was a halo image behind her.

"That's odd," Nathan said and pulled his glasses out of his suitcase.

He rubbed his fingers over the bright spot to see if it was merely a smudge upon the glass, but it wasn't. Whatever it was, it was imbedded into the glass itself. Upon closer inspection, Nathan noticed a silvery liquid moving under the surface and used his fingernail to try to pry apart the plates to see what it was. The shimmery liquid poured from the slit between the pieces of glass and fell into his hand.

"Mercury?" he whispered.

"Hello?" a woman's voice called out.

Nathan froze. Where had that voice come from? He was alone—or at least, he thought he was. He set the items on the nightstand and walked around the room with the mercury shifting and swirling in his hand. There wasn't anyone here.

"Please don't leave me. I'm here," the voice spoke again.

Nathan was rattled now, and that was saying something, considering all he'd endured when it came to creepy and odd things. He was an Egyptologist, like his father, and had seen countless bizarre and strange occurrences, but this—this was out of the ordinary for sure.

"The glass. Pick it up and look at me."

Nathan took care not to spill the mercury, but he didn't want to continue holding it either. It had long been suspected that its chemical properties caused men to go mad, but he couldn't imagine its effects would happen simply by holding it. Nathan found a small glass vase with a handful of wildflowers on the dresser and decided to pour the mercury into it, but as he started to tip his hand, the voice spoke again.

"No. Hold the liquid and the image," she demanded.

Nathan adjusted his glasses and picked up the glass slide. There on the surface, as clear as could be, was the beautiful young woman he'd seen earlier in the paper photograph. She was smiling a soft smile and holding her hand up in a faint wave.

"Hello," she offered.

"I've lost my damn mind," Nathan replied.

She shook her head. "No, you haven't, but I am so grateful to finally have someone who can see and hear me. Can you free me from this place?"

"Free you? What the hell are you?" Nathan stammered. "I mean, a figment of my imagination, for sure, but how—why?"

"I am trapped here in this prison, and I wish to be free."

CHAPTER 5

"Trapped? Free? What?" Nathan exclaimed in rapid succession as he stared down at the woman talking to him from between the two glass plates. She was *real,* as best as he could tell, and seductive—lord, was she seductive. The thin gossamer-looking gown she wore showed all of her curves along with details he wanted—no needed—to block from his mind, but he was too bewildered not to continue staring at her barely covered skin.

"Please don't be afraid. I do not wish you harm. I only ask to be released."

"Released from what? You have to be a figment of my imagination."

Nathan looked down at his hand and cursed. He was still holding the mercury. That had to be it. He dropped the glass plate onto the bed before hastily grabbing the glass vase. He pulled out the wildflowers, spilling the water out before pouring the mercury into the vessel. *There,* he thought.

He hesitantly glanced at the plate and watched as the female within slammed her fists against the glass. Nathan could see her, but could only faintly hear her cries for help. He eyed his hand and saw a thin residue of the mercury still coating his palm. He rubbed his hand vigorously onto his pant leg, and her voice fell silent. *See, it was the mercury messing with my head.* Nathan picked up the image and saw that she'd dropped to her knees and was sobbing into her hands. *Nope, you're still insane.*

Nathan sat there for a few moments, watching her cry, and began to feel guilty for causing her such pain. He didn't want to see his imaginary dream girl cry. Nathan ran his thumb over her hair and was shocked when she moved. She dried her tears and sat back, looking up at him with the saddest expression he'd ever seen.

"Even if you were real, I don't know what I could do to help you." He watched as her mouth moved, but he couldn't hear anything. "Oh, I understand. The mercury was how I could hear you. Hold on. Let's see." Nathan grabbed the vase and started to faintly hear her again, but it wasn't until he poured the silver substance back into his hand that he heard her voice clearly.

"Please do not be afraid of me. I won't hurt you. I only want out of here. I've been here for so long."

"How long, exactly? Because I cannot wrap my head around the fact that I am sitting in a hotel room, in a town I've never heard of, talking to a beautiful woman trapped in between the plates of a camera lost eighteen years ago."

She stared at him in disbelief. "What did you say?"

"Which part?"

"Eighteen years ago? Where?"

"Egypt. The tomb of Hatshepsut in the Valley of the Kings, to be exact."

Nathan lost sight of the beautiful blonde for a moment.

"Hello? Where did you go?" he called out as he sat up, spilling the mercury in the process. Nathan scrambled to get it back into his hand before she returned to view, but it wasn't working. He continued to chase it, like a spilled egg on a hardwood floor. The mercury was edging close to the Oriental rug, and he needed something to collect it before it soaked into the fibers. Nathan reached for the vase and began scooping its edge against the floor, using his fingers to coax the mercury back inside.

"Where is Samuel?" the woman asked in a rushed tone, her voice faint again.

"Excuse me?" Shocked, Nathan clenched his fist, breaking the vase in his hands. "Shit!" Blood pooled, and the mercury seemed to gravitate toward the cut on his palm. "No!"

Nathan ran out of the room and down the hall to the bathroom to grab a towel and ran back inside, hoping no one had seen him or heard his cursing.

"What's wrong?" he heard her ask when he was back within earshot.

Nathan ignored her as he tried to clean up the broken glass, but she persisted in trying to regain his attention. His hand, however, was bleeding profusely. There was a chunk of glass still embedded in his thumb. Nathan bit his bottom lip and pulled it out. Blood fell in droplets now, and he wrapped the towel around the gash. As he moved to sit on the bed, the glass plate slid off and fell onto the floor, cracking the top piece.

"I can't have this much bad luck." Nathan sighed as he leaned down to pick it up.

The plate had landed right where he'd spilled the mercury, and now the mercury moved, as if deliberately, toward the cracks and crevices. Nathan reached for the plate, but as he did, the edge of the blood-soaked towel he held fell away, and a few drops of blood dripped onto the glass. As soon as it did, Nathan heard a loud pop, and a flame appeared at the plate's center, growing higher and higher. It filled the room until, there before him, stood the beautiful blonde, in the flesh.

CHAPTER 6

$\mathcal{N}$athan sat back and stared with his mouth agape as he watched her move. She was real. Living and breathing real. This was not a figment of his imagination, and he was not insane. Good news, he assumed, but still utterly unreal and impossible.

"You freed me?" she said with a hint of disbelief as she took in her corporeal form.

"How? How did I do that?" Nathan stammered. "The mercury was in my hand. My cut. The blood and now, you're real? I must be dreaming."

She spotted the bloody towel and then gazed into Nathan's eyes. "May I?" she asked in a gentle tone.

Nathan was unclear at first as to what she meant, but watched as she reached for the towel. "It's just a cut. I'll be fine."

"I can help," she said, unwrapping the towel.

The blood was no longer gushing, but it was still flowing from the open wound. She touched her finger to the cut, and Nathan watched as gold streaks appeared on her skin. Some were lines, while others were symbols—hieroglyphics, he realized. The symbols pulsed and began to glow, bringing a liquid coursing through her veins and on a path straight to her fingertips, toward his thumb. A moment later, the gold liquid flowed into his cut, healing the wound almost instantly.

"How did you do that?" Nathan asked as he examined his hand.

She met his eyes. "I felt it was the least I could do for your sacrifice in releasing me."

"Yeah, about that." Nathan paused. "I am really confused. I don't know how anything that has happened tonight, or for that matter the events leading up to this past week, are even possible. Who are you? *What* are you? I mean, do you even have a name?" he rambled.

"Yes." She smiled. "My name is Amani."

"I'm Nathan," he replied in a rush.

"I can never thank you enough, Nathan."

"I will take my thank yous with answers, if you don't mind."

"I think you must be related to Samuel," Amani blurted. "I could see him once your blood touched my skin. I could see you as a young boy, though, and not the man you are now."

"You knew my father?" Nathan flinched.

"Samuel is your father?" Amani questioned. "I assumed someone more distant."

"No, Samuel is my father. How do you know him?"

"I don't *really* know him. I met him in Egypt the day my sister and I were planning to leave. That is all. The next thing I knew, I was trapped and alone."

"This doesn't make any sense. And where is your sister now?"

Amani shook her head as tears filled her eyes. "I do not know."

"Maybe my father and your sister are together, then?" Nathan offered, his tone hopeful again.

"Not likely. My sister was not very fond of humans."

"What?" He stood and stepped away from her. "What does that mean? Who are you?"

"I don't think the question is so much who I am, but *what* I am that may concern you."

"No. I am thinking both questions are pertinent here."

Amani sat on the edge of the bed, staring down at her hands. "I believe you were able to free me because your father was the one connected with my entrapment. I've played that day in my mind over and over again, but I come up short for answers every time. Maybe you can help fill in some of the voids."

"Not until you answer why your sister isn't fond of *humans,* as you say. I'm completely confused. If your sister is not human, then what is she? What are you?"

Amani moved to stand, but Nathan backed away, so she sat back down on the edge of the bed. "Please don't be afraid of me."

"I'm not afraid of you," Nathan snapped back.

"But you are. I can sense your fear, and I can hear your thoughts."

"But that is impossible. An improbability."

"I'm surprised, with all you've seen and uncovered, Nathan, that you still question the mystical elements of the world," Amani replied coyly.

He stared at her, but never spoke a word—out loud, that is. *Mystical elements. Like what?* he thought to himself.

Like the Egyptian gods and their purposeful goals of connecting what seems impossible to be connected, she replied in his mind.

Nathan's eyes snapped to his hand, checking for more mercury residue. "How are you doing that?"

"We are connected, your blood to me and my blood to you." She blushed. "We belong to one another now."

"We're *what?*" Nathan shouted.

"Connected," Amani said as she rose and stepped closer to him. Nathan started to move, but calmed the moment her fingers touched his chest. "I don't know how or why I ended up here with you, but I know the gods have their reasons. All I ask is that you give me a chance to explain—to show you we both want the same thing."

"And what is that?" Nathan breathed, uneasy at how close Amani was to him.

"The truth," she whispered.

CHAPTER 7

*A*mani stared at Nathan for a long moment before speaking. "Your eyes are the color of the lotus blooms I remember as a child. Were your mother's eyes blue?"

"Yes," he breathed, his heart racing as she stepped closer.

"And your tawny hair?"

"My father's side."

"You are young."

"I'm old enough to have experienced the world."

Her hand brushed his. "Why does your heart beat so swiftly?"

"Because you are a beautiful woman standing inches from me, and I know in my heart you cannot be real—this whole situation cannot be real."

"I'm here before you. Why do you keep asking if I am real?"

"Because you were in that camera not less than twenty minutes ago."

"You saved me. I am indebted to you."

"What are you, Amani? You're in my thoughts. I can feel you in my blood—my bones." He reached for her, but pulled back. "I feel an electrical current coursing through my body. Why?"

"The connection is possible because I am not like you. I'm otherworldly. Can that not be enough?"

"No. I wish it could be, but ever since I was a boy, I had to know what made things tick. I need to understand everything that has brought me here to this moment. Like how it is possible you are in these photographs," Nathan said, reaching for the pictures on the bed and holding them up for her to see. "And now here before me."

Amani shook her head. "I'm not sure how it is possible," she replied as she held out her hands to look at them. She flipped through each one quickly until she was back at the original image. "Khalida isn't in any of these? It's like she was never there."

"Who is Khalida?"

"My sister," Amani replied shakily.

"Both of you are . . . otherworldly?" Nathan asked as he reached for the photos.

"Yes."

"I was wondering about this one." Nathan pulled out the image of the blur and showed it to Amani. "Any chance, since you are *otherworldly*, you see something more than I do?"

Amani shook her head. "It doesn't look like anything, really," she said hesitantly as she handed him back the photograph. "Can you tell me how Samuel disappeared?"

"The camera and my father disappeared on the same day. No one knows what happened to him exactly, only that he was last seen taking a photograph of two young women—you and your sister, I suppose," he replied and sat back down on the bed. "And then he was gone. What do you know?"

"We met Samuel in the morning, not too long after we were released from our prison. Khalida had seen him with an odd box, and then images of items within the tomb visible on squares of paper. They talked, and he told her it was a camera—that it was used to take pictures of things you'd like to remember, or to document memories. She asked if he would take our photograph."

"And he agreed, obviously."

"Yes. He told us where to stand and not to move, but the flash was bright and startling, then it was over. We weren't certain what would happen next. Khalida wanted to know where the picture was, but he said he needed time to develop them and that he'd have them to us before lunch." Amani sighed. "When we met him again, he said the pictures didn't come out, and he'd like to take new ones. Khalida was angry at needing to do it again, but I convinced her to let him." Tears welled in her eyes. "Then I was trapped, and now I know Samuel went missing too. I'm sorry about your father, Nathan."

"Did he ask you any questions? Wonder why you were wearing what you are wearing? Anything?"

"No," Amani said, looking down at her dress. "Khalida told him our father was one of the men working nearby, and we were just looking at all the astonishing finds—that we were curious about the tombs being opened."

"But that was a lie," Nathan responded.

She nodded her head. "Tombs are sacred spaces and aren't to be disturbed—it is our custom. The fact that we were free was odd and unexpected. We never thought the goddesses would allow it. We were fearful the watchers would find us and trap us again. Khalida made me promise to stay quiet. I had no idea anyone would be hurt as a result. Do you understand?"

"Sort of."

"I can feel your judgment and disappointment, but you have no idea how long it had been since we had seen the real world," Amani added.

Nathan ran his hands through his hair. "It's just that I'd hoped when I found the satchel that it would provide me with clues. Hell, I even hoped when I received the letter from Calla Lily that I'd arrive here in Havenwood Falls and find him alive," Nathan rambled on.

"But instead you found me, and not him," she replied as she moved toward the window. "You said this place is in Colorado, and you received a letter that Samuel's items were here?"

"Yes, and everything about it is as odd as this situation. The last known sighting of this bag was in Egypt. How did it end up here?"

Amani paused before responding. "This place is filled with a magical energy. I can feel it, but I'm unsure of its origin. I cannot sense its source. Maybe magic brought it here."

"Magic? What are you talking about? Is that the explanation for you and the fact that you are *otherworldly*?"

"This Calla Lily you mentioned, may I meet her?" Amani blurted.

"I guess," he stammered, "but it's the middle of the night. I think we'll have to wait until the morning to try to speak with her."

Amani didn't respond. Instead she pulled back the curtain. The street wasn't empty. In fact, it was rather busy for the "middle of the night," as Nathan insisted. There were a few cars on the street and couples milling about, and Amani even saw a wolf heading off toward the woods behind the building across the street. Amani could feel the energy—feel the magic all around her. She laid her hands on the walls and listened to the sounds of the inn.

"What are you doing?" Nathan asked.

Amani remained still, but replied, "Can't you hear it? There are people all around, awake and enjoying life. Someone named Madame Luiza is serving up a plate of meatloaf to a wolf—no, a man— downstairs." Amani turned to Nathan. "What is meatloaf?"

"Wait. You are concerned about meatloaf when you just said there was a wolf man downstairs?"

"Yes," she replied flatly. "He is both man and wolf."

"How do you know this?" Nathan questioned as he reached for her hand. "Amani, please, you have to explain things to me. None of this makes any sense. Perhaps I am actually asleep, and you and all of this have just been a glorious dream."

Amani moved to sit next to Nathan, and when he shifted to the side to make room for her, she paused. "This is not a dream. I am as real as the bed you are sitting on. I told you, I am otherworldly. My kind do not speak of what we are. It draws attention to ourselves and makes the watchers aware. I do not wish to become a person of interest now that I am free. Can you understand that?"

Nathan shook his head slowly. "No, not really."

Amani sat down. "How familiar are you with ancient Egyptian texts?

"Pretty familiar."

"Do you know of the goddess Sekhmet and her brother Shu?" Amani asked.

"Of course."

"I am born of them."

"You are a goddess?"

"No. I am not worthy of such an honor. I am," she paused to find the right words, "I am a daughter of the goddesses Ma'at and Hathor." Amani beamed, pleased with herself.

"Wait, I am confused. I thought you said you were born of Sekhmet and Shu. Ma'at is the goddess of truth and the one all must meet in the Hall of Truth, yes? And Hathor is the goddess of joy and motherhood."

"Yes," she exclaimed, delighted he knew of whom she was speaking. "Khalida and I were both mistakes, but the goddesses Ma'at and Hathor took us under their wings and guided us—kept us safe," she said, her smile suddenly fading. "Sekhmet and Shu are the ones who created us. We are unnatural among our kind."

Nathan reached for her hand. "Okay, but what *kind* is that? Are you an angel or something? I don't know if they have angels in Egyptian mythos, but I think you could fit the bill."

The corner of Amani's mouth curved into a smile as she twirled a lock of Nathan's hair around her finger. "You had curly hair as a boy, too. It was longer then," she replied with a slight tilt of her head. "I think you are much more handsome now."

Nathan blushed and cleared his throat. "You're trying to change the subject."

"Have I upset you with my words?"

"Um, no," he stumbled. "Well, maybe. I'm not used to a woman as stunning as you speaking to me in such a way. The women I know are more," he paused, searching for the right word, "demure, maybe. I don't know. I'm not used to hearing such flattery."

"That is a shame, then. You have a beautiful soul. Any woman would be lucky to have you."

A spark shot between the two of them, but this time, Nathan took the jolt in stride. He knew now it was her. "Why is it sometimes when we touch, there is an electrical charge?"

"I'm sorry." She dropped his lock of hair from her hand. "I do not mean to hurt you. It is part of my curse. I don't like to release it, but I have to let some of it go, so I do it in short bursts. Please forgive me."

"A small price to pay."

"I suppose, but I wish I was different. I wish I was like you."

"I understand you do not want to say how it is we are different, and for now, I will accept that, but I hope that in time, you will trust me enough to tell me the truth. Because I, like you, do not wish to cause you any harm." Amani blushed, and he averted his gaze. "Can you tell me more about Ma'at, Hathor, and your sister?"

She shifted on the bed. "I love and honor the goddesses. They gave me a chance to be more than I was born to be. My hope is when it is time for my soul's heart to be weighed against the feather, that mine will be lighter. It is then the soul can freely be admitted into the Field of Reeds, where I will know nothing but peace and happiness."

"What happens if your heart is not as light as a feather?"

"Should the heart tip the scale, it is thrown to the floor of the Hall of Truth, where it is devoured by Amenti. The soul would cease to exist. This is a fate worse than death."

"I've read texts, but I didn't understand it the same way as you just described it. So this is the Egyptian belief? Does it tie in with why you cannot tell me what you are? Would your truth create an imbalance on the scale?"

Amani shook her head. "No, that is different. By speaking what I am, I put myself in danger, and thus would put you in danger. I won't risk it for either of us."

"Okay," Nathan relented. "Are you tired? Wait, do you even get tired?"

Amani chuckled. "I do, and yes, but not in the same way as you, I assume."

"I figured since we cannot go anywhere, we could rest until the sun is up, and then go to see Calla Lily."

"I would like that." She glanced around and saw nothing but a chair and the bed they were sitting on.

"I can take the chair," Nathan rushed.

"I was going to ask if you minded if I lay here with you. I won't be a bother, but a soft bed does appeal to me."

Nathan quickly gathered the items on the opposite side of the bed and placed them back into the satchel before helping Amani get settled in. He laid a blanket over her before he walked around to lie next to her. He didn't want to appear forward, but her fragrance was intoxicating. She smelled of cinnamon and lavender, and she was still wearing nothing more than a sheer gown that showed almost every inch of her body. She was by far the most beautiful woman he'd ever laid eyes on, and as if that wasn't enough, she was something other than human. For now, Nathan decided, she was his angel—a gift in return for all he'd had to suffer with the loss of his parents. Amani was a new light within his dark world.

CHAPTER 8

The abandoned monastery in Russia Khalida and Khaldun had been hiding in for the past few months had been a perfect refuge after all their wandering. They had traveled the world over, spending months at a time wherever they thought would be suitable. Khalida had never looked back when Khaldun freed her all those years ago. Instead, they reveled in the offerings of the world and made certain not to draw attention to themselves in any way. If the goddesses ever found out, they both knew the punishment would be swift, and they'd never see the light of day again. However, they'd made certain to cover their tracks. There was only one person who could stand in their way, and she would never be revealing their secret.

Khalida stared out the window and watched the sun as it started to make its ascent over the mountains. She hadn't thought about her sister, Amani, in years, and yet something stirred in her—something felt off.

"She's been released. Someone has found the camera and set her free," Khalida raged.

"I've heard nothing. Not even a whimper. How can you be sure?"

"I'm sure. Why would I be telling you if it wasn't so?"

"Calm down. I will track her, and I will end her."

"You cannot kill her, you fool. If she dies, I die, remember?"

Khaldun moved closer to Khalida. "I've forgotten nothing," he said as he loomed over her. "I will take care of the situation."

Khalida glared at him. "You'll need my help to do it. She is smart and will not call out our kind to draw the watchers. I can sense her only because of our bond."

"Then where is she?"

Khalida closed her eyes and did her best to sense Amani. She assumed Amani was shadowing herself, because the link between them felt like the flicker of a candle being blown by the wind—glowing but not steadily. "I'm not certain. She is not close, and it is someplace obscure and hidden from view."

"I'll need more to go on than that," Khaldun chided.

"You may be my savior, but you are not my master," she pushed back. "That is all I can see. The rest is nothing more than a view from a window. She could be anywhere," Khalida said, stepping away from him.

Khaldun grabbed her wrist and shoved her against the wall with her arms above her head.

"I love it when you are irate," he said as he pressed himself against her, tilting his head downward to taste her lips.

She smirked as his lips grew nearer. "I don't get irate these days. Nothing much to fret over, with you around."

"Well then, let me properly piss you off so I can have you the way I prefer you, my love," he said, tightening his grip around her wrists.

As he claimed her mouth, she moaned at his forcefulness and retaliated by biting his bottom lip, drawing blood. Khaldun laughed and ran his heavily tattooed hand up her torso, cupping her breast, tightening his grip. "I do not remember what my life was like before you, and I will die before I ever have to do without you."

Khalida ran her tongue over the blood pooling on his lips, and the silver symbols on her skin began to shimmer. Khaldun pulled the tie on the dressing gown she wore and let it fall to the floor. Her raven hair was a sharp contrast to her pale skin. All of her was exposed, and he groaned when she pressed up against him.

"I think you need to show me how much you love me and the lengths you are willing to go to keep the truth of me being alive hidden," she said against his lips. "Because if the goddesses find out I'm free, and have been for eighteen years, we will both be punished, if not killed."

Khaldun let his fingers dive into her sweet heat and assaulted her mouth with his tongue. He needed to claim her. No, they needed to claim each other before their djinn natures, then their budding passion would simmer, and they'd return to their human façades. Khaldun's true nature had been released, and nothing but sex or violence would settle the vibrant blue glow writhing within the lines of his tattoos. Khalida was the same, only her tattoos were not tattoos at all. They were hieroglyphs etched into her skin that shimmered silver, depending upon her mood.

She'd been forced all her life to hide who and what she was. The goddesses expected her to be more like her holier-than-thou sister, but ever since she'd been with Khaldun, she could be all she was, without fear of him shunning her for it. They were quite the pair, a watcher and the watched, in love and in hiding. Nothing else mattered but being together. They'd risked everything the day she and Amani were released. It had been a mistake or fate, depending on how you viewed it, but nonetheless, the outcome was exactly as it should be.

Khalida had met Khaldun when she and Amani were originally imprisoned. He was a watcher of wayward djinn—djinn who'd fallen out of favor with the gods and goddesses. Shortly after the twins were captured, Khaldun was assigned the duty of reporting any incidents that gave him pause—anything that could endanger the world if they were ever to be released.

The twin girls were unique and more powerful than expected. Their power was too great and thus was supposed to have been hidden away forever. No one could have predicted human archaeologists would unearth them and inadvertently release them. It was a misfortune Khalida and Khaldun took full advantage of.

Khalida didn't dwell on the day she was freed. She'd made certain she'd remain alive, but without Amani to keep her from living her life as she saw fit. However, now that she could sense her sister, things would have to change once again.

"Your mind is elsewhere, and I need your sole focus," Khaldun commanded as he moved his fingers purposely to bring her attention back to the present.

Khalida arched her back and moaned. "I'm focused."

"You are now," he said, hovering over her naked body.

Khaldun waited until she was ready for release before he entered her. The two writhed in pleasure until they both were sated. The moment they came, the symbols on their skin ceased to pulse. Their djinn sides were satisfied, and now they could focus on what lay before them.

Khalida sighed, and Khaldun pulled her closer. "I will find Amani, and I will fix this for us. Nothing has changed."

"I want to believe that, but I've evaded my fate for too long. I'm afraid now something drastic will have to happen to make any of this right, and we still haven't found a way to unlink my and Amani's lifelines."

"We don't need to. We will simply trap her again, and this time, we'll make sure she'll never be found," he said, and kissed her. "We'll make a plan tomorrow. For now, sleep."

Khalida was strong, hardened to the world, but in Khaldun's arms, she was a young girl in love with a man twice her age and three times her strength. Just as he was putty in her hands. She knew he'd go to the ends of the earth for her, and soon they were about to find out how far that journey would take them both.

CHAPTER 9

$\mathcal{N}$athan woke to the sound of Amani moaning and writhing on the bed. At first he thought something was wrong, but as he watched her, he realized she appeared as though she was pleasuring herself. He was shocked. Never before had he seen a woman like this. Nathan knew he should try to wake her, but he too was aroused as he watched her move her hands over her now exposed breasts. He wondered what she could be dreaming about that would have her doing what she was doing. However, when she called out the name Khaldun, he wondered who that could be. A lost love, perhaps?

Nathan moved to sit up and froze when he heard her gasp and cry out. Amani looked over at him, his hands in the air in hopes she'd understand it wasn't him touching her. She blushed and fixed her dress to cover herself.

"I—I don't understand. What was happening to me?"

Nathan shook his head. "I—I don't know," he replied in a rush. "I woke up, and you were—um, well, yeah."

Amani sat up and bowed her head. "I've never felt my sister's emotions so vividly and so . . ." She trailed off.

Nathan stood, grabbed the blanket that had fallen on the floor, and wrapped it around her shoulders before stepping away. "It seemed like you were dreaming or in a trance. You said the name Khaldun. Do you know who that is?"

Amani's eyes went wide, and she stared at Nathan, as though unsure of what to say.

"Is he your betrothed or something? Husband?"

"No," Amani snapped. "I am not mated. I've never been with a man in such a way."

"Oh, well, who is this Khaldun, then?"

"He is a watcher. Our guardian. Assigned to watch over Khalida and me. Nothing more."

"Okay, well, what do you think it meant that you were . . . um . . . ," Nathan stammered, "calling out his name?"

"There is only one way." Rage fell over Amani's features. "I was feeling my sister's emotions. She is alive and doing well, it seems."

"You two are *that* connected? Wow."

"We are twins. Forced to feel one another's emotions. Our lifelines are interconnected. If one of us dies, the other will follow. The same is true with everything else."

"Are you kidding?"

She shook her head. "No. I have not been able to sense her all this time. I assume it's because I was trapped in your father's camera, but now that I am free, our link will reconnect, and she will be able to sense me, too."

"Is that bad?"

"I don't know, exactly. I guess it will depend on if my sister is *with* Khaldun, or if she is his captive."

Nathan crossed to the window and opened the curtains. "It's morning. We can go talk to Calla Lily and see if she has any information about how the camera came to be in her possession."

Amani nodded and pulled the blanket around her tighter. "It's a start, at least."

Nathan checked his watch. It was barely seven o'clock, but when he opened the door to the hall, the smell of breakfast cooking tempted his every sense.

"Are you hungry?" Nathan said as he opened the door to their room. "They're serving breakfast downstairs. We can grab something to eat before going to see Calla Lily, if you're interested."

"Will they be serving the meatloaf you spoke of?"

Nathan laughed. "We do not eat meatloaf for breakfast."

"Then what do you eat? Grains and beer?"

"No, we eat eggs, bacon, toast, and potatoes."

"Okay," Amani said as she stood, the blanket slipping off her shoulders as she did. Nathan sucked in a breath, and Amani looked down at her dress. "What's wrong?"

"I think you should wear this," he replied as he reached for his coat and offered it to Amani. "At least until we can get you something *more* to wear."

"I don't understand. What is wrong with what I am wearing?"

Nathan paused to gather his words so as not to offend her. "Women of the day tend to wear more modest clothing. I'm not sure the people of Havenwood Falls will understand why you're not covered."

"Oh," Amani breathed.

Nathan held out the frock coat for her to put on, and she took it without another word. He buttoned the front and stared at her for a moment.

"You look great both ways," Nathan said, before he kissed her forehead and reached for her hand. "Besides, if I'm being honest, I don't want any other man looking at you the way I look at you."

Amani blushed and squeezed his hand.

The two walked down the hall and took the stairs to head toward the dining room. Madame Luiza grinned when she saw Nathan.

"Only here a day, and you've already found a beautiful young woman to accompany you to breakfast?" She cast a glance at Amani. "You're lovely."

"What are you?" Amani asked.

"That's an odd question, dear."

"Not really. You are something different, but nothing I've encountered."

"What can I get you two for breakfast?" Madame Luiza said with an emotionless smile.

"Two of whatever you are serving sounds great," Nathan blurted, hoping to ease the awkwardness.

"I'll get right on it. You can sit right over there, Nathan."

"Thank you, Madame Luiza. She's not familiar with the social mores of the time. I'm sorry. I don't think she meant any offense."

She patted him on the shoulder. "None taken. We'll get you fed and then you can take a walk around the town," Madame Luiza said before stopping short. Amani was walking toward the table, and Madame Luiza's eyes went to her feet. "Where are her shoes?"

Nathan's eyes went wide. *Shoes. How could I have forgotten shoes for her?*

"She must have forgotten them upstairs. I'll make sure to grab her a pair before we head out," Nathan said in a rush.

"Very well. I'll bring your food to the table here soon."

"Thank you."

Nathan looked at his watch as Amani was taking her last bite of toast. It was eight o'clock, and he was anxious to see Calla Lily—anxious to see if she could explain where she got the camera from. Maybe then he could understand who and what Amani was.

"Are you ready to go?"

"Yes," Amani replied after she swallowed her toast.

"Was everything to your liking?" Madame Luiza asked as she reached for their empty plates.

"Your food is wonderful. Almost magical, in fact," Amani replied. "I've never had toast before. Especially with this wiggly blue stuff."

"It's blueberry jam." Madame Luiza laughed. "It's homemade."

"I like it very much."

"Well, I will save you some for tomorrow."

Nathan stood and pulled out the chair for Amani. "Your cooking is delicious," he added.

"I'll expect you both for dinner later."

"We'll be here." Nathan grinned. "I was wondering how I get to Calla Lily's shop."

"That's easy. Out the front door and to the left. Go down Main Street, and it'll be on your left. She opens promptly at eight-thirty, and if I know her, she'll be expecting you."

"Normally, I would say that was odd, but after the past twenty-four hours, nothing is shocking. I will welcome her foresight."

When they walked out of the dining hall, Nathan asked Amani to stay put. "We don't have any shoes for you to wear, so I am going to grab a pair of mine until we can get you ones of your own. Okay?"

She nodded and watched him as he took the steps two at a time. Nathan returned a few moments later with a pair of work boots.

"Here, put these on," he said, kneeling down to help her into them. "They'll keep your feet warm too."

When he stood back up, they were face to face with one another. Amani reached up and touched his face. "You are so kind to me."

"It's nothing," he said offhandedly. "Ready to go?"

Amani nodded as Nathan reached for her hand.

The two of them walked slowly over the cobblestone streets, Amani tripping slightly in the boots that were at least four sizes too big for her.

"Can you smell the dew on the spruce trees or hear the heartbeat of the Aspens?" she asked distractedly, her head tipped toward the sky.

Nathan looked at her. "No. How can you?"

"I'm connected to the energy of all nature," she said as they reached the storefront, "and this place pulses with it."

CHAPTER 10

*I*t was 8:23 on the dot when Nathan and Amani arrived at Callie's Trinkets and What Nots, and as Madame Luiza had said, she was waiting for them.

"I trust you enjoyed your breakfast," Calla Lily said as she opened the door.

Nathan simply shook his head. "What is it with this town? You and Madame Luiza seem to just *know* things."

"I told you, Nathan. It's filled with a magical energy. Everyone here has a gift," Amani replied, matter-of-factly.

"Something like that," Calla Lily said, motioning for Amani and Nathan to come in. "Welcome to Havenwood Falls . . ." Her voice trailed off for a second before continuing, "I'm sorry, I don't know your name."

"Amani," she replied as she stepped inside.

Calla Lily tilted her head to Nathan as he stepped in behind Amani. "Your name means wishes and desires. How apropos."

Amani turned back to Calla Lily. "You are very gifted. Most do not know that."

Nathan watched the two women for a moment before shifting his focus to the store.

"Your shop is quite large and well stocked with treasures," he remarked, eyeing a glass chalice with a Greco-Roman scene featured on the front of it. "Is this a . . . ?"

"It is."

"And are these . . . ?"

"They are."

"How did you come to acquire such treasures?" The excitement in Nathan's voice was unmistakable.

"Sometimes in the same way I acquired your father's satchel."

Nathan arched his brow. "And how was that exactly?"

"Unexpectedly," she replied.

Amani, too, was mesmerized by the large space. It was filled with this and that—treasures or trash, depending on who was looking. To Amani, everything was beautiful, new, and interesting. She wandered over to a rack of clothes near the window and ran her hands over them. The unique fabrics, textures, and colors were all so different from what she was used to. She'd worn nothing but a sheer linen sheath for centuries. "These are beautiful."

"You're more than welcome to try on anything you like," Calla Lily said as she looked over at Nathan. "Your boots and coat, I presume?"

He sighed and crossed his arms in front of his chest. "Yes. She is in need of some clothes in the same way I am in need of some answers."

Calla Lily grinned. "How about we start with her first, and then we can move on to the questions and answers."

Nathan nodded and laughed as he watched Amani twirl with a dress in her hand. "That's probably a good idea."

Amani and Calla Lily worked together to gather some clothes and shoes to try on. When they'd narrowed it down to a few things, Nathan interjected his opinion. It didn't take long for Amani to find an outfit she looked amazing in, but then again, he was sure she'd look good in a potato sack. Nathan couldn't take his eyes off Amani. He watched Calla Lily fix her hair and wondered what it was about her that had him so enthralled. None of this made any sense, but even if he was willing to indulge the fantasy, what would the future look like for him, for her—for them? She wasn't human, and he was. How was that going to work? Perhaps Calla Lily's information about his father's satchel would come with answers about Amani and whether or not she could remain with him, but for now, he'd simply enjoy the moment.

"How do I look?" Amani asked.

Nathan stared at her for a long moment before replying, "Beautiful. It seems to be my favorite word to describe you."

Amani's smile radiated. "Oh, good. I was hoping it would please you. I couldn't tell what you were feeling when you were watching me try on all those garments."

Nathan took her hand in his. "It was joy. Nothing more."

Amani's smile faded. "Why are you lying?"

"I'm not lying . . . exactly," Nathan replied as he dropped his head. "I'm trying to understand all of this and thinking about how we go forward from here is all."

Amani reached up and placed her hand over his heart. "One step at a time until we find the answers we seek."

He exhaled a breath and put his hand on hers. "One step at a time then."

They both turned to see Calla Lily watching them from behind the counter. "How about we start with one answer at a time," she offered.

Nathan took Amani's hand, and the two of them walked over to Calla Lily. "We are going to be here a while. We have lots of questions."

"I've got all day." She grinned. "What shall we start with? I promise nothing but honesty."

"What are you?" Amani asked. "I know you are something, but I've never encountered anyone like you. You are otherworldly, like me, are you not?"

"I'm sorry. She keeps asking everyone that," Nathan replied nervously.

"It's fine, and she's right. I'm what's referred to as a gypsy," she said, and turned to show them the mark of the gypsies on the back of her neck. "I have the ability to *read* you," Calla Lily admitted.

"You're a mystic?" Nathan blurted. "I mean, not that there is anything wrong with that," he offered, realizing he may have unintentionally offended her.

"No offense taken, Nathan, and yes, I am, but I am more than a mystic."

"Do you know, then, what I am?" Amani asked.

"I have an idea, but I've never encountered your kind either. I can see more if you let me," she said, reaching for Amani's hand. "I can tell a lot by your palm, and I can tell you even more if I use my tarot cards."

"Can you fill in the missing pieces for us? We are lost. We do not understand how it is that I came to be here. I was in Egypt with my sister, Khalida, and I knew Samuel, well, met him," she corrected, "before I lost my sister and was trapped."

"And it seems like my father's disappearance is connected to Amani's entrapment."

"I'll do my best," Calla Lily said as Amani turned her hand over so her palm was visible. "You said you were with your sister?"

"Yes, but she was lost to me. I thought she had died, but now that I am out of the camera, I can sense her, but I cannot pinpoint where she is exactly."

"Havenwood Falls is a special place. The disconnect between you and Khalida may be due to the magic surrounding us."

"What?" Nathan questioned.

"Why are you shocked, Nathan?" Calla Lily laughed. "You had to have some clue. It's part of the reason you are here to begin with."

He rubbed his forehead. "Nope. Completely clueless. Just hoping I'd encounter a miracle."

She cast a glance at Amani. "In a way, you did."

Nathan blew out a burst of air and ran his fingers through his hair. "I guess you're right."

"Khalida is more than your sister—she's your twin. It is a bond stronger than siblings," Calla Lily said as she continued to examine the lines on Amani's hand. "Your parents were human, but they are not your blood. You are something different."

Amani nodded as she held her breath. "Yes."

"What are you, Amani?" Calla Lily asked skeptically, running her hands along the fate line.

"She can't tell you," Nathan interjected. "That is why we are here. I'd hoped *you* could tell me, because she can't. Amani is forbidden to speak it, or it will draw the watchers' attention, and that is not good, apparently."

Calla Lily released Amani's hand. "Hmm. Okay."

"Why hmm? What's wrong?" Nathan asked.

"I do not know what these symbols mean that are interlaced with the lines. I've never seen them before. I mean, they look like hieroglyphics, but I can't be sure."

"They are," Amani replied.

"May I see?" Nathan asked.

She gave Nathan her hand. "Hmm. Well this one is the symbol for life, and this one is the symbol for protection. Here," he pointed, "is the symbol for the Ka, and this one here is a feather, which could represent a few things."

"It is for the goddess Ma'at," Amani said, then pointed to the next hieroglyph. "And this is for Hathor, and this one here is . . ."

"The Eye of Horus," Nathan interrupted. "The all-seeing eye."

Amani nodded.

"Why would these be interlaced with your lifeline, Amani?" Calla Lily asked.

"I'm not certain." She shrugged. "I told you, I'm unique . . . Khalida and I both are."

Calla Lily sank back in her chair, disappointment furrowing her brow as she strained to look deeper. Unfortunately, within seconds, she released Amani's hand and confessed, "I'm not sure I can help. I see a lot, but with you, I am blocked from seeing your past or your future. It's all a hazy mess."

CHAPTER 11

"The tarot cards you spoke of. Can they show the past?"

"They can," Calla Lily replied and drew out her deck to set them on the counter. "They can tell the present and the future, too, but you have to understand how they work. Have you ever used this type of divination?"

Amani shook her head.

Calla Lily began to shuffle the deck, but Amani put her hands over them. "May I connect to you to understand them?"

Calla Lily gave her a quizzical look. "Of course."

Amani closed her eyes and used her power to see into Calla Lily's thoughts. She didn't want to pry into anything personal. She only wanted to understand enough to show Nathan and Calla Lily what she was unable to speak.

A few moments passed, and the cards began to fly one by one in a line from the table up into the air. In the open space at the center of the shop, the tarot deck swirled like a roaring tornado for a few moments before landing on the floor in a perfect Celtic Cross Spread.

Calla Lily was in awe. "You're a fast learner," she said as she walked over toward the cards.

Amani opened her eyes and smiled. "I promise I only looked into what I needed. Nothing more."

"I know. I could sense where you were in my mind."

"I have no idea what is going on," Nathan interjected, "but as long as you two do, that's all that really matters."

Calla Lily lifted the hem of her skirt and knelt down to get a closer look at the spread. The first card and the card related to Amani was the World. It was reversed with the Justice card lying across it. She looked over her shoulder at Amani. "You certainly know how to make things clear, now don't you?"

"I will need you both to brace yourself for what is to come when you get to the Temperance card. There is only one way for me to tell you without actually speaking it," Amani said as she wrung her hands together. "Before my mother died, I saw her memories. I've never told anyone this, not even Khalida," she said before swallowing hard. "I always feared the judgment if anyone knew the truth. I loved my mother and father and never wanted any harm to come to them."

Nathan was a little peaked, but he was also nodding his head in agreement.

"Okay then, what do you want me to do?" Calla Lily asked.

Amani closed her eyes. "Pick up the card."

Calla Lily glanced at the grounding card. It was the Tower. The card associated with shocking change and catastrophe. Mix that with the Temperance card in the reversed position, and this was going to be a journey. Calla Lily reached up for Nathan's hand. "I'm not sure what is going to happen, so please hold on."

Nathan gave her a quick, false smile and took hold of her hand.

The moment Calla Lily touched the card, the room began to spin. Suddenly, they were no longer in Callie's Trinkets and What Nots, but instead were in an unfamiliar place, watching as events played out before them like a motion picture.

NEEMA KNEW *it was odd to check in on adult children as they slept, but the day she had dreaded for twenty-five years was finally here. Where had the time gone? They were just babes in her arms, and now they were*

grown women. Beyond their prime, some would say, for marrying and having children of their own, but Neema and her husband had not pushed the girls toward marriage. Instead, they tutored them in multiple languages and various cultures, broadening their scope of knowledge. They were as smart as any man and as cunning as the pharaoh's own children. It had been a choice on their part to make them of supreme value. Neema even hoped maybe they could rule one day, if given the chance.

As Neema watched Amani and Khalida sleep, she was anxious to see what, if anything, would change. Would they even change at all? Would it happen when the moon was at its peak in the night sky? Maybe the prophecy had been false; maybe having her as a mother changed their fates. Neema thought back to the day when her world shifted. She wasn't the one who'd given them life, because she and her husband were both human. She was, though, the one who loved and cared for them every day and every moment. They were her treasures, yet as the days quickened toward their maturity, she began to fear the truth of who they really were.

Amani and Khalida were djinn, or so she was told, but to her, they were precious angels in need of love and care. She was warned to watch for any signs of peculiarity, because djinn could be tricksters, but the girls had never been anything other than sweet and kind. Every djinn aged a quarter of a century before their powers and talents were revealed. However, Amani and Khalida were not typical djinn. They were something else—something unique—and that was the reason they lived among the humans and not their own kind. Neema liked to believe their uniqueness was meant to save the world one day or to heal the sick.

The corner of her mouth quirked up as she looked down at her girls. Amani slept soundly, but Khalida was tossing and turning—nothing out of the ordinary. Satisfied they were okay, Neema decided to pray to Hathor and Ma'at for guidance instead of worrying the entire night away.

Neema plucked a single feather from a dove and placed it into a pile of burning embers. As the feather began to burn, she lifted the copper dagger from the altar she'd prepared and pricked her finger, letting the blood pool before swirling with her offerings. Neema removed the ankh from the cord around her neck and placed it over the ashes of the feather. She patiently waited for Hathor to appear. When nothing happened,

Neema sighed. Maybe it was a sign. She walked over to the chair on the open balcony and sat down stiffly, awaiting the goddesses' return. As she stared into the distance, a gentle wind caressed her skin, lulling Neema to sleep. Her thoughts drifted to the day the twins were born.

On the day of their birth, Neema gave Amani and Khalida names to enhance their souls, as was her belief. The soul was made up of five parts —the Jb: the heart; the Sheut: the shadow; the Ren: the name; the Ba: the personality; and the Ka: the soul—and it was Neema's plan to ensure they'd be worthy on the day they'd meet the goddess Ma'at by bestowing them with names to suit who they were as part of the universe. Neema honored all Egyptian traditions, and had since she was a young girl. Especially anything honoring Hathor and Ma'at.

Neema had been born of privilege and was married to a man of wealth and prestige, but she had a secret only she and the goddess Hathor knew. Neema had been unable to produce an heir, and her husband was growing weary of her infertility. She prayed night and day for Hathor to bless her with a child, and finally the goddess appeared before her with a proposal—one she would not refuse.

"I've heard your prayers, child, and I've come to give you what you ask," Hathor said in a gentle tone.

"I will do anything," Neema begged, "please."

"Twin girls were born of fire and air, but not human girls. These djinn will require watching over—careful watching. Do you believe you are worthy of the task?"

Neema dropped to her knees and looked up at the powerful deity. "I do. I only want my belly to swell and to feel the link of mother and child. Will they know I am theirs, as they are mine?"

"They will only know you as their mother, but you may never tell anyone of this night. Only you are to know, understand?"

"Yes, goddess. I will love them as my own."

"On the twenty-fifth year of their birth, you are to make a sacrifice in my name and burn it, letting the smoke rise and billow. When the flames recede, you are to place this ankh into the ashes, and I will come to you once again," Hathor said, handing Neema the golden symbol of life.

Neema bowed and held the ankh to her chest.

"Go now to your husband and seduce him. Make certain he is fully pleasured, and when you wake, the twins will be within your womb."

Tears spilled down Neema's cheeks. "Thank you, Goddess. Thank you for these gifts."

"I do hope by giving you these girls that they will turn into worthy beings."

"I will make it so. I will be a good mother."

"Be well, Neema. I will return to you when they come of age," Hathor said solemnly before disappearing from view.

Neema rose, fixing her hair and gown before going to do as the goddess asked. Her husband had been sleeping, but could easily be roused by Neema's touch. Tonight her belly would fill with not just one, but two children, and it pleased Neema to not only show her husband, Garai, how much she loved him, but also how virile he was to produce twins. Their children would not be male heirs, but they would still be a blessing. Neema caressed her husband until she had his attention and then let the thin wisp of material fall from her shoulders onto the floor, exposing her bare flesh and rousing every bit of Garai's senses.

The couple made love for hours, the moon's glow illuminating Neema's tawny skin as she writhed above her husband. They both seemed engulfed by the flames of desire. It was as if they'd never tasted one another, and this was their first moment of ecstasy. Neither wanted it to end.

As the sun began to rise, the couple lay in each other's arms, sated and exhausted. The slaves entered to bring them trays of fruit and beer, but noticed their sleeping masters and quietly left the room. Garai and Neema spent the day in bed, not bothering to rise until the sun began to set. Garai seemed pleased with himself, often commenting that their escapades of the previous night were sure to produce the child they so desperately sought. Neema contentedly ran her hands over her womb, knowing he'd be pleased with Hathor's gifts as much as she was.

Neema grabbed a handful of grapes and a few figs before striding back over to Garai. As he watched her walk to him, her breasts appeared fuller, and the gentle curve of her hips seemed to fill out with each step she took. His chest filled with pride in knowing his seed had taken hold. Neema's naked body was luxurious, and he wanted to taste her once again. When she reached his side, he pulled her into his arms and rolled her onto the bed. Neema giggled and fed him a fig.

"What has you so boyish, my love?"

Garai licked his lips and ran his hands over Neema's swelling belly. "This. You. Our soon-to-be family."

"But how can you be so sure?" she teased.

"You already have the glow of a woman bearing a child," he said and kissed her.

Neema grinned inwardly. "Then I shall praise Hathor for her gift and honor her in every way."

Garai grinned and let his hands roam until he could no longer control his desire. He entered her, and the waves of passion once again ignited between them.

Neema was jolted from the memory of her and Garai when the sound of footfalls resonated behind her.

"Mother!" Amani cried out. "Come quickly. Something is wrong with Khalida."

Neema jumped to her feet and ran with Amani to Khalida's side.

"What is wrong with her, Mother? Why is her hair alternating between dark and white?" Amani asked.

"I do not know." Neema's voice quivered as she watched gold symbols appear and disappear on Amani's back as well.

Khalida's eyes opened, and she stared blankly at her mother and sister. Neema gasped, and Amani cried out as they watched Khalida's eyes change from a golden amber to an opaque white, then back to amber.

"Oh, Sister. What has happened to you?" Amani pleaded.

Khalida reeled back and asked the same, as fissures of fire erupted over Amani's caramel-colored skin. Symbols took shape and etched words in ancient script over her entire body. Amani dropped to her knees and begged her mother for answers.

Tears welled in Neema's eyes. "I'm sorry. I should have told you long ago, but it was forbidden. I'm so sorry, my precious girls. Your Ren means wishes and aspirations, just as Khalida's means immortal. You two are my immortal wishes, and I love you both."

Neema ran to the altar and pleaded to Hathor to appear immediately, but nothing happened. Maybe the sacrifice was not great enough. She gripped the dagger in her hand and plunged it into her chest. "I beg of you, Hathor, protect my girls as I have protected your secret," Neema cried out. "I sacrifice myself to save them."

Amani ran to her side and held her dying mother in her arms. "Mother, no! Why would you do this? We need you."

Neema brushed back a golden lock from Amani's face. "You've been my greatest gift. Forgive me. All I did was for love—always love."

Khalida strode over to Neema. "What secrets?" she asked coolly.

Tears spilled from Neema's eyes as her blood pooled around her. Khalida had always been the mischievous one of the two. She always searched for trouble, while Amani kept the peace. As Neema looked at them now, their djinn sides revealing themselves, it became clear. Amani with her dark, dusky grey skin and flaming hair, and Khalida with her pure white hair and fawn skin. They were light and dark, merged as one yet split in two."

When the day comes for your souls to be weighed, make certain your heart is worthy," Neema whispered.

Khalida's eyes narrowed as she look at Neema. "Are you even our mother?"

Amani gasped. "You dare ask such a question!"

"Always the naïve one, sister. Look at us. Do we look like her?"

Amani looked down at her changed skin and then up at her sister's now white hair, still refusing to acknowledge the truth. Neema squeezed Amani's hand, shifting her attention back to her mother.

"I am your mother in all the ways that make a mother. I carried you in my womb. I gave birth to you and suckled you at my breast. I cared for you every day. Loved you like no other, but you are not of my blood. You are so much more than blood and bone. Be true and remember my peace and joy, and always my love," Neema said, the last three words in barely a whisper, before dying in Amani's arms.

Tears spilled from Amani's eyes, while Khalida stood defiant.

"Our life is built on lies," Khalida hissed.

"She may have lied, but she did love us. She was, as she said, our mother in all the ways that mattered." Amani cried as she stared down at her blood stained hands.

Just then the door slammed open, and Garai stormed in.

"What is all the ruckus?" he demanded. As he continued into the room, he saw a stranger holding his wife's lifeless body and flew into a rage.

Amani looked up at him with her now darkened skin and realized he didn't recognize her.

"What have you done?" he cried out as he tore Neema from her arms.

"We've done nothing. Neema did this to herself," Khalida spat.

"Neema? Never. Who are you to say such words?" Garai growled.

"Khalida means no disrespect, Father," Amani interjected.

"Father? I am not your father. Guards!"

"Do not call him Father. He is no more our father than she was our mother."

Garai narrowed his eyes at the two strangers before him.

Amani slowed her breathing and wished the changes that turned them into this would stop and he could see them as they truly were. Even as she thought it, her skin flickered and her hair fell in golden waves over her shoulders. "See father, it is us, your daughters."

"What are you?" Garai asked in confusion as he watched her change into the daughter he knew. He shook his head, whispering to Neema as he rocked her. "What have you done, my love? What have our daughters become? Demons? Sorcerers? Witches?"

"I'm sorry, father," Amani pleaded.

"Your mother gave everything to you, and this is the way you repay her—with lies?"

"Lies?" Khalida said as she moved to strike Garai.

Amani pleaded with her sister to back off and walk away, but when Khalida refused, Amani blocked Neema and Garai from her view.

"What is wrong with you?" Amani shouted.

"Different, it seems. We are powerful. Can you not feel it coursing through your veins? I want to see what we can do, don't you?" Khalida replied with a sinister grin, the djinn traits once again surfacing.

"You will never hurt them, Sister—never!"

"*Neema is already gone. He is all who remains, and he never did anything but force his will upon us. We are free now.*"

Amani's heart began to break as the truth began to settle in for her father. His beloved wife was now dead, and the truth that his daughters were not really his was sinking in. Lies begat more lies even as Amani tried to defend him and Neema against Khalida.

"*I have loved both you both equally, but Khalida, you have always challenged my authority. I know it must have come across as me treating you differently, but even in harsh tones, you had my heart and my love, Khalida. You both did,*" he cried.

Neema was gone, but he needed answers, so he pleaded for the goddess that Neema held so dear to show herself.

"*Hathor, I demand to know the truth.*"

No one answered.

"*Please, dear goddess. I must know why my beloved is dead and my daughters are not as they once were. I beg of you.*"

Amani and Khalida's argument stopped in an instant when the curtains began to whip near the balcony's edge. Smokeless fire and the scent of frankincense rose until it was pungent in the air. Three figures appeared before them, unseen until the fire cleared. They stepped forward, and Garai and Amani gasped as a larger-than-life guard with ebony skin and the face of a jackal stood holding a canopic jar, glaring down at the twin girls. Next to him was a frightening male, dressed all in black, his skin etched like Khalida's and Amani's, but glowing a vibrant cobalt blue. He, too, stared at them, his arms crossed loosely in front of his chest as if he were at ease, but nothing about his demeanor expressed calm. He appeared as if he could rip them limb from limb in a matter of seconds.

In the middle towered a beautiful woman dressed in ceremonial garb and adorned with jewels and headdress befitting a queen. Amani was the first to realize who she was and immediately dropped to her knees and bowed her head. Khalida stood defiant, and when Garai looked from his daughters to the goddess, he too bowed his head.

"*You will not honor me?*" Hathor asked Khalida.

"*I know not who you are, but can assume you have something to do with the lies that have been told here.*"

Hathor tilted her head in curiosity. "I believe you do know who I am, but still refuse. You will, however, pay me the respect I deserve." Hathor's eyes changed, and she stepped toward Khalida. "BOW!" she commanded.

Khalida unwillingly took to her knees.

"I am sick of your childish games," Hathor said as she hovered above her.

Khalida stared at her through opaque eyes. "I'm not playing games. I'm tired of being lied to."

Amani scolded Khalida under her breath, pleading with her to stop before the goddess killed them all.

Once Hathor was satisfied, she went over to where Garai knelt, Neema's lifeless body still in his arms. "May I see her?" she asked reverently.

Garai shifted so he could give Hathor access to Neema. "Why did she do this? Why are Amani and Khalida something otherworldly?" Garai questioned, the words catching on the lump in his throat.

Hathor brushed the hair back from Neema's face. "It is time for her to walk with Anubis. I know she will pass Ma'at's test and enter the afterlife without negative judgment. I will make certain Ma'at knows of Neema's love and good deeds."

"But she lied," he replied.

"A lie she was bound to by her commitment to me. She wanted to bear your children, but was unable. I gave her the twins as a gift—with one condition. She was to never reveal this to anyone, not even you, Garai. She honored her word and loved you and the girls as I expected her to."

"So why did she take her own life?"

"Sacrifice. She knew there would be one. This was never my intent, but no one knew what the twins would turn out to be—that is, until now."

"Will you take them from me?" Garai asked.

"I will have to."

"Then I ask only one thing of you. If you are to take my beloved daughters as you have taken Neema, then I wish to walk beside her in the Duat. Grant me this, please. I do not want to live a life without her."

Hathor bowed her head in acknowledgment, and the frightening male with the tattooed skin stepped forward, his markings calming from to cobalt to black. Amani cried as she stared at her father. There were no words spoken, no time before the man jammed a dagger into Garai's side. Garai's body slumped to the ground, and Amani was shaken. She knew she risked punishment, but she would hold her father as she held her mother in those final moments.

Amani cradled his head in her lap as he spoke his final words. "I love you, Amani. You and Khalida may not be of my blood, but you are of my heart."

"I love you, Father. Please be well until we can be together once more," Amani said as she slipped the ring and jewel-encrusted bracelet off her arm and placed them into his hands. "An offering, in case you should need it."

Garai squeezed Amani's hand and took one last breath. She swallowed hard and did her best to steady herself before responding to Hathor.

"Mother taught us your ways. To honor and obey the gods and to be ready when the day came to face Ma'at in the Hall of Truth. I know not what my sister and I are, but I will do as my mother commanded of me and honor her—and you."

Hathor reached into the altar bowl Neema had used to summon her. She lifted the ankh and held it tightly in her hand, the ancient symbol changing at once into a single gold feather. Hathor ran her hands along the tattered cord, and it too changed into a shimmering strand. "Rise, Amani."

Amani did as she was asked, never once risking a look at Khalida. She loved her sister, but could not for the life of her understand what had gotten into her this day. Hathor placed the golden feather and chain around Amani's neck and spoke words she couldn't interrupt. When Hathor fell silent, Amani thanked her in a whisper.

Hathor then turned to face Khalida. "Why today the change, Khalida? I've watched you for years be a loving and devoted child and sister, but now, as you kneel before me, I sense rage and disdain."

"Because today the truth was brought to light. Lies spoken brought to

bear, all except for one, that is. What are we?" Khalida looked between herself and Amani. "Why are we twins and yet now we are different? Why does Amani seem to have goodness in her heart and I anger? I feel nothing but pain."

Hathor nodded her head slowly. "I do not know, but I will find the answer you seek. I can tell you, though, your creation was a mistake. There have never been twin djinns born, so we all are uncertain of what to expect from you."

"Djinns?" Amani stiffened. "Mother told us stories, but we thought she was telling us of fantastic beings that didn't truly exist. Is this why all of these changes have occurred in us?"

"Yes. Today is your quarter-century birthday and the day when all djinn understand their particular talents. Yours have manifested into," Hathor paused, "well, it's still unclear. And it is the reason you will be coming with us."

"Never," Khalida spat as she moved to run. In an instant, she was but a wisp of sand and dust floating, and the next, she was trapped, with nothing but clay walls inscribed with ancient hieroglyphics and her sister to look at. "Where are we?" she hissed.

Amani wiped the tears from her eyes and straightened her shoulders. "The bronze ewer the jackal guard was holding. Thanks to you, we've been trapped. Had you held your tongue and not tried to flee, we might not be prisoners."

"Don't blame me. Blame Garai and Neema."

"I only blame you for this," Amani said as she stared at Khalida. "Hopefully, once we face our judgment, we will understand the details of who and what we are. That is, if you can manage to keep your anger under control."

Khalida started to protest, but Amani's human appearance had changed again—revealing her djinn side once more. Khalida held her tongue as Amani's sweet, delicate nature shifted dramatically to reveal her powerful djinn traits. She became something Khalida didn't recognize, but more importantly, Khalida needed to find a way to get Amani to see her point of view. If they were to be free, they'd need to work together.

"I can hear your thoughts, feel your energy, and I will do no such thing. Accept our fate, Khalida," Amani seethed.

Amani glared at her sister, and for the first time since all this happened, Khalida realized their twin bond was even stronger than it had been before. They were one being in two bodies. She pinched her arm and watched Amani react. Khalida smiled, but only for a moment before Amani sent a blinding pain into her head, knocking her to the ground. Khalida relented and found a comfortable spot to sit inside their new prison. Thankfully, it didn't appear small in size from the inside, but instead was laid out like an open room with basic creature comforts lining the walls.

Amani, calmed and returned to her human form, ventured to the bed covered in linen, while Khalida sat at the table covered with food and drink.

Amani and Khalida spent countless hours pondering their situation. Sometimes they argued, while others they remained silent, but most were spent discussing the possibilities of exactly what they were.

"Punished for being different," Khalida would rage.

"We'll be free soon enough. They must be still watching, and these malicious outbursts of yours are only delaying our progress," Amani would retort.

Khalida started to respond, but before she could, she and Amani were turned into wisps of sand again and sent swirling into the air. When they took human form, they were standing in an elegant throne room. There before them were Ma'at, Hathor, the jackal guard, and the tattooed man. All four of them looked down at Amani and Khalida from their elevated position. Amani was in awe. The room was gilded with blue accents amidst elaborate paintings and intricate carvings of hieroglyphics. And while all of that was impressive, what amazed Amani the most was the statue of the goddess Ma'at herself, with her winged arms outstretched, the feathers adorned in bright hues, accentuating each one as if they held a special significance. Amani bowed low. Khalida, defiant as always, remained standing, but silent, at least.

"Do you know why we have brought you here?" Ma'at asked.

Khalida began to speak, but Amani interrupted. "To tell us our fate?"

"In a way, yes."

"We've made a decision regarding your future, and we hope you will see its necessity," Hathor added.

"Khaldun," Hathor pointed to the tattooed man, "will become one of your watchers. He will monitor your actions and decide if reform will be necessary."

"May we go home?" Amani asked.

"No. We've created a place for you to dwell, but it will not be among the djinn or the humans. The djinn do not wish to have you, and you are too dangerous to be among the humans, as evidenced by the death of your parents."

Tears began to spill down Amani's cheeks at the thought of her mother and father.

"We did not kill anyone. Neema killed herself and he," Khalida pointed to Khaldun, "killed our father. We are guilty of nothing."

"Hathor warned me of your indignant nature, and while I value all opinions, I do not wish to hear the words of a petulant child. You'd do well to mind your tongue."

Amani reached for Khalida's hand and dragged her down to her knees. "Can you not be quiet?" she whispered through gritted teeth.

"No. If she is going to kill me, then so be it. It will be better than living out my days in a prison."

Hathor walked closer, the power she wielded radiating with each step she took. "I have no need of you, Khalida, but I do value Amani. Unfortunately, your lives are bound together in an unbreakable bond. Both must live or both will die."

Amani gasped, and Khalida stared at her in disbelief.

"Good. We finally have your attention," Ma'at interjected.

"As was your mother's way, Amani, you and Khalida will live out your lives in service to Ma'at's divine rules. When the day of your judgment comes, you will hopefully greet Anubis with honor," Hathor finished.

"The unfortunate circumstances of your creation and the actions we must take from this day forward are no fault of your own, but it is still a matter we must deal with. We've made every effort to make your new *home pleasant. Thoth has calculated all you will need and has created a home capable of serving you both. It will have all the amenities you had when you lived with your parents and then some. The one condition— and it is non-negotiable," Ma'at stated flatly, "—is that the watchers will be checking in on you often. Nothing you say or do can be withheld from them. There will be no escape, and there will be no release."*

With tear-stained eyes, Amani replied. "I will accept my fate and do as you ask, but I must insist you explain to us why we are to be punished simply for being born. Who are our real parents?"

Ma'at sat motionless, but Hathor moved closer to Amani. "You and Khalida, unlike true djinn—you are different. Djinn are born of searing wind and fire, between the ranks of angels and humans. They live long lifespans, but they also die. You have free will, which is why Khalida's temper rages against the choices before her," Hathor said as she lay her hand on Amani's cheek. "Your kind can be benevolent or evil, but that is where the link between you and djinn end."

"I'm sorry, I still do not understand. Why are we so different?"

"Because your birth came out of an argument between Sekhmet and Shu. Their rage in the moment bore twin energies carrying with it traits of the god and goddess themselves, making you two extremely powerful and unpredictable. No two djinn have ever been born at the same time. When you and Khalida are together, you think the same thoughts, feel one another's pleasure and pain. Now imagine if you someday felt the rage in Khalida's heart at the same time she was feeling it. It could be the end of us all. It is a risk we cannot and will not take. I'm sorry," Hathor said with a pained smile.

Khalida's rage began to build. Amani could feel it escalating like a sandstorm. She walked away from the goddess and stood before Khalida. "This upsets me too, but your anger will kill us both. Stop now, or you will not have to wait for their wrath. I will kill us instead, ending all of this now. Everything happens for a reason, Sister. We are destined for something. Let us take this gift of life and do what we can with it," Amani pleaded.

Khalida's palms began to burn, and Amani's did, too, reminding them both just how connected they were to one another.

"*Please, Sister. I do not wish to be in pain,*" Amani added.

"*Thoth promised to find the answer to the mystery surrounding you, but until that day, this shall be your home.*"

The jackal guard stepped forward with a unique-looking clay vessel in hand. It was different from the previous one he held. This one was large and cylindrical, but unlike anything Amani and Khalida had ever seen. From the outside, it appeared to be two jars connected as one, but they maintained their individual shapes—like the entrance to a private chamber. Before Amani could finish taking in the jar itself, they were all transported to a stone room, with stairs leading up to a massive double door. Two alabaster guards with their arms crossed in front of them stood at the base of the steps, while paintings and hieroglyphs covered the walls and columns.

"*Your home is beyond those doors. Once you enter, they will not open again,*" Hathor explained. "*Khaldun will escort you.*"

The tattooed man stepped forward and moved toward Amani and Khalida. "*This way,*" he said in a deep baritone.

Amani glanced down at where his hand was touching her and cast him a glance. He tilted his head in acknowledgment of her displeasure. He then attempted the same with Khalida, who met his eyes with an agreeable smirk. The two walked ahead, and Amani watched as Khalida seemed to be distracted by the truth of their fate. She was flirting, as she had done countless times with men their father did business with. They'd become smitten with her beauty, and she'd manipulate them to her advantage. Amani assumed Khalida was hoping she'd be able to do the same with their new watcher, but considering the look of disdain on his face, she doubted the effort would bring her sister much success.

Amani moved forward and made her way to the first step, before turning back to look at Ma'at and Hathor. After a few moments passed, she turned without another word and followed behind the watcher and Khalida. Her fate was sealed the moment she took the last step. A handful of Egyptian slaves opened the doors, and she and Khalida stepped into their destiny.

CHAPTER 12

With a gasp, the link between Amani, the Temperance card, Calla Lily, and Nathan was broken. It was as if no time had passed, and yet they were all drained from the experience. Amani's face was flushed, and her breathing was erratic just before her body went slack. Nathan leapt forward and caught her before she hit the ground.

"You don't look well. What can we do?" Calla Lily asked as she rushed to Amani's side.

"I need a moment to compose myself."

"Let me grab you some water," Calla Lily offered before running toward a sink at the back of the store.

When she returned, she handed Nathan the glass.

"Are you okay? That was some journey you took us on," Calla Lily said when Amani was sitting upright.

"I am, but it exhausted me. I've never done anything like that before." She feigned a smile. "I hope it helped."

"It did, but when you're up for it, I have a few questions," Calla Lily said.

Nathan shot her a sideways glance. He too had questions, but with the way Amani looked at the moment, he thought it would be better for her to rest. They could clear up the gray areas later.

"Or maybe we should go back to the inn and try again later," Nathan interjected.

"No, I will be fine. What is it you wish to know?"

Calla Lily paused and then blurted, "You had insight into your mother's deepest secrets. Do you have the sight?"

"No. With everything that happened that day, my mother's blood seeped into my skin, and I at once knew all of her memories—felt her every emotion. It's how I know Nathan's thoughts as well. His blood was what freed me."

"Hmm. Okayyy . . ." Calla Lily dragged out the words. "And since Khalida never touched your mother's blood, she never knew the depth of Neema's love for you both."

Amani shook her head. "And no amount of explaining would ever make her understand. She's angry. All she has ever wanted was revenge."

Calla Lily nodded her head. "She's a formidable force, from what I could see."

"Wait, so let me understand," Nathan interrupted. "Blood is the link to you being able to see a person's memories?"

"I see and feel everything," she said as she laid her hand on Nathan's cheek. "I wish I could ease the pain you are feeling with answers as to what happened to Samuel, but the only way I can tell you what happened is to have his blood or the blood of the one who had a hand in his disappearance. I'm sorry."

"We'll figure it out. For now, I'm only worried about you."

"Have you sensed Khalida since you've been free?" Calla Lily interjected.

"Yes. I felt her emotions, and I . . ." She blushed. "I think I was experiencing the connection between her and Khaldun."

"The watcher?" Calla Lily narrowed her eyes, trying to piece all this together.

"Yes, this morning before she woke, she called out his name and —" Nathan swallowed hard. "Let's just say she was in a precarious state," Nathan admitted as he helped Amani to her feet.

Calla Lily arched a brow, but from the bashful looks on both their faces, she'd use her imagination as to what they meant. "Well, this is not my expert opinion, but it is an opinion. I think you couldn't sense your sister because you were once again trapped, and now that you are free, the twin connection is working. The question remaining is what is your sister's link to this watcher."

Amani gripped her chest and cried out. "Khalida! She's near."

Calla Lily's eyes went wide. "Here in Havenwood Falls? Are you sure? We're hidden from most—even supernatural beings struggle to find us sometimes because of the magic surrounding us."

"And Khaldun is with her."

"Well, the Court is definitely going to need to know about this, then." Calla Lily sighed. "Let's get you two out of here, and I will find you later, after I have spoken with them. Don't worry. Our magic is strong. You'll be safe here."

"Thank you," Amani said. Nathan lifted her into his arms and carried her back to the inn. Calla Lily stopped to explain to Mihail, Irina, and Madame Luiza what was going on, while Nathan took Amani upstairs. There was still a lot to discover, but for now, all the two of them could do was relax and wait. Nathan laid Amani gently on the bed and covered her with the blanket. When she was comfortable, he grabbed his father's journal and began to read through it. The jars from the memory had stuck in his mind.

"Does this look familiar?" he asked, showing her the hand-drawn images.

She sat up and leaned against her arm. "Yes, but how do you have these?"

"My father drew them."

"I do not understand, Nathan. How does Samuel connect to Khalida and me?"

"If I had to venture a guess, I would say my father and his team of Egyptologists stumbled upon you by sheer accident. They were uncovering Hatshepsut's tomb, nothing more. Hathor and Ma'at's hiding place had to have been there. And based on my father's notes, you should have been safe. Your jar was sitting on a ledge with a barrier of red stones carved like scarabs and a shimmering liquid no one could identify. That, along with the mysterious hieroglyphs, should have kept most treasure hunters at bay, but for some reason, someone gambled on it being nothing more than for show." Nathan flipped through the journal and read further down the notes. "It says here the jars sat undisturbed for weeks, but one night raiders came in and stole several items from the belly of the tomb. Your vessel was broken and lay in pieces next to one of the men who tried to steal it. Apparently, his hands and face were badly burned, leaving him unrecognizable to the local workers." Nathan shrugged. "I don't understand that."

Amani shifted on the bed. "I do. I overheard the watchers talking about it once. Anyone who tried to move the jar would unknowingly awaken the protective magic surrounding us. The scarabs were made of carnelian, a powerful crystal used to protect the living and the dead. If touched, the scarabs would come to life and run into the mercury, creating a toxic combination. The person who dared to touch them would die a slow, painful death."

Nathan huffed. "Well, someone not only attempted, but succeeded in breaking the vessel, and in doing so, freed you and Khalida."

"We didn't know what happened, only that we were free. Khalida said it was our reward for good behavior." Amani paused, dropping her head. "And I believed her. I was so naïve."

"What reason would you have to doubt her? Besides, she didn't know you'd be released by human greed."

Amani sighed. "I'm not sure about that."

Nathan gave a quick shake of his head. "Why?"

"Remember when I said we met Samuel the morning we were released, and that Khalida saw a man using a box to capture people's images—said we should get one as a gift to ourselves?"

"Yes."

"And the blurred image along with the one that looked like I was standing next to someone?"

"Yeah, right here," he said, reaching for the stack on the nightstand.

"She was next to me, and the blur was her disappearing in a wisp of sand."

Realization dawned on Nathan's face, and he reached for Amani's hand. "You think she tricked you, and my father was collateral damage."

Amani nodded. "I think so. I doubt your father is alive, Nathan. I'm so sorry."

"None of this is your fault," he said as he squeezed her hand. "Khalida has a lot to answer for, but the question remains: with her close, how do we keep you safe and not susceptible to entrapment again?"

"You don't. I will keep myself safe. I'm wiser now, and my concern is for you and Calla Lily. I care for you both, and Khalida will try to use anything or anyone to get to me."

"Amani, I don't want to lose you. Yes, the circumstances of how this all came to be are insane and unbelievable, but I feel a connection with you. I . . ."

"I feel the same way, Nathan, but if I lost you after all this—after finally knowing what a life beyond my prison could be like—I would rather be dead."

Nathan caressed her cheek. "Well, if I have anything to do with it, that is not going to happen," he said before leaning down and kissing her forehead. "I want you to rest for a little bit. I'm going to go downstairs and see if Madame Luiza can make us some food," he said as he moved off the bed.

"I'll try," she replied.

WHEN THE DOOR CLICKED SHUT, Amani let her mind wander to her sister. The first weeks in their new home had been the hardest for her and Khalida, but the goddesses hadn't lied when they said Thoth had calculated all they'd need. The doors to the chamber led into an opulent palace fit for a pharaoh. It had servants and animals mingling about, with grassy knolls just beyond the gardens for the cows and chickens to graze. Sunlight and moonlight spilled onto the balconies as the days turned into night. It even had running water that fell into rectangular pools for them to either swim or bathe. They never wanted for anything. They had all the food and provisions anyone could ever need, all contained in the space of the dual vessels. They should've been happy, and they were for a time, but only having one another and the occasional visit from the watchers and Khaldun grew old quickly. Neither of them knew how long they'd live, and the infinite number of days and years hung over them like a boulder.

The pieces of the puzzle were becoming clearer to Amani after the stroll down memory lane with Nathan and Calla Lily. Khalida's flirting with Khaldun may have been innocent at first, but now Amani knew the initial manipulation must have turned into something more. Amani thought back to all the times he'd come to "check" on them. Khalida would disappear for long periods of time, but when it was happening, Amani assumed it was because she despised being watched and scrutinized by the watchers—she said she preferred to hide and avoid his questioning. How foolish she had been to think her sister was on her side.

～

"She's here. I can feel her. She's weak."

"Where?" Khaldun snarled.

Khalida waved her hand in a wide swath. "Down there somewhere. We have a connection, but it's not exact. It's still flickering for some unknown reason."

"You stay here. I'll go. I do not want you alerting her to my presence."

Khalida stood in front of him. "Actually. I think it's you who should stay. You she'd see as a threat, but me? She won't know if I'm a victim or a willing participant."

"She can sense your every emotion. She will know."

Khalida gave Khaldun a malicious grin before she dug her nails into her arm and dragged them downwards, leaving deep gouges. The open wounds began to ooze blood and the iridescent element that made her and Amani unique.

"Now hit me," she commanded.

He shook his head slowly. "There has always been something different about you, but this is taking it to the extreme, don't you think?"

"I think you're a vicious man who's kept me captive and made me his plaything for the past eighteen years, and you must be punished for your wicked ways," she teased.

Khaldun pulled her into his arms and kissed her hard and deep before biting her bottom lip. Blood dripped, and he grinned. "I'll expect you back in two days' time. If not, I will burn the town to the ground to find you, understand?"

"I do, my love," she answered before she kissed him once more. "Now hit me."

The blow Khaldun struck was hard enough to knock her out, but when Khalida came to, she was alone. She grinned. The marks on her arms were black and blue, and the blood was now dry and cakey. There was only one thing left to do—

"Amani, help me," Khalida cried out.

AMANI WINCED. She could feel Khalida's pain, but decided to block her link to her twin. It was something she had learned to do a long time ago, but never told her sister was possible. Khalida's rage was too much to bear, and sometimes Amani needed a break from the link that bound them together. It became a secret she held dear and something that was only hers. When they were young girls, Amani never minded sharing things, but after the change and the truth was revealed, she didn't want to be like Khalida anymore. Amani's heart was heavy with grief, and nothing Khalida said or did felt like she even cared about Neema and Garai. True, they weren't blood relatives, but the couple had loved the sisters and cared for them unconditionally nonetheless.

The fact she and Khalida were mistakes born out of anger weighed heavily on Amani. Was their only destiny to wreak havoc on the world? Could they not be something more than what was assumed of them? Khalida truly embraced the aspects of Sekhmet, while Amani tended to have more of Shu's traits, but the truth was they transformed often. Like the tide, their emotions and personalities shifted and changed. Amani knew now, after all the time locked away with Khalida, *that* was the reason for their imprisonment. They were too unpredictable. However, Amani never enjoyed the moments when her rage rose to the surface. She may have had this power, but she never wanted to use it to harm anyone. Disconnecting her emotions from Khalida was the only hope she had of freedom from this impossible situation.

CHAPTER 13

*N*athan ran into Calla Lily in the foyer of the inn. The look on her face spoke volumes.

"What's wrong?"

Calla Lily sighed. "The Court is worried. You were only supposed to be a visitor who'd be leaving in a day or two, but now, with Amani arriving unexpectedly and her sister and a watcher tracking her . . ." She paused. "It puts Havenwood Falls and all its residents in danger, and that is something they are adamantly opposed to."

"The court? Is this your judicial system here in Havenwood Falls?"

Calla Lily chuckled. "In a way. They govern the town and everything that goes on here. They have a vested interest in all visitors because they can adversely affect the balance."

"I understand, but what can we do? Where can I take Amani to be safe?"

"I don't know, Nathan. The Court members were split in regards to letting you stay and marking you with our protections. Did Amani say if she knew how close Khalida was?"

"No, but I left her upstairs to come get us some food. Maybe she'll have a better sense now."

"One of the members suggested trapping Khalida this time, thus keeping Amani safe."

"Oh sure, and how do I go about doing that?" He huffed. "I'm only human, remember? And what about this watcher? Does anyone know what he is capable of?"

Calla Lily shook her head. "No, but I do want to help you, Nathan. I want to help you both. Maybe the Luna Coven can help? Give me a little more time, and I will try to get you an answer, okay?"

"Yeah," he replied with a nervous laugh, "I doubt an hour is going to clear this up, but sure."

When Calla Lily turned to leave, Nathan made his way up the stairs with a pot of Madame Luiza's tea and some homemade biscuits and jam in hand. He hoped Amani would like it and that it would tide her over until lunch was ready. Madame Luiza said she'd bring a tray up right away. When he opened the door, he saw Amani sleeping. She looked so peaceful, and he wondered how in the world he was going to help keep her safe.

Nathan set the tray down and walked over to adjust the blanket. "All of this feels like some crazy dream, but it's become something I don't want to wake up from," he whispered. "You've gotten to me, Amani."

Nathan reached for his father's journal and went to sit in the chair across from her. He had too much on his mind to even think about resting. He read all of his father's notes—twice, in fact—but nothing stood out to him as anything he could use to help Amani. Everything here was benign, regarding the tomb and its contents, but now that Nathan knew the truth, nothing about this situation was normal. The quest to find his father's satchel had consumed him for so long that he felt off as he sat here with the truth before him. He'd lost his father a long time ago and had grieved that loss for too long, yet knowing he was truly gone was hitting Nathan hard. Amani stirred, and his heart beat a little faster. Would he end up like his father after all this was said and done? Amani was an innocent victim, but there was no doubt in Nathan's mind she had the ability to bring down entire cities if she wanted to.

"Nathan?" Amani whispered. "Are you okay? I can feel your sadness."

"I don't want you worrying about me. How are you?"

"I'm feeling much better."

"You had me worried. I didn't know how to help you or what I could do."

Amani sat up and let her legs hang over the edge of the bed, a sadness falling over her features. "From the moment you freed me from the camera, you've done nothing but take care of me. I'm so grateful for you, but I want you to know I need to leave to keep you and Calla Lily safe. I need to leave to keep everyone here in this town safe."

"You can't go alone. They'll get you for sure, and I don't want—" He stopped. "No. I will not lose you too."

"But if I stay, Khalida will use you and anyone here in Havenwood Falls against me. I think it's best to call on the goddesses and end this once and for all."

They stared at one another for a long moment. "But that will seal your fate for sure," Nathan responded.

Amani gave a faint smile. "I've never known anyone human other than my parents. You and Calla Lily have been wonderful, and I will never forget either of you."

Nathan cast his eyes to the floor. "Another impossible dream that will end in heartache," he mumbled.

Amani stood and walked over to where Nathan was sitting. She climbed into his lap and caressed his face. "If I had one wish, it would be to have you look at me every day the way you are now, but I know that is impossible."

"Why? Why can't your wish be possible? I don't want to lose you, Amani."

"You never know. Sometimes things turn in your favor. Fate has a funny way of shifting. Maybe we'll get lucky. All I know is I want to feel more of what I am feeling right now. Is that selfish?"

Nathan shook his head and then drew her mouth to his. "No," he said before he kissed her.

A knock at the door startled them both.

"That's probably our food. Madame Luiza said she'd bring it up when it was ready. Are you hungry?" Nathan asked.

Amani didn't speak. Instead she moved off of Nathan's lap and went to sit on the bed.

The smell of the food wafting from the other side of the door was a good distraction from the tension in the air. Sadness fell over Amani's features as she watched Nathan walk to the door and open it. There on a tray were two covered dishes with drinks, a white rose, and an envelope with his name scrawled on the front. Nathan brought the tray inside and set it on the dresser before reaching for the letter.

Dear Nathan and Amani,

Please eat and come downstairs when you are finished. We need to discuss a plan for the two of you to be safe. Calla Lily will be arriving with the Court of the Sun and the Moon in an hour. I hope you enjoy the meal. I added two slices of chocolate cake for you.

See you soon,

Madame Luiza

Nathan folded the letter and set it down before turning to Amani. "We have an hour before they want to meet with us."

CHAPTER 14

*N*athan and Amani made their way downstairs and came face to face with the Petran family, along with Calla Lily and nine other people. Amani tensed, and Nathan gave her hand a little squeeze. They were both caught off guard, but this was something they were going to have to do no matter what.

"Amani, Nathan, I'd like to introduce you to members of the Court of the Sun and the Moon. They are the governing body here in Havenwood Falls," Calla Lily said with a smile. "If you could please join us, we think we have a few ideas as to how to move forward."

Everyone made the proper introductions and sat at one of the larger tables in the dining room. The tension ebbed as Amani met each one of the Court members. She'd never met any other supernatural beings, and yet here before her were so many variations, all emitting an enormous amount of power as they sat in front of her and Nathan.

"What is your intention in being here?" the dark-haired mage asked with his arms crossed in front of his chest.

Calla Lily gave him a look. "Roman, we've already been over this. Amani didn't ask to be here. Neither did Nathan."

"Yet they're here and have brought their problems with them, which we now have to try to contain."

"I don't intend to be a problem. I plan on leaving. I do not wish to put Nathan and Calla Lily or anyone here in Havenwood Falls at risk," Amani interjected.

"But leaving with Khalida and Khaldun so close is not an option either," Nathan insisted. "That'll be two against one."

"We're not implying Amani should leave or face these two djinn alone, but we do have to decide how we are going to handle the safety of the town," Mihail replied.

"We received word before coming here that a woman was spotted in the woods just beyond Cooley Creek. Our belief is that this is your sister," Roman said, relaxing his posture only slightly.

"She was injured," Calla Lily added.

Amani looked at Calla Lily for a brief second before turning her attention to Roman and his visible disdain for her and Nathan.

"It's Khalida," she said coolly, "and I plan on taking care of it."

"What is your plan then?" Roman asked.

"I will handle my sister. Khaldun is not here at the moment. I cannot sense him."

"And what if he shows up?" Roman scowled.

"Then we will be there to intercede," Mihail countered. "I think all of us but you, Roman, are interested in the safety and survival of Nathan and Amani."

"Thank you," Nathan remarked, picking up on the hostility between the two men.

"That is all well and fine, but we need a plan to cover all contingencies," Roman said as he glared at Amani.

"What is your problem?" Nathan blurted.

Amani reached for Nathan's hand, turned away from Roman, and addressed the rest of the group. "I am going to go to my sister, and then we'll be leaving to meet the goddesses face to face."

"What about Nathan?" Calla Lily questioned.

Tears welled in Amani's eyes. "He understands that I have to do this to save everyone. I cannot trust Khalida, and if Khaldun does show up, kill him, because if you don't, he *will* kill you all."

A few at the table mumbled, while Roman huffed.

"We'll keep Nathan safe, Amani," Calla Lily said with tears in her own eyes. "I'm so sorry it is coming to this."

"Thank you," Amani replied. "For the small amount of time I've spent here, you mean a lot to me, and I'm grateful for all your help. I've never had a friend, but I consider you one. I will never forget you, Calla Lily."

"Oh, honey," she said as she moved to hug her.

As she did, Amani flinched and gasped in pain.

"What's wrong?" Calla Lily exclaimed.

Nathan didn't need to reach for her. He could see the agony in her eyes. It had to be Khalida. "What's wrong?"

"She's here!"

The Court members all rose at once.

"Everyone, do what needs to be done to protect the town. Saundra, alert the coven to strengthen our wards," Roman announced.

Amani's skin began to change, and previously unseen markings shimmered to life as they rose to the surface. She looked over at Nathan and mouthed "I'm sorry" just before she turned into a wisp of sand and disappeared.

*A*ll at once, the park in town square was filled with everyone who was just sitting at the table, with one addition—Khalida. Amani stood in front, with the Court members, Nathan, and Calla Lily taking up positions behind her. Thankfully, there were not a lot of other people wandering about, but with the energy surging, Amani assumed it was the Court's doing—their way of protecting the town's people. However, Amani could not concern herself with anyone other than Khalida at the moment.

"Sister," Khalida cooed, "it is so good to see you. I thought I lost you. I came as soon as I was able to sense you."

"Yes, I am certain that was your intent. Why do you look as though you've been in a quarrel?" Amani questioned.

"Why do you look like one of them?" Khalida hissed.

"Kindness was shown to me. My clothing wasn't suitable for this time, and I was offered something new. I see you are wearing the garments of our enemies. Where have you been while I was locked away?"

"I was being held prisoner. The day we took the picture in Egypt, I lost everything—you, my freedom, everything," Khalida said as she moved a step closer.

"No, it was I who lost everything while you were indulging in the pleasures of life. Prisoner or participant?"

"I couldn't stop his desire for me."

"Your lies end here, dear sister."

"What?" Khalida feigned shock even as her hair changed from black to white—her djinn side beginning to emerge. "Why would you say that? I have suffered."

"You never were good at hiding your emotions, Khalida. Besides, I already know the truth, and the only thing I'm interested in is for you to admit it, so we can go together to face Hathor and Ma'at," Amani said, remaining calm and unchanged.

Khalida laughed. "And what is it you think you know?"

"That the only person you care about is yourself."

"Actually, I care about quite a lot, and it all revolves around my freedom. I'm not going anywhere, but you are," she said as a watcher's vessel materialized in her hand.

Now it was Amani who laughed. "I was fooled by you eighteen years ago. I won't be fooled again, and I am certainly not going to let you trap me so you may live on."

"Then I guess we are at an impasse," Khalida said before she threw the first attack.

Ironically, it was Roman who executed the counterattack, deflecting a bolt of energy away from Amani. She wasn't sure if he doubted her ability to protect herself or if he genuinely wanted to thwart Khalida. Regardless, it was then that all hell broke loose.

Several Court members were casting blows and counterblows to what Khalida was throwing at them. Amani had never seen her sister like this. The only thing she recognized in her twin was her white hair and light eyes. Everything else was a magnified version of the night their parents died and the goddesses arrived. When one of Khalida's attacks hit Nathan in the leg, Amani reacted with an attack of her own, catching Khalida off guard.

"You care for someone," she taunted when Amani rushed to Nathan's side. "Well, well."

"These innocents have nothing to do with our conflict. Leave them be," Amani ordered.

"Then come willingly, and I will leave," Khalida countered.

"I know you too well, and if I agreed to those terms, you'd still kill them to save your lies from reaching the goddesses."

Khalida barked out a laugh. "You're probably right. Humans are of no value to me," she said as she eyed Roman, "not even magical ones."

Roman was none too pleased with her insult and began to conjure a spell. Energy radiated around him, and the ground beneath Khalida shook. Amani didn't waste any time. Instead she helped Nathan to his feet, and they made their way over to a lamppost. "I'm so sorry. I should have stayed in the camera."

"Don't say that." He winced as the cut in his leg gushed blood.

Calla Lily and Madame Luiza ran to them in a rush.

"He's hurt," Amani cried.

"We've got him. Go help Roman. I'm not sure how much longer he can hold her with the way she is shimmering," Madame Luiza said as Calla Lily knelt beside Nathan.

Tears were streaming down Amani's face, but she did as Madame Luiza asked and moved opposite Roman.

"Enough, sister," Amani yelled over the din in the square.

Khalida released Roman from her attack and turned to face Amani. "Poor you, always on the other side of things. Do these humans know who you really are?"

Amani saw the members of the Court battered, but still alive. This was all her doing. She'd brought Khalida here, even if it was inadvertently. It was time to end this. She reached for the feather around her neck and pulled it to her lips.

"No," Khalida screamed and flung her hand toward Amani. The chain holding the feather began to dig into the back of Amani's neck before snapping and flying into the air. With a flick of her wrist, Amani diverted it from reaching her sister, thankful when Mihail snatched it out of midair and vanished. Khalida raged at her missed prize, and Amani was grateful her sister didn't have the necklace.

Unfortunately, it was her only means to call the goddesses—now she'd have to fight.

Amani shouted for Calla Lily and Madame Luiza to take Nathan and leave, but before they could move, Khalida shoved the women aside and grabbed Nathan. He choked and spat as her fingers wrapped around his trachea.

"Leave. Him. Alone."

Khalida leaned in to Nathan. "Let me guess, she told you she was the innocent one, and I was the one to be feared?"

Nathan couldn't speak, so he only shook his head.

"Oh, you don't believe me. Have you seen what she is? What she can do? I *had* to trap her. She's a danger to everyone."

More gasps came from Nathan, and Amani started to lose control. Her skin changed from warm caramel to steely gray as the hieroglyphs underneath turned a vibrant gold.

"Let him go or I will kill us both, Khalida," Amani seethed.

"Did you hear that? She'll kill you both," Khalida taunted Nathan before she smashed her lips against his and turned to face Amani. "Show us all who you really are, sister. Let the world see why you should be contained."

Amani's blond hair began to blow wildly around her head by a violent wind erupting from the ground beneath her feet.

"There we go," Khalida goaded. "Show them all just how evil *I* am".

Amani wasn't sure what was going to happen next. She'd never fully embraced her powers or even knew what she was capable of—she never had an occasion to, until now, but as Khalida continued to taunt her, the thoughts in her head were becoming a reality. The ground started to shake, and the sand quivered as it hovered over the grass.

"I won't ask again," Amani ordered as she struggled to control her djinn side.

Khalida laughed. "You don't even know how to be a true djinn."

Amani's resolve ended, and she let the other side of her take over. Her hair was now alight and her hieroglyphs ablaze as she sent a blast of energy at Khalida, jarring her enough that she released Nathan.

"Don't, Amani," Nathan croaked. "You'll die, too."

Khalida snarled at him, realizing he knew the truth, and moved to strike, but Amani was quicker. Unfortunately, that was when Khaldun materialized near the fountain, making it two against one.

"Time for you to come home," Khaldun snarled as his cobalt markings began to glow. Khalida and Khaldun split up, obviously hoping to strike Amani from her flank, or so she thought. Khaldun came for her, while Khalida turned back to Nathan. Mihail and Irina tried to stop Khalida, but were tossed into Madame Luiza and Calla Lily, knocking them all to the ground. Roman raged and cast a spell to protect the other Court members. It was becoming abundantly clear that all they could do was save their own, because the battle brewing between these three djinn would not end well.

Amani used the connection between her and Nathan to send him a message. *I'm sorry. I never meant to hurt you.*

Nathan didn't have a chance to respond before Khaldun tossed the watcher's vessel in front of Amani. He began to speak in a language only a djinn would recognize, an ancient tongue that sounded frightening as it was spoken. Amani turned to face him, and as the final words came out of his mouth, she seized her opportunity. Turning herself into specks of sand, she vanished. Khalida suddenly remained the only viable djinn to be trapped within the bottle. When Amani re-emerged, she remained shapeless and used this to her advantage, attacking Khaldun. He swiped at her as she swirled around him in a tornado of fiery sand. When Amani finally appeared before him, her hair was still ablaze and the gold symbols on her skin glowed as bright as the flames.

"I've always despised you, Amani. I'm going to enjoy making you suffer."

"It will not be I who suffers this day," she replied.

Khaldun laughed and lunged for her, but Amani struck with unimaginable force. Khaldun stared at her blankly, the truth of what she'd done sinking in. Amani held his beating heart in her hand, watching it as it pulsed, absent of its owner. As Khaldun dropped to his knees, Amani crushed it beneath her fingers. She knew that wouldn't be enough to finish him, so she cast her eyes in his direction, setting him ablaze. Khaldun screamed as her djinn-enhanced flames engulfed him. In a matter of seconds, he was nothing more than ash. Amani dropped his stilled heart on top of the ashes and closed her eyes, trying to quench the rage.

She heard a voice calling out to her to come back, even as her body fell limp. "It's okay. Amani, please. I'm here for you," Nathan declared. "You did it. You saved us."

She took a deep breath in and composed herself, bringing her djinn side under control. When she opened her eyes, Nathan was there before her.

"There's my girl." He smiled.

"You're okay?"

"I am."

"And Calla Lily?"

"She's fine. We're all fine."

"You saved us all, Amani," Calla Lily replied with a faint smile.

"And Khalida?"

"She's in here," Roman said, holding the vessel in the air.

"I need that," Amani declared.

"Why would I give this to you?" Roman goaded.

Amani glared at him, the golden hieroglyphs on her skin beginning to surface again in a fluid rush. "Because my kind—and my sister—are not for you to possess. Khalida belongs to the goddesses," she said coolly as she extended her hand toward him.

Roman shoved the jar into her palm. "We'll see what is mine to possess or not."

"I don't want any trouble, Roman, but if you try to thwart what is right for the sake of your desires, I will take action."

"Is that a threat?"

"No," Amani said flatly. "But understand, I would destroy this vessel before you or anyone else could possess it."

Roman continued to glare at her, clenching his jaw, as Nathan and Calla Lily stepped up next to Amani.

"Are you okay?" Calla Lily asked, casting a look at Roman.

Amani shifted her focus to Calla Lily and whispered, "Yes, but I've never fully embraced what I am before, and it frightens me a bit."

"What happens next?" Nathan asked as he held Amani's hand.

"I face the goddesses and tell them the truth of what has happened."

"But how?" Irina questioned.

Amani turned to Mihail, who'd returned to the square. "Do you have the necklace?"

"I do," he said, pulling it out of his pocket and handing it to her.

"I'm very sorry this all had to take place here in Havenwood Falls. Is the town okay?" Amani asked.

Roman relented. "The fountain may need to be replaced, but other than that, the damage is nothing a little magic can't fix."

The energy died down, and the other Court members began to make their way to where the rest of them stood.

"Now what?" Irina inquired.

"Now I ask for a favor so that I may leave your town for good."

"And what is that?" Calla Lily asked.

"When the goddesses have been called before, magic was used or a sacrifice made. I don't really have a sacrifice, so I was hoping you could help me call for them."

"You want them to come here?" Roman balked.

"Do you want us out of here or not?" Amani shot back, finding her voice.

"Fine, what do you need, then?" Roman snapped.

"This," she held up the necklace, "a copper dagger, a dove's feather, and a pile of burning embers."

Calla Lily and Nathan grinned, but Roman glared at her.

"It was what her mother used to call Hathor," Calla Lily affirmed.

"So you want us to give you these items so you can call an Egyptian goddess to the town square?"

"No, I want you to give me those items to call *two* Egyptian goddesses to the town square."

Roman's lip curled. "I'm in no mood for games."

"This is not a game. I will say my goodbyes, and then I will face my judgment," Amani said as she lifted the ewer in her hand. "We'll be leaving together."

"I'll be back in five minutes with the items you've requested," Roman said as he reluctantly turned to leave.

CHAPTER 16

*M*ihail, Irina, and Madame Luiza walked with the Court members to the fountain. From where Amani stood, they seemed as though they were plotting the best way to repair it. When she heard voices chanting, she thought, *Good, they're fixing things already.*

Calla Lily watched as Nathan and Amani stood side by side, their hands clasped, and stepped back. "I'm going to give you two a minute."

As she turned to leave, Nathan called out. "Calla Lily?"

"Yes?"

"Thank you for sending me a letter about my father's satchel. You were right. The answers you seek don't always come the way you hope."

Calla Lilly's smile reached her eyes. "No, they don't."

Nathan turned to face Amani. "This trip has certainly not been what I expected."

"I'm sorry for that. I wish I had answers about Samuel."

"But that's the thing—you did give me answers. You're more than I could have ever hoped for," he said as he brought her hand to his lips. "I'll never regret getting on the train to come to Havenwood Falls, because every step has brought me straight to you."

Amani rose up on the balls of her feet and kissed Nathan.

"I have what you need," Roman's voice bellowed.

Amani blushed and squeezed Nathan's hand. "I was just saying goodbye."

She took the items Roman was handing her. "You'll need to light the sage for the embers, but everything else is there," he said as he moved to leave.

"Thank you, Roman."

"Once you do this and call on your goddesses, what protection do we need? I do not want any of the town affected."

"If you mean them no harm, no harm will come to you. It is Khalida and me they will want."

Roman gave her a clipped nod. "Then let's get on with it. The spell we cast to ward the rest of the town will be wearing off soon. No one but us needs to know what happened here."

"Very well," Amani replied.

"What can I do?" Nathan offered.

"I'd be grateful if you stayed close," Amani answered.

Nathan helped her put the items together while Roman went to talk to the rest of the Court. No one knew what was about to happen, but no matter what, it would end with Amani being gone and Nathan's heart left empty—again. *Love and loss seems to be your plight in life*, Nathan thought.

Amani closed her eyes and in a flash an altar appeared before her —her mother's altar, exactly as it had been so many centuries before. She lit the sage and waited until the smoke began to rise before laying the feather over the top. She cast a glance Nathan's way, and he tried to direct his heart and mind toward happier thoughts, since he knew she could hear and feel them. The last thing she needed right now was a distraction.

When Amani lifted the gold necklace and moved to lay it across the embers, Nathan blurted, "Can't we just keep her in there and run away? Hide for thirty or so years and then do this after we've spent a lifetime together?"

Amani shook her head and smiled. "I wish, but then I would be no better than my sister, and I don't want to be always looking over my shoulder for the watchers to come and take me away. It's no way to live. You deserve more than a life trapped within a wish, Nathan."

Nathan bowed his head. "It was worth a shot."

Amani took hold of his hand as she lay the necklace over the offering. "Hathor, I humbly request your presence, you and Ma'at. I surrender not only myself but Khalida too."

Thunder rolled, and lightning railed in the sky as the wind around them began to churn. The scent of frankincense was pungent in the air, and then sparks of fire appeared on the road in front of the nearby buildings. Four towering figures materialized before them, obscured until the fire dissipated. As they stepped forward, Amani immediately knelt, Nathan following suit, unsure of what else to do. Two larger-than-life guards with ebony skin and faces like jackals stood on either side of two elegantly dressed women, bathed in gold and jewels. Before their eyes, the two women transformed as they walked forward. They were no longer giant in size and stature, but gained more human qualities. However, their godly presence was still awe-inspiring.

"Amani?" Hathor inquired.

"Why do you summon us, and why are you here?" Ma'at asked before she surveyed the area.

"Khalida and I were freed for a time, but then she and Khaldun trapped me in a camera, where I remained a prisoner for the past eighteen years," Amani answered quickly.

"And where are they now?" Hathor thundered.

Amani bowed her head and held out the ewer. "Khalida is in here, and Khaldun is dead."

"I see," Ma'at acknowledged. "Your doing?"

"Yes."

Hathor walked over to Amani and took the bronze vessel from her outstretched hands. "And who is this?" the goddess asked, turning her attention to Nathan.

"This is the man who freed me from the camera and Khalida's

betrayal," Amani said as she offered her hands to Hathor and Ma'at. "See for yourself."

They took her hands, and Amani sent images of the past eighteen years into their minds.

"Nathan and the people here are all innocent. I humbly ask your forgiveness and beg to have this wrong righted," Amani said as the last image faded.

"And what is it that you wish for us to do?" Ma'at asked.

Amani steeled her gaze. "Erase any trace of this from their minds. Make it so they will be spared the pain of what has come to pass by no fault of their own."

"No, Amani," Nathan pleaded.

"I can feel the sorrow in your heart, Nathan." Amani lifted her eyes to meet his. "And I do not want you to pine for me once I am gone. You must live your life and be happy."

"I'm happy now."

"You've spent eighteen years searching for answers to your father's disappearance. I was tied to those answers." She gently touched his face. "You deserve more."

"I deserve you."

"Amani," Hathor interrupted, "who is the male to you?"

Amani turned to face Hathor. "Someone I care about very much. He saved me and in turn saved himself, along with the people behind me. The woman there," she pointed to Calla Lily, "she too helped me see the truth. I'm indebted to them both."

Ma'at turned toward Calla Lily and the Court. "And you? What do you say about what happened this night?"

Mihail stepped forward. "Amani did as she said. Her sister came to kill us all, and the watcher was with her. If not for Amani, we'd all be having a very different conversation."

"But is she not the reason Khalida and Khaldun came in the first place?" Ma'at questioned.

"From what I understand, that was not by her doing," Mihail replied.

"And this camera, how did it come to be here in your town?" Hathor asked.

Calla Lily stepped next to Mihail. "The simple answer—magical intervention. One day it simply appeared in my shop, and I contacted the person I believed to be its owner. Nathan responded to my inquiry, and the rest is history," she affirmed.

Hathor looked back to where Amani and Nathan were standing. "I am pleased. You did as I knew you would. The good in your heart won out over the wrath. Khalida never could see the truth of her existence and how she could change it."

"I'm not sure I am ready to declare judgment," Ma'at said flatly. "Instead I propose an offer." She paused. "Will you accept Amani as a temporary resident here in your home until we can confer with Thoth on the path we should take?"

Roman started to speak, but Saundra Beaumont answered instead. "We will gladly accept Amani and Nathan into Havenwood Falls. It is clear her intentions are only to help and not harm. It was not that long ago that our ancestors were faced with an unimaginable choice, and they too needed guidance to proceed."

Amani gasped, and Nathan stood silent.

Ma'at gave a gracious nod to the woman with the silvery white hair before she walked back over to Hathor. "We will send word when we are due to return. In the meantime," she said as she waved a hand over the square, "let your town be cleansed."

A golden-hued smoke wafted over the open space, clearing it of all trace of the battle that had raged. As the air cleared, four flames emerged, and the jackal guards, along with Hathor and Ma'at, stepped into the vermilion glow, disappearing into thin air.

Nathan pulled Amani into his arms, and Calla Lily ran to them. "Well, it seems we'll need to find you a place to stay, since you'll be here in Havenwood Falls for a bit."

"You're more than welcome to stay in one of the rooms at the inn, if you'd like," Irina added.

Amani turned to Saundra, Mihail, Roman, and the rest of the

Court, and bowed. "Thank you. I will honor this gift, and if I can in any way help you, I am at your service."

"Where is the ewer and Khalida?" Roman interjected.

"Safe where she belongs," she met his eyes, "with the goddesses."

"I certainly hope so," he said with disdain as he turned to walk away.

"We're happy to have you both. Come to see me tomorrow, so we can officially register you for your stay here in Havenwood Falls," Saundra smiled.

"Stop by the store too, and I'll help you shop for some more clothes," Calla Lily added.

With that, they all turned to go, leaving only Amani and Nathan in the square.

"Now what?" Nathan grinned.

Amani looked into his eyes. "One step at a time."

"One step at a time, then," he said as he leaned down and placed a kiss on her lips.

Released from a Curse, part two and the conclusion of Amani and Nathan's journey, available where books are sold.

ABOUT THE AUTHOR

Brynn Myers is an adult paranormal romance author. After considering writing a hobby for years, she finally turned her passion and talent into a career. She came into the paranormal genre later than most, but has always loved fairy tales and all things magical. Using that love, she creates charmed worlds by writing stories involving passionate, strong-willed characters with something to discover.

You can find out more about Brynn and her all titles by visiting www.brynnmyers.com and subscribing to her newsletter at www.brynnmyers.com/subscribe.

ACKNOWLEDGMENTS

I'd like to thank Ang'dora Publishing for asking me to be a part of the Havenwood Falls crew. I am thrilled to have had the opportunity to write in the Legends series. I'd also like to give a special thanks to Kristie Cook for allowing me to reference her characters, and to Randi Cooley Wilson for letting me roll with Calla Lily Mircea and Roman Bishop. It was my honor, and I hope I did them all justice.

Much love to my own publisher Amber Leaf Publishing. Thank you always for your love and support in all my work. I will never be able to thank you enough.

To my readers and anyone new to www.brynnmyers.com — THANK YOU!! Every time you pick up one of my stories and give my characters a chance to warm your hearts or royally tick you off, I AM BLESSED! Thank you for making this fantastic ride worth it with all your love and kudos! Much love to you all!

BLOOD AND DAMNATION

BELINDA BORING

Havenwood Falls

Legends

BLOOD AND DAMNATION

BELINDA BORING

ALSO BY BELINDA BORING

HAVENWOOD FALLS

Nowhere to Hide

The Collector: Awakening

Addicted to You

MYSTIC WOLVES SERIES

The Mystic Wolves

Forget Me Not

Testing Fate

Forever Changed

Savage Possession

Darkness Unleashed

Last Wolf Standing

Blood Oath

A Very Mystic Christmas

DAMAGED SOULS SERIES

Bittersweet Melody

Bittersweet Symphony

BRIANNA LANE SERIES

Broken Promises

STAND-ALONES

Loving Liberty

Enchanted Hearts

To my sweet little Odie,
If my love alone could've kept you here, you would've lived forever.

To Lin-Manuel Miranda,
Thank you for being such an inspiration!

CHAPTER 1

1868

*B*lood.

It was everywhere.

There wasn't a place I could lay my hand that didn't come back covered. As I lifted my fingers to my brow, the fading sun caused the redness of the liquid to take on an even more sinister hue.

As if being bathed in blood could get more sinister, I chuckled silently.

There really wasn't anything funny about the situation, but for the life of me, I couldn't stop the wave of hysteria that threatened to overcome my sensibilities. It started somewhere in the base of my chest and rose with such force that to ignore it, to stifle it, would cause more pain than it was worth.

So I let it out.

Ripples of laughter echoed in my ears—sounding completely foreign and unhinged.

I shuddered to think what would happen should someone stumble by and find us like this. I imagined I would look like a madman sitting in the middle of a dirty, rat-infested alley, quietly cradling the lifeless body of a woman in his arms.

They may have witnessed the precise moment her heart stopped— the last of her lifeblood trickling slowly from her wounds.

I knew I looked disheveled, my clothes caked with blood that was already beginning to dry, my exposed skin smeared with the sticky gore. I also knew that people would not stop to ask questions. Instead, they would run screaming for the authorities.

Sounds slowly filtered back into my awareness, and the abrupt slap of reality returned me to my senses. My bloodstained hands roughly smoothed over fine black hair as if to comfort her in death.

My victim, I thought without hesitation.

I had somehow done this. Bile bubbled up into my mouth while I observed my gruesome surroundings, the bitter scent of copper made me gag, and numbness spread through me, shock wrapping its icy fingers around my heart.

I turned the woman's face so her lifeless eyes stared back at me, as if in death she continued to accuse me. Her name had been Primrose, or was it simply Rosa? Letting out a hasty breath, I cursed my stupidity for not remembering her name.

Whoever she was, she had been beautiful, her skin still holding a slight warmth from being held so close.

She'd caught my eye earlier in the evening as I strolled through the crowds attending the annual town fair. With her long raven-colored tresses and green twinkling eyes, I'd spent the better half of the evening exchanging glances and sensual flirtations.

London gossiped about my "rakish" ways. I had a useful talent of layering my seductive charms on so thick that it always guaranteed me getting what I wanted—whoever I wanted. My goal was that before the night was over, she'd be beneath me, writhing as I drew out every ounce of pleasure within her.

She'd responded so freely to my suggestions that it wasn't long before she'd led me to this very alley, secluded from prying eyes. I'd immediately pressed her up against the wall as my mouth devoured hers.

Her eagerness had stoked a fire in me. Gone was the frigidity I often met from my own fellow countrywomen, and my urgency was met with her own brand of fire.

With each caress, each flick of her tongue, she sent me

careening out of control. When she'd softly moaned over my touching her covered breast, I'd instinctively deepened our passionate kiss.

She'd tasted of mead and sunshine.

Even now, the thought of that fevered kiss made my mouth water.

She'd felt so good and responded so well to my attentions that I'd lost track of time. One moment she was racing toward release and the next she was lying in my arms.

Dead.

I frowned, my mind desperately trying to piece the events together, but all I could sense was an oppressive fog—one that was unwilling to succumb to my frantic probing.

Something had happened, but still it remained elusive.

Shock wouldn't hold it from me forever.

Moments passed, and more sounds filled the night air.

"They'll discover us soon," I murmured, still unable to do anything but stare down at the woman who had previously set my entire body aflame.

My skin pebbled from the chill now settling over me. The sweat clinging to my once pristine shirt caused a slight tremble to begin.

Where was my coat?

My hands slowly released her, and that's when I discovered I'd taken it off to cover Rosa.

Primrose?

The body.

Muscles groaned from suddenly being forced to move, and I gingerly pushed the weight from my lap, careful to not disturb the woman further. This caused another chuckle to erupt.

The time for gentleness and consideration had passed with her last breath, but still I couldn't bring myself to think of her as dead. It felt wiser for my dwindling sanity to consider her asleep, and as if to prove that point, I leaned over one more time and tentatively laid my lips to her cool forehead for one last kiss.

My lips came back wet, no doubt glistening from her blood.

That was all the truth and reality I needed.

As my resolve snapped, I toppled to the side and began violently heaving.

"Dear God," I groaned, too weak to wipe at my mouth.

The feeble contents of my stomach mingled with the drying pool of blood as if taunting me, forming a macabre mixture.

The smells of the alley—the smell of her—assaulted my senses again, driving me to purge my stomach until all that was left was a repeated gag.

I gasped for air, my chest struggling to drag in enough oxygen to compensate for the violence. My stomach screamed from my muscles being roughly contracted.

It took everything I had to stand, staggering slightly as the world began to spin. Unable to take my eyes away from the body, I suddenly realized that I'd lingered too long.

With the alley open at both ends, a channel between two streets, it was only a matter of time before someone else would seek to use it. I had to flee. I couldn't be found here . . . not like this.

I'd made it a mere two steps before a hysterical shriek pierced the air.

Panic blasted through me as the scream evolved into guttural sobbing, revealing two strangers. One of the women threw herself to the ground and scooped Primrose up into her arms, pinning the now stiff body to her chest. Tears cascaded down her wrinkled cheeks.

Words flew out of the older woman's mouth in short spurts of some foreign language, one that sounded familiar. She wore a haunted expression, her hands frantically searching over the person I assumed was someone she knew and loved.

She was feeling for the fatal wound.

I stood transfixed, held tightly by the women's grief. Chivalry screamed for me to go comfort her, but even I knew how badly this appeared. Her loved one was dead and there I stood—smeared with her blood.

The other woman, much younger in appearance, maybe a sister or cousin, finally reached the spot of despair and flung her arms around the rocking figure. She added her sobs to the melee, and something within me jolted.

I shouldn't be watching this. This was too private, too intimate, and it wasn't for me to witness.

My traitorous foot crunched on discarded litter as I took a step away. The movement caused the air to suddenly silence as two pairs of tear-filled eyes snapped on me.

Anguished.

Wretched.

Furious.

Frozen by the honesty I couldn't ignore, I willed myself to move, to break contact with the piercing gazes that scrutinized me. It wasn't difficult to read the judgment filling their faces. They took everything in—my appearance, the blood, what I assumed was my guilt-stricken expression.

The younger woman gasped as she made the sign of the cross, her hands trembling with strong emotion. Even though she was at a distance, the word *mulo* reached my ears.

Death.

That word. I knew it. It meant death.

Pieces clicked together as my brief lover's face flashed through my mind. Primrose had been my escort for the evening. I would've recognized her heritage, had I not been so fixated on bedding her.

Guilt. Waves of guilt pulsed through my veins as memories finally surfaced.

The spell that held me broke, and without thinking, I stepped forward, moving toward the women with my hands outstretched in a sign of submission. There was no denying my sense of survival begged me to run, but honor compelled me to stay. There were explanations to be made, questions to be answered, and somewhere amongst the emotions churning thickly in the air, I hoped to uncover some of my own.

Evidence be damned. I couldn't have done this. My lust ran toward the flesh and losing myself between a pair of willingly spread legs. It wasn't in death, murder, and violence.

It was with these thoughts that my confidence slowly strengthened. Romani people were often present on my family's estate when I was growing up. I'd spent many a childhood summer running and playing with the children of different traveling families, so dealing with the two women wouldn't pose too difficult a problem.

"Hello." My voice croaked from being unused.

Angry stares answered. Neither woman spoke, which caused me to stop mid-step.

Perhaps I'd underestimated the situation. How could this be resolved if they refused to acknowledge me?

I did the only thing I knew to do—I tilted my head forward in a respectful bow. We English prided ourselves on having impeccable manners.

With a scratchy throat and my mouth feeling as though I was trying to swallow fireplace ash, I tried again. For a brief second, I wished I had a tankard of mead, anything that would help so I could make this speech and leave.

I took in a deep breath, and thankfully my voice didn't hold the weakness from before. I sounded strong, diplomatic, trustworthy even.

"My name is Marcus. Lord Marcus St. James of Smithersby Field . . ."

A cold tone interrupted my friendly introduction.

"We know who you are." It was the older woman, the grandmother, if I'd judged correctly, who spoke. She then punctuated her statement with a sharp noise as she spat on the ground angrily.

"We know exactly who you are. *Chor.*"

My brow crinkled as I hurriedly tried to translate the foreign word. Something tugged at a distant memory. I was sure I'd heard it before, but the stress of the evening was causing me to draw an annoying blank.

"I'm sorry. I don't know what that word means," I mumbled in response.

Again, the woman interrupted.

"*CHOR.*" The word rang out with a blistering force as her finger shot out, pointing straight at me. Accusation and hatred exploded across her face.

There was no withstanding the vehemence of her verbal attack. Stuttering, struggling to find a way to placate her, all I could do was stand there—speechless. For the life of me, I had no idea what she was saying.

"She's calling you a thief," the grief-stricken voice of the younger female revealed. She must've been a few years older than Primrose.

"I assure you, I am no thief. Allow me to say again . . . my name is Marcus St. James. Believe me, there's an explanation for this. This is not what it seems."

"It matters not what your name is. It's your actions that label you a thief. You stand there covered in the blood of our beloved, hoping to slip away into the night after stealing the life of sweet Primrose. You are a thief, a black-hearted stealer of innocence."

"Please, let me continue." I took another step forward. "I didn't do this. I didn't kill her. I'm not quite sure what happened. One moment we were becoming . . . *acquainted*, and then she was dead."

The moment it passed through my lips, I knew how dubious and feeble my explanation sounded. Even the most uneducated of commoners could poke a hole through it with enough certainty to convict and then hang me.

"What do you mean *acquainted*?" The question thundered brashly in the alley.

My face flushed, and I tried loosening the tightness of my shirt collar, only to find blood flaking away when I pulled my fingers back. The small pieces fluttered to the ground, some snagging the thigh of my trousers. Repulsed, I jerked violently as I tried to brush them away.

Some would say it was a compelling act of guilt—the killer unable to face the truths of his sins.

Everywhere I looked, I saw blood. *Her* blood. In some places it was so thick, it caused my clothing to stick and dry to my skin.

I gagged again, quickly covering my mouth. This wasn't a moment to show weakness, but there was no helping it. With each passing breath, my hope of escaping this nightmare grew dimmer.

"What do you mean *acquainted*?" the woman repeated. "Do you mean to stand there and say that not only did you murder my sister, but you also corrupted her with your debauched and vile ways?" Her gaze narrowed on me as if she'd already judged and condemned me.

Images from earlier returned to invade my mind.

Primrose squirming against me, her hand rubbing hard against my erection. Based on her nymph-like response, she'd definitely been corrupted, but not by me.

If there was even an inkling of possibility that they'd believe me, I would tell that to her family. I would give them a quick education on how very *unvirtuous* their precious Primrose was.

The older woman drew herself up slowly, finally coming to a stand. She'd been quietly rocking back and forth with the deceased as she watched the interaction between her kinswoman and me. She was small, as women went, the years beginning to hunch her over with a stoop. I would've sworn that as she stood there, vengeance blazing in her eyes, she grew in stature—rivaling my own height.

"*Chor!*" she accused. As she stepped around the body she'd lovingly been holding, an energy began to fill the space around them. Somewhere in the distance, I heard dogs howling as thunder shook the air. Something was stirring, and it felt as though its focal point was solely on me.

The words were coming thick and fast as the woman launched into a rhythmic speech that was occasionally broken up by her quick gasps for breath. She droned on and on for what seemed like a lifetime.

I was able to pick out the occasional word, but what I heard next chilled me to the core.

Bibaxt. Bad luck.

Marime. Outcast.

Naswalemos. Sickness.

Strazhno. Danger.

Amria. Curse.

That word hit me the hardest. She was cursing me, and as I propelled myself forward to stop her, a pain like nothing I had *ever* experienced drove me abruptly to my knees with a demonic roar of agony.

Fire blazed through my veins, heating then boiling my blood until I was positive my insides were liquefying. Sweat dripped from every pore as my body trembled with vicious convulsions that threatened to render me insane.

Now writhing on the floor, words failed me.

All I could see—feel—was excruciating pain.

Deep within my chest a humming began, the sensation causing my heart to beat erratically. All I wanted to do was beg for death as I felt something inside me explode. Whether from mercy or approaching unconsciousness, the pain began to fade as everything dulled. My vision darkened.

I wept with relief. As I curled up into a ball so I could welcome oblivion like a long-lost friend, a single word reached out and branded my soul.

Shilmulo.

A small shard of alarm pierced me the moment I recognized it, but I was without hope, the world finally crashing around me.

Shilmulo.

Vampire.

CHAPTER 2

10 YEARS LATER

"*E*nter."

Annoyance flickered through me at the interruption. A new lead about the band of gypsies who'd cursed me to this blasted existence had surfaced, but instead of leaving to pursue it, I was stuck here, collecting a debt.

With heightened senses, I could hear her lurking outside the door as if trying to will her feet to move. This lack of spine was something I wouldn't tolerate once she became mine to do with as I pleased. Cowardice was an ugly trait—especially for a woman of her breeding.

Pity it hadn't stopped her father from being a squandering fool who believed I would show mercy and forgive his mismanagement of funds.

Hesitation seemed to still delay her in obeying my command, and my annoyance was quickly evolving into impatient anger. I had a reputation for crushing those who thought they could keep me waiting.

She wasn't the one controlling this meeting. She was merely property exchanging ownership—from the keeping of her father to mine.

"I won't ask again," I called out, knowing full well she heard me. My voice was one no one could ignore without paying the price for it.

There was a microscopic part of me that was impressed her hesitancy was because of fear and not because she was inherently rebellious. She knew who I was.

I was the fearsome Marcus St. James.

A monster.

Cruelty personified.

And unfortunately for her, her newly betrothed.

Her heart picked up its pace, that telltale sign she'd finally made the decision to act. She may be terrified of me, but she had a deep, abiding love for her father, and it was that devotion that turned the door knob.

Perhaps she still doubted that her father meant to force her to marry me. We hadn't officially met, although I'd sensed her hiding in the shadows when I'd attended her father's request that I become his financial benefactor. Her family was facing utter destitution, and he had approached me out of desperation.

I wasn't ashamed to admit I had also overheard part of the discussion between them when he broke the news of the conditions. I had no real need for money or a wife, but I saw the sense in having a blood source readily available. If anything, she was at least good for that.

"But, Father!" she'd cried, the sound of her heart breaking ringing out. "His heart is ugly . . . blackened . . . cruel. Surely, you've heard the town gossip? How can you ask this of me?"

I heard the tears in her voice, but they did nothing to move me toward empathy. Let her believe I was guilty of the foul acts I was often accused of. Her opinion meant nothing.

I could've been the very Devil himself, but she was a woman, and they had no say in the affairs of men.

Catriona finally stood, shuddering, in the doorway. Her gaze scanned the room, no doubt looking for me, but I remained hidden. Let her panic. It would teach her not to keep me waiting in the future.

"Girl, this will be the last time I repeat myself. You are to obey my every word without qualm." My voice, harsh and filled with bitterness, drew her attention in my direction.

Catriona closed her eyes and absently crossed herself before stepping completely into the room, closing the door behind her. She kept her eyes to the ground, losing what little bravery she'd somehow managed to muster.

I let out an amused chuckle.

"God won't help you. You would be wise to abandon whatever faith you cling to. He cares not for his supposed children." It was a lesson I was all too familiar with. A decade ago I had reached out— begged with all the sincerity my young, naïve heart could rally for His intercession and benevolence—only to find silence and betrayal.

Judging from her expression, the room was nothing like she'd thought it would be. She no doubt expected to find opulence and extreme finery, with my entire wealth on extravagant display. Without thinking, she raised her eyes, her mouth opening in surprise as she drank in our surroundings.

I had the room decorated for this precise reason. I loathed meeting the expectations of others. I had quickly realized the power that came from allowing others to underestimate me. It gave me the upper hand in every situation—throwing each person off their game and leaving them at my whim.

The room was definitely beautiful and unbelievably simple in its decorations. Floor-to-ceiling bookcases flanked the room on two of the four walls, and I saw the instant she fought the urge to run to the impressive library and see what treasures were displayed. The comfortable chairs and settees were strategically placed because it was the room I most used for quiet solitude. Elegant crafted lamps placed on side tables were positioned to offer the best light.

This room was my sanctuary. Very few had been granted entrance.

Silently, I watched as she turned around, momentarily transfixed. Her gaze was drawn to the portrait hanging on the wall next to the door she'd just come through.

Each brush stroke, each choice of vibrant color presented the image of a man who had no problem dominating those beneath him.

The artist had been able to capture the strength of his subject, a power and authority that filled the room by the mere presence of the painting. It reflected a man who could command armies, yet held a glimmer of something else—a trace of humor and mirth in the way the eyes seemed to twinkle and the gentle lifting of the lips into a smile.

My lips.

My eyes.

Or should I say, the person I should've been, had I not been in that damned alley all those years ago. I had been tempted to smash the portrait into pieces, to set it aflame until all that remained were ashes, but oddly enough, it comforted me. At least this way, that version of me still existed.

Looking at the small brass placard at the base of the frame, Catriona reached out, letting out a gasp when she recognized the name.

Marcus St. James.

"Do you like what you see?" I teased, reminding her I was still in the room, and her focus on my portrait hadn't gone unnoticed. Let her fall in love with the illusion. Let her find peace in her fate.

My voice held a strange softness. She raised her hands slowly, rubbing the sides of her arms as though she was suddenly cold.

"I do. It's hard not to. This man is definitely attractive, and there's something mesmerizing about the way he presents himself," she uttered, unable to drag her gaze away from the image in front of her.

"Would he be a man you could fall in love with?" My brows furrowed. Why the hell did I care what she thought?

"I hardly think that's an appropriate question, sir."

"Answer the question." The gentleness of the moment was shattered by the ruthless command I barked out. "And don't presume to lie to me, Catriona." Her name rolled off my tongue with ease. "I've a way of always finding out the truth, and heaven help the fool who thinks they can deceive me."

Raised goose bumps danced across her skin, causing her to

tremble slightly. Swallowing nervously, she answered. "Yes. Yes, I think this is a man I could fall in love with."

She let out a soft sigh, realizing that such romantic hope was folly, because the man she was to marry wasn't the image before her but the monster behind her.

"Will you not turn and address your betrothed . . . your *beloved*?" The last word was spat out with such vehemence and scorn that it caused her to jump from its force.

She slowly turned. Her confused expression elicited another chuckle from me.

I cleared my throat, a reminder that whatever she had fantasized about meeting her future husband had been in vain. She wasn't here for loving gestures and thoughtful acts.

"How do I address you, sir, if you won't show yourself?" Try as she might, she wasn't quite able to hide the curt frustration in her voice.

"Are you sure you are ready to come face to face with me? Have you fortified your delicate sensibilities? You are, after all, about to meet the Beast of Smithersby Field. Are you not scared, trembling in your corset?" I all but mocked her.

Raising her right hand to eye level, she revealed the unsteady tremble that had come over her. "As you can see, I am afraid, and wish the introduction over. If you are so concerned for my *sensibilities*, as you put it, please reveal yourself and let us speak freely. I assume there is much to discuss."

I stepped out from the curtains. I didn't bother withholding my grin as another gasp escaped through her lips.

A beast I may be, but I also knew the effect I held over the weaker sex. It was encouraging to see that I could use my physique and appearance to weaken her knees, so to speak.

I stood at almost six foot one and had been described as the epitome of masculine perfection. I could see she agreed with that sentiment as she all but licked her lips. I had inherited my father's strong face, with a defined jawline and a cleft in my chin that many females had stroked with soft fingertips.

We also shared the same hair color, that of the darkest black oil, but unlike my father, I didn't tie it back with a ribbon like most men of the time did. I'd grown accustomed to letting it hang loose.

It was my piercing blue eyes, however, that many confided bored deep down into their souls, digging about for whatever secrets they kept hidden, and I could exploit. That wasn't what made me appreciate them, though.

They were the eyes of my beloved mother—my champion. She was the one, had she lived long enough, who would've kept her only son from becoming a broken shell of his former self.

As much as I hated to admit it, my mother would've instantly approved of Catriona—pleased her darling son had found such a beautiful woman to marry. I could barely remember her voice, but something told me she would've uttered with pride how pleased she was.

I tried to view my bride-to-be as though I was peering out through my mother's eyes. What would've caught her attention? What traits would she admire? I shook away the thought softly murmuring that there were plenty of attributes I found attractive. As my gaze attempted to take in Catriona's appearance, there was no need to closely study her features—I already knew what I liked.

Her eyes. Philosophers shared that they were windows to the soul and everything you needed to know about the measure of a person could be found by taking a few moments to peer into their depths. Catriona's eyes terrified me because the briefest of glances—the tiniest of peeks—had felt like the strike of a match . . . an instant desire. Not in a sexual way, although there was definitely a stirring of lust within me. No, her dark eyes all but promised that should I linger . . . should I cave to temptation . . . I would find myself lost. The clarity and intelligence that stared out at me struck a chord of warning that once distracted, I would gladly walk away from the life I knew and follow her to the ends of the earth.

I didn't like that. I hated it. I refused to let another person control me or alter the path I had chosen to walk. A woman had been my downfall once before, and now this temptress stood before me— unaware of the power she held, the power that beckoned.

Her smile, a voice in my head gently pressed, forcing me to drop my gaze to Catriona's mouth. While her lips were only slightly curled upward, there were moments where a smile came as the result of her seeing something that pleased her. I'd caught a glimpse as she stared up at my portrait, and there was a growing need building within my chest that wanted to see it again.

This was absolute absurdity. I didn't want love. I wasn't looking for it. I was half convinced to take her by the arm, drag her back through my home, and toss her out on her behind. I didn't need a wife, or any kind of distraction, especially one that would no doubt prove to be trouble.

Yet all I could do was stare. By some miracle, I managed to keep my mouth shut, because I had the sinking suspicion that I would make myself look like a blithering buffoon or a lunatic incapable of speech.

I would need to act cautiously around her, never lowering my guard or showing any sign of softening.

I could see Catriona gathering her resolve, so she could push her fear aside.

I needed her afraid, however. If not for her, for me.

One moment I stood by the wall, and the next I was before her, grasping her hand with the intent to kiss it. Questions rose in her mind, shining out through her eyes. There was no need to ask her what they were—I had heard most of them before.

How did I move so fast?

Why did I toy with her like a cat plays with a mouse?

Why wasn't I acting completely monstrous, instead keeping her unbalanced?

She lowered her eyes out of habitual respect, yet the nicety of the moment vanished when I flipped over her hand and buried my mouth in her palm, nudging the soft flesh with my lips. Her skin heated when I pushed her buttons further, the tip of my tongue caressing her skin in light swirls.

Her knees buckled this time, and without thought, my arms banded around her waist, pulling her flush against my hard body.

Propriety demanded she ask to be released, and truth be told, I wasn't quite sure I would honor it.

I liked how she felt.

Damn.

She couldn't help but shudder with pleasure as I nipped at the meat of her palm with my teeth. Whatever resistance she'd felt all but melted away as she softened against me further.

Intriguing.

I curled my finger under her chin, raising it until she was looking up into my eyes. Common sense finally took back the reins, and she tried to back away, but I refused to release her.

I should have.

I should've returned to where I'd been standing and kept the space between us until I understood the lust now bubbling up within me. It was hard to believe such a frail female could be dangerous, but I could feel her presence chipping away at my intentions.

All I had wanted was to put a greater fear in her—help her understand that the life she'd once dreamed about was gone and lost forever.

Instead, my mouth came down over hers.

It was as if the heavens opened and a chorus of angels began to sing their praises. Passion burst through me, and as inexperienced as she was, it didn't take her long to know what I expected.

As my tongue flicked out against her closed lips, she parted them willingly and actually groaned when I caught a taste of her.

Her hands moved up over my shoulders and wrapped around my neck. It sent off an alarm inside my brain—that she was taking liberties I hadn't yet granted her. I was the master here—*her* master—and she touched me as though we were consensual lovers.

We would never be lovers in that sense. Ever.

My body betrayed me, and I tugged on the back of her head, my hands fisting in her thick, silky hair. I deepened the kiss, and with it, I almost lost what remained of my sanity.

Time seemed to stand still.

Her body began to rub against me, and I felt that familiar pressure building—one that felt urgent, hot, and needy.

I moved us, pinning her against one of the bookcases. Catriona gasped as my hands found her breasts, kneading them with my fingers.

Gripping onto my shoulders, gathering fistfuls of my shirt, she dipped her head back, and the movement exposed her throat.

I exhaled sharply—instantly stopping.

Her breath now came out in heavy pants, but that wasn't what held me hostage.

My lips found her skin again, my tongue tracing the contour of her neck. It was the one spot that always controlled me, although I fought it with everything I had.

Her pulse.

Gently, I began sucking on the spot, and it caused her heart to race so fast, I could feel it against my mouth.

That was when I realized she wasn't the one in the most danger.

It was also when I began second-guessing my decision to accept her as payment. There was nothing sweet and innocent about the young woman limp with pleasure in my arms.

No, she was much, much more than that.

There was a good chance she was one of Satan's sirens—sent to tempt me to Hell with lust—the one who believed it would be her to bring me into submission.

It was that last thought that acted like a much-needed slap in the face.

Dumping her unceremoniously on the floor, I fled from the room, driven from my own sanctuary like the Black Plague had returned to claim me as its victim.

I was no one's victim—not anymore.

Never again.

CHAPTER 3

*W*e didn't talk again until a week later.

She was already moved in, Knox having placed her in a room that was as far away from me as possible. I didn't want her entertaining any kind of illusion that she could tame me, or that she was in fact *wanted*.

She was a means to an end.

If there was one thing she could rely on from me, it would be that I was consistent.

I would *consistently* keep her at a distance.

I would *consistently* remind the annoying female I was not her knight in shining armor and there would be no happily ever after in her future.

It was the only offering I would bestow on her.

She ranked just below the discarded furniture stored away in the wing she now lived in. I felt some kind of emotion toward the antiques passed down through the generations, however.

I could at least see some functional use for them.

She'd finally spotted me passing through the kitchens quickly, having spent the past hour walking the estate. It had become my nightly routine and was one of the very few rituals that brought me any semblance of peace.

That contentment shattered as soon as I heard her shriek my name.

Truth be told, this confrontation was days overdue. Part of me had expected her to barge into each and every room in the house, searching to see where I'd been hiding.

What she didn't understand was it wasn't really hiding when you had zero intentions of spending time together in the first place.

My hands clenched by my side, and even though I willed them to relax, they simply tensed up again.

Would I ever be able to roam freely about my home again without being pestered?

"What happened?" Her voice was filled with accusation and anger.

I replied with stony silence. I didn't care how much that unsettled her.

She reached out to touch me, an unforgivable act, and stumbled back when I moved like lightning, roughly grasping her wrist with a steel-like grip.

Tears flooded her eyes at the pain.

Bending her wrist slightly, I added enough pressure to elicit another moan of pain.

Damn, the sound was like a shot of pure, unadulterated lust to my groin. As she looked up at me, her rage was replaced with undiluted fear.

Gone was any semblance of defiance. In her eyes, the *monster* was fully unleashed.

I towered over her smaller form, forcing her to cower before me.

"Don't *ever* make the mistake of touching me. You will not survive the consequences." I kept my tone cold on purpose.

"I'm sorry." Catriona cringed at the way her voice had quickly devolved from confident to whimpering. "I didn't mean to interrupt you. I just wanted to know what happened."

"What do you mean? Nothing happened." I spat the words out impatiently, releasing her wrist and brushing past her. I didn't have time for such feminine nonsense.

"But the last time we spoke . . . you and I . . . we—" She had the decency to appear humiliated about bringing up last week, and the fact that I feigned ignorance.

I knew exactly what she referred to. Memories of the kisses we'd exchanged and the way she roused the man in me still plagued me at the most inopportune times.

I whirled around, wearing what I hoped was a look of complete derision. All I could see was the ghost of her swollen lips and the breathless way her chest had heaved with passion. Each step I now took toward her caused her to retreat—as though she recognized the predator in me and that she was prey to be stalked.

I shoved her to the door, finally pressing her body against the frame with my own.

It was infuriating how perfectly we fit and how incredible she smelled as the subtle perfume of her skin infiltrated my senses.

The wind blew, rustling the leaves on the tall trees that stood proudly in the gardens. There was no one but Knox around, but I had no idea whether she'd met him yet—whether he'd deemed her worthy of his attention. I kept him busy on projects of vital importance. It wouldn't surprise me if he avoided her just as much as I did.

"There is no one to hear you scream, Catriona. No ally to protect you." Without thinking, I traced the curve of her cheek with my finger. Too soft for her own good.

"Should I be crying out for help?" she countered bravely. I could see the thread of restraint that kept her from shrinking back from my touch. *In some other lifetime . . .* it was a thought I couldn't indulge.

Loneliness could be something we held in common—separately.

She clutched the doorframe for strength.

"You think that inconsequential display of affection meant something? Did you suppose it's something you can look forward to once we're married? Or are you hoping for another taste, perhaps?" I searched her face for the answer and replied with a deep throaty laugh that flushed her cheeks with a mottled shade of red. "You did, didn't you?"

She tried to hide the hurt she was feeling and failed. It was her own fault that she'd gotten caught up in the moment and romanticized me into someone with a heart. Someone with the ability to show and enjoy passion.

"Poor fool of a girl. How about some brutal honesty since we're to be married? I took one look at you gazing at my portrait with such lovestruck eyes and felt nothing but pity for you." I reached up and pushed a lock of hair back from her face. Instead of lowering my arm, I traced the side of her face as I crooned softly into her ear. "So soft. So innocent. So horribly naïve."

Catriona tried to fight her way out of my tight embrace, but came up short because she was no match for my superior strength. Clutching the sides of her arms now, I shook her. Hard. The force caused her head to roll back and slam against the door.

My cruelty was rewarded with an unwanted twinge of guilt.

Had I truly become the very creature people accused me of being —that I often told myself I was? How had I completely lost sight of the young man I had once been before that fateful evening a decade ago?

I instantly squashed that emotion. It would only undermine the person I *had* to be in order to survive the curse.

"Let. Me. Go," she demanded through gritted teeth.

"Not until we get this foolishness of yours resolved. Consider what happened a gift, the only one you will ever receive from me. The man in that portrait is dead, and no amount of girlish charm will resurrect him. Accept that and we may be able to reside alongside each other in tentative peace. All thoughts of affection, loving gestures, sweet whispered words are fruitless. You will receive none from me. This is an arrangement that comes from the ridiculous begging of your father. The man is a fool who squandered his fortune and then expected someone to reach into their pockets and save him. Nothing in this life is free. Everything has a price, and you, Catriona, are the price for your family's pride and vanity."

Her temper rose again in her eyes. I'd besmirched her father's name directly to her face. Her hands formed into claws, and I knew she wanted to reach up and scratch my eyes out for showing such dishonor.

I grasped her arm and brutally squeezed.

"That got your attention. Learn now that I won't be ignored. When I speak, you would do well to hang on my every word as though it came from the mouth of God. I'm to be obeyed and maybe, just maybe, you will survive this farce of a life forced on both of us."

"You bastard!" She raised her hand to slap me across the face and almost connected before I wrenched it away. I'd finally found the limit to her patience and self-control.

"So you're not the submissive mouse you pretend to be. Good to know. It can be beaten out of you, if you think to push me. Don't ever think you can raise your hand to strike me. In three days, I will own you, and you'll be mine to do with as I please. Play the role of the dutiful wife well, and I may just leave you alone. Annoy me, and you'll wish you'd never stepped foot in this house. Do I make myself clear?"

Catriona refused to look at me, another rush of defiance keeping her from caving to my demands. It was as if she silently challenged me to do my worst.

Foolish. Very, very foolish. I hoped she never got to witness firsthand the extremes I had, and would go to, in order to get what I wanted.

"I asked you a question."

Resentment shone from her eyes as she met my gaze. She realized she truly was a prisoner here, that I was her warden, and that returning to her former life was a hopeless cause. Tears flowed down her cheeks as she fully understood the extent of her situation.

What she didn't know was that I was just as much a prisoner to this life as she was.

"I understand, sir."

"Good. Now go away and do something. I'm sure you have things that will occupy your time here. If you don't, talk with the maid I've hired for you, and see what she suggests. I trust we won't have to meet too often once we're married. It may serve you well to find a friend."

Catriona nodded her head, biting on her bottom lip. She wiped at her cheeks with the back of her hand, and when I finally let her move freely, she turned to retrace her steps out of the kitchen. Right before she left, with her back to me, she asked one last question.

"What about children?"

My incredulous gasp answered it.

"What makes you think I would want to bring children into this shamble of a life?"

Her mouth popped open with a gasp. I'd shocked her.

"You want no sons? No heirs?" Judging from her response, the idea was beyond anything she could understand. It was something that society drummed into us from childhood—that the greatest accomplishments a man could achieve was his ability to pass his legacy on to his children. Her gaped mouth showed she'd never met anyone who thought the idea of it a joke.

"You don't want to pass your legacy on?" The question flowed from her mouth without thought.

"You have no idea what you're asking, Catriona." I'd grown tired of the conversation and brushed her away with a hand gesture. "Go away. Your questions offend me." This would be the last warning she got.

With my hand on the doorknob to go back outside into the twilight air, I ignored the melancholy that descended across her gentle features.

Let her be sad.

Let her be disappointed.

Welcome to the ways of the world, wife-to-be.

Welcome to reality.

CHAPTER 4

$\mathcal{F}$iddling with the last cufflink on my sleeve, I quickly glanced over my shoulder to the only person with permission to enter my bedchambers unannounced.

Phineas Knox—manservant and trusted confidant. Our relationship was a far cry from the business-driven contract I'd initiated when I first met him. Back then, he had merely been a necessary cog in the machine—someone to run my errands while I chased every rumored gypsy sighting across England and into Scotland.

It had taken me a while to call him by the correct first name. Who he was personally was inconsequential and I hadn't cared enough to learn anything about him—other than to exact his complete obedience. By chance, I'd discovered that his talents and skills lay beyond the superficial running of an estate and ensuring his master's needs were met.

Knox was a man who held great value.

He would bring me the cure on a silver platter—most likely with hands splattered with the blood of those he forced to bend to my will.

"You plan on wearing that to the ceremony?" he asked quizzically. He strode over to where I stood before the full-length mirror and began brushing along my shoulder blades—straightening the fabric of my shirt.

"Am I expected to dress up?" I retorted, checking my appearance. My linen shirt was pressed to perfection, and my black trousers held a sharp crease down the front. I didn't move as he finished his own inspection.

For all intents and purposes, to the outside world, he was my valet. When we were alone, we often continued the façade, even when there was no one to witness it.

"Honestly, Marcus?" he offered me a respectful bow and came to a stop beside me. "I anticipated finding you in your underclothing, clothes crumpled and creased from the lack of care. You've made it perfectly clear that today's formalities are simply that and that you hold no affection for the girl. I've seen you show more excitement over the prospect of inspecting new horses for your stables."

"Well, one usually dresses to impress for their wedding, Knox." I didn't bother hiding the sarcasm or smirk that danced across my lips.

My wedding.

How the hell did I allow things to get this far?

"Have you seen her yet? Did you deliver the outfit I requested she wear?"

Part of me wished I'd been a fly on the wall when he presented her with the garment I'd found stuffed in a long-forgotten storage trunk that once belonged to a dead ancestor. Insects had eaten jagged holes in the yellowed lace, thread hanging loosely from various hems. I had no idea whether it could be laundered back to its former glory, but deep down, I felt it was an appropriate representation of this whole fiasco.

She wouldn't be the blushing bride, and I wasn't the doting husband.

If it fit her, that was sufficient for me.

Knox cocked his eyebrow before nodding his response. "And she was far from . . . enthusiastic."

He'd searched for the right word—always in his role as a

diplomat. It's why I had kept him in my services for so long. He knew how to soften my edges when interacting with others.

I shrugged on the last item of my outfit he held up behind me, sliding my arms into a dark blue jacket. "How she feels is not my concern. She could always attend the ceremony wearing nothing, if that is more to her liking."

He burst into laughter. "Why does she irritate you so much? She's pleasant to look at, and I'm sure if you treated her with even a shred of civility, she would warm your bed quite nicely. Do you truly have to act like such a bastard toward her?"

"How I treat my betrothed is not your concern," I quietly warned, catching his gaze in the mirror's reflection. I all but spat out the word betrothed. The truth was, I still felt resentful this was becoming a reality.

Women were good for only a handful of things.

They were nuisances, otherwise, always getting involved in affairs that didn't involve them. One look at Catriona, and I had instantly recognized that same defiant spirit, one that would no doubt become a thorn in my side for years to come.

"I beg to differ, *friend*." He added his own weight to the word. "Surely you see that this borderlines on cruelty. Set her free and let her at least claim some semblance of contentment. Marriage to you will not be easy."

"Don't forget your place."

"How can I, when you enjoy reminding me on a daily basis?" There was no malice or resentment in his response. In fact, his grin revealed that as always, his loyalty lay with me. "Sometimes twice, if I'm a good boy."

"Have I told you how much I hate you?" I grumbled, my mind already flickering forward to what was about to happen. Marriage had once been the ideal—the expectation bequeathed on every son to carry on the family lineage. I'd abandoned all hope once I realized that life was no longer compatible with the one I was now forced to endure. "Summon her to my office."

I didn't wait for an answer.

Knox would obey, and this farce would be official within the hour. The last thought I had as I left my bedchambers was a hollow one.

I should've seized control of his estate instead. That would've at least made a hell of a lot more sense than this did.

A wife.

One more cursed achievement to add to a growing list of many.

TRUE TO HER SEX, Catriona was late, no doubt using her tardiness as one last, failed attempt at showing her defiance and reluctance to follow through with her father's deal.

I refused to pity her. She had been born a female and therefore knew this was her lot in life—to never have control over her own destiny. Unfortunately, that had been placed in my hands.

Even the local minister whom I'd overpaid an exorbitant amount to hurry along the process and abandon tradition was impatiently shifting his weight back and forth on his feet. He knew better than to try to engage me with small talk.

There was no commiserating over the weather we were experiencing. He hadn't so much as peeped about a possible donation to the parish. Instead, Father Thompson stood in his worn priestly garb and stared at the closed door—as if to will Catriona's appearance so he could then flee the house and my presence.

Finally, the doorknob jiggled, and despite my efforts to not turn and greet the person entering, I obediently glanced over, and that's when I experienced something I had long thought dead.

Speechless. I was utterly, unbelievably, uncontrollably . . . speechless.

She was positively angelic.

Despite the fact I had given her a nightmarish dress to wear, she'd somehow managed to make it look regal—her head held high. The material hung on her smaller frame, a partially ripped hem dragging across the floor behind her.

But you wouldn't have known that she noticed the pitiful garment and that it was a far cry from what she'd imagined wearing as a small girl.

That wasn't what almost brought me to my knees—what left me with an overwhelming need to run as far away from the creature now standing before me.

She was exquisite.

She was perfection.

She is mine, a voice whispered, claiming her instantly.

"Let's hurry this up," I growled, grinding my teeth tightly to prevent any soft-hearted platitude from escaping. "There are more important affairs to take care of."

I barely managed to drag my gaze away from Catriona's features to glare at the priest.

"Is my father not coming?" Her words came out broken, and I could sense the tears that lay barely beneath the surface. She didn't dare look about, in case it confirmed what I was about to say.

"No. This is not a celebration. I assume he is off enjoying his newfound freedom, having escaped debtors' prison." I resented the pressing urge to look at her—to comfort her. This was not part of the arrangement I'd committed to.

"Could we . . ." Her request died on her lips.

For some bizarre reason, I wanted to hear her complete it. "Could we what?" I pushed, gruffly.

"Nothing. As you said, this is strictly business, and I am merely your chattel." Catriona kept her gaze trained on the floor, patiently standing still with her hands clasped in front of her. Even in her misery, she held an ethereal quality. One might've even suggested she was fae-like.

"At last, something we agree on." Nodding to the priest, I indicated that it was time to begin. Father Thompson began droning on about marital bliss and the wonders of a man and woman joining together in the sight of God.

"Father," I corrected, reminding him that this was not the speech I had given him permission to do. Platitudes were wasted in this room.

We would never be a typical husband and wife, so there was no need for flowery poems and heartfelt vows.

Catriona would obey me, and in exchange, I would tolerate her presence in my life.

The priest coughed and cleared his throat, flipping through the small brown leather book in his hands until he found what he was looking for. With as little feeling as possible, I recited back the words that I would take Catriona Livingston as my wife—excluding any promises that I would cherish and care for her until death did us part.

Catriona's bottom lip trembled when it was her turn to pledge her fealty and devotion to me—her new monster of a husband. Her eyes didn't quite meet mine, and her fingers were white from constantly gripping her hands so tight. Silent tears fell down her cheeks—the blasted liquid somehow increasing her appeal.

Energy pulsed through me, and I ached to move. It was becoming more and more unbearable to remain in the room with her, each ticking sound of the clock wearing on my nerves.

No sooner had the priest declared our union official when Knox burst into the office. His dark hair was windswept, his eyes bright with excitement. I hadn't questioned his absence from the ceremony, because looking for him would require time I didn't want to waste.

"Yes?" I asked, already dismissing Father Thompson and Catriona. I was more interested in knowing what made Knox practically brim over with enthusiasm. "You have something."

"A lead!" he exclaimed triumphantly.

It had been months since we'd received any new information about the gypsies responsible for my curse. It had left me no choice but to learn years ago the importance of patience. Sometimes answers required a lengthy wait.

I would never rest until I found them.

"Let's go," I fired back, the thrill of the hunt already stirring within my breast. I was already halfway to the door when I noticed Knox hadn't moved, his own gaze directed to those behind me.

Catriona.

Barely remembering my manners, I spun about and bowed.

"Excuse me, wife." There was a slight mocking tone to my words. "It seems business waits for no man. I trust you can take care of yourself until we return."

She nodded, and I could almost detect a hint of relief. There would be no wedding night. "When shall I expect your return?"

I drank in one last sight of her.

"When it is time to return."

And with that, we departed—racing away into the night.

CHAPTER 5

FOUR MONTHS LATER

Soft footsteps approached my office door. It was the same sound I heard each evening as I sat at my desk, looking over papers. At first I had felt irritated by the disturbance, knowing that it was Catriona who lurked beyond the closed door. I could almost imagine her standing there with indecision warring across her features while she tried to decide whether or not she would knock.

Would tonight be the night that she found her courage and ventured inside? And how would I react to the interruption?

I'd like to think that I would answer consistently—with a stern and impatient retort, shooing her away like whatever it was that brought her to me was inconsequential.

On the odd occasion when she'd entered the study and found me sitting by the fire, reading one of the many books I'd collected over the years, she nervously licked her lips before asking if there was anything she could get me.

I wasn't a fool. I recognized the bravery needed to approach me. I hadn't made it easy for her since our pathetic excuse for a wedding. I'd warned her afterward that I wasn't to be disturbed and that for her own good, it would be best that we try to avoid one another.

There was no mistaking the crestfallen expression that glimmered in her eyes. Despite every attempt I'd made to keep her at arm's length, she was determined to breach the barrier I'd placed between us.

I found small trinkets throughout the house—items that she'd somehow known would please me. Countless nights I'd entered my study for solitude and there would be some type of treat. I'd even walked in to discover freshly cut flowers from the garden arranged in a crystal vase in my bedroom.

My first instinct was to hunt down my disobedient wife and rebuke her for violating the sanctuary of where I slept, but something inside me counseled that I tread carefully. For what reason I didn't know. Sure enough, the next time I passed by her in the house, the words that formed in my mouth went unspoken.

Even with all the precautions I took to not allow her closer, she was changing me with her small acts of kindness.

She still lurked outside, and as I closed my eyes, I could faintly hear the beating of her heart. I held my own breath this time and silently willed her to enter. If only to see what her reasoning was tonight.

She fascinated me.

She terrified me.

"Catriona," I called out, summoning her to come in.

The door handle jiggled slightly, and then it stopped moving. What would she do?

A few moments later, she retreated, making her way back up the hallway from where she'd come. I guess tonight wasn't a night for conquering fears.

I sat there staring at the door, but it was my thoughts that kept me from returning to my reading. I'd lost count of how many conversations I'd had with myself since that night when I'd been cursed. I tried not to think about what might've happened if I'd been far away from that alley, or better yet, had never laid eyes on Primrose. I'd allowed my lust to override common sense and had been punished for that decision ever since.

I could've been anything I wanted—anyone I wanted—because

the world had truly been mine to explore. Having been born into wealth and privilege, very few doors had been closed to me.

Yet, here I sat behind one, shut away from the world. I had what many would call a beautiful wife, a woman who appeared to at least try to bridge the distance between us.

For each small kindness she extended, I returned it with indifference. She didn't deserve such treatment. What scared me even more was the voice that had started whispering to me since I met her —that I didn't deserve such a life either.

Monster or not, I was at a crossroads. I would either need to let Catriona in or squash any hope she may have of melting the iciness in my heart.

Pushing away from my desk, I decided to seize the moment and follow her. I needed to understand what drew me to her—what made her so different that I was finding it harder and harder to resist.

Instead of going upstairs, however, the sound of Catriona's footsteps revealed she wasn't heading to her bedroom suite. Curiosity piqued my interest. She was hurrying in the opposite direction, and if I guessed right, toward the rooms reserved for Knox.

Interesting, I murmured beneath my breath.

Then, to my complete surprise, she briefly knocked on his door before entering. There was no waiting to be granted entrance. There was no gruff appearance of Knox—annoyed that she would dare to invade his privacy.

Anger rose sharply, followed by jealousy. How often did they meet late at night? What could they possibly have to discuss? And even though I'd shown no interest or intention of ever treating her like a true wife, there was no mistaking the word that came rushing to the forefront of my mind . . .

Mine.

Ready to burst through the door and catch them in the midst of their indiscretion, all logic and reason abandoned by the irritating sense of possessiveness, I abruptly stopped in my tracks when I caught the first sound of her voice.

She was crying.

Something—someone had upset her.

Reduced to spying on others in my own home, I reserved judgment for a moment and listened in, my ear close to the door. Despite the fierce pangs of mistrust I was feeling, there was one thing I did know with certainty . . . Knox had never given me a reason to doubt his loyalty. There was something else happening—another motive for Catriona to enter his room like they were friends meeting. Like she belonged there.

A muffled noise broke through her sobs.

"Why won't he let me in?" came the broken words of the woman crying like her heart was splintering into pieces. I pushed down the guilt that surfaced. I owed her nothing.

Or did I?

I could almost picture Knox standing there, unsure of how to handle someone so emotional. He'd shared that he'd had sisters growing up, but from the stories he'd confided in me over the years, he wasn't particularly close with them.

"What happened, Catriona?" he asked with compassion. It was strange hearing him speak so softly and tenderly. The only time I'd heard him talk in such a way was when he soothed a spooked horse down in the stables. He had a magic touch with animals, the creatures instantly calming under his touch and guidance. It was a trait I often envied. It was as if they could sense the beast I was . . . the predator I was cursed to be.

"I wanted to wish him good night. I remember you told me that such simple things might work in softening his attitude toward me."

Knox had told her that? How often did she come to him? Questions flurried around inside my head, each one left unanswered. Part of me knew I could barge in and demand the information I wanted, but it was a wiser part that urged for me to remain hidden. Sometimes the things you seek can only be revealed through being still and silent.

"And?" There was a hint of concern in that one word. I didn't blame him. I knew who I was and how others saw me. No amount of counsel had managed to tame my rough edges. I'd assumed he'd given up trying.

There was silence before she quietly answered. "I was a coward. I left before he could yell at me." There were a few more betraying sniffles. "I don't understand why he hates me so much, Knox. He doesn't even know me! Am I to be condemned to a life of misery because of my father's foolishness with money?"

The guilt had returned, and it frustrated me. I was tempted to flee back to my office where I could put more distance between this blasted woman and me. Maybe I would show her how truly cruel I could be and send her away to live in a nunnery. There she could curse my existence to her heart's content. She would at least find some semblance of peace.

"Give him time, Catriona. I told you. Marcus is not the man you assume him to be. I warned you it wouldn't be easy, but you were adamant that you could break down his walls. Remember, I told you it was a foolish waste of time."

It was interesting to hear him speak so freely about me.

"How can you sit there and defend him? Why won't you talk to him on my behalf? Tell him how lonely I've been and how much I wish to at least be friends? Food I take him, hoping that it will tempt him, is left untouched. The other day I found the freshly clipped roses I'd gathered tossed in the pile to be thrown away. It's as if he's doing this on purpose to drive me crazy!" As she uttered each word, I could hear her anger growing stronger and stronger. I didn't blame her. I would never accept such treatment myself. I wanted to not care, but that lack of sentiment felt like it was slipping through my fingers.

"Catriona, my loyalty belongs with him. He is my master, and no matter how many tears you shed, or how often your lip quivers, there's nothing I can do to change your circumstances here. You asked for my advice, and I gave it."

I bent forward and tried peeking through the large keyhole. There they both were—Catriona standing still with her arms wrapped around herself, and Knox, perched on his workbench stool, turned about so he could face her. Just as I had assumed, there was a hint of frustration at being kept from his work, but he was also staring at her with sympathy.

"So, you truly won't help me?" Tears began welling in her eyes. Catriona looked longingly at him . . . beseechingly. "I am all alone."

He slowly stood and walked over to where she stood. I expected Knox to guide her toward the door, but instead, he wrapped an arm around her shoulder for comfort. "Don't give up. If this is something you really want, then you will have to use that stubbornness I've seen in you. Fight for what you want. If at first you don't succeed, step back, re-evaluate, then try again."

Wiping her face with her fingers, Catriona slumped with resignation. "I didn't imagine it would hurt this much, Knox. I told myself that hope would be futile when it came to this marriage. I knew I was merely property exchanging hands. I didn't wish for a love-filled marriage . . . I'm not that naïve. But what harm could come from being friends? Am I really that unlikable?"

I couldn't see Knox's face. He squeezed her shoulder once more before dropping his arm. "You're asking questions I don't have the answers to, and what I do know, I can't share without betraying his confidence." Fingers raked through his ash-blond hair, a gesture I'd seen him make countless times. He was ready for the conversation to be over. He was ready to return to his work that beckoned him to finish.

Catriona let out a loud sigh. "Then I will keep trying." She gave one last glance about the room, and headed toward the door I was hiding behind. "Just tell me one last thing. Was he always like this?"

"Like what?" Knox asked over his shoulder, having already turned his back.

"Unapproachable. Cold. Indifferent."

He caught her gaze and held it. "He has good reason to be untrusting. Earn his respect, and you'll see he's not the monster you believe him to be." Having said all he intended to say, Knox returned his attention to his work, dismissing her.

I quickly stepped back to hide in the shadows, not wanting to let them know that I had been eavesdropping like a common thief. There was a strange mixture of emotions flittering about in my head.

There was pride and gratitude that Knox had kept my secrets, proving that my faith and trust in him were well placed.

There was a growing sense of apprehension that Catriona was determined to establish some kind of relationship with me—despite my many protests. But I was also impressed that she wasn't relying on her beauty or feminine wiles in seducing me. She had known immediately that such attempts would fail, and instead, tried to find ways to please me.

Watching her finally retreat in the direction of her own rooms, I stayed where I was for a moment, trying to absorb everything I'd heard.

"It's safe to come in now, Marcus."

He'd known I'd been there. Clearly I'd underestimated how observant he could be.

"I'm glad she has someone to talk to," I countered, entering his work space.

"She wants to be free to speak with you . . . her husband." He didn't bother disguising his bold smirk.

"I am her husband in name only," I retorted, completely unamused with this side of him. He was getting more and more brazen when we talked. It usually didn't bother me, unless, like now, he was not agreeing with me.

He cocked his brow, his boyish features turning hawkish. "I believe it was you that decided that, Marcus. I am but your obedient servant."

I ignored his last comment, choosing to focus on the more important issue. "You're to stop giving her advice. If she comes to you again, send her away. We don't have time for comforting a lonely female. Your focus is best placed elsewhere." I gestured to the experiments that covered his workspace. "That is why I hired you."

"Yes, master," he replied, with only a hint of contrition in his voice.

"No more," I reiterated, reinforcing that whatever alliance Catriona believed she had with Knox would be ended from this moment forth. "There is too much at stake."

I didn't wait to hear his response. He knew that what I said was law, and that whatever flights of fancy he might be entertaining by encouraging Catriona's visits would no longer be tolerated.

It didn't stop me from dwelling on it the rest of the night, though.

I didn't want her.

I didn't love her.

So why did I hate the idea of his arm around her shoulder, her turning to him for comfort so much?

CHAPTER 6

TWO MONTHS LATER

There was something peaceful about a quiet room where the only noise was the gentle crackling from the fireplace. Winter had descended with a vengeance on the estate, and with the colder weather came unavoidable duties to perform.

For the most part, we were ready for the long months where glistening snow covered every inch of the Suffolk countryside. I didn't allow it to hinder my true work, however. With my extended life, I braved the chilly conditions, pushing on when most men would retreat, because truth waited for no one.

One of these days I was certain I'd find the gypsies who cursed me, and if not them specifically, at least their clan. I wouldn't rest until I held their lives in my own two hands, satisfied only when they had removed their magic.

My heart screamed for vengeance, and even having the curse removed wouldn't curb my thirst for retribution. They had judged me without knowing all the facts. I would return that favor tenfold.

The leads Knox had brought to me months earlier had dwindled away into nothing, just as the fire in the hearth would do. It was part of the frustration that slowly ate away at my psyche. Every tidbit of information had to be explored, but not every morsel bore fruit.

We'd hit a dead end, and for the last few months, had heard little else.

I was itching to get out on the road and far away from the estate accounts that now demanded my attention.

And from her, I silently choked back, trying to ignore how easily her face surfaced in my mind. She was like a plague that decimated my hard-earned resolve. I didn't want to think about Catriona, or the way her defiance tugged at my focus.

I should be furious.

I should seek for ways to teach her a lesson, but the maddening woman didn't care. She spoke her mind whenever she managed to corner me, and I'd finally taken to avoiding areas of the house I knew she frequented.

My threats often fell on deaf ears, something Knox liked to rub in my face.

The knock at the door disrupted the peace, and I mentally prepared myself for who was on the other side.

"Go away," I called out.

The handle turned, and Knox entered, his face filled with tension. "Marcus—" he began.

I didn't bother looking up from the page I'd been reading. "She is your problem, Phineas. Whatever she's done, deal with it."

Dipping the quill in the black inkpot, I scribbled out the numbers I was tallying. The estate was in better shape than I'd assumed.

"Trust me, I've tried." His voice was filled with exasperation and annoyance. I didn't envy him. She was infuriating enough that even the pope himself would jump into the deepest ocean to escape her.

"Well, obviously not hard enough, if you're standing there expecting me to intervene." I placed the quill on the desk and folded my arms across my chest as I sat back in the chair. "Let me guess. She wishes to go to London for some pretty trinket?"

The affairs of women were lost on me. What they wanted was beneath my attention.

Knox cocked his eyebrow at me, unimpressed. "Do you really

think that little of me? That I would need to come have you hold my hand over something so trivial?"

He was right. While I hadn't told him such, his patience with dealing with all the unpleasantness that infiltrated my life was commendable.

"I'm sorry, my friend." I bowed my head respectfully. I'd interrupted him before even giving him the chance to explain. "What's the matter?"

"She's found him."

My gaze narrowed on him. I'd heard no horses approaching the house, no cloaked riders delivering messages. There was only one *she* he could've been referring to.

And by found him . . .

The chair I'd been sitting on teetered close to tipping from the force of my standing. Estate business came to an abrupt end as I stormed toward the door.

"How did she find him? What the hell have you been doing?" I didn't wait for him to catch up as I continued to rant over my shoulder. "How difficult is it to keep track of one pesky female?"

He was wise to not answer, choosing instead to hurry behind me as I headed toward the one place in the entire house Catriona had no business venturing.

Angry footsteps resounded in the air as we raced down stone steps to the rooms I'd affectionately dubbed my dungeons. The only people, besides Knox and myself, who saw the inside of said rooms were those unlucky enough to cross me.

Right now, that title was reserved for one man, and one man alone—my only souvenir from my search months ago.

I heard her before I saw her—Catriona's voice growing louder and louder on my approach.

"Marcus," Knox warned, calling out right as I put my hand against the door and pushed. "Remember who she is."

"She's a nuisance and a thorn in my damn side," I countered angrily, my response the only alert to those in the room.

Catriona jumped as guilt skated across her features. She knew she'd been caught and that there would be hell to pay, but that didn't stop her from then positioning herself in front of the chained man in the center of the cell. Her arms spread out as if to protect him somehow from more harm.

Little did she know how close she came to feeling the full weight of my wrath.

"You are a monster!" she screamed, fire blazing in her eyes. "How long has this man been here? Why do you have him chained like some animal?" When she couldn't get the response she wanted from me, she turned to Knox. "Free this man now!" Catriona punctuated her demand by pointing at the motionless form on the chair.

Knox simply stood there with his hands behind his back. He wasn't there to jump to her every command. He knew better than to listen to anyone but me. While we enjoyed a close relationship, Phineas never forgot who his master was.

"So, you are a coward, too!" she spat out, running forward to beat her small fists against his broad chest. "You made me believe that you could be trusted . . . that you were just as much a prisoner in this place as I am."

"Are you finished?" I asked, disappointed that she hadn't turned all that passion and fury my way. When she stood there—chest heaving from a shortness of breath and her body rigid from indignation—I moved closer to my prisoner. "Knox, take her back to her room and see that she stays there."

"I refuse to leave until I know he's safe." She crossed her arms across her chest, the motion pushing up her breasts. The muscles in her jawline twitched from being tight, her nostrils flaring with insolence. "So help me God, I will rip those chains from him myself if you deny me!"

I didn't know who laughed first—Knox or me. Glancing his way, I saw him shrug, and I chose to instead lean against the wall closest to her. "Then by all means, Mrs. St. James, dazzle us with these feats of strength."

Her face reddened until it rivaled the color of the apples that grew in the estate's orchard.

"What is wrong with you?" she asked, studying me like I was some carnival display she couldn't quite understand. "What could he possibly have done to warrant such treatment?"

She crouched down beside him, her clean hand resting tentatively on his dirty pant leg.

"His business doesn't involve you." It was the only answer she would receive.

Judging by the incredulous look on her face, she wouldn't be accepting it.

"Knox," she pled. It was quaint how she believed he would somehow rally to her side—pitting them both against me. "This man needs sustenance. He may even need a doctor."

"What he needs is none of your concern," he replied, woodenly, without emotion. He glanced my way. "I'll return her to her room and lock the door behind me."

This stirred up wildness in Catriona that was both intoxicating and amusing. It was the kind of expression I imagined she would make in the throes of passion—an expression I wouldn't allow myself to witness. What fascinated me, though, was the belief she still held tightly to. That, somehow, she still had control over her life.

"When you're done, return here so we can deal with this mess." I gestured to the still form with disgust. Our reluctant guest hadn't stirred since I visited his cell late last night, attempting once more to get the information I needed.

"Noooo!" Catriona screeched, kicking out as Knox wrapped his arms around her to carry her out. "You can't treat me this way!"

Her furious tirade continued to echo outside as Knox removed her from the lower levels of the house.

The room descended back into blissful silence.

"Kill me," came the barely audible whisper. "Kill me and be done with it."

I still hadn't managed to uncover exactly who my prisoner was within the gypsy clan I was hunting, but I knew enough to determine he wasn't being truthful.

Sooner or later, with enough incentive, they always confessed.

With enough applied pressure, even the most resilient and determined babbled like babies.

"You wish for death?" I asked, equally quiet. Pacing about the young man, I wondered what it would take to finally break him. Torture had yielded very little result, and frankly, he was beginning to reek from the lack of bathing. "Perhaps I should release you so the wolves can fill their bellies with your flesh."

"It would be an honorable death compared to this." His tone was the same as the long line of others who had sat in that same seat, filled with misplaced pride.

His bitter response filled me with mirth. "You believe yourself honorable?" I barked out an abrupt laugh. "You and your people create monsters, justifying your misuse of magic in the name of family. There is no honor in you or your ancestors." I kicked out at the legs of his chair, gaining his attention.

Black eyes glared up at me—their inky depths revealing how blackened his soul was. There would never be a time when I believed gypsies were a force of greatness in the world. In my mind, the only good gypsy was a dead one.

He tried spitting at me and failed, his mouth too dry to form any kind of spittle. Slumping back in the chair, his head lolled forward, his chin hitting his chest.

"Nikolai," I crooned, walking around him again like he was my prey and I was playing with my dinner. "Your suffering can come to an end . . . you can go home to your family." I trailed my hand across his shoulders, relishing the way he managed to flinch despite being exhausted. "You know what I want. Give me the information, and all this will end. You have my word."

His words came out mumbled, but I still understood them. "The word of the Devil means nothing."

I struck him hard against the side of his head. My patience had limits, and I was growing tired of this song and dance. "Tell me!"

Laughter bubbled out of Nikolai, and with great effort, he lifted his head to stare at me with contempt. "You will never find the cure. You are blood and damnation. Accept it."

155

I seized hold of his chin, squeezing it tightly between my fingers. Thin lines of blood welled where my fingernails broke his skin, and I resisted the urge to lap up the red liquid. Monster or not, I still had standards, and I refused to feed on gypsy scum.

"You walk a thin line," I threatened, again.

"And you talk too much." He mumbled something in Romani, the sound filled with scorn.

I stopped and got down close to his face—close enough that I could feel his faint breath across my skin.

"You're right." I held his gaze as I made sure he understood my next meaning. "And that is the beauty of your clan. When one won't talk, there are others more fragile who are easier to break. Perhaps a sister . . . mother . . . daughter?"

I studied his reaction, knowing that sooner or later I would hit the mark.

Daughter.

He had a daughter.

"I will give your apologies to her. It's unfortunate that you won't get to watch her grow up. That she won't enjoy growing old."

It took a few moments, but the second he understood, he strained against his restraints, heated threats rushing out in a mixture of broken English and Romani.

Reaching forward, I placed both of my hands on the sides of his head and twisted, snapping his neck. He wasn't going to relinquish the information. I wasn't wasting any more time on the dead gypsy.

"Where do you want me to dispose of his body?" Knox had returned in time to see me execute the prisoner.

"With all the snow, you might be hard pressed digging a grave to dump him in." Wiping the grime off my hands, I couldn't help feeling disappointed that once again, we had come up empty-handed. "Ride out a few hours, then drop him into a river or something. Do it far enough away from the estate so as not to raise suspicions."

"And Catriona?"

I let out a heavy sigh. "Inform her that I did as she asked. I gave him his freedom."

It wasn't the complete truth, but it should at least appease her.

I was almost out the door when Knox spoke up.

"Don't give up hope, Marcus. We will find the cure by either finding the gypsies who cursed you or through my experiments. We just need more time."

Nodding, I left him to take care of the body, trudging back up the stairs to my office.

Alone.

CHAPTER 7

*L*ife was about ritual—at least that's what mine had been reduced to. The carefree days of my youth were but a distant memory now, and it was often painful dwelling on what might have been.

Making my way to Knox's study was part of the nightly routine that dictated everything—superseding temptation and any form of nostalgia. Just once, I wished I could abandon all the safeguards I'd placed in my life, and simply *be*.

Free to be whoever the hell I chose to be and not the persona—the monster—I had become.

Ever since Catriona had moved into the house, these kinds of thoughts plagued me, causing waves of self-doubt to surface from the emotions I kept buried deep inside me.

It didn't pay to feel or have a heart anymore. Every decision I made was one of life or death. When it came to seeking vengeance—pure unadulterated revenge—feelings simply got in the way. I'd learned quickly once I started changing into the blood drinker those two women cursed me to become, that I would drown trying to hold tight to my humanity.

It was one of the first things I relinquished of my old life—like a snake shedding its skin. What was needed was the ability to be one hundred percent ruthless, to be such a force of nature that even the trees would bend to my will.

I lived in a world now saturated in deviousness and darkness. It was one where you were either the predator or the prey—the invincible or the destructible.

What was left of that former Marcus wasn't enough to brave falling in love. There was barely enough of my true self to maintain the friendship I had with Knox. He knew that and accepted it anyway.

What begun by chance had evolved into a symbiotic relationship where we both benefited. I'd found him a homeless beggar on the streets of London, and there was something about the young Phineas Knox that whispered his value. I'd learned not to judge others too quickly, and it had definitely paid off.

Down on his luck, his tall form lanky and thin from malnutrition, Knox hadn't thought twice about my offer to become his employer. All he saw was a way out of the cutthroat streets—a way to always have food in his stomach and a warm place to sleep.

I saw an urchin who was street smart—someone who could slip by unnoticed—a boy who would know the value of loyalty.

So it came as a complete surprise when he confided that he'd been an apprentice to an obscure alchemist. That brand of magic and science was a mystery to me, but something had impressed on me that, one day, such knowledge would prove useful.

It didn't matter that he claimed he'd burnt his master's home down from a spell gone awry. I overlooked the way the tips of his ears reddened as he confessed his complete lack of skill—his mouth full of the fresh warm bread I'd given him.

Knox had looked me dead in the eye—every inch the man he was beneath the grime—and vowed that should I give him a chance, he would never fail me. He would always serve me to the best of his abilities.

Here we were, after all this time, and he'd honored his word.

There were a few small incidents where he'd set fire to the bed in the connecting room, and then to the draperies hanging heavily over the only two windows in his study. Those things were inconsequential compared to the work he slaved over at the desk.

Knox had preserved my sanity, and for that, he would always have a home with me—servant or not.

Knocking briefly on the door, I didn't wait for him to welcome me into his sanctuary. It was a given that no door would ever be barred against me. There would never be any secrets. He knew mine, and I knew his—what little there was to know.

"I wondered where you were," came a deep baritone voice. "I would've brought the elixir to you, Marcus, but as you can see . . ." Knox waved his hand over the large wooden bench he'd made to work on. The surface was covered with all manner of tools he needed—glassware, candles, endless stacks of papers with weird symbols and scratching on them, empty ink bottles, and herbs.

I crinkled my nose. How he managed to work in such chaos was beyond me, but he'd once said that all creative geniuses preferred working in a mess. It quieted the voices in his head, apparently. I didn't argue.

"Please tell me that stench isn't for me."

While I was his master, I recognized this was his domain. Careful not to disturb anything, my gaze skimmed over the work in front of him. Knox didn't bother covering it up—he knew full well I couldn't read the alchemist symbols.

He let out a chuckle. Pushing back from the bench, the wooden stool scraping across the bare floor, Knox picked up a glass filled with thick, red liquid. That was another thing we removed from his study—carpet. We considered it a wise choice considering the amount of liquids and potions he spilled on an almost daily basis.

"Would you prefer the alternative?" he fired back, holding out the drink.

This was how I drank my blood. It was mostly human with different concoctions added—whatever Knox was testing to see if it would help curb my cravings and keep the beast at bay.

Before his help, I'd resorted to slipping into town every night and gorging until I couldn't swallow another mouthful of blood. My hunger all but consumed me, and there were still whisperings in the nearby counties of a monster that scoured the countryside in search of new victims.

I'd left death and carnage in my wake. There were times when I'd been too lazy to cover up my kills, launching the town or village into mass hysteria. Banners were placed all around with generous rewards for anyone who could bring the killer to justice.

Once I knew that Knox could be trusted, I'd confessed who I truly was, and he'd set about trying to find a cure for the curse. He'd been adamant that perhaps alchemy could hold the answers, and that I couldn't wait to find the gypsies.

And here we were. I was drinking his god-awful elixirs, and my appetite for blood was under control. Unfortunately, he still hadn't figured out a way to fully restore me.

He was the only thing in which I had any faith left. Sooner or later, he would be successful. He was too stubborn to admit defeat.

"Sometimes I miss the pleasure of sinking my teeth into something warm," I murmured, bracing myself to take my first swallow. "The way the blood flowed freely into my mouth . . . the ecstatic way it left a blazing trail of fire down my throat." I took a deep breath and decided to swallow the contents in one gulp.

The sensation was a meager substitute to the real thing, but it did its job. The uneasiness I always felt began to subside as it heated my stomach, and the loud, growly presence in my head grew quiet.

"Was this new?" I asked, placing the now empty glass beside Knox on the bench. "There was something . . . different about it." I gestured to the red liquid still staining the cup.

He nodded. "Gold. I added gold flakes to it with the hopes that as it builds up in your system, I may be able to alter your organs. By perfecting *you*, I will have created a vessel that can transform to whatever I wish it to be."

Like always, whenever he tried explaining the science behind his experimenting, my head began to throb. "So, I'm essentially a creature you're testing your theories on." It was more of a fact than a question.

Knox paused long enough from swirling about some clear liquid in his bowl to glance at me. "You disagree?"

It had been a long time since I'd lingered after taking my nightly tonic. He was more used to me gruffly accepting the blood, drinking it, and then leaving in a similar manner.

Yet here I was—trying to start a conversation and interrupting him from working.

"I trust you, Phineas," I assured him. "I sometimes wish I understood exactly what it is you do down here." Picking up one of the loose leaves of paper, I turned it about to show him. "This looks like utter nonsense, but if you tell me this brings us closer to removing this damn curse, that'll be enough for me. It will have to be enough."

Abandoning his work for a moment, Knox turned about, his hands resting on his knees. "I gave you my word that I wouldn't stop until I helped free you. You saved me that night in London, and I owe you a life debt." He chuckled as he took the paper back. "As for these, even the failures are a step forward. I don't possess the same skill and clarity of my former master, but what I lack in expertise, I make up for in sheer stubbornness."

"And gold flakes are the latest?" It felt weird knowing the precious metal was now pumping through my veins.

He shrugged. "It's just a thought. In alchemy, gold is considered a source that promotes human renewal and regeneration. My theory is that by infusing your very organs and blood with it, perhaps it will trigger that transformation within you—that it will help your spirit fight against the evilness of the curse, and triumph." Knox glanced at the empty glass, his brows furrowed in thought. "Again, that's the notion I'm exploring right now."

"And here I thought you were merely throwing in different ingredients to see which one made me sick," I teased, suddenly struck with appreciation for my friend. He had grown to be much more than someone who served me. I gave his study one more sweeping look. "Do you require anything?"

It wasn't uncommon for Knox to come to me with a long list of the items he required. I learned not to question some of them, especially if they would end up in my elixirs.

I could already see his focus returning to his work.

"Yes. I may need to go to London for the supplies." He wasn't even looking at me now. Whatever he'd been writing had snared his attention again, and his silence was a loud indication that our discussion was over.

"I may join you then." There was a certain seer I'd been trying to gain an audience with, but each time, I'd been denied. Knox wasn't the only one who refused to admit defeat. I was determined to finally meet with the infamous Lady Hannah.

Knox mumbled something in return.

One more nightly ritual was complete.

As I headed toward the door, he called out again, surprising me. "One of the added ingredients in your drink will help you dream walk. Just in case you wanted to visit anyone . . . understand anyone."

His comment stopped me dead in my tracks.

Dream walk?

"You don't need me to explain that, Marcus. You now have the ability to visit someone while they're asleep."

"Why?" I asked, curious how he'd deduced that. I didn't sleep very often, and therefore, didn't dream. I wasn't interested in making social calls that way either.

It was his turn to look at me, bewildered. "I had the thought the other night when I went to dispose of the gypsy. What if instead of trying to break his body and spirit, we attack from a place where he wouldn't be expecting it? A man can tolerate unimaginable pain if he believes it's for a just cause. In our dreams, we are more vulnerable . . . more susceptible to coercion."

I was impressed. Knox's reasoning was sound, and if it worked, could save a lot of time. In fact, it was a brilliant idea that I hoped prove fruitful. "I can't wait to see the results then. We'll bring home a subject to test it on."

The corners of his mouth curled in a mischievous way, and I instantly saw he had an ulterior motive. "Why wait? There's someone who resides under this roof you could understand better." And with that, Knox looked up in the direction of Catriona's bedchambers.

"No," I retorted, my response loud and forceful. "Absolutely not."

"Do you have so many friends, Marcus, that you can't stomach to nurture another ally?" I had his full attention again, which made me wonder how long he'd been preparing to tell me this. "I am good at what I do, but there are certain places even I can't enter. Don't you think it a good idea to have Catriona help you break this curse as well? Women talk—a lot. They gossip. Why not befriend her and see what she can uncover?"

I loathed the suggestion with a fiery passion. The thought of confessing my secrets to the female forced into my keeping felt intolerable. It would require my being vulnerable with her— discarding the persona I'd adopted with her and being someone . . . softer.

"She thinks me a monster."

"She only sees what *you* show her. You already know my thoughts on that." Knox gave me a shrewd stare. "She should never have been placed in the role of an enemy."

"Who is the master here?" I thundered, uncomfortable with the way the conversation was going. It wasn't because I thought it was ridiculous. No, slowly but surely, I was beginning to see the sense in it.

"You, but that doesn't change the fact that my advice bears consideration."

I didn't speak another word. His words bounced around in my head, and no amount of refusal and denial on my part dimmed the truth.

She would make a better ally than enemy.

If she was going to remain here with me, it would be better that I find a use for her, instead of letting all that pent-up frustration and hostility percolate. Sooner or later, it would need an outlet, and I had a sinking suspicion Catriona would level me with her anger.

Part of me wanted to witness that.

But common sense won.

"Let me consider it," I muttered, heading for the door again.

"All you need do is think of her before sleeping and you'll find yourself where she is."

I'd sworn I wouldn't rest until I was fully human again and my cursers dead by my hand. If dream walking helped me accomplish that—if it finally uncovered the answers I'd spent over a decade looking for—then it was time to win over my wife.

CHAPTER 8

*S*leeping was such a foreign concept to me, something that I required less of as the years passed. Mostly, I reserved it for those moments where I needed a break from the drudgery of everyday living. The brief respite seemed to soothe my nerves around the edges, making it possible not to completely lose my mind.

Now I was seeking sleep for a different reason, and I wasn't quite sure how I felt about that. Once upon a time, I thought knowing the innermost thoughts and feelings of others would be a useful trick to have, but I still wasn't convinced understanding Catriona was a good idea.

There was so much that could go wrong. Tampering with another person's psyche, especially when they were vulnerable, could only complicate matters further. Something told me that my wife wouldn't appreciate the violation, either.

But my curiosity, once stoked, was a hard thing to quell.

Laying back on my bed, I tried to make myself as comfortable as possible. Slowly I could feel my muscles releasing their tension, and the first telltale signs of sleep started trickling through my body.

It wouldn't be long now before I ventured into unknown territory.

"Think of her," I whispered beneath my breath. Images of the beautiful brunette surfaced, and despite the countless times she'd irritated me, there was no denying that my wife was in fact an extremely attractive woman.

I pictured the way her dark locks seemed to have a mind of their own—hanging in long curls that framed her pretty face. I hated admitting that my fingers often itched to tangle in the thickness, missing the way it had felt that day back in my office when we first met. What had started as a way to undermine her confidence had turned around and bitten me hard, because it was often all I could think about.

I wanted to trace the soft curve of her face, relishing the way heat flooded her cheeks at my touch. She was unspoiled and virtuous—the brief taste I'd stolen confirming she would open up like a beautiful flower, each petal begging to be admired.

Her red lips held my attention regardless of what she was saying. Whether it was the way she softly sang to herself when she thought no one was watching or the way they pursed when she disapproved of something I had done, they drew me to her. Her mouth—her kiss—would be as intoxicating as a flagon of ale. I doubted there was a man alive who would escape becoming drunk on such a taste.

But it was her temperament that drew me in like a moth to a flame. She was both fire and tenderness—chaos and stability—strength and fragility. She was a walking contradiction to me, because one moment she would flay me on the spot with her shrewd brown eyes, and in the next breath, gently cradle a wounded bird in her hands. The way she viewed the world was at complete odds with how I had been forced to see it.

She saw injustice and sought to correct it by showing kindness to others.

I saw injustice and wanted to rain down blood and violence until I gained my revenge.

Drowsiness beckoned until I couldn't keep my eyes open. With one last murmur of her name, the world dissolved, and I found myself someplace strange.

"Marcus?" The breathlessness of her voice caused a ripple of awareness to pulse through me. She'd never spoken to me like that before, and the part I had tried denying flared back into existence. I felt greedy for such softness.

"Catriona," I replied, finding her sitting on a brick wall covered with green moss and vines. "Where are we?"

I couldn't tell if this was a figment of her imagination or if she was visiting a place she knew.

"The ruins where Lancelot and Guinevere would meet secretly." There was a wistfulness about her as she looked around with fondness that told me she was a romantic at heart. "At least, that's what I've told myself. I'm sure this is merely the long-forgotten home of someone." Catriona stroked the brick wall she was still perched on. "But I like to come here and think."

She gave me a pointed glance that told me I was often the subject of such musings.

I slowly started walking around, noting how secluded it was, half believing that this was actually a place that lovers rendezvoused— stealing kisses and heated embraces away from the prying eyes of the world.

"I could see that," I confessed, gingerly touching a rich green vine with budding white flowers dotting it. "We live in a world where the forbidden intrigues us."

"And where we can't always act on our passions."

Her response caused me to stop long enough to study her next. "You have passions, Catriona?"

Females in society didn't have the luxury of acting upon their own, let alone acknowledging openly that they were stirred by the same instincts and cravings men were.

"Why are you here, Marcus?" she gently pressed. "I've never dreamed of you before, yet here you are as though you belong here with me."

Like a queen on a throne, she hadn't moved since I'd come across her, the height of the broken wall making it so she sat higher than me.

With the light shining from behind, she looked ethereal.

"How do you know you haven't brought me here yourself?" I

countered, unable to keep myself from being somewhat honest with her. I held her gaze as long as I could before lowering my eyes.

I was completely out of my element here and unsure of how to proceed. In the waking world, I would exert my dominance and force her to cower and answer whatever questions I had. I wasn't used to being asked my intentions.

"So, at last, you are my prisoner." Her smile was genuine and void of any malice. I couldn't say I would be as gracious if the roles had been reversed. "Seeing as you are intruding on my dream, I would say I also hold all the control." A twinkle sparked in her eyes, revealing a side of mischievousness I hadn't seen before either.

"So it seems," I replied and bent at the waist, offering my respect. "What would you wish of me, my lady?"

I added a flourish with my hand and was rewarded with the soft tinkling of her laughter. Another sound I hadn't known I needed until this precise moment.

I had nothing to lose by dropping the persona I held in the waking world. If there was ever an opportunity to lower my guard and simply enjoy something carefree and innocent, it was now.

Sadness skated across her features. "No matter how much I would love for this to be real . . . for us to hold a genuine conversation where we mutually liked one another . . ."

A stray tear fell from her lashes. It killed me not to reach over and capture it with my thumb. These emotions—the foreignness of feeling compassion after all these many years—churned up confusion inside me. Bit by bit, I could feel the façade I had cloaked myself with fall, until all that was left was . . . me.

I didn't like it.

I hated it.

But I also embraced it, stood in awe of it—of knowing such affection was still possible for a monster like me.

"Pretend with me then," I encouraged, and finally moved from where I'd been standing to her. Knowing this was only a dream, I bravely took her hand and held it between my own. The warmth of her skin felt real enough to send a shiver up my spine.

Warning bells sounded in my head—cautioning that to proceed would only result in heartache and would be dangerously reckless. In truth, the last time I had allowed myself to feel anything remotely close to the romantic feelings swirling about in my chest, I'd woken to find myself holding a dead body in my arms, and the wrath of a gypsy clan dragged down upon me.

Drop her hand, a voice screamed inside me. *Wake up. The way before you is folly and you know it.*

My fingers twitched as if they longed to obey, but I held on tighter. This was what I had been secretly craving—yearning for. Human connection. Revenge had kept me warm throughout the years, but it hadn't brought me a speck of solace.

I was bone weary of constantly fighting.

Just once, I wanted to see what it felt like to find that peace in another.

"Catriona," I murmured, finally cupping the side of her face, my thumb softly circling over her skin. "We are quite impossible."

She nodded, holding herself still as though with one wrong move, this would all fade away. I could see the questions bubbling up in her eyes, each one waiting to be asked. I was sure she was biting her tongue, unsure about whether to give them voice, or whether she should remain silent—waiting to see where this moment might lead us.

"I never wished this life for you. In another lifetime, I know I could grow to love you deeply, to delight in growing old with you. You are quite a remarkable woman . . ." I struggled to find the right words, my tongue tripping over my own thoughts. "A treasure to any man."

"Then why do you act so abominably toward me? Why must we be enemies?" The earnestness in her voice was almost strong enough to break me. There was nothing more I wanted in this moment than to promise her things would change and that the happiness she desperately longed for could be ours.

But we weren't part of some fairy tale of star-crossed lovers, fighting against the odds to be with each other. My reality was set in stone—at least until Knox and I found a cure. By then, it might be too late for anything to grow between Catriona and me.

"What do you want from me?" I finally asked, holding the side of her cheek as I tilted her head to look deep into her eyes. "Ask now, because once this dream is over, what we want can never be."

Catriona slowly slipped from the wall and stood before me, her hands hanging by her side, fingers loosely gripping her nightgown's material. She looked so unbelievably small amongst her surroundings, but her request revealed the magnitude of her heart.

"Love me, Marcus. Even if it's just for the briefest of seconds. Let me have something to hold on to once this is over." Tears began to fall again. "I know I mean nothing to you, but please."

For some reason, her request came as a shock. I'd expected her to beg for her freedom or to have more control in the waking world—to even be friends. That made more sense to me than a request for love, no matter how temporary and fleeting it was.

I responded instinctively, pulling her into my arms as I rested my forehead on hers. It was the most intimate position I'd ever been in, regardless of how many times I'd shared my bed with another. It was as though our spirits gently spoke—communicating the emotions I knew I couldn't even dare to voice.

"You don't know what you ask."

"Am I so unlovable that you can't even muster the smallest of sympathy for me? I am lonely, Marcus. I am your wife in word only . . . and even that is viewed scornfully by you. Give me something that I can hold on to when we return and you . . ."

Again, she struggled to complete her fevered petition. Her body relaxed into mine as a signal that she was done trying to convince me. She was accepting that any hope for a relationship was a feeble one. I'd watched that belief disappear in reality, and now . . . now I was witnessing its death in her dreams.

It was that realization that obliterated any kind of resistance in me. Let them believe I was a monster, because I knew I played my role masterfully, and their hateful opinions meant nothing to me.

But hers . . . somehow, along the way, she had come to matter.

"Catriona," I whispered again, the thudding of my heart loud in my ears. "Will just one moment be enough? I can't give you what you want, but if a small token will appease you, then . . ."

My words faded away as I cradled her face in both hands.

What I was about to do was extremely dangerous. Not for her, but for me. It threatened to unravel any hope of being the particular beast needed to exact my revenge.

Love and hate couldn't exist within a person at the same time.

Catriona claimed that it would be enough for her—that she would cherish whatever morsel I offered, but the truth was this:

I didn't know if it would be enough for me.

Could one more taste last a lifetime?

Lowering my head, my mouth hovered over hers, lips barely touching. We were both lonely. We both craved an intimacy that had so far been withheld from us. It made sense to find that comfort with each other.

But at what cost?

Was loving Catriona worth abandoning my thirst for retribution?

Which battle could I live with—the violence and singular focus required to hunt my cursers to the ends of the earth, or the agonizing restraint needed to ignore my need for this remarkable woman?

She had shown no fear when facing me, a man who had no qualms about treating her worse than the horses in his stables. She'd shown incredible courage, facing days filled with the unknown, her life no longer her own to control.

Knox had been right. I'd been wrong this whole time. Perhaps trusting Catriona and giving in to the feelings we both shared could only bring happiness to my dark existence.

Maybe.

Hopefully.

I couldn't think any more. Closing the distance between us, I seized her mouth and surrendered. I kissed her as though everything depended on the electricity passing between us. I poured every piece of me into it, and she replied with her own intensity.

I was drowning in her.

I lost myself in her.

For the briefest of seconds, I would've given up everything for her —my mission, the search for a cure, every twisted thought that had consumed me and shaped me into the man who now clung to her like a lifeline.

It wasn't until a thought brazenly infiltrated my mind that I dared to pull away, breaking the seal of our mouths.

We both stood there with heaving chests, desperately trying to slow our breathing, lips bruised from our outburst of passion. Her hair was mussed, and I longed to drag her back against me, to embrace her and never let go.

But there was no denying that one traitorous thought.

She doesn't know who you truly are.

And with that singular sentence, I woke up with a start.

CHAPTER 9

I couldn't remember the last time I'd come into this room.

Catriona lay peacefully under the covers, still locked in the dream we'd shared. The dwindling flame of a candle slowly burned, offering a small amount of light in the darkened bedchamber.

Turn around and leave, an inner voice cried, trying to reason with my heart. *This path will only lead to misery.*

I agreed with the thought blaring inside my head, but it didn't prevent me from completely entering her sanctuary and closing the door behind me. The effects of the kiss we'd exchanged—her plea for something more than merely coexisting in the same house—all these things wreaked havoc over my senses.

It felt as though my entire being was at war with itself, and for the first time, I was undecided how to move forward. It didn't matter that I'd instantly rushed to her side, hoping to continue the kiss that had ravaged my self-control. The truth still rang loud and clear.

Catriona St. James had no idea with whom she was begging to have a meaningful relationship. Whatever ideals she imagined while she hid away in this room—whatever fantasies she concocted in her lover's dream hideaway—I could never be that man for her.

The sooner she understood why it was impossible, the faster she could relinquish those expectations and accept the bitter hand Fate had dealt us both.

I needed to wake her and take her to the only place I knew that would remove any confusion and release me from the temptation of wanting what we couldn't have.

She let out a faint sigh and shifted slowly, not resting until she found a comfortable spot. It felt like a sin to wake her—to shatter the tranquility that graced her beautiful features and replace it with one of revulsion and disgust.

There would be no gazing up at me, no sinking into my embrace, once she'd heard my complete confession. She would be confined to a doomed marriage and left to live out the rest of her days in bleakness, always hoping for the one thing she couldn't obtain.

"Catriona," I whispered, nudging her arm to rouse her. I was on the verge of losing my nerve, of bargaining with my conscience that a few more minutes of ignorant bliss would be worth it.

A coward's choice, but it was all I could do not to take a seat and continue watching her sleep. Such beauty right before me was a heady invitation to refuse.

I repeated her name again, this time louder.

Thick eyelashes fluttered open, and it took her a few moments to completely wake up. I knew the instant she recognized she wasn't alone, because she quickly sat up and tugged the bedding up under her chin, as though it would protect her from my cruelty.

She was no longer the Catriona from the dream.

I mourned that it was seeing me that destroyed it.

"Mr. St. James?" she asked, her voice shaky. Strands of her thick black hair were messed from her pillow, and I watched in fascination, wanting to smooth it out for her.

"There is something I want to show you," I answered, shaking myself to dislodge the lovesick thoughts that threatened to addle my brain. This was the very reason why I didn't want to get close to her—to allow myself to feel anything toward Catriona beside obligation. "Come, you'll need to put on your shoes and an overcoat."

She didn't move. She simply stared at me as though I was some apparition delivering a message that made little sense.

"Did you hear me?" I asked, this time going to retrieve her coat myself. "There is a conversation we must have that is long overdue. All I ask is that you hear me out and make your decision once you've heard all the details." Holding out the jacket, I waited as she quietly slipped on her shoes.

It wasn't until she'd finished buttoning up her winter coat that she spoke. "Can this not wait until the morning?" Her words were muffled behind her hand as she stifled a yawn. As she came closer to me, she sniffed the air. "Are you drunk? Is that why you're dragging me from my bed?" She had the sense to look apprehensive.

I did my best to feed her fears. "You need to be afraid, Catriona." It was difficult not to take offense when she flinched away from my extended hand. "I won't hurt you. You have my word."

With a trust I wasn't worthy of, she placed her hands firmly in mine, and nodded. "Then show me, Marcus."

We walked through the house in absolute silence, neither of us breathing a word. Only our footsteps echoed in the still hallway as I slowly led her out through the kitchen door into the cool early-morning air. The sun had yet to peep above the tree line, and the chirping birds that often sang their song each morning were still nestled in their nests.

There was a crispness that left me feeling alive. It was chilly enough to set goose bumps across my skin.

"Slow down, Marcus," she begged, tripping over the hem of her nightgown and clutching my arm for balance. "I'm not familiar with the path we're on, and I don't want to fall."

In my haste, I'd forgotten that she often kept to the house and inner gardens. I'd chosen the place where I went to reflect specifically for that reason. Not even Knox ventured this way.

"Only a little farther, and then I'll explain everything," I promised, and gripped her hand tighter. The hero in a story might have gathered her up in his arms, offering to carry her safely, but I was already skating on thin ice. Even if Catriona was able to look past the curse, I wasn't her hero.

It was everything I could do not to be her own personal villain.

There was always a solemn hush whenever I entered the clearing, and it was no different now. It was only a small glen, but surrounded by tall trees, and with the full moon shining above, I was reminded why I chose to build the gravesite for Primrose here.

Her body was buried far from here, but I'd erected the gravestone as a reminder of what had been lost that night. I came here every day to offer my penance for somehow playing a part in her death. I'd eventually remembered being knocked across the head by cutthroats, after trying to protect Primrose from their advances. It truly had been a case of being in the wrong place at the wrong time, but I'd still been there.

I'd spent hours trying to convince myself that I'd done everything I could to defend her honor. The strangers had spewed out such filth at the young gypsy woman, I was surprised God didn't strike them down for such depravity.

Many prayers had been offered up as I knelt beside the simple stone carving, pouring my heart out with the hopes that somehow God would show mercy and pity my feeble attempts.

In the beginning, I came looking for redemption.

All I had left was bitter prayers that I would one day meet my maker having found my vengeance.

"Who is she?"

It was my turn to jump. I'd forgotten she was standing there, my thoughts consuming me again.

My voiced cracked from thick emotion. "Her name was Primrose."

Catriona stepped between me and the headstone, trailing her fingers lightly across the top. "Did you love her? Is that why you can't love me?"

She squinted at me, hoping to catch the truth through my reaction to her questions.

It was on the tip of my tongue to lie to her, to sugarcoat what I wanted to tell her, so I would at least be seen in a favorable light. But that wasn't the reason behind me bringing her here.

Just as the night gave way to the day—the moon setting as the sun rose—I couldn't remain in the shadows with her anymore. I needed her to see me . . . to see all the horrible flaws and choices I'd made. Nothing was as brutal as that first ray of light, because there was no hiding from its blinding honesty.

Guiding her to the wooden bench I'd spent many evenings sitting on, I paced back and forth in front of her, suddenly nervous.

"Listen to what I have to say in its entirety. Once I'm done, I will answer whatever questions you might have. I only ask that you reserve judgment until the last detail has been confessed."

She nodded in agreement. "What's brought about this change in heart, Marcus?" There was a soft smile when she realized she'd already disobeyed my request. "I only ask so I don't dwell on it."

"How were your dreams tonight?" I countered, bracing myself for her anger. "Did you enjoy your time in the ruins?"

Her mouth dropped open with astonishment, and she shrank back against the bench, her hands clutching at her gown. Each time she began to speak, Catriona shook her head, dismissing the thought.

"I took a potion so I could visit you in your dreams," I continued, studying her to see how she might react. She appeared eerily calm and not the feisty woman who'd threatened to sneak into my room at night and chain me to my bed so she could escape. "Catriona?" Her silence was unnerving.

"That was real?" she finally asked, her eyes wide as saucers. "That means we . . ." Her fingers pressed against her lips as if she was remembering the passion between us.

I nodded. "Invading your dreams is one of many sins I need to confess to you." I took a step toward her and thought better of it. I didn't trust myself right now, and as my hunger flared deep in my gut, I realized I should've gone to Knox for fortification before attempting this heavy conversation. "Will you listen to what I need to say?"

It looked like she didn't trust herself to respond, either. Nodding, she folded her hands in her lap and gave me her full attention.

Suddenly at a loss for words, I glanced over to Primrose's memorial, praying that somewhere in her afterlife, she could see I was trying to do the right thing.

Taking in a deep breath, and with the morning's first rays brightening the sky, I then prayed for courage to see this retelling through to the devastating end.

For Catriona.

For Primrose.

For the broken pieces of my soul.

~

WAITING for her to speak was an exercise in agony.

I had divulged it all, leaving no detail untold as I gave a faithful account of that night in the alleyway, of Primrose's death and the subsequent cursing by her kin.

I described the person I had transformed myself into—the reasoning behind embracing my new life as a blood drinker—how easy it had been to become cruel and hostile to those around me.

I spoke about that night, how in desperation and anguish I'd vowed my most solemn oath of vengeance. I shared each failed attempt in finding the gypsy clan. I spoke of the carnage I had wielded—the bodies and blood I had consumed in my pursuits.

I had resembled a feral animal in those days before Knox planted those few seeds of faith that he could find the answers I needed. Story after story, I confessed my thirst and hunger for blood and gore, of leaving trails of dead behind me, of being the very killer many in the country whispered about.

I didn't stop—even when her gasps grew louder and louder—or the look of horror remained across her face. With each syllable, the possibility of ever kissing her again, of truly being a husband to her, faded away until it blinked out of existence.

This was what I wanted.

I wanted her to see me for the beast I was, and to give up her futile attempts to tame me.

I wanted her to run away from me screaming.

I wanted her to declare her own oath—that for as long as she drew breath, she would fight to stop me harming innocent people.

There was so much I needed from her—from her reaction—but it didn't keep the whole ordeal from feeling like I was slowly being gutted, one agonizing cut at a time.

I needed her to loathe my very presence.

I needed her to curse my birth and wish for my speedy death.

Yet she did neither, and that was what devastated me.

She didn't offer her condemnation nor her acceptance.

I wasn't foolish enough to think she'd give me her forgiveness, but something—anything but her silence—would've been enough.

Finally, she let out a faint breath, and looked at me. "Why tell me all this?"

Her stare unmanned me. "Because it's the only thing I can give you, Catriona. You showed me your heart in your dreams, and I felt you deserved the same in return. While I can never give anyone my love and affection, I can at least help you understand why."

She slowly nodded as if she was struggling to digest it all. "Well, I appreciate that, Marcus."

Her brow crinkled from the heavy thoughts mulling about inside her head. At least, I assumed they were heavy. I knew mine were.

"Do you have any questions for me?" I asked, hoping that might alleviate some of the tension. "I promised you I would answer them all as truthfully as I can."

"You drink blood." Fact.

I bobbed my head.

She nervously raised her hand to her throat. "Do you want to drink mine?"

I took a step back to grant her some space. "There was a time when I would've taken from you, whenever I wanted." Her eyes widened again, and I almost expected her to get up and flee. "However, Knox has made it so I only need to feed once a day. He procures the blood I need and then adds his special ingredients to it.

It enables me to control that part of me without becoming a ravaging beast."

That surprised her. "You want to live like this?" Her incredulous tone was understandable.

"All I had was my honor when I walked into that alley with Primrose. I wasn't guilty of the crimes they accused me of, yet they cursed me anyway. They reduced me to this." I didn't hide the bitterness I felt, smacking my hands against my chest in anger. "Justice demands to be appeased. They will pay for what they've stolen from me."

I wanted to smooth out the permanent wrinkle on her brow. "In one breath you speak of honor and justice, yet you thirst for your revenge. They are at odds with each other—you can't have revenge *and* remain honorable."

"Watch me," I fired back, my own annoyance flaring. "Endure what I have and see whether you still believe that. I didn't ask for this life, but I will use whatever *gifts* it has given me to claim some semblance of peace."

She had the audacity to laugh. "You call this peace, Marcus? Let go of your need to make those who've harmed you pay. Embrace this new life and make the best of it. Imagine the great things you could do with your extended life. Think of the legacy you could leave in your wake . . . of being someone who rises above the harshness of life and makes the world a better place."

I shook my head, already dismissing her words as folly. "Can you not see that this is the path I am destined to walk? I used to believe I held some control over what Fate did . . . that I chose the life I wanted. If there was one thing the curse has taught me, it's that I was a fool, and in order to survive, I needed to kill that side of me."

"Then I pity you, Marcus, I truly do. You're wasting the chance given you to find meaning and purpose."

Anger continued to bubble up inside me. While I'd granted her the freedom to talk to me as she wanted, to ask her questions, it still rankled. Her fear I could handle. Her disappointment and disgust were expected.

It was her pity that irritated me, because I didn't need her sorrow.

"This is why we can never have the kind of relationship you yearn for."

"So, you chose to act like a barbarian because you felt I was too weak and feeble-minded to understand your plight?" She finally stood and approached me, placing her hand over my chest. "Do you really think so little of me?"

It was my turn to be speechless.

"Thank you for confiding in me. Your secret is safe with me." Patting my chest affectionately, she left me with a smile that tugged at my heartstrings again. "Let us be friends." And with that, she kissed my cheek and turned to head back to the house.

Right before she disappeared from my sight, I found my voice.

"Catriona, thank you," I called out. Then, as a new thought arose, I threw caution to the wind. "Prepare to journey to London later this morning."

She stilled ever so slightly, then nodded.

Falling onto the bench, exhausted, I couldn't help but wonder if this had been yet another mistake in a long line of many.

Friends.

It was more than I deserved.

Much more.

CHAPTER 10

*M*rs. Pickering was worth every pound her services demanded.

Upon our arrival in London, I quickly sent Knox to see whether the popular seamstress would see us. Those who recommended her were adamant there was little chance of her granting our request because of how highly in demand she was. I'd listened to them all attentively, but I also recognized a greater truth.

Lengthy waiting lists could often be obliterated when enough money was placed on the table. I had extremely deep pockets and no problem spending the wealth I had accumulated.

Sitting on the gold brocaded chaise longue in the corner of her workshop, I couldn't keep the smug expression from settling across my face.

Catriona had been so anxious about being dressed by the woman who boasted about a client list containing some of the most elite aristocrats in our country. Hell, Mrs. Pickering had even adorned the king and his queen with her fineries.

After glaring at my speechless companion, I reminded her that her new wardrobe was a gift from me—my way of showing her how truly sorry I was for my former treatment of her.

As far as I was concerned, the moment we were able to, I would order a bonfire to destroy the tacky clothes I'd forced on her.

"What do you think, Mr. St. James? Does your wife not look stunning in this emerald green dress?" The older woman stood back from her creation, gesturing to Catriona, who was raised up on a wide stool so Mrs. Pickering and her apprentice, Harriet, could move about easily. "With the rich darkness of her hair, and her flawless skin, you may wish to hire a guard to keep this one safe." Gazing up at Catriona, the seamstress continued. "You, my darling, are quite stunning."

She rattled off a long string of instructions to her apprentice, who in turn faithfully jotted it all down on a small pad. I'd told her the outfits I believed Catriona would need and that she was to spare no expense.

She'd simply chuckled softly and patted me on the arm like I was a child. "My dear, I have no doubt that you are quite accomplished at what you do. However, you don't see me come into your office and tell you how to do your work. Do you doubt my abilities? My skills?" She cocked an eyebrow as if daring me to challenge her. "I didn't think so. You've come to me because you heard I am the best. Perhaps you should've left with your manservant?"

Answers bounced around in my mind, but something warned me that this was not a woman to argue with. Resigning myself to the corner, I'd spent most of the past few hours watching the process.

And watching my wife . . . who wasn't truly my wife . . . who was barely a newly formed friend . . . the woman who continued to complicate my life.

"What do you think?" Catriona asked, chewing her bottom lip as she twisted, the dress swishing about her. "You don't think it's too elaborate for spending each day at the estate?"

I heard the question within the question she asked.

Why was I going to such an extreme when all she would ever see were the walls within my home? So far, I had not taken her out into society, refusing any invitations to balls and dinner parties that were extended.

People would always be curious about me—the reclusive heir of Smithersby Field—but she was something else entirely. Rumors had labeled me a confirmed bachelor after my constant refusal to court the local beauties. Yet, here I was, married.

They wanted to meet *her* with the hopes of understanding how she'd managed to tie herself to such an affluent family.

Let them wonder, I silently grumbled.

I nodded my agreement. "You look beautiful, Catriona."

I added a smile to my words, hoping that it didn't reveal the true depths of my feelings. She wasn't just beautiful—she was extraordinary.

She flinched as Harriet accidently pricked her with a long dressmaking pin. It earned the poor young girl a slap from Mrs. Pickering, and the admonishment that should she spoil the fabric with blood, it would come out of her meager wage.

The mention of blood tugged at my senses, and my mouth watered. The elixir Knox had brought the previous night had all but left my system, and oddly, my hunger had roared back with a vengeance. There might not be time enough to wait until we returned home.

There was a knock at the door, and to my relief, Knox entered, his eyes glued to Catriona's svelte figure on display.

Whistling softly, he dragged his gaze away from her, and approached me. "Marcus, we have a problem." He crouched down beside me so he could whisper. "I tried to get you an audience with her, but she is unmovable. I couldn't even gain entrance to her home to ask her personally and share your plight with her."

It was as I thought. We had been lucky with Mrs. Pickering, but meeting with the infamous seer of London proved to be impossible. People came from near and far to have Lady Hannah read their futures. I already knew mine, but I had desperately hoped she could grant us some insight into the curse I bore.

"Perhaps I should try," I answered, already moving to stand. As pleasant as the view had been, Catriona's new wardrobe would not restore me to the man I was. It wouldn't help me gain my revenge. It was simply a means of distraction.

"I'm afraid I need to take my leave, ladies," I announced, tilting my head forward with respect. "It seems that my associate here requires my help with another errand." Catching Mrs. Pickering's gaze, I added, "How long will you still be needing Mrs. St. James?"

It felt odd addressing Catriona that way, but I knew it was a title that removed suspicions. No one needed to know we were far from the typical married couple.

She waved me away impatiently. "You can't rush perfection, Mr. St. James. Go, take care of your business, and return in a few hours. By then I should have most of the measurements needed to create a wardrobe fit for a queen."

To show me just how unimportant my being there was, she then turned her back to me and continued talking with Catriona and her apprentice quietly.

Thoroughly dismissed, I bowed once more and left the house, Knox in tow.

"Good God," he complained once we found ourselves out on the street. "How are you not tearing your hair out from boredom?" Knox threw one last glance over his shoulder before climbing into my coach behind me. "All that material and lace." He shuddered hard.

"It paled in comparison to where I placed my focus," I chuckled, giving him a knowing look. "Heaven help me, but I've grown to appreciate my . . ." It was on the tip of my tongue to call her my wife. Thankfully, I caught myself in time. "My new friend."

Knox snorted, recognizing my explanation as the falsehood it was. He was gracious enough to let me continue fooling myself, anyway.

"I hate to tell you, but I don't think you'll have any better luck talking to her Ladyship's footman. He was quite firm in her refusal." Knox bounced up and down as the carriage wheels hit an uneven portion of the cobblestone road. "I tried every kind of plea to convince him. I even took a page out of your book and offered to throw an obscene amount of money for him to turn a blind eye."

It was a dig at my spending a year's monetary allotment on Catriona's wardrobe.

"And you told them it was a matter of life and death?" I asked, trying to think of any other way to approach the London seer. "That my sanity hangs in the balance?"

"Does it?" Knox fired back, that ridiculous smirk on his face again. He was thoroughly enjoying the way Catriona had gotten under my skin. I hadn't breathed so much as a syllable regarding the change of heart that was currently happening, but somehow, he still knew. It was the consequence of assigning him the very specific role of ensuring that I didn't lose what little humanity I had to the beast that lurked inside. "I would have said your control was slipping the moment you announced Catriona was going to join us today so she could go shopping."

I couldn't deny it. It was definitely a sidestep from my usual behavior. "It seems I need to remind you, again, that I am the master in this relationship, Phineas. Although—" I let out a heavy sigh. "I'm tempted to side with you. Love is a fickle thing that has turned on even the strongest of men and rendered them blithering idiots. Maybe, instead of petitioning Lady Hannah, you should take me to the nearest asylum and have me committed."

I knew the second I closed my mouth that I had revealed the secret I'd been harboring in my heart since I'd woken from our shared dream.

"Love?" Knox was too damn observant for his own good.

"Shut up," I grumbled back. "My feelings aren't a subject for discussion."

I peered out the carriage window at the passing scenery. London was always a bustling town—filled with people going to and from—both the upper and lower classes coexisting. They didn't acknowledge that they all walked the same paths and needed each other to maintain whatever level of lifestyle they enjoyed.

"So, do you really want to try again?" Knox asked, his fingers drumming against his knee as he studied me.

"With Catriona?" I replied absentmindedly.

He burst out laughing. "No, with the sole reason you journeyed to London. You wanted to ask the seer if she could shed any light on the gypsies and where they were hiding." Knox shook his head at me, a look of bewilderment on his face. "Or does that no longer matter? Maybe I should give up my attempts to break the curse as well. You know . . . now that you've found love."

I banged hard on the roof of the carriage, demanding that the driver stop immediately. I kicked at the door, making it fly open.

"I'll say this once: whatever I may feel for Catriona is not up for discussion or ridicule. Nothing and *no one* will stand in my way, do you understand? My first priority—my *only* priority—will always be to undo that bloody curse and then destroy those who dared harm me. Everything," I thundered passionately, small flecks of spit flying from my lips, "everything I do—that I order you to do—is for that one purpose. All I have is my revenge, Knox. I would caution you to never forget that."

I expected him to argue back, or to at least act indignant that I'd chastised him, but he did neither. He actually grinned wider, and it made me wonder who was the crazier of us two.

"Good to hear that, master," he replied, acting submissive by bowing low. "The apothecary had many of the ingredients I needed for my new experiments. It would be a shame if they went to waste because you've been struck with Cupid's arrow."

And with that, Knox reached over and closed the coach door, signaling the driver to continue on.

"I'm sure you presented my case well, but refusing a servant as opposed to a master and gentleman . . . I would feel much better talking with her footman myself." I relaxed back into the seat and gently smoothed out the creases forming in my trousers. "I can be quite persuasive."

As we jostled toward the seer's Cavendish Square residence, I vowed that I wouldn't leave until I had gained what I wanted.

And should she continue to refuse?

Then I would take what I needed by force.

CHAPTER 11

*T*he tension in the carriage was practically palpable.

Gone were the plans to spend a few days in London, introducing Catriona to society, and showing her that I could be the reformed "monster" she wanted. While I wasn't promising her sonnets and a showering of hothouse flowers, a night listening to a popular opera singer would have gone a long way toward softening the damage I'd already done.

All plans came to a crashing halt when the front door of Lady Hannah's home slammed shut in my face—denying me entrance to talk with her.

The force I'd threatened to use was extinguished as easily as blowing out a candle. Before Knox could pull me back, I had pushed against the door with my body, determined to rip it from its hinges if needed.

A pulse of explosive magic zapped across my body, sizzling the hair on my arms with its current and almost throwing me off my feet and down the steps onto the street. It made sense that the famous seer had taken the necessary precautions to protect her residence, but it didn't help my wounded pride any.

A crowd quickly gathered at the gate, watching with astonished faces when I repeatedly tried breaking through the spell that now barred my entrance.

It had been a humiliating waste of energy, but that hadn't kept me from my repeated attempts. It wasn't until Knox finally dragged me away, whispering the need for decorum, that I remembered who and where I was. Word would spread like wildfire and make me the brunt of the gossip mill's mockery.

Amidst my cussing and vehement promises to burn the damn town to the ground for this slight, Knox had gotten me back into the carriage. We returned to Mrs. Pickering's seamstress shop without another word spoken and retrieved Catriona. Arrangements were made to have the new clothes delivered to Smithersby Field, and we were gone within the next hour.

Since then, I'd sat fuming in the coach, staring out the window while Knox and Catriona quietly talked to each other. Every now and then I caught a furtive glance from her, but after a while, she gave up trying to ease me into a lighter conversation.

As if to match my mood, a dark storm was rolling in from the east, making it all the more important for us to reach our destination. The roads were treacherous enough without having to navigate around potholes filled with water.

Knox seemed to have the same thought as he studied our surroundings. A crease lined his brow, and for what seemed like the hundredth time, he massaged his temple gingerly with his fingers.

"What?" I barked, noticing that his concern wasn't lifting.

He didn't answer immediately, instead leaning forward to get a better look outside.

"Something doesn't feel right, Marcus," he murmured, loud enough that I caught his response. "I know you'd rather continue traveling until we reach home, but I can't shake the feeling that we would fare better if we traveled during the day, and not during this storm."

I glanced at Catriona to see if she also felt the same. She remained tight-lipped, but her features gave away her similar worry. Her hands fidgeted in her lap, crumpling the material of her dress.

"We should be safe, Knox," I answered, peering forward to where the driver sat, controlling the horses with his leather rein. "If we push the horses, and don't stop as often, we should arrive with no problems. Unless you're truly worried about a mere storm?" I ribbed him, knowing it would gall him to admit his fear.

"Does that look like a mere storm to you?" he countered, challenging me. "It looks as though the gods themselves are angry and have unleashed their wrath on us petty mortals."

I exhaled sharply. "When did you become so dramatic? You sound more like a woman than a man, your delicate sensibilities all aflutter." I raised my voice until it sounded more like Catriona's than mine. I was in no mood to be argued with.

"Damn you," he answered angrily, his gaze narrowing on me. "I would follow you into Hell itself, Marcus, and that may make me a fool, but mark my words—there's an ill wind out tonight, and we need to find shelter."

"Do you agree?" I turned my focus to Catriona. "Do you believe we'll be struck down by lightning if we don't find a place to spend the night?"

She raised her hands in defense, as if she could somehow hold off my frustration and annoyance. "Will you not listen to common sense? If you're not afraid of getting caught in the storm, are you at least aware that the darker it gets, the braver ruffians will be as they see us traveling the road home?" Then with that steel and spitfire nature I'd grown to admire, she threw in another consideration. "Is your pride that important that you would risk your life—our lives? What of your holy mission to bring down the vengeance of heaven against your enemies? You can't do that if you're dead, Marcus. Please, take a deep breath and think."

I slammed my mouth shut—unable to see a way to counter her opinion. She was right, and it rankled me down to my very last nerve.

"She's right, and you know it, master," Knox added, his own sarcasm evident as it dripped from the title he used for me. "You have a right to be angry. What you don't have the right to is taking risks with everyone else's lives."

I let out another drawn-out breath, my fists clenching and unclenching. Before I could change my mind, I caved, and banged on the roof once more. "Driver, stop at the next town so we can find shelter."

"As you wish," came the muffled reply.

"Thank you." Catriona rested her hand lightly on my arm, the warmth of her touch breaching the barriers my clothes provided. "We can start again tomorrow and together," she added, making sure I understood that I wouldn't be alone. "Together we'll find a way to meet with the seer. I promise you that I won't rest until I can help you. Both Knox and I stand with you."

It was her humbled compassion that broke through the bitter fog I'd cloaked myself with, and I finally relaxed. She'd somehow managed to reach deep inside and find the right words to calm me.

"We'll leave at dawn," I grumbled.

"And not a second later," she promised, an enchanting smile tweaking the edges of her mouth.

Knox huffed his disbelief, and he reclined in his own seat, arms crossed over his chest. It would seem his own pride had been pricked with my buckling under the words of Catriona, but he would have to get over it.

With the decision made, and the tension in the carriage slowly dissipating, I closed my eyes, the rocking of the coach lulling me softly into a light sleep.

CATRIONA'S SCREAM filled the air, causing my heart to immediately sink with dread.

The coach had come to a stop only moments ago, and as my eyes flew open, I saw that we were no longer traveling the dusty road alone. Assailants with faces darkened by shadow approached by horseback, their murderous shouts disturbing the peace we'd been enjoying.

Despite my protests to continue on with the hopes of outrunning the attackers, we'd been brought to a halt.

One look was all that was needed between Knox and me. We were no strangers to danger—of protecting ourselves from those with nefarious plans. There was no doubt in my mind that those rapidly surrounding our carriage weren't merely asking for directions.

A sense of foreboding settled over me and with a quick nod—paired with a knowing glance—to Knox, we both flew out of the carriage fully prepared to unleash our fury at being disturbed.

The scent of blood on the air slapped me in the face, and it triggered my throbbing hunger. I didn't always let the darkness that I kept heavily restrained deep inside me free. But the second I caught that familiar coppery scent, mingling with the adrenaline coursing through my veins, I launched myself at the closest assailant to me.

He was no match for the strength I fired at him. As he lay bleeding on the ground, my fangs punched out from my gums, but there would be no time to feed.

I assessed the situation.

Knox was currently trying to hold off three attackers with clubs, his feet kicking out while one of the men struggled to hold him. Rage like I'd never seen from my friend radiated from him, and it was all because two other attackers were dragging a screaming Catriona away from the coach to where their horses stood, waiting.

In the second it took to calculate a response, I ripped off my jacket so the tight item wouldn't hinder my movements. With hands curled up into fists, I threw myself at those beating the hell out of Knox—my hands pounding against soft flesh over and over again.

"Catriona!" Knox bellowed, surging toward her. "Marcus! They mean to take her."

Her kidnappers were almost to their horses when I abandoned helping him and leveled the full weight of my fury toward them. Horses whinnied and reared back as they sensed the beast inside me surge to the surface.

Her look of relief was fleeting when one of the brutes

manhandling her released her and came thundering at me—his knife extended, slashing through the air.

"Release her!" I ordered, my voice loud above the ruckus. Its volume rivaled the thunder rumbling in the distance. "This will be your only warning." I swung at the older man with straggly brown hair, mud used to obscure his features and darken his eyes. "You have no idea who you are dealing with."

My fingers grasped tightly on his arm, and I pulled hard, catching him off guard. With hands that now resembled claws, desperate to rip out his throat and gouge the eyes from his head, I let go of whatever humanity I'd managed to safeguard, and fully embraced the monstrous nature that had plagued me all these years.

I didn't hold back.

I had no desire to restrain the demon.

With a ferocity unlike anything I'd ever experienced, I slashed at the man, disarming him easily, but instead of using his knife against him, I bared my teeth—intent on ripping the flesh from his bones myself.

Horror blazed in his eyes, and I reveled in it.

He knew he was facing death. I would personally deliver him to the gates of Hell for ever thinking he could take from me what was mine.

Blood sprayed everywhere as chunks of flesh fell to the ground.

Weakened by the intensity of my counterattack, the man made the sign of the cross, offering a brief prayer to a God I knew would not be listening. As far as I was concerned, he had better chances of survival by petitioning for my mercy, not some invisible deity in the sky.

But I was in no mood to dispense mercy.

As Catriona continued to scream and fight for her freedom, I gave one last kick and slash at the man in front of me and stepped over him as he toppled to the ground—dead.

In a cold, still voice that carried over the melee, I stooped down long enough to retrieve the knife and pointed it at the fool who held my wife.

"Are you next?" I paced toward him, my steely gaze never leaving his stoic features. "Tell me, shall we bury you beside your dead companion?"

I wiped at my face, my fingers coming back wet with blood. Without thinking, I licked at the ichor, receiving strength from the taste. My response was met with a look of disgust as Catriona's sole kidnapper now grasped her tightly from behind, slowly backing up to his horse.

"I am saving her from you," he growled, spitting on the ground. "I know who—*what* you are."

"Marcus," Catriona begged, desperately trying to break free so she could rush toward me. "They knew we would be traveling tonight. They were waiting."

I took the briefest of seconds to look at her—to really look at the woman who had first been such a hindrance, but had over time worked her way into my heart. I'd been a fool to deny that happiness didn't have to be sacrificed in order to honor my vengeance. All these months, I could've savored our time together, instead of acting like the bastard I'd been.

"I know," she mouthed. That's when it hit me—I may have held her at arm's length, but Catriona had used her time more wisely. She'd quietly been studying the man she'd married, learning to read my body language so she could better understand me. And now—when what she needed was for me to be her hero—I realized that was exactly what I wanted.

Revenge be damned.

She was now the driving force behind my wanting to be a better man, even if that meant living with the curse for the rest of her days.

"Catriona," I roared, and with a strength I hadn't felt since before the alleyway, I stalked toward her, ready to gut the man who restrained her.

My focus zeroed in on him.

All sound seemed to fade around us.

My heart thudded loudly in my ears, my chest trying to adjust to the raggedness of my breathing.

I was death.

I was retribution.

I was a man defending the woman he loved.

"Marcus!" It was Knox who yelled now, from somewhere behind me. I didn't turn, however, not willing to give the bastard holding Catriona a chance to gain the upper hand. If he reached his horse, he could whisk her away in a heartbeat—each stride taking her farther and farther away.

"I will gut your bitch," the man hissed as he pressed the knife's blade into her stomach. "Like the filthy swine she is."

"Marcus!" she screamed again, her eyes wide as saucers, and with what little energy she had left, Catriona raised her hand, pointing to something behind me.

I didn't think. Later, I would relive this precise moment over and over—my failings repeating in different ways as I agonized over what happened next. Instead, I turned about to see what had caught her attention.

Everything slowed.

Knox was racing toward us, a wild desperation radiating from his features.

In front of him by a few strides came a bulky mammoth of a man with his fist cocked back, aimed at my head.

It was all the distraction they needed.

The giant collided with me, knocking us both to the ground. Knox reached shortly after, and began pulling to get me free.

"Not me, you fool!" I exclaimed. "Protect her!"

But it was too late.

I watched in absolute horror as Catriona was whisked up onto the horse's back, and with a loud crack of the reins, disappeared into the dark surroundings with the gloating ruffian.

A gurgled laughter broke the spell.

"She wasn't yours, *shimulo*." His lips were curled up into a smug smirk. Blood streamed from the open cuts on his head, the scent dancing around me like a siren.

"She is mine!" I thundered, cocking back my fist and striking him with every ounce of strength I possessed. "Where did you take her, gypsy?"

His use of the word had told me exactly who our attackers had been.

"To freedom." He laughed again, and this time spat in my face. "Which is more than you gave my brother Nikolai."

Vengeance.

Why did it always come back to it?

"Marcus, we can still follow. Forget him. Let's go."

For as long as I lived, I would never forget the expression the gypsy wore as I used his body to gain my balance and stand. It was a mix of ruthlessness and gloating satisfaction. In his mind, we would never reach them in time to stop whatever plans they had for Catriona.

"Give my regards to the Devil," I sneered, bending over one last time. "Make sure he knows that your clan will be joining you shortly." And with one violent swipe of my clawed hand, I tore at his throat, exposing his jugular to the air. Blood gushed out, and within moments, he was dead.

"Hurry," Knox urged, having retrieved two horses that had somehow remained despite the melee.

Swinging up into the saddle, I left everything behind and galloped into the darkness, uttering yet another promise I fully intended to honor.

"If she dies, they all die."

CHAPTER 12

*T*he scent of blood and carnage hung in the air.

Wiping my hands down the sides of my pant legs, I surveyed the damage Knox and I had delivered.

The justice we had served.

All around us, battered bodies lay where they had fallen—an entire gypsy clan wiped out. Nowhere did I feel an inkling of remorse. They'd brought this destruction down upon their own heads when they dared kidnap Catriona, attacking us as we traveled home.

This was the price of the war we waged—both parties hoping to deal out vengeance.

Nikolai had been one of their kinsfolk, and I'd made sure that his wife and child knew that he'd died quickly by my hand. Had the clan released Catriona into my care, I may have shown them some kind of benevolence and spared at least the children.

But as Knox tore apart their camp site, rifling through caravans and tents, there was no hint that she'd even arrived. When she didn't respond to our calls—no sign of the beautiful woman who'd changed my entire world for the better—a cold seething began building inside me where all I could see was red.

Knox knew better than to warn me against unleashing the storm that still boiled within my veins. When I had the leader down on his knees—begging for the lives of his family—there was no room for negotiating. Tears fell from his eyes as I vowed to wipe out his lineage before slitting his throat.

I had rained down death with no qualms or hesitancy.

One brave fool had stepped forward with the derisive taunt that Catriona would be defiled and murdered before I could ever hope to reach her. That this vile act was to repay the anguish I'd inflicted by killing their beloved Nikolai.

Over and over, clan members tried bargaining for the lives of others—offering hollow promises that they could somehow produce Catriona, whole and unharmed.

But I saw their words as the lies they were.

From my experience, twisted as it may be, gypsies were a ruthless, amoral group of people that deserved the wrath I was about to rain down on them.

And I had.

Side by side with Knox, we had systematically erased the entire group from existence, tossing their soulless bodies to the side as we made sure there were no survivors.

"She isn't here," Knox cried, his voice thick with emotion. He had loved her too—he was her protector from me when I had failed to see her for what she was.

A treasure to be cherished.

A woman who had somehow managed to tame the beast.

"Then we will hunt her kidnappers to the ends of the earth until we find her." I lashed out to the pot of food hanging over the fire someone had lit. The fragrant stew splashed across the ground, flecks of gravy splattering the lifeless body of the woman responsible for it. "They will all pay for this!"

I stood there, shaking my fists at the sky, and all the bitterness I'd felt over the past decade came flooding back until all I could feel was the vampire nature I'd been cursed with.

Marcus the man had been obliterated, and I didn't mourn the death of him.

I'd lowered my guard, allowing the light to touch those parts of me, and for what? So someone could come crashing in and steal what was most precious to me—again.

Knox's hand fell hard on my shoulder, his fingers squeezing in an attempt to comfort. I shrugged him away. There would be no more solace or peace.

"She was mine to protect," I uttered, slowly regaining my breath. Adrenaline still coursed through my veins, and the bloodlust still stoked my anger. "She was mine, and they took her."

"We can still catch them," Knox stated, convinced the odds were still in our favor. He was covered in blood, and judging from the red patch at his side, he was also injured. When I pushed my fingers against the material, he winced.

There was no hiding it.

"You're in no condition to ride. I will go. You'll only slow me down." My foot caught on something, and I looked down to find my boot had snagged a small doll made from rough material—the toy still in the tight grasp of a child.

I couldn't think about the ramifications, of the people I'd made victims by my rage tonight. Any chink in the armor I now wore would weaken my resolve. Right now, I had one mission . . . one focus. Catriona was still out there, and by all that was holy, I *would* be her knight in shining armor.

"You need me," Knox gasped, pain hitting him again, and his stance faltered, his knees threatening to give out under him. "Just get me on my horse."

I shook my head. "I can't wait for you, Phineas. Every second we waste here is another second they have her."

He tried to stop me from walking away, but his own blood loss made him drop to his knees finally. Frustrated that he was now useless, Knox pounded his fist on the ground. A flurry of words coated with resentment and outrage burst from his lips. He was angry —justifiably.

"I will bring back her kidnapper. He will be yours to administer justice to. You have my word." I extended my arm quickly, clasping his in a warrior-like handshake, slowly pulling him to his feet. "Ride for home. Seek medical help at the next town." Consumed with a sudden feeling of family, I grabbed him at the back of the head, pressing our foreheads together. "Live for me, my brother. Live for her."

"Go," he ushered, waving me on. "Go with God."

As I swung my leg up and over my new ride, I let out a cynical laugh. "I don't know about God, but I would be grateful for any kind of divine assistance tonight."

With one last look as my horse turned in a circle impatiently, I kicked in my heels and spurred the beast onward.

My new enemy had a head start, but I had one thing aiding me that he'd underestimated.

I would never rest until I found her.

I would never rest until I held her safely in my arms.

CHAPTER 13

ONE WEEK LATER

*M*y heart hurt.

As in it physically hurt me to arrive home empty-handed.

Despite my most valiant efforts, the one who'd taken my Catriona had disappeared like a thief in the night, and all my attempts at tracking him had failed.

I'd been so cocky and sure that I would find them. Each hour that passed fueled the fantasies I created, where I punished the fool for his audacity in stealing her. She truly was an innocent in all of this—and they'd chosen their target well when he'd taken off with her.

Kill me, and it would end this pitiful existence I endured.

Kill Knox, and it would slow down the search for a cure, but ultimately, he was replaceable. I didn't like that thought, because Phineas had become more like a brother to me. It wasn't something I ever acknowledged, but all my beliefs and opinions had been blasted to smithereens now that I'd lost everything.

But to touch her, to defile her virtue, to sully her very body—that was unforgivable.

No matter how hard I rode, or the many villages and towns I stopped at, the results were the same.

No one had seen her or the villain who had stolen her. There were no leads. No witnesses came forward, despite the generous reward I offered for information. I didn't care how insignificant the news was, either. I was prepared to pay handsomely for a mere glimpse of her.

It had rendered me a desperate man, and that irritated me. What was needed now was force and ruthlessness. Instead, I acted like a panicked, lovesick male who'd lost his mind over a woman.

On and on I rode, chasing shadows until I had to finally admit defeat. I was tired. I was hungry. I had to return to feeding on stragglers late at night as they stumbled home from the local tavern. My impatience made me brutal—my thirst demanding its fill.

Yet, here I was again at Smithersby Field, alone.

Stabling the horse and leaving instructions with the boy I'd hired to care for the beasts, I headed toward the house, but found myself lured to the private glen in the woods.

The headstone seemed to glow beneath the moonlight, an eerie beckoning from the ghost that still haunted me.

Primrose.

It had all begun with her, and now another grave would be dug to hold my beloved Catriona.

It would be a testament to the two women I had failed terribly.

Sinking onto the bench, I buried my face in my hands and wept. Hot tears streaked down my cheeks, clinging for a moment under my chin before falling to the ground. I didn't bother hiding the raw emotion consuming me.

I felt it—all of it.

"Marcus?"

The sound of my name made me jump with surprise. I hadn't heard anyone approach, and while my soul rejoiced in hearing Knox speak, it couldn't extinguish the sorrow that filled me.

My sobs grew louder, and as he wrapped his arms around my shoulder, I let go and fully gave in to my grief.

"I couldn't find her." My words came out in ragged breaths, my chest heaving. "I searched. I begged. I threatened, and it was all in vain. I failed her, and by not bringing her home, I have failed you, too."

He didn't speak, allowing me to purge the twisted feelings that had been buried inside me for so long. I didn't bother wiping away my tears. There was no need for masculine pride. When I finally looked up, I instantly saw I wasn't the only one who was caught up in misery.

His expression was one of absolute solemnness. He knew what it meant for me to bare my soul to him, to expose myself so completely that it would forever change our friendship.

We were no longer master and servant.

We weren't really friends and comrades either.

We were family.

We were brothers.

All we had seen and experienced had forged an unbreakable bond, and as we fell back into silence, we mourned our loss together.

Eventually the cool air became impossible to ignore, and wiping my face, I let out an exhausted sigh.

"What have I missed in my absence?" Despite what had happened, the estate still required my attention. I hated it, but honoring my responsibilities would give me an outlet until I devised a new plan.

Catriona may very well be dead.

I would add her name to my list of grievances.

Knox reached into his coat and pulled out a sealed letter, handing it to me. "This came a few days ago with the strictest of commands that only you could open and read it."

"Do you know who it's from?" I asked, turning over the folded paper and lightly tracing the waxed seal keeping it together. The insignia wasn't familiar, but that didn't mean anything. Perhaps it was a petition from the nearby town for aid to make it through the winter. As one of the big houses and estates in the area, people often looked to me for help during the tough season.

I often refused them, or sent them meager supplies, but for Catriona, I would grant whatever they requested. She had changed me. I refused to dishonor her memory.

Cracking the wax, I slowly unfolded the letter, and started reading.

"What does it say?" Knox asked, peering over my shoulder. "Who is it from?"

I couldn't answer as a lump formed in my throat, hope flaring within my chest. The second I finished the short message, I read it again . . . and again. Over and over as if it would somehow explain itself.

When I couldn't keep quiet any longer, I crumpled the message in my hand and stood—a new excitement sweeping away my despair.

There was an emotion at the forefront, one I'd assumed I'd never feel again.

Hope.

"Come, we need to pack. I want to be gone within the hour." I didn't offer any other explanation, and to Knox's credit, he acted immediately, following me back to the house.

We each retreated to our bedchambers, throwing clothes into trunks before meeting at the bottom of the grand staircase. I'd already left instructions with the hired help that would stay behind. Even though the message wasn't from the town, I'd still asked that food from the storehouse be taken to the people there.

"Are you really going to keep me in the dark, Marcus? Where are we going?" Knox threw me an impatient look that warned me should I not include him in the mystery, he would take the letter and read it himself. Forcibly, if needed.

I didn't answer. I offered him the letter that I'd placed in my pocket.

His lips moved as he silently mouthed the few words contained in the message. Nodding, he met my gaze.

We were united.

We had purpose.

We had a lead.

"Let's go," I said. Without a second thought, I walked through the door, unsure whether I'd ever return to my ancestral home, but not caring.

I didn't know what dangers we might face. The future was as murky as ever, but for the small flicker of hope that now burned within my heart.

I was blood and damnation.

I would finally lay claim to what was mine.

I would become wrath and retribution.

I was Marcus St. James, and in my pocket, I held the key to the answers I was seeking.

EPILOGUE

ONE YEAR LATER, 1879

*W*ith dust-covered clothes, we arrived at the designated place. I still wasn't sure why there was a need for all the secrecy, but after traveling this far, there was no way I would be turned from my goals.

Lady Hannah's note may have been short, but I chose to see it as certainty. This was where she said I would find the answers I was seeking. She was a celebrated seer—someone who was well known within the supernatural community for her accuracy. I'd asked, and she'd responded by using her gifts of foresight.

Glancing about, I was shocked to see that this was where our journey had ended. The rugged wildness of Colorado was breathtaking, and so different from the world I'd left behind in England. I could see why so many were flocking to the Americas—in particular to the land they now called the United States of America. People came in search of freedom, of finding their fortune, of changing the circumstances of their upbringing. The beauty that surrounded Knox and me right now, with majestic mountains and greenery—the fresh air a testament that it remained untouched by civilization—I could see myself joining the others in staking my claim here.

Perhaps if this lead failed to provide the answers I was seeking,

Knox and I could remain and see where a new life might take us. No one would know us here. No one would know me. It could be a fresh start for a monster like me.

"Are you sure this is where we were to meet our contact?" Knox murmured, scanning the area, looking to see if anyone approached.

I nodded, remembering the conversation we'd last had at the town miles away. After a week of asking around, of trying to find anyone who knew about the town Lady Hannah had named on the paper she'd sent, we'd almost given up and moved on.

Why would she send us on a wild goose chase across the ocean to a place that people had never heard about? Did such a town even exist?

Finally, after we finished our evening meal, a stranger approached us in the saloon where we were staying, discreetly asking us to follow him outside. Once we were out in the alleyway, he'd asked us about our queries, not once giving away whether he held the answers we needed or not.

If anything, the idea of being there in that alleyway—another one in another time and place—had given me the sense of coming full circle. Knox felt the same wariness, never once taking his hand off the concealed knife that he had strapped to his thigh. Desperation wasn't an excuse to lower our guards. We hadn't come this far to meet our end in the Colorado mountains.

The stranger had listened, and then with a sweeping look, told us to await further instructions. Sure enough, early this morning, I found a note slid under the door of our room with the directions for a secret meeting.

"We've come this far. Let's see what happens next," I replied, licking my lips nervously. There was a weariness about Knox, his expression tired from the constant traveling. I was grateful for his company, happy that he was standing here beside me.

There was a crunching sound that told us immediately that we weren't alone.

"Be on guard," I uttered beneath my breath. Knox touched the side of his leg, where the large knife was. I readied myself in case this was an ambush. If there was one thing I'd learned from my experiences with the gypsies I'd met, it was that it was deadly to walk into a situation unprepared.

"There will be no need for violence," a deep voice spoke. A second later, a tall man appeared—one whose demeanor screamed authority. Whoever he was, he was a leader. "I called for this meeting so we could talk, not fight."

I assessed him quickly—was he friend or foe?

He was neatly dressed with his dark hair slicked back. There was a small scar under his left eye—which was the darkest blue I'd ever seen. Sizing him up, I stepped toward him.

"My name is Marcus St. James, and this is my companion, Phineas Knox." We both bowed our heads with respect, hoping that it would work in our favor.

I wasn't the only one sizing people up. He gave me another once over and nodded. "My name is Roman Bishop. I understand you've been asking questions about my town." There was a strong sense of pride as he spoke. "I hope you understand that I'm protective of the people I lead. I can't let just anyone into our home."

He definitely gave off a no-nonsense attitude. I knew it would work against us if I was completely honest and told him I was here on a mission of revenge. Half-truths would have to be enough for right now.

Wetting my lips, I answered. "I can respect that, Roman Bishop. I feel the same about my own kin; in fact, that's what's brought us here. My wife was kidnapped over a year ago, and our search has led us here, to your town."

I watched him as I spoke, trying to gauge his response. I caught the flicker of anger at the mention of Catriona being kidnapped and the furrowing of his brow. It gave me hope.

Knox chose to speak up next. "We're not here to cause any trouble. We've experienced enough during our travels. All we want is to find her so we can return home to England." The earnestness in his tone was convincing.

Roman Bishop looked back and forth between us. "There are rules you will need to follow should you be allowed to enter my town. Do you agree to abide by the law?"

We both nodded. I knew I wasn't the only one curious about the town now. "You have my word as a gentleman."

I extended my hand in agreement and with only a slight hesitation, Roman shook it. His handshake was strong and firm.

"Then welcome to Havenwood Falls, gentlemen. May you find the answers you seek."

Marcus St. James' story continues in *Wrath and Retribution*, coming Spring 2019.

ABOUT THE AUTHOR

International and #1 Multi-Genre Bestselling Author Belinda Boring is known to many readers as the Queen of Swoon and also the Queen of Cliffhangers. Her Mystic Wolves series has topped many charts, along with receiving several awards and nominations such as Paranormal Book of the Year, Best Debut Book, as well as being in the Top 3 Best Rated on Amazon. With additional titles like Wanderlust, Enchanted Hearts, Loving Liberty and Broken Promises, it's easy to see why readers are captivated by this swoon-worthy author!

A homesick Aussie living amongst the cactus and mountains of Arizona, Belinda Boring is a self-proclaimed addict of romance and all things swoon-worthy. It wasn't long before she began writing, pouring her imagination and creativity into the stories she dreams. Whether urban fantasy, paranormal romance or romance in general, Belinda strives to share great plots with heart and characters that you can't help but connect with. Of course, she wouldn't be Belinda without adding heroes she hopes will curl your toes. Surrounded by a supportive cast of family, friends, and the man she gives her heart and soul to, Belinda is living the good life.

ACKNOWLEDGMENTS

I fell in love with Marcus St. James immediately. From the moment he stepped forward in my mind, I knew he had a story that would reach in and claim my heart. He's not the typical hero. He's a jerk, and there were times were I had to pause, cock my own eyebrow, and say, "Really? You're going to be THAT kind of guy?" But what can I say? I love the broken hero, the reluctant hero, the hero who thinks he has it all figured out, only to realize he is CLUELESS. I hope you fall for him like I did. I hope that you can see his heart . . . it's there, I promise. I like to believe that the harder someone falls, the greater their redemption is. He's worth it—they all are!

I wanted to thank everyone behind the scenes who helped bring this story to fruition:

My husband and family, who are always so supportive and patient while I'm writing. I sometimes wish that brainstorming came with a frequent driving card or something because Mark and I totally racked up the miles driving about our small town. #LostWithoutYou

My beta readers who faithfully read each chapter and gave amazing feedback. You guys are invaluable to me so *lick* you're mine FOREVER! Thank you for always being there and begging for more. Your comments made me chuckle! #StuckWithMe

My author coach, Jessica Gibson, who cracks that whip of hers with expertise! Thank you for keeping me focused and motivated, especially when I have a tendency to squirrel over a bazillion things OTHER than what I'm meant to be writing. Thanks for always being in my corner. #BabeBossForever

Lastly, I wanted to thank Kristie Cook and all my fellow Havenwood Falls authors, for being part of my journey. I LOVE Havenwood Falls. I LOVE the stories that have been shared and what each of you bring to this incredible world. Thank you for welcoming me with open arms and being part of my book world family. I'm proud to stand amongst you and call you all friends! #SappyBels

For those who love author insights, I wrote this entire story to one song: It's Quiet Uptown by Lin-Manuel Miranda. I'm obsessed with all things Hamilton and when it came time to build this story's playlist, this was the ONLY song I could write to. It sets the tone beautifully so, please, if you're curious, have a listen to the music and see if it helps capture your heart.

Happy reading, everyone! Thanks for visiting Havenwood Falls with me. ❤

Belinda

xoxo

FATED BEGINNINGS

E.J. FECHENDA

A Legends of Havenwood Falls Novella

HAVENWOOD FALLS
LEGENDS

FATED
BEGINNINGS

BURGER BAR

OPEN 24 HOURS · HOME COOKING · AIR CONDITIONED · HOME OF THE FAMOUS TWENTY RING

E.J. FECHENDA

ALSO BY E.J. FECHENDA

THE NEW MAFIA TRILOGY

The Beautiful People

Clean Slate

Endings & Beginnings

Enforcer (a prequel novella)

THE GHOST STORIES TRILOGY

End of the Road

Havoc

The Triangle (Fall 2018)

HAVENWOOD FALLS

Fate, Love & Loyalty

HAVENWOOD FALLS HIGH

Fata Morgana

Mom and Dad, thank you for everything. I love you.

CHAPTER 1

SUNSET CREEK, COLORADO AUGUST 1947

*D*ust billowed out behind the truck, and the dirt road had grown increasingly bumpier and narrower the higher Daniel McCabe's dad drove up the mountain. The truck bounced over ruts and rocks, causing Daniel to bounce in his seat. The last sign of civilization he recalled seeing was a homestead with two sickly looking horses in the corral, emaciated to the point he could count the ribs. He had wanted to stop and give them his apple that was packed with his lunch, but his dad refused. He said there wasn't time to dillydally. He wanted to get to their destination before noon.

Judging by the sun high overhead, that time quickly approached. They passed a sign for Prospector Gulch, and Daniel noticed his dad's grip on the steering wheel tighten, as did the set of his jaw. Sheer determination pushed him forward on this task. When his dad asked him if he wanted to visit Sunset Creek, Daniel didn't hesitate to say yes. Sunset Creek had only been spoken about in whispers, accompanied by expressions of sadness. Daniel knew something bad had happened that had resulted in his grandfather dying, but he didn't know what. Now that they were approaching the old mining town, the place of his father's birth and his grandfather's death, hopefully he'd learn the whole story.

They rounded a bend in the road, and his dad slammed on the brakes, sliding to a stop on the dirt. An aspen tree lay on its side, blocking the way.

"Well," his dad said with a sigh, "looks like we're walking the rest of the way." He grabbed the satchel that contained their lunches and canteens of water before opening the door. Daniel scrambled out after him, eager to stretch his legs. They had been driving all morning. Sunset Creek was located in the mountains in Gunnison National Forest, about two hours west of where they lived in Colorado Springs. Daniel's dad was quiet as they marched along the narrow road so choked with overgrowth, it was hard to believe it was a road at all.

"Dad, how can anyone live out here?"

"Nobody does . . . anymore."

"Why?"

His dad paused and fished out a canteen from the bag. He screwed off the top, took a few deep gulps, and handed it over to Daniel. That's when he noticed his dad's hand was shaking. His dad didn't respond, just turned around and kept walking. Daniel easily kept up. Since he had turned fifteen three months ago, he had gone through a growth spurt. Now his long strides matched his dad's. The forest grew thicker around them, and it was so much quieter out here than in the city. Daniel itched to roam through the woods and smell everything. He was getting better at controlling his shift, and out here, where they hadn't seen any humans and he didn't detect any with his enhanced senses, the urge to be one with nature became increasingly difficult to contain.

As if sensing this, his dad grabbed his wrist. "Not yet," he said. "There will be time later."

Daniel let out a small growl, but nodded in understanding.

"I used to know these woods—they were like my second home once. Before . . ." His dad trailed off, staring off into the distance, but Daniel could tell he was lost in his thoughts. His forehead crinkled before he shook out of his trance and started moving again.

They walked side by side in silence until they reached an old wooden post. On the ground in front of it was a sign. The wood was half rotted, and the white paint faded to the point where some of the letters were gone, but he could still make out the words: Sunset Creek est. 1867. That was eighty years ago, he thought to himself as he took in what was left of the town laid out before him. There were structures left—a few homes and stores—but no sign of life. He could see where the mines had been carved out of the hillside above the town. Rusty machinery dotted the stripped earth. As they walked down the main street through the center of town, Daniel shivered as if ghosts followed them. Looking over at his dad, he could tell he was haunted by memories. Shells of buildings remained. Some of them were half burnt and leaning at a dangerous angle.

"Dad?" His voice shook with fear. "What happened here?"

"Humans. Humans happened." His dad's shoulders slumped as if exhausted, and he focused his blue eyes just past Daniel's shoulders. "Come, it's time you know. You're old enough."

He led them to the front steps of what was once the general store. The windows were busted out, glass littered the front porch, and the wooden door swung in the gentle breeze, rusty hinges letting out an occasional squeak. Once they were settled on the steps with sandwiches that his mom made in their hands, his dad started talking.

"Sunset Creek was a booming mining town in its heyday. The vein of gold they discovered made a lot of men rich. My father—your grandfather, Ian McCabe—arrived here from Ireland in 1875 with his oldest brother, Robert. Robert was seventeen at the time, and my father only thirteen. Even though it was a few years after the vein was first discovered, there was still plenty gold left for him to acquire some wealth.

"In 1878, Sunset Creek was still thriving. Even though the gold vein had been depleted, one of the largest silver veins had been discovered, attracting prospectors like bees to honey.

"As Sunset Creek grew, the boundaries encroached upon unclaimed land where wildlife was plentiful. Hunting and fishing provided a much-needed food source. According to what my father told me, in 1878, William Jenkins, a Sunset Creek resident, had gone out hunting with his twelve-year-old son, Johnny. He returned on the second day without any fresh kills. Instead, the bloody body he carried in his arms was his son. Johnny had been mauled by a mountain lion. William had shot the beast before it could snap his son's neck. A priest was brought in, and last rites were read at Johnny's bedside as he fought for his life. William and Judith Jenkins kept a vigil through the night. Fortunately, he survived, but there were more attacks by mountain lions. Your grandfather was one of the victims."

"What?"

"That's how he became a shifter. He was bitten. Imagine the shock and surprise when he first shifted."

"Holy Toledo!" Daniel sat back in awe. He'd always assumed his grandda was born a shifter like everyone else in his immediate family.

"The mountain lion attacks continued for several years, and multiple residents were bitten. Only after Johnny Jenkins shifted in public during an argument with his father, in front of the assayer's office, did your grandda figure out there were more mountain lion shifters like him. The reaction to Johnny's public change also made him realize he needed to be very careful about who knew his true nature."

"Why?" Daniel asked, leaning forward with his arms propped on top of his knees.

His dad sighed and ran a hand over his beard, which was a deep reddish brown that had only recently become threaded with some white hairs.

"Humans are easily afraid and easily suspicious of anyone they consider different. I mean, you've seen the reservations and the internment camps."

Daniel understood what he was saying. Even though the Second World War had ended two years earlier, pictures of Holocaust survivors that ran in newspapers were burned into his memory. Here in Colorado, the Japanese Internment camps, which the governor fought against, still existed. They were empty, the prisoners released to go back to their lives, but the structures remained as a reminder of how quickly people could turn against a whole group considered different or a threat.

"According to your grandda, it was late one night when a group of men who worked at the mines formed a mob. They had been drinking at the saloon and got riled up. Somebody mentioned Johnny Jenkins, and it escalated from there. They left the bar and marched down Main Street to the Jenkins house."

Daniel's dad paused and stared off across the street at the shell of what used to be the bar. A faded sign that read Silver Spur Saloon had come loose on one end and hung at an angle, partially blocking the doorless entrance. He swallowed once before continuing. "They burnt the fucking house down. Johnny and his family barely escaped."

Daniel's eyes widened, and his mouth hung open in shock, partly because of how horrible the story was, and also because his dad swore. He rarely said cuss words in front of him.

"Apparently, Johnny and his family left that night, and were never seen or heard from again, but things were different after that. Anyone who had been associated with them were cast under suspicion as well. My father kept hoping that things would settle down, but seeing a person transform into a wild animal is something people don't easily forget."

"But he stayed. I mean, you were born here. Why didn't he leave?"

He snorted, and his mouth twisted up in a smile. "Us McCabes are a stubborn lot," he said and winked at Daniel, who returned his grin. "He and his brother had settled in Sunset Creek and that's all they knew. They refused to leave. Also, I think love had something to do with it."

"Oh," Daniel responded with a knowing tone. "Gran."

"Yup. He met my mother, and she didn't have any desire to leave either."

Daniel scratched his head and swatted at a fly buzzing around his ear. The sun had shifted, and he was baking in its full afternoon heat. "Was Gran already a shifter when they met?"

"Yes. She had been bitten, too. As you are learning, we have enhanced senses, so it's easier to pick out nonhumans in a crowd.

Soon the mountain lion shifters of Sunset Creek were holding their own gatherings in secret. These gatherings were the only way of exploring the animal side; they were a safe place."

Once again, his dad grew quiet and stared off into the distance. Daniel noticed his eyes shone with tears that never spilled. His dad cleared his throat and stood up. He paced in front of the steps where Daniel sat.

"When I was ten years old, I was with your grandda and gran and my sister at one of these gatherings. Now, mind you, the mines were almost depleted by this time and the population was growing smaller each month as people had to find work elsewhere. This also meant there were a lot of desperate people around. Desperate and angry people are like powder kegs waiting to go off. We thought our gatherings had gone unnoticed, but in a small town, it's hard to keep secrets. Unfortunately, someone noticed, and that was enough to light the fuse."

"What happened?" Daniel was leaning forward by now, completely engrossed in the story. He was finally going to learn what his dad and gran kept secret.

"They came for us. Tried to slaughter us all and came really close to succeeding." His dad's voice was rough with emotion, and he stopped pacing. With a sigh, he sunk down on the steps next to him. His shoulders were hunched over like he was physically burdened by the memory. "Homes were torched, friends were shot in the street . . . it was swift and brutal. I don't know how many survived. We scattered. My dad managed to get us to safety, urged us to head for the nearest town, and said that he'd catch up to us. He went back to fight, and we never saw him again."

Daniel shuddered as he absorbed the information. He had no idea his family history would be so dark. "Did you try to find him?" he asked.

"I wanted to go back and look for him, but your gran insisted we stay far away. She scoured newspapers for any coverage of the violence, but nothing was ever published. She thinks the government covered it up. It's possible. Just look at what's happening in New Mexico. That fellow found a spaceship on his farm, and now the news is saying it's a weather balloon. They probably are testing on aliens right now in some underground bunker. Hell, they probably captured a shifter or two and are testing them, too. All I know is Sunset Creek has been wiped from the map and was left to sink back into the earth. Humans can't be trusted, Daniel. Remember that. They can't handle anything out of the ordinary."

His dad's warnings were nothing new. Daniel had been hearing them his whole life, even more since his first shift, which took place three months ago, not too long after he turned fifteen. Now, knowing the history, he understood why.

He took his dad's warning to heart that day, adapting it as a rule that would follow him into adulthood: be careful who you trust, especially humans.

"I needed to tell you the history, Daniel. It's why we move so much. We can't afford to get too comfortable in one place. Your mother and I know it's been difficult, especially with you getting older."

The images Daniel's imagination conjured up flashed vividly through his mind, the carnage worse than any war movie playing at the local cinema. He pictured streets running red with blood and the empty street before him a scene of total chaos as shifters were slaughtered. His dad was right—he hated moving all the time. Just when he started to settle in and make friends, his family would pick up and move on. It had gotten to the point where he didn't bother making friends.

"Are we moving again?" Daniel asked, hoping to disguise the disappointment in his voice. His dad's expression said it all, in the tight set of his jaw and slight frown.

"I'm afraid so, son. This time we're heading east. West Virginia, to be exact."

Daniel's shoulders dropped, and he hunched over, curling inward and turning his head so his dad didn't see the tears welling in his eyes. It was worse than he could have imagined. Not only were they moving again, but they were leaving Colorado, the only constant—the only state he had always been able to call home.

Two weeks later, they left, Daniel crammed in the cab of the truck next to his mom, who sat in the middle. The truck's bed was piled high with their belongings, covered by a large black tarp to protect their things from rain.

The farther they drove, the more uneasy Daniel grew. He wanted to go back, felt it in his bones that they were heading in the wrong direction, but he was powerless to do anything, forced to follow his parents.

As they crossed the state line and entered Kansas, Daniel made a promise to himself: he would come back. As soon as he was able, he'd make his way back to Colorado.

CHAPTER 2

*D*aniel grabbed the paper sack of groceries, the bottles inside clinking with the movement. He thanked the cashier and started to leave the variety store that was on the corner of his street. He'd had a long day, and all he could think about was the cold six-pack of Coors he was carrying. His current foreman was a grade-A asshole who tested Daniel's temper. Fortunately, he had been training since he was a teenager to keep that temper in check. Sprouting claws or partially transforming into a mountain lion when he was surrounded by humans was a recipe for disaster.

He was about ready to leave the store when a flyer pinned to the community bulletin board caught his attention:

LOOKING FOR A CHANGE?
CONSTRUCTION FOREMAN NEEDED
MUST BE EXPERIENCED
MUST HAVE OWN TOOLS
Spend the summer in the mountains and be part of an exciting new opportunity.

229

Call 6-4511 for details and to apply.

Daniel unpinned the flyer and tucked it inside the bag. He *had* been looking for a change, and escaping the confines of the city appealed to him. With the prospect of something new ahead, his steps were lighter as he walked down the street to his apartment. Daniel and his mom lived on the bottom floor, while a young family lived upstairs in their two-story building. His mom, Margaret, was sitting out on the small porch, which was just large enough to accommodate the rocking chair she occupied. Late afternoon sun blanketed her in golden light, changing her hair from light brown to blond.

"Ah, there's my boy! Come sit, tell me about your day. Dinner will be ready in about ten minutes."

He complied and sat on the top stoop, stretching his long legs out in front of him. Dust covered his well-worn denim carpenter pants and his heavy boots. He paused for a moment with his eyes closed and his head tilted back as he scented the air and listened to the noises surrounding him. With his heightened senses, he could pick up so much more than a human. He could hear people talking two streets over, and he smelled someone grilling chicken, the sweet tang of barbecue sauce lacing the air. His stomach rumbled, and he opened his eyes. Reaching into the bag, he pulled out a beer. Holding the top against the railing, he smacked his hand hard on the cap, and it popped off, landing on the small patch of grass next to the walkway.

After a few long swallows, he sighed in contentment and grinned up at his mom. "What's for dinner?"

"Steak and potatoes. The potatoes are finishing up in the oven now. I made extra, in case you're hungry." She raised an eyebrow at him when his stomach rumbled.

"Thanks, Ma. I could eat a horse. It was a long day."

They chatted while he finished his beer, then went inside. As he pulled his beer out of the bag to put the rest of the bottles in the icebox, his finger brushed against the flyer, slicing his skin. He winced and examined the paper cut. It was small, only a tiny drop of blood bubbling to the surface. Shrugging, he stuck his finger in his mouth and sucked, shoving the flyer in his back pocket. For some reason, he didn't want to show his mom. Once he knew more and if he was offered the job, then he'd tell her. It would mean leaving her temporarily, but he knew she would be fine. She was strong, tough as nails, and had been through so much that he didn't want her to relocate with him. He'd send money back to take care of the bills that his dad's life insurance policy didn't cover.

"I'm going to go wash up before dinner," he told his mom, who was pulling potatoes out of the oven, and walked down the narrow hallway to his bedroom. Once inside, he stripped off his shirt, the fabric stiff with dried sweat, and tossed it in the hamper. The paper in his back pocket crinkled, reminding him of its presence. He pulled out and unfolded the flyer then immediately dropped it like it was on fire. The wording had changed.

COME BUILD YOUR FUTURE
AND HAVENWOOD FALLS' FUTURE
Call 6-4511 for details and to apply.

"Daniel, dinner's ready." His mom's voice drifted down the hallway. He lifted up the paper from the floor very carefully with two fingers and held it away from him like it was poisonous. He set it on top of his dresser and quickly left the room, needing time away to process what just happened. Maybe it was the beer on an empty stomach that was making him see things. That was the only logical explanation.

He was quiet during dinner, and his mom noticed.

"What's going on in that brain of yours?" she asked when she started to clear the table. "You hardly said a thing tonight."

"Mom, do you believe in magic?"

She paused and tilted her head to the side before answering. "Of course I do. Remember those witches who lived on our street in Pueblo? They cast some pretty incredible spells. Then there is us. I think a little magic was involved to create shifters. Why do you ask?"

Daniel chewed on his lower lip as he debated whether to tell her, but not one to keep secrets from his mom, he stood up.

"I'll be right back," he said and hurried to his bedroom. He grabbed the flyer, cautiously looking to see if the message had changed, but it was still the same. He strode into the kitchen and set it on the counter next to the stove with a dramatic flourish.

"What do you see?" he asked his mom.

She set the dish she was washing back in the sink and dried her hands on a towel before coming over to look. He watched her eyes dart as she read the brief summons.

"It's an advertisement for a construction job. Are you thinking about calling?"

"You don't see anything about building a future in Havenwood Falls?"

His mom frowned, deepening the lines around her mouth and the furrows in her forehead. She looked down at the sheet of paper again and slowly shook her head. She glanced up at him, her expression changing to one of concern. "Obviously you're seeing something different. Is that why you asked me about magic?"

Daniel let out an exasperated sigh and buried a hand in his thick, russet brown hair. He started pacing the length of the kitchen, a habit he learned from years of watching his dad do the same thing. "The original message was a generalized one for a construction foreman, like the one you are still seeing, but it's changed, for me. Holy cow, I sound crazy! Someone is going to lock me up in the booby hatch."

"Don't be ridiculous, Daniel. Come here and sit down."

His mom tucked her skirt behind her knees before she sat at the dinette table. The white top had already been scrubbed clean. The napkin holder and glass salt and pepper shakers stood in their usual place at the center. She lifted up the paper to the overhead light and examined it closely. Daniel sat down across from her and watched, his fingers tapping the table. She brought it close to her nose and inhaled deeply, her eyes briefly changing to their cat shape and flashing their bright amber color before turning back to human.

"There's something faint—an essence that's definitely magical in origin. I believe you, son. I think forces are at work here."

"Is it a trick, though? A trap by humans? Should I trust it?" He stood up and walked to the icebox, yanking on the chrome handle hard enough that the entire unit scraped forward on the floor. He slowed and took a deep breath. Even though he was home and away from humans, he couldn't get in the habit of displaying his strength. His father had taught him to always stay contained and control his emotions, which was easier said than done when he was a teenager. Now that he was twenty-five, it had become easier, but the rare display of his supernatural side, triggered by emotion, still happened.

He grabbed a beer and popped the cap off with his bare hands. Daniel didn't sit back down. His shifter side was itching to break free. It felt like the mountain lion was pacing just beneath his skin, its tail swishing from side to side with agitation.

"I think it would be highly unusual for humans to employ magic to lure you into a trap. Besides, we're fairly new to town, and we haven't given anyone any reason to suspect we're different. We've been so careful over the years."

What his mom said made sense. His dad had been so adamant that they move often enough to not raise suspicions. Daniel was raised to be as human as possible. When they did shift, to appease their other nature, his dad scouted out unpopulated and remote locations in advance. He and his mom continued all of these practices after his dad died. Did Daniel think his dad was a little paranoid at times? Yes, but he hadn't witnessed the horrors his dad had. They kept to themselves and interacted with humans only out of necessity. They didn't forge friendships with neighbors, because they were never in one place long enough. Daniel longed for a community, though, for relationships and for an existence that wasn't so . . . lonely.

"I'll admit I'm intrigued, and who or whatever is behind the message has my attention."

"Same here. What are you going to do?" his mom asked.

"I don't know. I need to shift and go for a run to think." Daniel set the empty beer bottle on the counter.

"Go and be careful."

Daniel went outside to his truck—the truck that used to be his dad's—pausing to run his hand along the dent in the driver's side door. He'd avoided bringing it into a shop to have the damage fixed. His mom thought it was morbid that he kept that reminder of the accident that took his dad's life, but it was a reminder for him that while his kind may have enhanced strength, reflexes, speed, and senses, they were mortal like humans. His dad's head had cracked against the window upon impact and broke open like an egg.

The door creaked on its hinges when he opened it. The truck was over ten years old now and had seen a lot of miles. He imagined his joints would be protesting like that someday, if he was fortunate enough to live a long life. He turned the key in the ignition, and the engine roared under the hood. Daniel pulled away from the curb and headed out beyond the city limits.

It hadn't been difficult to convince his mom to move back to Colorado. While West Virginia and Kentucky had some beautiful forests, they never felt connected to the East as they did with the wilderness of the Rockies. They had chosen Fort Collins since it backed to the Arapaho and Roosevelt National Forest. Acres of mountains and untamed land were a short drive away and offered plenty of space to discreetly shift and roam for hours. Away from the noise and distractions of civilization was where Daniel did his best thinking.

He found a deserted place to park in the shadows and climbed out. He raised his head, his nostrils flared as he scented the air, picking up all sorts of wild scents. His inner mountain lion itched to be free. *Soon*, he said to it and moved across the field toward the edge of the forest and the cover the tree line provided. Once there, he unlaced his boots and stripped off his clothes. His skin practically glowed in the moonlight, every muscle rippling with movement when he bent over to hide his clothes underneath a bush. He stayed in a crouch and called his animal forth. The familiar sting of claws breaking through the ends of his fingers and toes before his hands and feet transformed into paws came first. His bones snapped and muscles pulled as they made his new form. It was over in seconds, and then Daniel was loping through the woods, squirrels, birds, and rabbits scattering before him, ever wary of the predator that had just joined the night.

Dawn was approaching when he shifted back to his human form, his bones feeling heavy from exhaustion. Daniel slipped on his clothes and made his way back to his truck with purposeful strides. Listening to instinct, or whatever longing tugged at him from inside, he had made a decision. He was going to take a chance and call about the job in Havenwood Falls.

CHAPTER 3

"*P*arker's Perfect Placement Agency, this is Patty. How can I help you?" The woman who answered the phone had the chirpiest voice.

"Uh, hi, I'm calling about the construction foreman position."

"Oh, great, and how did you hear about this job?"

Daniel sat down at the table in the kitchen with the phone in his hand, a pencil in his other hand poised over a notepad. "A flyer was posted on the community board at Art's Variety in Fort Collins."

There was a pause, and all Daniel heard in the background was the *clack-clack* of keys on a typewriter. "Fort Collins. Wow, that's pretty far."

"Where exactly is Havenwood Falls?" Daniel asked. "I looked at a current map and couldn't find it anywhere."

"Well, that's because we're Colorado's best kept secret!" Daniel moved the phone away from his ear. The woman's voice was so sweet, he expected syrup to start pouring out of the receiver. "Now tell me your name. If you have the time, we can do a phone interview right now. The fact that you're calling because of the flyer pre-screened you."

"It did?" He thought that was strange, but he had never worked with an agency before, so he shrugged it off. "My name is Daniel McCabe."

Patty asked him about his construction background, of which he had plenty. He learned his trade from hands-on experience starting in high school. Once he graduated, he entered the industry full time, starting as a day laborer and working his way up. He provided three references and their phone numbers. Patty explained the job was for a new commercial building, but there were ample opportunities beyond that.

"Daniel, thank you for calling. I just need to call and check your references. Hopefully I'll have good news by the end of the day!" she chirped.

After the call disconnected, Daniel stared down at the notepad. His one question he had written down in advance remained unanswered: *Where is Havenwood Falls?*

Later that afternoon, Patty Parker called back and offered Daniel the job. They agreed that he would start the following Tuesday, but he needed to be there Monday to do paperwork. When he asked for directions, he was instructed to meet a shuttle bus in Grand Junction, and he could either take the shuttle or follow it into town.

"We're kind of in the middle of nowhere, and it's easy to get lost if you've never been here before," she explained.

Daniel clenched the steering wheel tight with anticipation as he drove past a sign constructed out of river rock, a blend of muted blues and grays. Black wrought iron lettering spelled out *Havenwood Falls*. His journey had been long, but uneventful. He took his time, keeping the shuttle in sight, but not taxing the old truck as the winding road climbed to higher elevations. With his windows down, the air was cool yet sweet from the lupines that lined the road, creating a colorful border for the dense forest that lay beyond. A hawk cried and circled in the sky ahead before disappearing in the tree tops. He sensed he was being watched. That something or someone was concealed in the woods, tracking his progress, and had been following him for a couple of miles, since he passed through an invisible border made of magic. It was subtle, a tickle across his skin, but magic nonetheless. He didn't sense a threat, so he had kept going.

Now the trees began to thin, and driveways appeared on the side of the road leading to small homes. Daniel continued on, following the shuttle, but he sensed he would have found his way on his own, if he focused on the internal tugging. It was like a magnetic attraction or an internal compass leading him in the right direction. The shuttle continued on the road that became Main Street. He drove past the high school, a three-story brick structure with arches marking the front entrance. A sign out front said "Congratulations to the Class of 1957! Go Dragons!"

Across the street, a restaurant was hopping. He spotted waitresses on roller skates expertly balancing trays full of food. He inhaled the aroma of grilled meat, and his stomach rumbled. Burger Bar was definitely going to be one of his first visits. There was a sign in the parking lot behind Burger Bar that said: "Miller's Plaza Coming Soon!" and he wondered if that was the project he would be involved with.

He continued on, and sun filtered through the trees that lined the street. He slowed down as he approached the shopping district, as there were a lot of pedestrians. People watched him drive by. Typical behavior for small towns, where the residents probably knew everyone and their vehicles. With the two-tone buttercream and brown paint job, plus the large dent in the driver's side, and the distinctive growl of the engine, his truck was one of a kind, and it was obvious, based on the stares, that they didn't recognize it.

He took note of Campbell's Market, the dark green canvas awning providing shade for fresh ears of corn, cucumbers, and tomatoes for sale in bins underneath a large window. He drove past a saloon and made note of that, too. The town square appeared to his left. A giant fountain in the middle sparkled in the sun. A jazz band was set up in the gazebo, playing to a small crowd. All of the buildings he saw were well maintained. He had entered a town worthy of a postcard.

As he drove through the center of Havenwood Falls, he became aware that not all of the people were human.

The shuttle parked along the curb in front of a gorgeous Victorian house, but Daniel kept going around the square. He pulled in next to a police cruiser when he parked in front of City Hall and caught the distinct odor of wolf. He turned in the direction of the scent and noticed the sheriff's deputy sitting in the cruiser, also scenting the air. Daniel hadn't gone undetected, either. The deputy narrowed his eyes, and they flashed a deep gold before returning to brown. Leaving his truck unlocked and windows down, figuring it was going to be searched anyway, Daniel left to find Parker's Perfect Placement Agency. According to the directions Patty gave him, it was located on Eleventh Street next to the bank, Havenwood Falls Savings & Loan.

A secretary sat behind a wide metal desk, typing away. Her fingers hitting the keys made a loud clacking noise. Her gray hair curled out at the ends and brushed the tops of her shoulders. She had a matronly look about her, and when she glanced up at Daniel, she pushed her tortoiseshell horn-rimmed glasses up her nose.

"Can I help you?" she asked in a no-nonsense tone, while still typing at a rapid-fire pace.

"Yes, my name is Daniel McCabe. I'm here to see Patty Parker." He handed her the flyer, and she gave it a brief glance before sighing and handing it back to him.

"Hold on, please." She stood and walked down a narrow hallway. There were two doors on the right and one on the left. She knocked on the door on the left before opening it and disappearing inside. She returned a moment later to bring Daniel back.

They stopped in front of a closed door. The bottom half was dark wood and the top half frosted glass, and etched in the glass in block letters was the name Martin Parker. A woman sat behind a cluttered desk. Her hair was brown and twisted up into a beehive. He showed her the flyer, and she grinned at him, her blue eyes sparkling behind her black-framed glasses.

"Mr. McCabe, pleased to meet you, finally. Patty Parker," she said and stood up to walk around the desk. She was taller than he expected and wore navy capri pants with a short jacket. "Please have a seat and pardon the mess. It's my husband's, and I'm attempting to organize."

Daniel took a seat in one of the two available chairs, and Patty handed him a clipboard with a bunch of forms. About fifteen minutes later, he was just finishing the last form when his nostrils flared. He scented the presence of a vampire—it had been a few years since he last encountered a vampire, but he'd recognize their scent of dusty blood anywhere—and two other creatures he wasn't familiar with. Suddenly the office door opened, and three people filed in: a tall older man with intense blue eyes and silvery blond hair that draped down to his lower back; the man next to him was the vampire, his grayish green eyes unlike any color Daniel had seen before; and the other man's scent was spicy, but his species eluded Daniel. What was going on? Everything about this situation was unusual, but things just kept getting more bizarre. His gut was telling him to proceed and that he wasn't in danger, so he decided to stay.

"You're a mountain lion shifter, correct?" the tall man with silvery hair asked.

"Yes. How did you know?" Daniel sat up straighter in his seat, taken aback at the man's directness.

"We have our ways, Mr. McCabe. I know you sensed we're not human, and there are others in town like us."

"Yes, I did."

"My name is Elsmed Fairchild, and I'll tell you, so you can stop guessing—I'm a fae. The vampire is Mihail Petran, and he owns Whisper Falls Inn. This other gentleman is Del Augustine, and he's a mage. Havenwood Falls isn't like other towns. Sure, there's the chamber of commerce, city hall, and city council, but the supernatural population requires a different structure and type of policing. That's where we come in. We sit on the Court of the Sun and the Moon and make sure everyone behaves in this town. If not, there are consequences." His blue eyes flared at this, driving his point home.

Daniel tapped his fingers against his leg, waiting for the other shoe to drop. So far everything had been going too smoothly.

"Relax, Daniel," Patty reassured him. "If we didn't think you'd be a good fit here, you wouldn't be sitting there."

"Exactly," Del said, his voice a soothing baritone. "The flyer you saw was spelled to only be seen by supernaturals."

"Oh, that makes sense. My mom said she smelled magic."

"Either she has a very keen nose, or I'm slipping," Patty said with a laugh that broke some of the tension in the room.

"The rules are simple, Daniel," Elsmed continued. "You can't show your shifter form or abilities in public, specifically in front of humans. This includes hunting. You also need to know that wards are in place that will alter your memory. If you leave Havenwood Falls, your memories of this town will fade until they're gone forever. Finally, you will be marked with a tattoo that identifies you as a supernatural and has certain magical qualities. For example, you'll have better control over your shift. We'll start you off with the temporary one and if you decide you like Havenwood Falls and want to live here long-term, we'll upgrade your tattoo. A permanent tattoo has benefits, such as being able to leave the wards for a full lunar cycle, or twenty-eight days, without your memories being affected. Any questions?"

"You want to tattoo me because I'm not human?" Daniel stood up, prepared to walk out. "Identifying a certain group by marking them is a tactic of war. I'm not comfortable with this." He crossed the room to the only window and peered out onto the side street. A mountain, one of the many peaks that surrounded Havenwood Falls, loomed above the neighborhoods behind the agency, and the evergreen tree line beckoned him, a promise of nocturnal romps within the forest. *Perhaps this town is too good to be true, after all*, he thought to himself.

"It's a temporary tattoo unless you choose to stay and make it permanent. It doesn't even have to be visible. It is a requirement if you plan to take the job and stay here." Del Augustine approached Daniel. He wore a three-piece suit, and gold cufflinks with the letter *A* inlaid with onyx stuck out from beneath the sleeves of his tailored jacket. Daniel tensed up when Del drew too close, and the mage backed off. "You don't trust easily, do you?" he asked Daniel.

"No."

"I understand, believe me. Our kind have been persecuted for centuries. Right, Patty?" Del called out across the room.

"We sure have. My ancestors fled Salem. Left in the dead of night before they could be accused."

"You see, all of us have been hunted or treated differently. Havenwood Falls was built as a safe haven for our kind. The rules we have are to ensure that safety isn't threatened."

As Del spoke, Daniel listened with all of his senses, and he didn't detect any type of deception. Taking a deep breath, he turned away from the window and faced the room.

"Fine. I'll agree to a tattoo, but it has to be invisible."

CHAPTER 4

$\mathcal{T}$he sun was beginning to set when Daniel left PPP Agency. In his hands he had the keys to a cabin and the paperwork to start his new job the next day. His right shoulder blade itched. True to their word, his tattoo was invisible, but he still felt the tendrils of magic seeping into his skin. Still in shock and unsure what to make of his good fortune, he sat in his truck for a few minutes, letting everything sink in. First, he had to call his mom and let her know he'd made it to the town, and as his stomach growled, he realized had to find something to eat. Remembering the market he passed on the way in, he fired up the truck and backed out of the parking spot. Within minutes, he was pulling into a space along the curb right in front of Campbell's Market. A strange sensation, like his pulse beating along the surface of his skin, began when he stepped onto the sidewalk, and it grew stronger when he entered the store.

To the right was a single register and checkout counter, and next to it a stack of baskets. He grabbed one and made his way over to the refrigerated case along the back of the store, where all the meat was kept. Apparently, the cabin he was renting came fully furnished, including dishes and pots and pans. Daniel was used to his mom cooking for him, but he thought he could handle frying up a steak on the stove and making a potato. It couldn't be that difficult. Throwing a steak and a package of bacon in the basket, he made his way down the case and added a dozen eggs. As he walked down the canned goods aisle, the thrumming sensation on his skin increased in intensity, becoming more of a buzz, like he was on the receiving end of continuous low-level jolts of electricity. *What in the world?* he thought to himself, thinking it was the tattoo causing the sensation. And then he saw her, and he forgot about everything.

A young woman stood behind the register, ringing up a customer. Her hair was silken gold, and her skin the peaches and cream described in fairy tales. She reminded him of Grace Kelly, but he thought she was far more beautiful. She was the most gorgeous creature he had ever laid eyes on. The woman smiled at the customer, her full lips parting to reveal straight white teeth. Daniel stood frozen in the aisle, staring like an idiot. Even his inner beast had stilled, captivated by the tiny beauty.

Slowly he breathed in deeply through his nose. He filtered out extraneous odors, like the onions and peppers in the produce section and the bananas that were too ripe. Her perfume was a soft floral and so very feminine, but masked her true scent, and that was what Daniel was after. Buried underneath the perfume and soap was a scent that reminded him of sunshine and moonlight all at once. It called to him, and without realizing, he had taken a few steps forward, his body being pulled to her. Then his brain finally caught up with his senses when he fully processed what was unexpected about her scent.

She was human.

This fact stopped him cold, and he almost dropped the basket. Daniel was positive this woman was intended to be his mate. The visceral response to her left little doubt, but how could she be? He couldn't be with a human. That was an affront to his kind. As if he were standing next to him, his dad's voice echoed in his head. *"Humans are the predators, son. They seek out and destroy or try to control anyone they see as different."* Daniel knew this; history had proven it. So, with a heavy heart, he set the basket down and quickly left the market, ignoring the instinct that was urging him to claim the woman.

Sitting in his truck with the windows down, Daniel took several deep breaths in an attempt to clear his head, which was at war with his heart. The papers for his job and the keys to the cabin lay on the passenger seat. The promise of a life with some permanency was within reach, and he didn't realize how badly he wanted that until it was offered. The human woman complicated things.

A rap on the passenger door pulled Daniel from his thoughts. He turned his head to look at the older man who was bent over, elbows on the sill of the door, peering into the cab of the truck. He had deep wrinkles around his mouth and eyes, which were shrouded by wiry, bushy eyebrows that resembled steel wool. His gray hair was slicked back with pomade.

"Well, I'll be. You're the spitting image of him."

"Of who?"

"I wasn't sure, I mean McCabe is a common name, but when Elsmed told me you were a mountain lion shifter, I had to see for myself."

"What are you talking about and who are you?"

"Jerome Brewster. Are you heading to the cabin? I'll explain along the way." Daniel watched in disbelief as Jerome opened the door and climbed inside, sliding the paperwork and keys along the bench seat toward him. "Well, don't just sit there and stare at me catching flies. Drive. I'll give you directions, since you're new to town."

Shaking his head at the audacity of the strange old man, Daniel started the truck. He was curious who Jerome was and who Daniel reminded him of. Hoping the saying "curiosity killed the cat" didn't hold true, he pulled out onto Main Street and followed Jerome's instructions.

Once they were out of the downtown area, they followed the main road back out of town, until the sign showed it changing to County Road 13, although Jerome called it Burdorf Pass. When he turned right onto a dirt road, he recognized the cabins he had driven past on his way into town. Several log cabins were scattered among the trees, many partially hidden in shadows as the sun dipped behind the mountains to the west. He spotted cabin number four and pulled up in front of the single-story building. It was a simple structure with a window and a door on the front. A metal stovepipe rose from the roof.

Grabbing his suitcase from the bed of the truck, Daniel climbed up the three steps that led to the door and unlocked it. Pine-scented cleaner and wood polish assaulted his nose, and it took him a few minutes to adjust. Opening up a few windows to air the place out helped. On the counter there was a basket of cheese, sausage, crackers, and some apples as a welcome. Between that and the few sandwiches his mom had packed in a cooler for him, at least he had something to eat, since he left the market empty-handed.

The living room consisted of a love seat in the most god-awful pattern and a rocking chair.

"Have a seat." Daniel sat in the rocking chair, which creaked under his weight, and Jerome sunk down onto the loveseat, his equally creaky knees popping.

"Your grandfather saved my life," Jerome announced.

And the revelations kept coming. Daniel was surprised he wasn't dizzy from all the information being dumped on him. First the supernatural secret society of Havenwood Falls and now this. "What?"

"I was at Sunset Creek that night everything went to shit. You do know about Sunset Creek, don't you, son?"

Daniel nodded. "Yes, my dad told me—he even brought me there."

Jerome shook his head and frowned. The wrinkles around his mouth deepened. "I know Ian got his wife and son out. Then he came back to help others escape. I was the last one he saved. As I was running with my son in my arms and my wife running alongside me, I briefly looked back over my shoulder just as a burning building collapsed. It was like a wave of fire washed over your granddad. Only a fire dragon could have survived that."

"Wow." That's all Daniel could say. After seeing the decades-old ruins in Sunset Creek when he was a teen, it was easy to imagine his grandfather's painful death.

"What are the odds that you show up here," Jerome said and rose to his feet with a groan. "I can't pay your grandfather back for saving me, but I can return the favor to you. Anything you need, boy, don't hesitate to ask. My family has a cabin just around the bend —number 9."

"Thank you." Daniel shook his hand and watched as the old man sauntered down the driveway.

"What are the odds, indeed?" Daniel muttered under his breath.

CHAPTER 5

One minute the handsome stranger was standing in the aisle, resembling a deer trapped in headlights as he stared at her, and the next minute he was gone. He had set his full basket down on the floor and bolted out the door like his Levi's were on fire. Before Colleen could call after him, the door had swung shut.

Maybe he forgot his wallet, she thought to herself, and shook her head. That wasn't the first strange thing to have happened in town, and surely wouldn't be the last. She did wonder about the man. He wasn't from around here, for she would have heard about him from her girlfriends. A man that looked like he did would not escape their attention. He was tall, muscular, and had the most incredible blue eyes that were accentuated by his dark eyebrows. His reddish-brown hair was thick on top and had a slight pompadour. Sideburns added to the definition of his sharp cheekbones. If she hadn't been busy ringing up a customer, she probably would have been caught up in his intense gaze. Sighing, she smoothed the apron she wore over her Madrid print capri pants and salmon-colored blouse, before retrieving the stranger's basket and putting back the items, taking note of the toiletry items and the thick steak swimming in blood.

Perhaps he was a tourist passing through Havenwood Falls, here to take advantage of the hiking and fishing. Maybe he was visiting family. Colleen hoped he came back, so she could at least learn a name to go with the handsome face. She grinned at the memory of doodling her name in her school notebooks and adding the last name of whoever she had crushed on at the time. Sadly, none of those crushes had panned out. Some turned out to be jerks, and others left Havenwood Falls after graduation and never returned. Now some of her friends were beginning to settle down. At twenty years old, she was already past the age her mom was when her parents were married. So far, Colleen hadn't found anyone even remotely close to husband material, and in the small town, her chances of finding someone were slim.

She shook her head and scoffed at the direction her thoughts had taken. Just one glimpse of the handsome stranger and she was already thinking marriage. Perhaps planning her friend Peggy's bridal shower was responsible.

The small bell above the front door to the store chimed, and Colleen looked up from where she was dusting and straightening the rows of canned vegetables. Her dad walked in, carrying a wooden box with the Stone Falls Winery logo burned into the side.

"Howdy, pumpkin!" he called and set the box down next to the register. The bottles inside rattled slightly with the movement.

"Hi, Daddy!" Colleen said and walked over to meet him.

"The Blackstones gave me a great deal on this case of cabernet." He pulled out a bottle and held it up to the light. "I can't wait to bring this home for your mother. Her bridge club will love it."

He winked at her and set the bottle back in the crate. While he went to the back of the store, where his office was located, Colleen counted down the register and started closing everything down for the night. The sun had set, and the dinner rush was over. At seven o'clock on the nose, she locked the door and flipped the sign from *Open* to *Closed.*

Together they walked out to the street where her parents' station wagon was parked. Her dad was quite proud of the fact that they had the only wagon in town with the wood paneling on the sides. The drive home only took about five minutes. They lived at the end of

Fairchild Lane where it dead-ended. Their house backed up to Bels Creek, which Colleen could actually see through the trees when she looked out her bedroom window.

Instead of going to college or moving to a big city after she graduated high school, Colleen had stayed home and taken on more responsibilities at her family's business. She had recently become the assistant manager, and she was salting her wages away into a nest egg for when she did move out on her own or got married.

As if reading her mind, her dad broke the silence inside the car. "Pumpkin, I appreciate you taking on the assistant manager position. It's nice knowing I can leave to run errands and know the store is in good hands."

"Aw, Daddy, thank you." She leaned over and pecked him on the cheek, which crinkled when he immediately smiled.

"I know it won't be long before someone comes along and sweeps you off your feet, then you'll kick your old man to the curb."

Colleen shook her head, causing her blond hair to bounce. "I don't think that will happen anytime soon," she protested, but immediately thought of the mysterious man who had run out of the store earlier. A vision flashed of her holding his hand while her free hand rested on her belly, swollen with child. A gasp escaped her lips and snapped her out of the daydream. She was surprised to find she was holding her stomach, like in her vision.

"Are you okay, pumpkin?" Her dad's brown eyes were full of concern when he turned to look at her.

"Yes, I'm fine," Colleen said and quickly moved her hand onto her lap.

Before her father could say anything else, they had arrived at home, and he was pulling into the driveway. The azaleas and rhododendron in the front flower beds were in full bloom. Some of the blossoms reached as high as the porch railing. The Campbells lived in a Victorian painted a light lavender with darker purple trim. The garage used to be a carriage house, back when horses were the main mode of transportation. It was just large enough to accommodate the station wagon. Her dad didn't pull into the carriage house, though, and before he turned off the engine, Colleen ran on ahead inside, leaving her dad to get the sack of groceries. The screen door slammed shut behind her, and she slipped off her white Keds before running up the stairs to her right.

Once in her room with the door shut, she took a few deep breaths to collect herself. That vision had felt so real, like she was really pregnant, and as she ran a hand over her flat stomach, she actually mourned for the child that never existed. *What on earth?* she asked herself, bewildered at the range of emotions.

After running a brush through her hair, pulling it up in a ponytail, and tying it with a ribbon that matched her shirt, Colleen went back downstairs to join her family for dinner. They were already in the dining room. Her dad was seated at the end of the table with his back to a window that looked out over the side yard. Her seventeen-year-old sister, Kelly, and her fourteen-year-old brother, David, were seated to his left. Colleen's mom was just setting the platter containing a roast on the table right next to a vase displaying a gorgeous arrangement of fresh flowers. Colleen sat down to the right of her dad and her mom took the seat at the other end of the table. They joined hands and said grace before diving in. Bowls and platters were passed around until everyone had full plates. David's practically spilled over onto the lace tablecloth.

"Ellen, you outdid yourself with this fine feast," her father praised, and Colleen grinned when her mom blushed from the compliment. Forks scraped against porcelain as they ate and chatted about their days. Callum presented a bottle of cabernet from the crate, and Colleen's mom opened it, filling the wine glasses for her and her husband, as well as Colleen.

"So, David, what did you do today?" Callum asked.

"Oh, my day was real swell, Dad! I spent the day on Mathews River with Billy and Dewey. We went fishing and swimming."

"Did you catch anything?"

"No. Well, Dewey hooked an old boot, but that's it. Oh, and we saw a giant wolf. Billy claims he saw its eyes glow, but I didn't see anything like that." David's face lit up as he recounted his adventure.

"Callum, this is why I get nervous with David running around all day. What if he had been attacked? Lord knows what else is in the woods."

Colleen finished taking a sip of wine before chiming in. "The animals were here first. We're encroaching on their land. It's only natural they're going to be seen by the river. It's one of the few water sources around here. Imagine how they feel. We've moved in and taken over, just like with the Indians."

The room grew quiet, and Colleen looked around the table. Her mom's lips were a straight line, her eyes narrowed in disapproval. "Being vocal about such controversial viewpoints won't win you any suitors, Colleen," she said.

"Well, I'd prefer a suitor who shares my views and doesn't mind a woman who speaks her mind."

Kelly snorted, and Colleen turned to look at her sister. She had clamped a hand over her mouth, but it didn't cover up the grin she was trying to conceal. They both had opinions about being stuck at home to be housewives and spent many nights sneaking into one another's bedrooms to discuss their dreams of changing the world. For Colleen, she saw how the town was creeping farther and farther into the wilderness that surrounded them. She wanted to protect the animals and their habitat. Kelly wanted to break barriers and become the first female fighter pilot in the Air Force. Watching films about the daredevil heroes who flew bombers during World War II had left quite a lasting impression on her sister.

"Callum, say something," Ellen pleaded, but he only winked, his brown eyes twinkling with amusement.

"I agree with Colleen. I want both my girls to find men worthy of them and their passions. Just like you, Ellen. It wasn't so long ago when you were coordinating letter-writing efforts for our troops and supporting the young wives left behind."

"Not me. I'm never getting married. I'm going to stay here forever," David announced, before stuffing a piece of roast beef in his mouth. "Mom's cooking is too good to leave behind." This statement was muffled as he chewed and spoke at the same time. Ellen gave him a pointed look in reprimand at his poor manners but couldn't help but laugh at his declaration. This dissolved any tension in the room.

Later that night, Colleen tossed and turned, her dreams invaded by the stranger from the store. His blue eyes as his gaze traveled the length of her body, warming her from the inside out. She could even smell him in her dreams, and when she woke up, the scent lingered. A mix of balsam and something spicy. Blaming it on the open bedroom windows and the smell of the forest being carried in on the slight breeze, Colleen got up to close the window closest to her bed.

The moon was full and illuminated everything in a silvery light. Looking out into the backyard, she almost missed the animal partially shrouded in shadow, until it moved. The movement caused the creature's eyes to glimmer in the moonlight. Colleen gasped and took a step backward, even though she was on the third floor and safe inside the house. Once over the initial shock, she returned to the window and leaned forward, her elbows on the sill. After a few minutes, the animal stepped out of the shadows to reveal a gorgeous mountain lion. Muscles rippled beneath its fur coat as it moved. Then it sat down on its haunches and raised its gaze to meet Colleen's.

She wasn't sure how long they stared at each other, but she was captivated by the odd interaction, which was interrupted by a yawn. Her skin was chilled by the night air, and she shivered. When she stood upright, the mountain lion got up, too. She raised her arm and waved farewell. Colleen watched as the giant cat slipped in between the trees that grew along the edge of the yard and disappeared, before turning away and climbing into bed, burrowing under the covers.

The next morning, she woke and stretched, not feeling completely rested because of all the vivid dreams. When she walked past the window, she paused and looked outside for any sign of a mountain lion. The only wildlife in the backyard was a squirrel. The light of day gave her a new perspective on the previous night's events. *It was just a dream*, she convinced herself, and continued on with getting ready for work.

CHAPTER 6

*W*ith a groan, Daniel sat up, swinging his legs over the side of his bed. He was buck naked, and shredded bits of clothes were strewn all over the hardwood floor in the cabin. Streaks of mud stained the bright white sheets, and pine needles fell from his hair when he ran his hand through it.

"Damn it," he muttered under his breath and stood up, stretching out his body.

Between the full moon and the lure of his mate being so close, he was unable to resist shifting and seeking her out. While he thought he may come to regret his actions later, he enjoyed observing his mate at her home. When she appeared in the window, he practically froze. Her blond hair was rumpled from sleep, and he saw the outline of her curves through the fabric of her nightgown. With his keen eyesight, he noticed when her nipples hardened right when she saw him. She was like Rapunzel in her tower, and everything about her called to him. It took every ounce of control to stay in one spot when all he had wanted to do was scale the wood siding of her house to reach her. Fortunately, he hadn't done anything that would make her think he was anything but an ordinary mountain lion.

It was his first night in Havenwood Falls, and he had already showed himself to a human. When he met with Elsmed Fairchild the day before, the fae had explained how the town came to be. That the founding families were made of various supernatural species, from werewolves—including the town's sheriff, Ric Kasun—to vampires, witches, fae, and more. They were all seeking a safe haven and found it in the picturesque box canyon. The surrounding mountains provided a natural barrier, but wards and spells provided a magical boundary for additional protection. The humans who lived in town, with the exception of a few, like the town mayor, didn't know that supernaturals existed, and the Court—the supernatural governing body made up of members of the founding families—wanted to keep the humans as uninformed as possible. That meant not doing anything supernatural in front of them. At least he hadn't shifted in public. Only a mountain lion would have been seen roaming through town, if there were any other witnesses, which he hoped there weren't. He was lucky he didn't get shot. His new beginning was off to a stellar start.

Crossing the bedroom to the tiny bathroom, Daniel peered in the mirror at the stubble that had sprouted up overnight. After shaving, making sure to shape his sideburns, he showered, removing all evidence of his nocturnal romp.

The parking lot at Burger Bar was deserted when he drove past to reach the jobsite. A Silverstream trailer was set up in the packed down dirt directly behind the restaurant. He parked next to it and got out of his truck. Daniel had been told to report at seven o'clock, and had arrived a few minutes early on purpose. He wanted to get a feel for the landscape and scope of the project. The ground had been broken during a big ceremony with the mayor cutting a ribbon and everything, but after that, Miller's Plaza had stalled because of labor issues. Apparently, Ross Builders had been experiencing a string of bad luck in keeping people employed. The last foreman had disappeared overnight. This was why the owner, Herschel Ross, had started recruiting in other parts of the state.

Miller's Plaza was a big commercial initiative that would create more retail and office space beyond the town square. An excavator was parked off to the side near a flatbed trailer stacked with steel beams.

Patty told him the day before that Herschel had said the city was ready to run sewer and water lines once the holes were dug. That would be step one. Then they'd dig a hole and pour the basement. From there, the buildings would go up fairly quickly.

Daniel leaned against his truck and poured some hot coffee from his Thermos while he waited for Herschel and the rest of the crew to show up. He was anxious to take a look at the blueprints. From where he stood, he had a good view of Main Street. Traffic was light, but he imagined once school was back in session, it would be busier.

A pale green International pickup truck turned into the entrance and came to a stop next to Daniel's truck. "Ross Builders" was written on the side with dark blue paint. An older man stepped out. He wore faded dungarees and a dark green Western-style shirt. The buttons looked strained as the shirt stretched across a rotund belly.

"You must be Daniel McCabe," he said and extended his hand. "I'm Herschel Ross."

"Nice to meet you, sir." Daniel shook Herschel's hand. He had a strong grip and plenty of calluses. Those came with the trade.

"Well, Patty Parker from the temp agency spoke very highly of you. Are you ready to get to work?"

"Yes, sir."

Daniel followed Herschel into the Airstream trailer, which served as the jobsite office. The dinette area on the right, with the built-in table, served as the desk. Blueprints, invoices, and newspapers were scattered everywhere. The sink and counter in the kitchen area to the left were spilling over with dirty dishes. Several grease-stained waxed paper wrappers with the Burger Bar logo were on the floor. Cigar smoke permeated the air, making Daniel want to stop breathing. He imagined if Herschel went camping, he'd leave his garbage behind in the forest. Another reason he disliked humans—they didn't appreciate the environment.

"Have a seat. We'll go over the plans."

Daniel shoved some papers aside and sat down on the bench. Herschel dug through the pile and pulled out a roll of blueprints. He unrolled them across the top of everything. There were so many lumps pushing up from underneath, it resembled more of a topographic map.

They spent close to thirty minutes going over the plans and schedule. When the rest of the crew arrived, Herschel introduced Daniel. The crew was small, and half of the eight men looked like they were approaching retirement age. One of the crew members, a tall man with olive skin and dark hair named Mickey, shook Daniel's hand. As he did, a gust of wind blew, and Daniel caught his scent. Mickey wasn't human either. A subtle nod passed between them, an acknowledgment that they both recognized each other's supernatural side.

As the day progressed, the cool morning burned away under a cloudless sky. The sun beat down on the crew as they worked. Daniel paused to wipe sweat from his brow and take a drink of water from the canteen he brought. The water was no longer cool, but it was wet and kept him from dehydrating. He took off his shirt and tossed it onto the seat of his truck through the open window. When he leaned back against the hood, enjoying a hint of breeze, he stared up at Main Street. Traffic had picked up, and Burger Bar was hopping. Waitresses wearing pink dresses with white aprons, notepads hanging out of their front pockets, whizzed through the parking lot deftly, carrying trays loaded with burgers, fries, and shakes. They navigated around cars and people with the grace of dancers and were a mesmerizing sight. The smell of grilled meat and fried food made his stomach growl, and the sandwich in his lunchbox was suddenly unappealing.

At high noon, Herschel came out of the job trailer and sent everybody to lunch.

"Be back in an hour—sharp!" he yelled before disappearing back inside.

Daniel shook his head. No wonder Herschel had a hard time keeping people. His management style was awful. Daniel had seen his type before, the kind who hired people to do the dirty work while they stayed clean and barked orders. Daniel preferred to work alongside his crew. Not only did it help to earn their respect, but working hard made the day go by fast.

Reaching into his truck, Daniel grabbed his shirt and lunchbox. He walked past Burger Bar and made a right on Main Street.

He remembered seeing some benches in the town square and found an empty one underneath a large oak tree and completely covered in shade. Daniel sat down with a groan. His shoulders and back were already tight from the morning spent shoveling and moving dirt. It was at least ten degrees cooler in the shade, and he took a moment to close his eyes and lean his head back. His roaming the night before had cut into his sleep. Between being tired and his sore muscles, he felt like an old man. The scrape of his lunchbox sliding toward him on the bench and the most irresistible scent caused him to open his eyes and sit up with a jerk. There, sitting next to him, was the woman from the market. She had a paper bag on her lap and was looking at him with deep brown eyes. A shy smile lifted her pink lips.

"I hope you don't mind. There's room for two." She gestured at the respectable distance between them.

"Uh, no, you're fine," Daniel responded stiffly and popped the latch open on his lunchbox, hoping the distraction of food would help him to ignore the woman. Now that she was sitting right next to him, his senses were overwhelmed. His whole body coiled tight—even his toes in his work boots were curled. He needed to keep from making a scene. He wanted to pounce on her, touch her, rub against her, bite her, and mark her. He'd be hauled away in a second. The police station was within eyesight.

Out of the corner of his eye, Daniel saw her pull out a book from the bag, and she opened it up on her lap. She held a sandwich in one hand, taking dainty bites whenever she turned the page. Her blond hair was just long enough to brush the tops of her shoulders and curl up at the ends, and her bangs curled down over her forehead. She had an adorable nose that turned up slightly at the end. A bread crumb clung to the corner of her mouth, and he became fixated on it. How that crumb teased him. All he had to do was lean over and lick it off, but one taste would lead him down a rabbit hole, and he'd be lost in his own Wonderland and simply mad.

"Aren't you hungry?" Her soft voice broke through his haze. He forced himself to look away from the taunting crumb and meet her eyes. She was blushing and chewing on her bottom lip like she was trying to stop from laughing.

"What?" He felt disoriented, like the first time he got drunk on whiskey. It was right after he had watched his dad get lowered into the damp ground. He remembered staring at the dirt under his fingernails as he held a tumbler in his hand. Dirt from the handful he had tossed on top of the casket. He sat at the bar in a room full of strangers, isolated by his grief and his lack of close relationships. Daniel's dad had been his rock. They had moved so much that faces, except for his family's, became a blur. Now he looked at this woman, and her face was so clear, while everything else was blurry.

"You haven't touched your lunch." She pointed at his lunchbox. He had gotten as far as opening the darn thing but had been too busy staring at the human woman, making a fool of himself.

"Oh, I guess not." He ran a hand through his hair and looked away. Daniel didn't embarrass easily, but this woman had him all out of sorts. Then he glanced at his wristwatch and cursed. He had five minutes to get back to the job site. He mumbled an apology and grabbed his stuff.

A faint giggle followed him as he rushed off.

"I'll be here again tomorrow, same time!" she called after him.

Her invitation caused him to slow down. He spun so he walked backwards, wanting one last glance at his fair-haired temptress. That's exactly what she was, a temptress. Why would fate be so cruel as to make his mate a human? Committing his final glance to memory— the way her hair blew in the gentle breeze and how her brown eyes lit up when she smiled, which revealed a dimple. And she was smiling, smiling at him. His inner cat growled when Daniel turned away and ran through the square, his lunchbox knocking against his leg. By the time he crossed Fourth Street, he slowed down and walked the rest of the way. When he reached the jobsite, it wasn't just his inner beast growling, but his stomach. He'd just have to eat lunch in his truck from now on.

~

THAT VERY NIGHT, he found himself in the woman's backyard. He paced in the shadows, his paws barely making a sound, muffled by soft earth and grass. Clouds had moved in, rendering the dark an extra inky black and lending a stillness to the damp air. The dampness amplified the scent of everything. The sweetness of roses blooming and the aroma of rosemary in the herb garden were strong scents, but not strong enough to cover up that of his mate. He'd recognize her anywhere.

All of the windows in the house were dark. The occupants had been asleep for hours. Daniel had watched as an older woman, who bore a strong resemblance to his mate, washed dishes before turning off the light. A young boy in a bedroom on the second floor had been playing a record, and the twang of Johnny Cash could be heard through the open window, but he eventually settled down. Anytime there was movement in his mate's window, his eyes were immediately drawn to it. When he was at just the right angle, he saw her at a vanity, brushing her hair. He longed to run his fingers through those silky strands. She, too, went to bed, and yet Daniel stayed, unable to pull himself away.

When the sky began to lighten to the east, he reluctantly stepped into the thatch of trees and ran along the river, following its curve through the forest until he crossed County Road, reaching his cabin, where he fell into bed.

Managing a little less than three hours of sleep, Daniel arrived at the jobsite looking as refreshed as a hungover hobo, or his boss. Herschel rolled out of the job trailer wearing the same sweat-stained clothes as the day before, and reeking of beer. He squinted his bloodshot eyes and peered out at the crew, which had decreased by one. After barking out orders and announcing the foundation would be poured that afternoon, Herschel disappeared back inside his trailer, leaving Daniel to manage the day's work, not that he minded. The group of six sweaty men smelled better than his boss.

When lunchtime rolled around, Herschel didn't make an

appearance, so Daniel dismissed the workers. Mickey, the shifter, asked if he wanted to go to Burger Bar. At first, he was going to say yes, because he wasn't going back to the square and back to that bench, but ten minutes later, Daniel found himself in the same spot, waiting for his temptress to arrive.

He saw her when she emerged from underneath the shade of the awning in front of Campbell's Market. She waited for a 56 Merc to drive by before crossing Eighth Street. When she looked up and saw Daniel sitting on the bench, she flashed a wide smile and waved. She was wearing a pair of navy-and-white-striped capris, white Keds, and a white shirt. She skipped over and sat down next to him.

"I'm Colleen, by the way." She held out her hand, and Daniel grinned at her forwardness.

"Daniel," he said and shook her hand. The moment they touched, he knew he was doomed. It was like his pulse jumped to meet hers. Her brown eyes, which were framed by the longest, thickest lashes, widened, and she gasped. This was how he knew she felt the connection, too.

They stayed like that for a few moments, hands and eyes locked on each other. Only when two teenage girls walked by giggling did they separate. Colleen blushed, her fair skin flaring a beautiful dusty pink. Reaching for her lunch bag, she pulled out a sandwich along with a bottle of Coca-Cola, followed by a hardcover book. This time, Daniel glanced at the cover. She was reading *Peyton Place*, one of the previous year's best sellers. He heard it was being made into a movie.

Actually eating his lunch this time, Daniel ate his sandwich and took time to observe the town. Here in the square, he was basically sitting in the heart of Havenwood Falls. Whisper Falls Inn, a beautifully restored Victorian, sat kitty-corner. Baskets of purple and pink petunias were hanging along the eaves of the front porch. The bank, located next to PPP Agency, had a steady stream of people coming and going. He could see two ladies in the window of the beauty parlor sitting in chairs with their heads underneath some sci-fi-looking contraption.

"You're not from around here, are you?" Colleen asked out of the blue. Turning to look at her, he saw her book was closed on the bench between them. She had finished her lunch and had moved so she sat at an angle, facing him. Her legs were crossed at the ankle and her left arm was draped over the top of the back of the bench, her fingers inches from his face. This position caused the buttons on her blouse to gap slightly, and he caught a glimpse of her white bra.

Swallowing hard and tearing his gaze away from her breasts, he met her eyes. "No, I'm not. This is my first week here."

"I thought so. Everyone basically knows everyone in Havenwood Falls."

"Have you lived here long?"

"Born and raised." She stared wistfully off toward Mount Alexa. The peaks were still capped with snow even though summer was already underway. "I've never really been anywhere else. Where are you from?" she asked, turning her attention back to him.

Daniel sighed and stretched his legs out before him, settling in to the conversation. "All over really. My family moved around a lot. I'm from Colorado originally, though, and just moved back after spending ten years in Kentucky and West Virginia."

"Golly! What was that like?"

"Different, but the same. People don't really change, just the landscape."

"Huh." Colleen contemplated his statement. "I never really thought about it that way." She moved her arm from the back of the bench and started gathering her things together. Tucking her hair behind her ear, she stood up. "I have to get back to work and I'm off tomorrow, so maybe I'll see you Friday?"

"Maybe."

Her smile faded slightly at his noncommittal response. "I understand. It was nice meeting you, Daniel."

With a final wave, she rushed off in the direction of the market. He watched her until she was safely across the street and inside. The moment she was gone from sight, a small ache formed in his chest, like a mild case of heartburn, but not quite. Frowning, he rubbed at it and kept rubbing at his chest as he walked back to the jobsite. It grew increasingly worse as the day progressed.

"You look like you need a drink," Mickey said as he helped Daniel clean up at the end of the day. The concrete had been poured, and there wasn't much else they could do until it cured enough. That meant they had the next day off.

Hoping a drink would take the edge off the burning sensation, Daniel agreed. Half an hour later, they were parked on two bar stools at the Haven Saloon. As soon as they were seated, Mickey ordered them each a shot of whiskey and a mug of Coors beer.

The whiskey had an interesting golden glow to it, and Daniel's inner lion became piqued with interest, making him realize this wasn't ordinary hooch. He lifted the shot glass and raised an eyebrow at Mickey.

"Apparently there's a secret ingredient. Warded Whiskey, the Tinker's Drink, has been distilled right here in Havenwood Falls since the 1800s. There was a couple who owned a shop right on the square, and they made clocks, puzzle boxes, all sorts of early engineering type gadgets. The guy, Gregory, built a still, and it took off from there."

Mickey raised his glass, and they both tipped the whiskey back with one swallow. Daniel coughed, and his eyes watered as the liquor burned a path down his esophagus. Once the liquid hit his stomach, warmth bloomed from within, like a mushroom cloud had erupted from his core. His already acute eyesight sharpened, and his other senses became more heightened so suddenly, the saloon, which was already loud, became almost painful to his ears. Chasing the whiskey with a gulp of Coors was like dousing flames with water, and his body returned to normal except for the looseness of his muscles, which usually took a six-pack to achieve.

"Holy Toledo, that is some potent juice!" He wiped his mouth with the back of his hand and noticed his lips were slightly numb, like he had been out in the cold too long.

"One of Havenwood Falls' best kept secrets," Mickey said with a wink.

"What's yours?" Daniel asked, keeping his voice low. "I know you're a shifter. I just can't tell what kind."

"Hawk. And you're some kind of big cat, am I right?"

Daniel nodded and took another swallow of beer. "Mountain lion."

"In the normal animal kingdom, we wouldn't be getting along like this. Cats and birds don't mix well," Mickey said with a grin and waved the bartender over for another round. "How are you at darts?"

Turned out, with their preternatural eyesight, they became competitive and kept playing to one up the other. Five rounds of drinks and five games later, they stumbled out the door into a town transformed by dusk. This was Daniel's first time in town during the evening as a human, and he stopped in his tracks to take in the soft glow from gas-lit street lamps. They cast a flickering light on the sidewalk and sides of buildings. Garlic and other spices laced the cool air, and his stomach growled.

"I'm famished, too. Been to Napoli's yet?" Mickey asked, and Daniel shook his head. "Come on. Their food is cheap and tasty."

Daniel fell into step alongside Mickey, their strides evenly matched. Mickey was about Daniel's height, which put him around six feet tall. They crossed Main Street and walked down Eighth Street on the storefront side. Daniel paused outside Campbell's Market and raised his head, scenting the air and inhaling the faint traces of Colleen that seemed to permeate the building. The store was closed, and all of the lights were off except for those of the cooler that ran along the back wall. Bottles of milk and blocks of cheese and butter lined the shelves.

"Hey, blockhead." Mickey tapped Daniel's shoulder, getting his attention. "They're closed. Food is this way."

Backwoods Sport & Ski was still open. The front window displays featured mannequins dressed in the latest summer hiking and fishing gear. A wooden canoe filled the whole length of one of the two windows. Daniel made a note to stop in and replace the Levi's he destroyed in his uncontrolled shift the other night. The scent of garlic grew stronger as they made a left on Stuart Street. The fire department, a two-story brick building with two arched garage bays, was all lit up. One of the garage doors was open, revealing a shiny red firetruck. A Dalmatian lay in front, watching the street with alert eyes. It was a scene straight out of a Norman Rockwell painting until the dog turned its head toward them and growled slightly, most likely sensing the animals lurking beneath their skin.

Napoli's was a small restaurant around the corner from the town square. A screen door let out the noise of several conversations as well as the tantalizing smell of food. A teenage girl greeted them when they walked in. She wore a black poodle skirt and a white shirt. Her brown hair was pulled back in a ponytail tied with a red ribbon.

"Welcome to Napoli's!" she chirped, greeting them with a bright smile and more enthusiasm than an entire glee club. She grabbed two menus, and they followed her down a narrow aisle between tables, her wide skirt brushing against chairs and patrons as she charged ahead. There was something about the girl that seemed familiar to Daniel, but he knew he hadn't met her before.

They were seated at a booth in the back near the kitchen. Minutes later, a woman closer to their age came to take their orders. She introduced herself as Karine. She had thick dark hair, the tight curls pinned close to her head, and large green eyes that were accentuated by thick, contoured eyebrows. Daniel was briefly distracted by her red lips before noticing the apron tied at her waist showed off her curves. She could have easily been one of those girls painted on WWII fighter jets. He realized the normal attraction he should have experienced wasn't there. This woman paled in comparison to Colleen. *Geezum crow*, three days around her and she was deep under his skin. The bird taking their order didn't do anything for him. All he wanted, all his inner mountain lion wanted, was Colleen. A human.

Suddenly, his buzz dissipated, and after the waitress left, he let out an exasperated sigh and leaned back heavily in the booth.

"What's eating you?" Mickey asked, before taking a sip of Coca-Cola through a straw.

Daniel surveyed his new friend. Mickey was a shifter, and by the looks of him, an Indian. Out of anyone, he had to understand.

Leaning forward in his seat, he gestured for Mickey to lean forward too, so other diners in the cramped restaurant didn't overhear.

"I met my mate. She's here in Havenwood Falls."

"That's fantastic, daddy-o! Why do you seem so gloomy about it?"

"She's—" Daniel paused. "She's human," he whispered.

Mickey's face transformed from a smile to a scowl, and he moved away. He tapped his fingers on the table and regarded Daniel.

"Are you a purist?" he finally asked.

"A what?"

"A purist. You only procreate within your own kind and shun everything else. You didn't strike me as one, but if you have an issue with your own mate—which is a gift not to be spurned—because she's human, then I guess I was wrong about you." Mickey made a move to leave, a look of disgust on his face.

"Hold on," Daniel said. "Let me explain."

At that moment, Karine returned with their food. They had each ordered a large pizza and an order of garlic knots. As soon as they were alone and in between mouthfuls of food, Daniel told Mickey about Sunset Creek and how that history was behind every move his family had made.

"That's how I was raised. That's all I know, but Colleen—she's mine. I can feel it here." Daniel pounded on his chest above his heart. "How can she be my mate? It doesn't make sense."

Mickey set his slice of pizza down. "My ancestors helped to build this town alongside the founding families. All of the founders were either hunted or cast out because of their supernatural abilities. Witches and witch hunters helped to build Havenwood Falls— together. My great-great-grandmother was a white woman and a witch. My great-great-grandfather is from the Chickasaw tribe. Their relationship was forbidden by society, yet they found a way. You can figure this out. But to deny your mate? You know what that means, right?"

Daniel nodded and looked away from Mickey's intense dark gaze. He knew what it meant, and as the whiskey wore off, the physical effects were no longer masked. The ache was back.

After eating, they walked back to the jobsite where Daniel had left his truck, but as they passed Burger Bar, which sat dark and quiet, Daniel caught the scent of blood in the air. He raised his head slightly and inhaled deeply through his nose. It had the distinct smell of humans. Animal blood had a richness to it that human blood lacked. Mickey came to a stop, his head tilted to the side and his eyes closed. Suddenly his eyes popped open, and he started running toward the jobsite. Daniel immediately followed, not wanting his friend to go into an unknown situation alone. He could see at night almost as well as during the day. A man was laying on the ground, moaning.

They each came to a stop on either side of the man, whose face was beaten to a pulp. Daniel almost didn't recognize Herschel, if it wasn't for the clothes. They were stained with sweat earlier, and now they were soaked with blood. Alcohol wafted off his body like he had been soaking in a vat of whiskey.

"Mr. Ross, can you hear me?" Mickey asked. He rolled Herschel onto his back, and the man let out a hoarse cry that tapered off to a whimper.

"Christ, he's a mess," Daniel said, noting the crushed nose and eyes swollen shut. Herschel tried to say something, but his jaw hung at an angle, making it impossible for him to produce words. Drool, tinged pink from blood, dribbled down the side of his mouth. "Help me lift him up. He needs a doctor."

Herschel cried out when they lifted him off the ground. Mickey was at his feet, and Daniel supported the almost unconscious man with his hands hooked underneath his arms. Together they carried him up the slight incline to Main Street and the short distance to the medical center, which looked more like a house from the outside, not a hospital.

There was one nurse on duty, and she came running from the reception desk when she saw them outside the front door. She held it open so they could carry Herschel inside. He had passed out during the brief walk. Daniel noticed her nametag pinned to her starched white dress uniform when he passed by: Sharon Heller, RN.

"What happened?" she asked as they followed her down a short hallway, austere and sterile in its white brilliance.

"We found him like that," Daniel answered. "But I don't think he got this way from falling down the stairs."

Mickey snorted and almost dropped Herschel's feet. The jostling woke him up, and he started to thrash.

"Getoffme!" His swollen lips and lopsided jaw garbled his words.

"Herschel, knock it off!" Nurse Heller commanded, causing Daniel and even Mickey to stand up straight. "These fine young men are trying to help you." She continued to chastise him after they had set him down on a gurney.

"You know him?" Daniel asked.

Nurse Heller looked up at him, the stethoscope still stuck in her ears. "We grew up together, and he's always been a grump. It's a chronic ailment," she said with a wink before shooing them out of the cramped exam area.

A small waiting area, to the right of the main entrance, was where they wound up. Several wooden benches, which reminded Daniel of church pews with their straight backs, lined the walls. He leaned his head back against the cool plaster and stretched his legs out in front of him. Dust coated the tops of his boots. Mickey sat down next to him. He leaned forward with his elbows on top of his knees. His head hung down, almost like he was in prayer.

Moments later, the roar of an engine caught their attention, and their heads swiveled in unison to look out the large front bay window as an ambulance pulled up. It was all white with a red roof, the front round wheel wells merged with running boards that had seen some wear and tear. A single light just above the windshield flashed red. Two men wearing white jackets and red caps hopped out and ran around to the back of the wagon, where they unloaded an empty stretcher. They rushed inside the medical center, steering the stretcher between them. They disappeared down the hall, in the direction of where Herschel had been deposited. Instantly, Mickey and Daniel were on their feet.

"What do you think is happening?" Mickey asked.

"I don't know, but I don't think it's good." Daniel immediately started making a contingency plan in his head. If Herschel Ross was seriously injured or—heaven forbid—dead, then he would most likely be out of a job. He'd have to move back to Fort Collins and find work there. Suddenly, an image of Colleen flooded his mind at the very thought of leaving Havenwood Falls. Like his heart was held in a vise that was being tightened, pain pierced his chest. He doubled over gasping, and when Mickey whipped his head around, Daniel covered it up with a cough.

"You okay, Hoss?" Mickey asked, a thick dark eyebrow arched in question.

"Yeah, I think I strained a muscle carrying our boss." Forcing himself to stand up straight, he winced and rubbed the area over his chest that still burned.

A flurry of activity exploded in the hallway as Herschel Ross was wheeled out, strapped to the gurney. Nurse Heller rushed after them and passed off a dark brown file to one of the medics like she was passing a baton in a relay race. Within seconds, Herschel was loaded into the back of the ambulance. With sirens blaring and tires squealing, the rig raced off into the night.

As the siren faded, Daniel began to accept that he would have to move again. The idea didn't appeal to him. Despite finding his mate and discovering she was human, Daniel was beginning to like Havenwood Falls.

"Where's he going?" Mickey asked.

"Grand Junction. His injuries are too severe to treat here. His jaw will most likely need to be wired shut, and I suspect he has bleeding on his brain. One of his pupils was dilated and the other was fine, which is a good indicator without taking X-rays," Nurse Heller said. "I really shouldn't be telling you since you're not kin, but Herschel doesn't have anyone, and you found him."

They made to leave, but Nurse Heller called out. "Hold tight, boys, the sheriff's going to want to talk to you."

Daniel paused and swallowed deep. He hadn't thought about a crime having been committed, and here he was, new in town without anyone to vouch for him except for Mickey, but how well did he know Mickey? Would the sheriff be like other small-town cops and find someone easy to pin the blame on?

Minutes later, a sleek black truck with whitewall tires came to a stop in front of the medical center. A large man stepped out and adjusted his gun belt. He wore jeans and a denim shirt with the sleeves rolled up to his elbows, the gold star badge reflecting the overhead lighting the only indication this man was law enforcement. As the officer walked toward the waiting area, he tipped his tan cowboy hat at Nurse Heller, who blushed before pretending to be busy shuffling papers at the registration desk.

"Mickey," he said and pulled out a small notepad from his back pocket. "And you must be Daniel McCabe." Piercing blue eyes landed on Daniel, and a blast of wolf washed over him as the sheriff projected his scent, sending a message that in addition to sheriff, he was also a wolf shifter.

"Yes, sir," Daniel answered, standing straighter and squaring his shoulders, not only hiding his surprise, but sending his own message that he wouldn't be pushed around. They eyeballed each other, and Mickey shifted nervously next to Daniel the longer the stare down lasted. The sheriff finally smirked and extended his hand.

"Sheriff Ric Kasun. You mind telling me what happened?"

Daniel shook his hand, making sure his grip was tight, then he and Mickey launched into telling Sheriff Kasun where they discovered Herschel.

An hour later, satisfied with their answers, Sheriff Kasun dismissed them.

Insects danced in the beam from his truck's headlights as Daniel drove back to the cabin with eyelids so heavy, they threatened to close. Normally he had more energy at night, a side effect of being part feline, but his emotions had been all over the map. Once he was away from the town center, darkness descended, and he struggled to focus. When he turned off on the dirt road that led to the cabins, he slowed down. Trees loomed on either side of the road, their bark looking like leathery skin when illuminated by the headlights.

Stumbling into the cabin, he tossed his keys on the small rustic dining table and continued straight into the bedroom. Within minutes, he was asleep.

Chirping birds and the early tendrils of morning sunshine woke Daniel from a restless slumber. He sat up in bed, the top sheet pooling around his waist. Looking around, he noticed his clothes on the floor where he had stripped them off before climbing into bed. His sheets were clean, with no evidence of dirt and leaves, which meant he hadn't shifted and gone roaming the forest to stand in the shadows, watching Colleen's house. Relieved it was just a dream, he let out a sigh and fell back against the pillows.

As he lay there, he thought about Herschel and how the man's health left his job hanging in the balance. Daniel looked around the room. His suitcase was open on the floor next to the dresser. He hadn't bothered to unpack yet, so it would be easy to pick up and leave. He was used to it.

Sitting up, he swung his legs over the side of the bed. His feet landed on the hardwood floor. Scratching his head, he walked to the window that looked out upon the forest that surrounded the cabin. A light breeze caused tree tops to sway, and birds swooped and flew in their own random dance. A deer stepped out from the tree line and froze, its head raised and eyes alert as it surveyed the area before crossing a small meadow and disappearing into the trees on the other side. Daniel tracked the deer's movement, the urge to hunt surfacing briefly before his humanity shut it down. How easy it would be to slip out the back door and shift without being seen, but as the sun rose higher in the sky, the urge to hunt faded. He knew he'd have to soon, though. It had been almost a week since his last kill. The longer he went without hunting, the harder it became to curb his urges, and his mountain lion became difficult to contain.

That was one of the things that appealed to him when Elsmed Fairchild explained Havenwood Falls and how the supernaturals coexisted with humans. He still had to be careful about displaying anything unusual in public, but protections were in place to avoid anything catastrophic. Knowing he would be leaving those safeguards behind, as well as his mate, hurt more than he imagined.

Despite the internal objections from his mountain lion, Daniel turned away from the window and crossed the bedroom. He hoisted his suitcase onto the bed and tossed in the few things he had unpacked.

isappointment hung around Colleen's neck like a weight, causing her shoulders to droop. She scrunched the paper bag from her lunch into a ball. With her book tucked under her arm, she walked along the brick walkway that wove through Town Square Park. As she left the square, she tossed the paper bag into a trash bin before waiting at the intersection to cross the street. Daniel hadn't shown up for lunch at the bench as she had hoped.

Apparently, the attraction was one-sided. She doubted he dreamed about her at night the way she did about him. Dreams that left her wanting. Dreams that made her entire body hum and her skin flush from heat that burned deep within. Every morning that week, she woke up feeling like she needed to go directly to church and confess her sins. Did impure thoughts count when they were your subconscious and the thoughts occurred in dreams? She was a good girl, still a virgin and planned on staying that way until her wedding night. The night before, she dreamt she was pregnant and Daniel stood behind her, cupping her swollen breasts. She woke up completely off kilter and longing to see the man who was still a stranger to her in reality, but so familiar to her in her dreams. By the time her lunch break rolled around, Colleen was practically crawling out of her skin with anticipation of seeing Daniel and getting to know him more. She kept checking her watch and scanning the square looking for him, her book abandoned on the bench next to her. But he never showed.

Sighing, she pushed open the door to her family's market. The bell chimed, announcing her entrance, and her dad looked up from the register.

"Hi, pumpkin, what's wrong?" He peered at her over his bifocals. Slapping a smile in place, she walked over to him.

"I'm fine, Daddy. Just a little tired is all. It sure is warm out there today." Nothing distracted her father more than talking about the weather. He could spend hours gabbing with customers over the ice storm of '39 or the drought of the summer of '46.

"They say it could be a record breaker. I better bring in an extra fan from out back." Just like that, he was gone, and Colleen let her smile fall as she slipped her store apron over her head and tied the strings around her slim waist.

At around two in the afternoon on Fridays is when business started to pick up. People stopped in for last minute dinner items or to grab things for the weekend. When school was in session, it became even busier at three, when students came in after school to raid the penny candy display and buy bottles of pop. Colleen was ringing people up when she overheard how Herschel Ross had been assaulted, nearly beaten to death and dumped in a dirt lot like a piece of garbage. When she heard Daniel's name mentioned, her ears perked up.

"That new foreman, Daniel McCabe, and Mickey Ahusaka found him. They carried him to the medical center, bless them," Hilary Monroe shared with Melba Ferguson, who stood in line behind her.

"What do we know about this Daniel McCabe?"

"He's a mystery. Patty Parker refuses to say. She acts all high and mighty, claiming employee confidentiality. I think we should pay him a visit." Melba Ferguson and Hilary Monroe were on the town's unofficial welcoming committee and two of the town's biggest busybodies.

"I think we should. Will he be around, though?"

"Patty did say he is going to step in and help run things until Herschel has recovered," Hilary added.

"Is he still in a coma?" Melba asked.

"A coma? I hadn't heard that!"

"Well, Cindy Adams heard it from Calista Harmon at the library bake sale this morning . . ."

Colleen rolled her eyes at the gossip mill. Calista owned Callie's Trinkets, a designer consignment store around the corner from the market. Her shop was frequented by just about every housewife in Havenwood Falls. Colleen knew from watching her mother's friends, whenever it was her mom's turn to host bridge club, that idle housewives loved to talk. By tomorrow, Herschel will have achieved martyr status even though he was probably one of the biggest jerks in town. Whenever he walked through the door of the market, she had to brace herself, because he inevitably would complain about something just to get a discount. He liked to wink at her and make suggestive comments, too. One piece of information she overheard, that Daniel was staying on as foreman, she hoped was true and not a rumor.

After closing, Colleen straightened items on the shelves and made notes on what needed to be restocked or reordered. She wiped down the cooler doors of the hundreds of fingerprints and smudges on the glass, counted down the drawer, and swept the floors. Her dad was in the back office when she went to retrieve her change of clothes. She was meeting her friend Sally Andrews at Burger Bar to talk about Peggy's wedding. Sally was a bridesmaid and had offered to help plan the bridal shower.

"All set?" her dad asked, looking up from the ledger when Colleen set the bag of cash and checks in front of him.

"Yes. I'm going to meet Sal at Burger Bar."

"That's nice. Be safe."

"I will, Daddy." She leaned over the desk and kissed the top of his head, which was already bent over the ledger again.

Grabbing her bag, she slipped into the restroom and changed out of her capris, slipping on a black pencil skirt that stopped just below her knees. She pulled on a hot-pink short-sleeved knit top. Looking in the mirror, she fluffed her hair and put on a little bit of makeup, just a touch of mascara and pink lipstick. She kept her saddle shoes on because her feet ached after standing all day.

Less than ten minutes later, she was entering Burger Bar, bypassing the area where people parked their cars and placed their orders. There was a separate dining area like a regular restaurant. The juke box was blaring "Be-Bop-A-Lula" by Gene Vincent, which put a little sway in her step as she crossed the black and white checkerboard floor to the booth where Sally was sitting. Her friend wore a yellow blouse that stood out like a beacon, making her easy to spot. Sally's thick brown hair was pulled back in a ponytail and she wore tortoiseshell horn-rimmed glasses that framed gorgeous hazel eyes. Sally was sipping on a Coke when Colleen slid into the booth.

"I'm starved!" Colleen proclaimed and snagged a menu from the end of the table, even though she already knew what she was going to order. She always ordered the same thing: a regular cheeseburger with pickles on the side, French fries, and a Coke.

Sally shook her head and laughed.

"What?" Colleen asked, scanning through the limited options.

"You always order the same thing. Why bother looking at the menu?"

Colleen shrugged and set the menu down on the Formica table. "Maybe something will jump out at me. You make me sound predictable."

Sally snorted. "That's because you are! That's okay. I still think you're swell."

Colleen frowned at her friend's opinion. She was too young to be considered predictable. Granted, there weren't a lot of options to do anything wild in Havenwood Falls, except run with the Greasers who liked to drag race on Blackstone Road late at night. There weren't any homes along the stretch that ran between County Road and Havenwood Heights, the upscale neighborhood where most of the old money families lived. She could spend time at the Haven Saloon, but she didn't want to just drink in a bar. That wasn't fun for her, and darts . . . well, darts could be dangerous. Throwing sharp objects through the air while inebriated didn't seem like a good idea.

A waitress came by to take her usual order and rushed off. Friday nights were always busy. Colleen glanced around to see who all was there. Herne Fairchild was sitting at the booth across from hers. He lived down the street from her and his looks always made her pause. With his blond hair, blue eyes, and bright white smile, he reminded her of a model from a Sears & Roebuck catalog, right down to his perfectly creased chinos.

The Bishop brothers, Ronan and Roman, were in another booth. They were a few years older than Colleen and both incredibly handsome, with dark hair and blue, stormy eyes. The Bishop family helped to found Havenwood Falls. With their looks and old money, either one of the brothers would have been a good catch, except there was something about them. They made her think of a bright red apple that looked perfect on the outside, but hid bruises and rotten spots just underneath the skin.

A man sat in the corner of the restaurant, and Colleen's lips parted in surprise. She had never seen Viktor Azimov at Burger Bar before. He was always an interesting character—very dark and brooding with thick black hair and eyes a bottomless midnight blue that stood out against skin as white as milk. In the winter, he wore a long black wool coat with a tall top hat, reminiscent of Abraham Lincoln, and he cut a striking figure whenever he walked through town. When Viktor passed by one of the gas-lit streetlamps, he seemed like a ghost from a different era. Now he wore a black leather jacket over a black shirt and denim jeans. His table was empty except for an untouched strawberry milkshake. Ice cream dripped down the side of the glass, and it looked like wax on a candle. He was in observation mode, too, and as if he felt Colleen watching, his dark eyes met hers. Blood rushed to her cheeks when she blushed, and she quickly looked away, embarrassed that she was caught staring.

The waitress returned with her dinner, and Colleen placed her napkin across her lap before diving in with both hands. Sally filled her in on how she spoke to Irina Petran at the Whisper Falls Inn and secured the dining area for Peggy's bridal shower. They were going with a traditional tea party theme and agreed the majestic Victorian inn would be the perfect venue. Once they mapped out a list of what needed to be done and who should be invited, Sally steered the conversation back to Colleen's predictability. Sally's hazel eyes glittered mischievously behind her glasses, and she flashed a sly grin.

"Sally, no. Whatever it is you're thinking, no. The last time you had that look, I snorted salt up my nose on a dare."

Sally pouted and crossed her arms on the table. "You're no fun."

Just then, someone came to a stop next their table, and Colleen's nose filled with the most delicious scent. It was like dark chocolate and raspberry. The two women peered up at the man standing beside them. Up close, Viktor Azimov literally took Colleen's breath away. His skin was flawless perfection. His lips were full, his cheekbones sharp, and his eyes hypnotizing. Once she met his gaze, she couldn't look away.

"Dance with me?" he asked and held out a hand to her. "In the Still of the Night" had just started playing on the jukebox. An internal voice urged her to look away and to decline his offer. She opened her mouth, starting to form the word no, when Sally answered for her.

"She'd love to. I was just telling her she needs to live a little."

Viktor smiled, exposing a glimpse of really bright teeth. They practically reflected the light.

"No. I really can't." Colleen managed to break eye contact and nervously fidgeted with the napkin on her lap.

"One dance can't hurt, Colleen. Go. I dare you." Sally winked at her, and Colleen sighed dramatically.

"Fine." She tossed the napkin on the table and slid out of the booth. "One dance." She placed her hand in Viktor's and almost yanked it back. His skin was ice cold. Before she could pull away, his fingers wrapped around hers, and he was tugging her over to a small area where tables had been moved to the side to make room for dancing.

Viktor moved in close and placed his hands on Colleen's hips. She put her hands on his shoulders. He was much taller than her, and she had to shuffle a bit closer to ease the stretch in her arms. His dark hair was just long enough to brush along the tops of her hands. Chocolate, raspberry, and the heavy scent of leather from his jacket washed over her, and Colleen closed her eyes. She didn't realize she was nuzzling his neck until the music switched to "Tutti Frutti." The upbeat tempo and Little Richard's raspy howl broke through her haze. Her heart was beating so fast, and she felt her cheeks heat with embarrassment. Viktor looked at her like he wanted to devour her, the way she had looked at her cheeseburger.

"Come with me," Viktor said. His voice was clear as day over the music, yet she could have sworn his full lips hadn't moved. Dazed, she nodded and turned to say goodbye to Sally, who was staring at them like the Cheshire cat.

"Go live a little, Colleen. Be unpredictable."

Viktor led her through the crowded restaurant and outside. The cool night air was a relief against her hot cheeks, and she took a few deep breaths that helped to clear her head. She came to a stop, and Viktor's hand almost slipped from hers, but he clamped down at the last second and turned to look at her. Once again, their eyes met, and any doubts about leaving with Viktor disappeared. Tucked in the back corner of the parking lot, a black Corvette shone in the moonlight. Had it been a cloudy night, the convertible would have been camouflaged in the shadows of two cottonwood trees.

Viktor held the door open for her, and Colleen sunk down onto red leather. The convertible top was down, and Colleen held her hair back to keep it from blowing in her face. Taking a left on Farnsworth Road, just before the turnoff to Blackstone Road, Viktor sped along until he reached the covered bridge. The road led to an abandoned mine and was hardly ever used. Inside the bridge, the sound of rushing water from Mathews River was amplified. Leaving the radio and headlights on, Viktor put the car in park and in one swift movement, wrapped his arm around Colleen's shoulders and leaned in close.

"You smell amazing," he said and buried his nose in her hair. "Did you know hamburgers are a good source of iron?"

What a strange thing to say, she thought, but was immediately distracted when Viktor slid a hand beneath her top and skimmed his fingers along her back, his icy touch making her shiver.

"Let me kiss you," he breathed in her ear. "I need to taste you." The longing in his voice made her breath hitch. Her thoughts weren't her own from that point on.

"Yes, please. Kiss me," she practically begged, slamming an imaginary door on the inner voice that was screaming in her head, telling her to run, effectively reducing it to muffled sounds of protest.

Viktor's mouth descended upon hers. His tongue teased the seam of her lips, and she opened for him. His tongue was cool at first, but after a few seconds of the deeper kiss, everything warmed up. He sucked her bottom lip between his teeth, and she gasped at the pinching sensation, but the pain quickly changed to pleasure that traveled down deep. He sucked and sucked. With each pull on her lip, something built inside of her that felt incredibly wrong, but also so good.

A sharp cry of a hawk pierced the night, startling Colleen. The way the call echoed, it sounded close, like the hawk was under the covered bridge with them. It startled her enough that she pulled away. Viktor released her lip with a pop, and she scooted away from him, appalled at her brazen behavior. Raising her fingers to her lips, she discovered they were hot and swollen to the touch. Viktor's eyes looked almost completely black. Blaming it on a trick of the shadows, she quickly looked away.

"I'd like to go home now," she said, her voice huskier than usual. Viktor brushed her hair away from her cheek, his hand much warmer than before, and she felt him observing her as if waiting for her to change her mind. She refused to look at him, afraid of losing control again. Sally wanted Colleen to live a little; well, this definitely had to count. She licked her lips, tasting chocolate and something rich, almost metallic.

Honoring her request, Viktor drove her home. They didn't say anything to each other, and as soon as he pulled up in front of her house, she climbed out of the car and ran up the brick walkway to the front porch. She heard the low purr of the Corvette as he left, and she ducked inside her house, staying in the foyer until her breathing and her pulse were under control. It was after eleven, and her family was already asleep. She quietly climbed the stairs, avoiding the spot that always squeaked, and once Colleen was in her bedroom with the door closed, she collapsed on the bed. Touching her lips again, she discovered they were still swollen and a little sore. Shame washed over her when she realized she had never even properly introduced herself to Viktor. He didn't know her name. They didn't know anything about each other, and she let him paw at her like she was easy pickings. A vision of Daniel popped into her head, and the sense of shame deepened, as if she had actually been unfaithful to yet another man who was a stranger.

"I'm losing my mind," she whispered and curled up in a ball in the middle of her bed, where she fell into a fitful sleep.

CHAPTER 8

$\mathcal{J}$ust as Daniel had climbed into bed, ready to get some sleep for his long drive back to Fort Collins the next morning, there was a sharp knock on the front door. He looked at his clock. It was almost eleven, and since he didn't know too many people in town, he had no idea who was paying him a visit. Lifting his nose in the air, he breathed in deep, separating the layers of scents around him and picking up on a familiar one: Mickey.

He opened the door to find Mickey wearing shorts and nothing else. His hair was free of the leather band he usually tied it back with when they were working. It hung loose in thick dark waves around his broad shoulders. Sensing agitation rolling off his friend, Daniel quickly invited him in.

"What's going on?"

"The other night you said your mate was Colleen Campbell, right?"

"Yes, why?"

Mickey paced the tiny living room, his heavy footsteps causing the hardwood floor to vibrate.

"She was making out with Viktor Asimov. He was feeding off of her."

Daniel's blood ran cold, and he placed his hands on Mickey's shoulders, forcing him to stop pacing.

"Who is Viktor, and what the hell do you mean he was feeding?"

"Viktor is the head of the Gothic vampire nest here in Havenwood Falls. I think he compelled her to go with him."

"Tell me everything," Daniel demanded. His hands curled into fists. Claws burst through the tips of his fingers, piercing his palms, the pain helping him to keep from shifting as Mickey told him he had been flying overhead. That's what he did—he was a watcher and kept watch from above. He saw Colleen leave Burger Bar with the vampire. He followed them to the covered bridge. His cry had interrupted them when things were getting hot and heavy.

"When they drove away, I flew right here. If she's your fated mate, you need to know. Viktor tends to lure humans in and make them his blood slaves."

"The Court allows this?"

Mickey shrugged. "He doesn't kill them, and he needs blood to survive. He might be looking to recruit Colleen."

Daniel growled, which his inner cat echoed. Stripping out of his underwear, he let his mountain lion free and shifted there in the living room. He didn't even feel the pain this time, he was so focused on getting to Colleen and making sure she was safe. He bounded out the front door and heard a hawk cry overhead. Looking up, he barely made out Mickey's dark wings against the night sky.

Daniel ran along the river until he reached the trees that surrounded Colleen's backyard. He paused, ears flicking back and forth as he listened for any witnesses or threats. All was quiet except for the rustle of feathers as Mickey settled on a branch above his head. Crouched down low and alert, he stole forward and approached the back of the house. A faint trace of vampire scent was in the air, and he followed it around the side of the house to the curb. The vampire hadn't breached the walls. This was good.

Mine ran on repeat in his head at the idea of a vampire touching his mate, taking her blood. His cat wanted to send a message, and before Daniel could assert his will over his animal, he was spraying the front bushes and proceeded to spray the perimeter of the house, marking his territory with musky urine. Daniel ran back into the woods and traced his steps back to the cabin, with Mickey following him. As soon as he was inside his cabin, he shifted back to his human form. Mickey flew in behind and shifted mid-air, coming to a running stop like a skydiver. He doubled over laughing, slapping at his bare thigh.

"You peed on her bushes! That's a riot!"

"Just staking my claim."

"So, you've decided then, you're going to pursue her?" Mickey asked as he pulled on his shorts that had been left on the floor.

"Yeah, I am." At that proclamation, his inner cat let out a contented purr and settled down. His reaction to another supernatural sniffing around his mate made it clear, and he couldn't deny it any longer. As far as Colleen being a human, he'd have to find a way to make it work.

Daniel bent over and picked up his underwear and slipped them on, covering up his nakedness. Nudity didn't bother shifters, though, so he wasn't uncomfortable around Mickey. He understood.

"All right, I need to get some shut-eye. It's at least a seven-hour drive tomorrow."

"So, are you going to stay on as foreman, run things until Mr. Ross is back?"

Daniel nodded. "I'm going to get my mom. She needs to see Havenwood Falls. I think she'll be happy here. We'll be back sometime Sunday."

"See you then."

As Mickey turned to leave, Daniel called to him. "Thanks for looking out for Colleen. Do you mind keeping an eye on her while I'm gone?"

Mickey grinned. "That's what friends are for." With a final wave, he slipped out into the night.

Shutting the door behind his friend, Daniel smiled. Assimilating to life in Havenwood Falls was surprisingly easy. Mickey was proving to be a loyal friend, already looking out for his interests. It had been a long time since Daniel allowed himself the luxury of friendship.

CHAPTER 9

Something hit the side of the house beneath Colleen's bedroom window, waking her up. Sunlight streamed in through her windows, the pink gingham curtains blowing in a light breeze. She climbed out of bed and crossed her room to see what hit the house. Looking down on the backyard below, she saw her mom, hose in hand, spraying down her roses. The sound that had woken Colleen was the water hitting the house.

Colleen quickly showered and dressed for work before going downstairs. Her mom had left a place setting at the small dinette table, which was located in the far corner of the kitchen, close to the back door. She poured some Chex in a bowl and grabbed a bottle of milk from the refrigerator. Taking her breakfast with her outside, she discovered her sister was sitting on the small deck, reading.

"Mom, didn't you water the roses yesterday?" Colleen asked, taking a seat next to her sister.

Her mom stopped the spray of water and glanced up, tilting her wide brimmed gardening hat away from her eyes so she could see.

"I did, but some animal sprayed them last night—sprayed around the entire house—and it smells awful."

Colleen sniffed the air and shrugged. "It doesn't smell bad, almost like cinnamon or cloves."

Kelly snorted. "Cinnamon? Have you gone mad? It smells like a bunch of feral cats had a party last night."

"Are you sure it wasn't David, Mom? You know he liked to pee in the backyard when he was little. What if the neighbors saw him?" Kelly hid her laughing face behind her book.

"Girls," their mom responded with a shake of her head, "I'm pretty sure I would have heard about your brother peeing in the bushes by now. Especially since I already heard about you leaving Burger Bar with Viktor Asimov last night."

Her mom stood with her hands on her hips. She was still holding the hose in one hand, looped out from her side like a lasso.

"Really?" Kelly's eyes were huge as she leaned toward her sister.

Colleen blushed and groaned. "Honestly, this town. Rumors spread faster than wildfire. It's just like Peyton Place. It's a wonder anyone can keep a secret around here!"

"Are you and Viktor in looooove?" Kelly asked, making kissy sounds at her.

"No. It was one kiss, and I don't plan on seeing him again."

"Good," her mom said. "I won't have any of my daughters running around with strange men. Your father and I didn't raise you to be that way."

"Ugh, honestly, mother, you think anyone who dresses differently and who doesn't attend at least one church social is strange." Colleen stood up, her empty bowl in hand. "I'm going to be late for work." She stomped across the deck, kissy sounds following her into the house.

Pedaling her bicycle to work helped to calm her down, and by the time she was propping her bike up against the lamppost in front of the store, she had a genuine smile on her face.

How quickly that smile faded when she overheard several of the ladies who were in her mother's bridge club gossiping about Daniel. Two of the women, Melba Ferguson and Hilary Monroe, were full of information. Apparently, Melba had gone over to the cabin where Daniel was staying with one of her famous apple pies to welcome him to Havenwood Falls, but was too late. She saw him loading a suitcase into his truck right before he drove out of town.

"Such a shame," Melba said. "I'm beginning to wonder if Miller's Plaza will ever be built."

"Oh, don't you worry, Melba," Patty Parker chimed in. She reached across Hilary and plucked a can of Kitchen Klenzer off the shelf. She briefly examined the label before placing the can in her basket. "I have it on good authority that Daniel is staying on as foreman. He just went to go pick up his mother to bring her here for a visit."

"So he does have family?" Hilary asked.

"Yes, it's just him and his mother. His father died a few years ago. He's been taking care of her ever since—he simply dotes on her."

"Oh, the poor dear."

"So tragic," Hilary said with a sigh.

"She's lucky to have such a devoted son," Mrs. Wilson said with a sniff. Her son, Wally, had left Havenwood Falls right after he graduated high school and never came back.

"He isn't married. I wonder who we can introduce him to? He'd make a fine match for someone."

The ladies moved to the next aisle, and Colleen strained to hear who they were hypothesizing about. The very idea of them playing matchmaker with Daniel made her want to yell at them to mind their own business, that Daniel was hers. Surprised at the possessiveness of her thoughts, Colleen ground her teeth together to avoid an embarrassing outburst and regarded the gossipers through narrow eyes. Patty stepped forward to the register, setting her basket down on the counter.

"Relax, dear." She placed her hand on top of Colleen's, which was curled into a tight fist. "You have nothing to worry about," she said cryptically and winked.

Before Colleen could ask her what she meant, Patty was walking away, the brown paper grocery bag tucked against her hip like she was carrying a child.

That afternoon was busy since it was the second Saturday of the month, which was when Movies in the Park took place. Havenwood Falls was too small to justify a drive-in movie theater, so the city council and local businesses created the next best thing. Practically the whole town gathered to watch a recent family-friendly flick, and then adults and teenagers stayed for the second movie. That weekend they were showing *Tarzan and the Lost Safari* first, followed by *I Was a Teenage Werewolf*. The latter had created quite the buzz with all of the female high school students because the actor, Michael Landon, was positively dreamy. Colleen laughed out loud when she realized that what her brother David and his friend saw by the river the other day wasn't a wolf with glowing eyes, but just a figment of their imagination. They had been obsessed with this movie. Hollywood and books featured creatures of the night and shape-shifting beasts, but she knew they didn't exist in real life.

The market usually closed at seven, but by six thirty it was dead, so her dad decided to close early. Colleen stayed at the front of the store cleaning and straightening for over an hour while her dad went to the back office to do some paperwork. When she was done, she peeked her head in his office and waited until he finished counting out a stack of money before telling him goodbye.

"I'll be over in a bit, pumpkin. Save me some popcorn."

Colleen promised she would and reminded him to put her bicycle in the back of the station wagon. After hanging up her apron and grabbing her purse, she went back through the market and out the front door, making sure to lock it. She stepped onto the sidewalk and froze in place when she saw a sleek black Corvette parked alongside the curb. The convertible top was down, and Viktor sat behind the steering wheel. He had an arm stretched out along the front seat and his other arm propped against the top of the door. This position put him at the perfect angle to watch the market entrance.

"Viktor, what are you doing here?"

"I came to see you." He got out of his car and moved toward her. The way he walked, with his intense dark eyes focused on her, he came across as predatory, and she instinctively took a step back. Just then, she heard someone running, and she turned to see Mickey

Ahusaka running down the sidewalk, his hair streaming behind him like a thick, black ribbon. He came to a sudden stop, in between her and Viktor.

"Shoot, you're closed?" he asked, looking over her shoulder at the darkened storefront window.

"Yes, we are. Sorry."

Mickey frowned and let out a sigh. "My mom called because my little brother is sick. Since I live around the corner, she asked me to pick up some Pepto-Bismol."

Colleen glanced at her watch. The movie would be starting at eight thirty, once the sun set. She still had time.

"Come on," she said and pulled the store keys out of her purse. "We can't let Nahele suffer all night." Unlocking the door, she flicked on the lights and called to her dad, knowing he would have heard the bell above the door. She crossed to the hygiene and home remedy aisle to grab a bottle of Pepto. "Is one bottle enough?" she asked Mickey.

When he didn't answer, she looked up to discover he wasn't in the store. Walking over to the window, she peered out and saw him talking to Viktor. It didn't look like a friendly conversation either, by the way they squared off. Seconds later, Viktor spun around and climbed into his car. Mickey watched him leave before coming into the store.

"Sorry," he said.

"What was that all about?"

"Nothing." Mickey shrugged nonchalantly, and Colleen didn't believe him for a second. She knew male posturing when she saw it, and if she wasn't mistaken, Mickey scared Viktor off, but why? "Thanks for opening the store back up. You're a real peach." He flashed a brilliant smile, which stood out against his darker skin.

They walked out together. Mickey stood with his shoulders hunched and hands in the pockets of his Levi's as he waited for her to lock the door. She pulled on the handle, double checking that it was secure.

"Well, good night, Mickey. I hope that fixes your brother right up." Colleen made to leave.

"Going to the movies?" Mickey asked, catching up to her at the crosswalk. Colleen nodded and started across the street, since there weren't any cars in sight. "I'll walk with you."

"Don't you have to get that to your brother?" She glanced at his hand holding the bottle of pink medicine.

"I'll see you safely to the park first."

"If you insist." Colleen shook her head, unable to imagine what dangers Mickey thought she'd encounter on the short walk.

Picking her way in between people sitting on the grass, using only the flickering light from the giant movie screen to see, Colleen made her way to the large oak tree, where her family had planned to sit. Mickey followed her like a shadow. Pausing occasionally, Colleen was distracted by the movie. She had arrived just as a plane had crashed and Tarzan, a big strapping beast of a man wearing only a loincloth, heroically rescued the passengers. She found her family sitting on a large plaid picnic blanket. Her mom had brought a Tupperware container of popcorn and a cooler full of bottles of Coca-Cola. Once Colleen was situated next to her sister, Mickey whispered good night.

"What was that all about?" Kelly asked. "Are you kissing him, too?"

"No!" she hissed, thankful it was dark so nobody saw her cheeks flare red.

Her dad joined them not too long after, and they finished watching the movie. Once it was over, her parents left. They didn't have any interest in watching a horror movie about a bunch of teenagers.

"We already know what living with teenagers is like," her dad joked before leaving. As soon as they left, Kelly slipped away to hang with her friends and to swoon over Michael Landon. David's friend Billy appeared out of nowhere and immediately descended upon the popcorn. Colleen stood up to stretch, and that's when she noticed Mickey's brother sitting not even twenty feet away, looking as healthy as a horse. This caused her brow to wrinkle in confusion. Between Patty, Viktor, and Mickey, just what the hell was going on?

CHAPTER 10

*H*aving only been back in Fort Collins for one night, Daniel already missed the peacefulness of Havenwood Falls. He hadn't realized how loud and confining city living could be. Being around more people, more traffic, more noise, more everything made his skin crawl. How quickly he had adjusted to his temporary cabin in the woods.

Shuffling into the kitchen, following the smell of coffee percolating on the stove, he smiled when he saw his mom stirring a pan full of eggs.

"I missed your cooking," he said, kissing her on the cheek before reaching over her head to grab a mug out of the cabinet.

"Soon you'll find yourself a wife, and you'll only want her cooking," she teased. At the mention of a wife, Daniel's shoulders tightened. He felt them draw up like he was a puppet on a string. Of course, his mom noticed. She didn't miss anything. "Daniel?"

Sighing, he sat down at the table and wrapped his large hands around the mug. He hadn't told her about Colleen, because he was still coming to terms with finding his mate. His mom carried the pan of eggs over and dropped several scoopfuls on his plate. A platter of bacon and toast was already on the table. He grabbed several slices as his mom sat down across from him.

"Is there something you're not telling me?" she pried.

Daniel finished chewing and swallowing before answering. "I found my mate, Mom, in Havenwood Falls."

"Oh, that's wonderful, Danny!" She set her fork down and reached across the table, giving his hand a squeeze. "What are the odds—a new job and finding your mate, all in the same week." She must have seen the conflict written on his face, because when she looked at him, her expression morphed into one of concern. "What's wrong? This should be a joyous occasion."

"I know, it's just, well, it's complicated."

"How so?"

"She's human."

His mom paused and slowly brought the napkin up from her lap and wiped the corner of her mouth. "Well, I can see that would be a complication if she doesn't know shifters exist, but it won't be the first interspecies relationship. We're compatible with humans."

"That's just it, Mom. We're not compatible. Humans are dangerous. What if I tell her and she flips out? Next thing you know, I'm either being put down or I'm held prisoner in a government lab somewhere, being experimented on."

"Oh, Danny, no! God damn him!"

Daniel sat back in shock when his mom threw her napkin on the table and stood up.

"Who?"

"Your father."

"What? Why?" Now it was Daniel's turn to jump up out of his chair.

She started to clear the table, angrily scraping food into the trash can. Filling up the sink with hot sudsy water, she tossed the dishes in, sending a burst of bubbles into the air. Daniel had seen this reaction many times before. Whenever his mom was angry or upset, she cleaned. She scrubbed every surface until she calmed down. It took a few minutes for that moment to come. Finally, with her head lowered and shoulders hunched, she dropped the dishcloth in the soapy water.

"I love your father, but . . . ," she started, turning around to face him. Tears shimmered in her blue eyes, but they didn't spill. "His mistrust, his fear of humans—he poisoned you with it. His experience in Sunset Creek shaped his entire life. I could never understand, because my childhood was normal, safe. I've never felt hunted or threatened. Your father and I argued something fierce about how he was letting his prejudices rub off on you." She sighed and smoothed the skirt on her pale blue dress before crossing the room to sit back down in her chair. "Not all humans are bad. You know that. You've worked alongside them, gone to school with them."

"I know that," Daniel said, sitting down across from her. "But I kept my distance and for good reason. Remember, in Kentucky, that colored man who was beaten for making a pass at a white woman? Remember the segregation? All because of different skin color." Daniel cringed whenever he saw a sign posted at a business announcing it was for whites only. It didn't take much to imagine a sign that read "humans only." He didn't see that ever happening in Havenwood Falls, though. There the supernatural went about their lives unbeknownst to the humans.

"Don't you realize how hypocritical you sound?" she asked. "You're just as prejudiced, and I'm sorry I didn't raise you better. Despite our arguments, it wasn't my place to go against your father. There was no convincing him, and he became set in his ways, but there has to be hope for you, Danny. This girl is your mate for a reason. Human or shifter, you have to learn to accept her."

"I'm trying, Mom. I'm going to ask Colleen out on a date and see how things go. With her being human, is it even possible she can feel the same mating call? Besides, someone else has been sniffing around her, and I can't let that stand." If he was in his mountain lion form, his hackles would have been raised. Just the thought of another man, let alone another species, making moves on his mate made him see red.

"Daniel Matthew McCabe, you need to go claim your mate!" His mom chastised him and stood up. "Let's go. We need to get you back to Havenwood Falls. Good thing I packed already. I can't wait to see this town."

Daniel went to his room and grabbed more clothes from his closet. The Court had granted him a special pass to leave Havenwood Falls without immediately losing his memories of the town. It had taken a few minutes for his temporary tattoo to be enhanced, and the instructions were firm: as long as he was back before midnight on Monday, he would be fine. Looking around his room, he knew it wouldn't take much to move. They had moved so much that their possessions were few, and they often never unpacked completely. His parents' china set, a wedding present from his mom's parents, was stowed away in a box in the hallway closet. His bedroom walls were bare, with the exception of the green-and-brown-striped wallpaper. The few pictures he had were on the top of his four-drawer dresser. There was a large framed picture of his mom and dad when they were first mated. Another picture was of Daniel when he was three years old. He sat in a straight-backed rocking chair with his baby sister, Katherine, on his lap, holding on to her so tight you could see the strain in his smile. According to his parents, Katherine passed away just six months later from pneumonia. He had vague memories of her, mainly just her scent, which was imprinted on him. After the first warm spring rain caused blossoms to open and sweetened the air, he always thought of her.

Snapping out of the memories, he closed his suitcase. No, it wouldn't take much to move, and he had a feeling he'd be moving to Havenwood Falls permanently. His mountain lion rumbled in agreement.

WHEN DANIEL PULLED up to the cabin later that afternoon, Mickey was waiting for him. He sat on the front steps wearing Levi's that were folded at the bottom, forming wide cuffs. He was barefoot, and his shirt was partially unbuttoned. Daniel recognized the disheveled look as someone who had recently shifted and put their clothes on in a hurry.

He climbed out of the truck and briefly stretched before walking around to the passenger side to open the door for his mom. She'd brain him if he forgot his manners.

Mickey sauntered over to meet them.

"Mickey, this is my mom, Margaret McCabe. Mom, this is Mickey Ahusaka. We work together."

"Pleasure to meet you, Mrs. McCabe," Mickey said, shaking his mom's hand.

"Oh please, call me Maggie. It's nice to meet you. Daniel doesn't have many friends." This set Mickey off, and he started laughing.

"Mom!" Daniel said with a groan, and his mom walked away giggling.

"Were you planning on waiting out here all day until I got back?" Daniel asked Mickey as they unloaded the truck.

"Nah, I was flying, keeping an eye on things, and saw you coming."

"Is everything okay?" he asked, while his mom was busy unpacking the food from the cooler into the icebox. Mickey told him how he warned off Viktor from Colleen the night before.

"Thanks, man, I owe you."

"No big." He shrugged. "I'm glad I was there. Viktor definitely had his eye on her."

"Where is she now, do you know?"

"She's at a church picnic with her family. I doubt any vampire will try anything on church property."

Daniel nodded in agreement and went back outside to close up his truck.

"I'm going to ask her out tomorrow," he told his friend, who had followed him.

Mickey stayed for a few minutes, but soon left so Daniel and his mom could get settled. The cabin was small. Daniel moved out of the one bedroom to the loft. Not quite a second floor, the loft was basically a small platform that extended out from the wall separating the living room from the bathroom. It cleared the ceiling by about four feet and overlooked the living room. The only access was a narrow ladder, which Daniel climbed up before tossing a pillow and sleeping bag onto the wood floor.

After one night of sleeping in the cramped space, Daniel decided that if they were going to stay in Havenwood Falls, they were going to need a bigger place.

The next morning, his mom drove into town with him. He showed her around the jobsite before she ventured off to explore, taking the truck in case she did any shopping. Daniel chuckled to himself as she drove away, because he knew there was no doubt that she would shop.

As noon approached, he found himself checking his watch more frequently. He'd normally be starving, his breakfast long worked off, but nerves kept his appetite at bay. What if Colleen rejected him? She could very possibly not be attracted to him or affected by the mating call at all. He had no idea what to expect since she was human. Finally, it was lunch time, and he dismissed the crew. Mickey clapped him on the back and wished him luck. Daniel needed it—he had no idea if Colleen would even be there.

Worry was replaced with nerves as he approached the bench and saw the back of her head, her blond hair a beacon in the shade of the tree. As he drew closer, he saw she was reading. He had already noted that was one of her hobbies, and he wanted to build her a bookcase. Hell, when they made a home together, he'd build her an entire library. *Way to put the cart in front of the horse, McCabe*, he cautioned himself and cleared his throat when he came to a stop in front of the bench.

"Is this seat taken?" he asked, and Colleen jerked her head up in surprise. When she saw him, she smiled a brilliant smile that was all dimples.

"It's all yours," she said and shifted over slightly to give him more room. She was wearing tan shorts that barely came to mid-thigh and showed off her gorgeous long toned legs. "I heard you left town?"

"Only to go pick up my mom and bring her here to visit."

She seemed relieved at that. Daniel noticed her posture soften a bit as she relaxed against the bench.

"I should warn you that you're quite the talk of the town, and the busybodies are already making matchmaking plans. You should have run while you had the chance." She teased, but he detected an edge to her tone. Was it jealousy?

"What if I already found a match?" he asked her, reaching out and brushing a stray curl away from her cheek. Her lips parted as he tucked the hair behind her ear and gently trailed his fingertips down her neck. Her eyes, deep brown with striations of amber, seemed to darken, and her eyelids lowered slightly.

"What do you mean?" Colleen whispered and grabbed his hand as he was pulling away. Everything snapped into focus the moment her fingers entwined with his. His hands were calloused and rough from work. They were darker than hers, tanned and freckled from hours spent in the sun. Hers were pale and soft, yet they fit together perfectly.

"I know you don't know me and that I'm not from around here, but I feel drawn to you—that we're connected somehow. I'm not going to ask if you feel it too, but I am going to ask if you'd be interested in going on a date?" He watched her closely to gauge her reaction, fully expecting her to retreat at some point, but she never did. Instead she squeezed his hand and smiled.

"Yes! I am very interested." Her smile was brighter than the sun and the most dazzling he had ever seen. Her natural beauty left him awestruck. The moment she said yes, a tightening in his chest released, and it was like he could breathe again. "And yes, I feel the connection, too."

Her cheeks flushed red when she said this, and she looked away. Her scent changed, heavy with pheromones and arousal, causing Daniel's nostrils to flare. Keeping himself in check was akin to wrestling an angry alligator. Desire coursed through his veins after the first inhale. She wanted him as much as he wanted her.

Colleen met his gaze again, and she slid closer, not breaking eye contact. When she sucked her lower lip in between her teeth, he was done. Closing the gap between them, he reached out with his free hand and cradled her cheek, his fingers sliding into her soft hair.

Closing her eyes, she leaned her head into his touch and released her lower lip, exhaling a soft sigh.

Initially, Daniel wanted to wait until they were on a date to kiss her, but the longer they touched and the closer they moved together, the more he felt his control slipping, like a tethered rope giving way thread by thread. Any concerns about her being human vanished, replaced with the overall sensation that this was right. Tilting her head slightly, he leaned in and captured her lips with his.

He'd heard others tell of their experience kissing their mate for the first time, and he'd thought they were exaggerating. Nothing could have prepared him for the earthquake that shook him from within— the force of two souls coming together and colliding. Not until they consummated would they be fully joined, and Daniel ached for that joining with every cell of his two beings.

A car horn blasted from nearby, breaking their connection, and they slowly separated. Colleen's cheeks were flushed a gorgeous pink, and her lips glistened from their kiss. Brown eyes, dark with lust, stared back at him. Drawing in a shaky breath, she moved back, slipping free of the gentle hold he had on her head.

"Wow," she whispered and touched her lips.

"Wow is right." He raised their joined hands and placed a kiss on the back of her hand. That's when he noticed the time.

"Crap, I'm going to be late."

"I'll walk with you," she announced and stood up with him, slipping her hand in his. It felt so natural, like something she had done countless times before.

"You don't have to work?"

"No, I had today off, but I came here hoping you'd show."

"I'm glad you did."

"Me too." She grinned and tugged on his arm, urging him to move. They walked hand in hand through the square and crossed Main Street at the crosswalk by the high school. Daniel told her how he and Mickey had found Herschel Ross. She gasped at the gory details and squeezed his hand when she thanked him for taking care of the man.

When they reached the entrance to the parking lot for Burger Bar, Daniel turned to say goodbye to Colleen, but she wanted to see the jobsite, so they continued on. Catcalls and whistles greeted them. Mickey stood in front of the crew with a big grin on his face.

"Way to go, boss!" he said and clapped Daniel on the shoulder. Colleen turned beet red at the attention.

"Yeah, yeah, whatever. Get to work," Daniel said with a laugh. The beginnings of the structure had been put in place, steel beams forming a grid. They had a tight schedule to meet the developer's deadline. Daniel explained this to Colleen as he took her inside the Airstream, which he had cleaned considerably in Herschel's absence, and showed her the blueprints and plans. Her face scrunched up like she had bitten into a lemon when she looked at the rendering.

"What's wrong?" he asked.

"It just looks so industrial. For the longest time before you started building, this empty dirt lot just sat here. Everything was barren. So many trees and shrubs were cleared to make room. I just wish the environment was taken into consideration."

"I agree with you."

"You do?" She looked up at him. They were side by side, leaning over the table, and he couldn't resist moving over and kissing the tip of her slightly upturned nose.

"I do. If I ever build something of my own, that's not part of someone else's design, I'm going to preserve as much of the natural environment as possible."

Smiling, she leaned into him, resting her head on his shoulder. "That's good."

Reluctantly, Daniel had to say goodbye. He needed to work, and he liked to be alongside his crew.

"Friday night. I'll pick you up for our date at say seven o'clock?"

"You know where I live?" Colleen asked.

Daniel, realizing his misstep quickly, recovered by laughing and smacking his forehead. "Of course not. That was going to be my next question."

Colleen found a piece of paper on the table and grabbed a pen.

She wrote down her address in perfect penmanship. She even drew a little map.

They left the trailer, and Daniel walked her to the edge of the Burger Bar parking lot, where she turned and, standing on tiptoes, pecked him on the cheek. This caused another chorus of catcalls and whistles, which made her blush again. Daniel watched her walk away, amazed at how easy she was to be around. Having overcome the obstacle of asking her out with success, the next hurdle was the actual date, and if their relationship progressed, that's when Daniel would face the biggest challenge of all: telling Colleen he occasionally turned into a mountain lion and that she was his fated mate.

CHAPTER 11

The walk home was a blur. Colleen basically floated down Main Street, ignoring anyone who called her name. She was too busy walking on clouds to stop. Her entire body hadn't stopped humming since Daniel kissed her. While she'd had her share of kisses, none of them compared.

As soon as the front screen door slammed closed, her mom appeared at the end of the hallway by the kitchen. She wore an apron over her dress and held a wooden spoon in one hand. "There you are! Sally has been calling here for you nonstop. She's getting on my last nerve."

As if on cue, the phone rang. Colleen dashed into the living room to answer it.

"Hello, Campbell residence."

"Colleen, you have some explaining to do!" Sally's shrill voice practically shattered her eardrum.

"What are you talking about?"

"Oh, don't be a ditz! I'm talking about that stud I saw you looking cozy with, strolling through town holding hands, and not one word to your best friend. How long have you been dating?"

"Um, well, we're not . . . not really. We're going on our first date on Friday."

"Gee whiz, Colleen! You all looked real comfortable with each other."

Colleen sighed and sat down on the sofa, curling her legs underneath and settling in to tell Sally everything: how it felt like she and Daniel were old friends, not new acquaintances, how he smelled better than anything, and that was when he was sweaty. She stopped short of telling her about the dreams. Those were a little too personal to share.

"You have it bad," Sally said with a note of longing.

"I think," Colleen peered around to make sure no one was listening before whispering into the phone, "I think Daniel's the one."

"Whoa."

"I know."

They chatted for a few more minutes, and Sally made her swear she would keep her updated. After she hung up the phone, Colleen remained on the sofa, lost deep in thought. She thought love at first sight was a myth reserved for fairy tales, but the way Daniel energized her, listened to her, and actually looked at her, and especially the way he kissed her, made her believe it was possible. Without even searching for him, she had found the perfect man.

Apparently keeping her newfound bliss a secret was easier said than done. The moment she sat down at the dinner table that night, her parents zeroed in on her.

"What?" she asked, the fork in her hand paused halfway to her mouth when she noticed her mom and dad looking at her.

"You look different," her mom answered.

Setting the fork down, Colleen patted at her hair, but everything felt in place. She smoothed her hands over her white sleeveless blouse, but all the buttons were secure. Picking up the cloth napkin from her lap, she dabbed at her mouth, but it came away clean. "Different how?"

"You're practically glowing," her dad said, which made her mom gasp.

"Colleen Morgan Campbell, are you pregnant?"

This question caused her brother to spray the milk he was

drinking all over the freshly pressed tablecloth, and Kelly's mouth dropped open.

"What? No! Oh my word, how could you think that?" Colleen's bliss extinguished with that one question. Anger and embarrassment made her cheeks burn. "For your information, I'm still a virgin, Mother."

Poor David practically choked on this announcement.

"All right, rein it in," her dad said loudly. She looked over at him, and his cheeks were just as red. "Pumpkin, we were just making an observation."

This was one of those moments where Colleen realized she was outgrowing her childhood home. She was an adult, yet as long as she lived with her parents, they were going to treat her like a child. Even at work, while she was the assistant manager for the market, her dad still called her pumpkin. She didn't have the typical boss/employee relationship. Realizations like these made it hard to breathe, like the walls were closing in on her.

"I'm fine, Daddy. Can I be excused?"

He nodded, and she folded her napkin, setting it back on the table before grabbing her plate and bringing it into the kitchen. She scraped her half-eaten meal into the garbage and set the plate on the counter next to the sink. Movement caught her eye, and she looked out the window into the backyard. Dusk was setting in, and the shadows were long as the last bit of sunshine filtered through the trees. There, along the tree line, she saw it—a gorgeous mountain lion. Its amber eyes seemed to be locked on her. Instead of fear, she felt comfort with its presence. They stared at each other until she heard someone coming in from the dining room. Looking over her shoulder, she saw her sister.

"What are you doing?" Kelly asked.

"Come look at this mountain lion." Colleen waved her sister over to the window, but when they both peered through the screen, the big cat was gone. "Oh, too bad you didn't get to see it. He was beautiful."

"He?"

"Maybe, I don't know. I saw him in the backyard before one night when I couldn't sleep."

"Huh, I bet that's the animal that sprayed mom's bushes. Should we leave a saucer of cream out for it? Adopt a big cat as a family pet? Here kitty, kitty!" Kelly called.

"You're such a goof!" Colleen said with a laugh.

"What are you two carrying on about?" their dad interrupted.

"Colleen just saw a mountain lion in the backyard. We're going to adopt it."

His eyebrows rose with surprise, and then his expression grew serious. "You girls be careful. Wild animals shouldn't be approached. You let me know if you see this animal again, Colleen. I don't like the idea of a mountain lion sniffing around our house and getting comfortable."

"Oh, Daddy, relax. Remember, they were here first." With one final look out the window, Colleen left the kitchen. Grabbing her book from the table in the foyer, she turned on the porch light and slipped out the door to read on the porch. Within minutes she was lost within the pages of *Lord of the Flies*, her knuckles white from clenching the book so hard. The descent into cruelty and chaos as boys turned against each other and darkness and lightness of humanity fought for dominance kept her enthralled. So enthralled she didn't hear twigs breaking and leaves rustling as the mountain lion moved close and lay down between the bushes and porch, hidden from view.

CHAPTER 12

Throughout the week Daniel kept a nightly vigil on Colleen, needing to be close to her. Once her bedroom light turned off, he went back to the cabin. His mom actually joined him one night. The older she became, the less she needed to shift, but ever since she had arrived in Havenwood Falls, she told him the call to the wilderness was hard to resist. He enjoyed hunting alongside her. They took down a deer together and feasted on the fresh kill. During one of their many late-night conversations, she confessed she didn't want to go back to Fort Collins. She, too, had fallen under the spell of the small town.

So, while Daniel was busy running the Miller's Plaza job during the day, his mom was working with the local real estate agent on finding a larger place for them to live.

"But small enough for me to manage by myself when you and your mate settle down in your own home," she had said with a wink.

Finding a place to live was proving to be a challenge, though. Apparently Havenwood Falls had been experiencing a surge in population, resulting in a housing shortage. Ross Builders was the only construction company in town, and from what Daniel learned from Mickey, Herschel's unreliability and surly demeanor didn't make his phone ring for bids. After cleaning up the Airstream, Daniel

305

imagined Herschel's lack of organization had something to do with it too. He had unearthed a stack of unpaid invoices and several requests for bids in one of the kitchen cabinets.

In addition to keeping watch over Colleen at her house, he still met her for lunch in the square at what he considered their bench. They shared more kisses, held hands, and learned more about each other. Daniel opened up about his sister Katherine's death and his father's passing. He shared how they moved a lot when he was younger, so he didn't have close relationships. He learned that Colleen was the oldest of her siblings, and that in addition to reading, she liked to ride her bike and spend time with her friends, several of whom she had known since kindergarten. Their lives were significantly different, but they discovered they had things in common: conserving the environment and a love of cheeseburgers and Elvis Presley's music.

By the time Friday arrived, any apprehension Daniel had had over his first date with Colleen not going well was gone. Their lunches together had already forged a strong bond between them, enough that he could sense her emotions, like he was attuned to her specific frequency. Her scent was imprinted on his brain, too, and he could single her delicate floral fragrance out of a crowd, a heady mix of lilac and sunshine.

Instead of meeting Colleen for lunch that afternoon, Daniel stayed behind to finish paperwork and run some errands. He was in the Airstream, hunched over the table putting together a task list for the following week, when the door opened, and Herschel limped inside.

His face was almost back to normal. The swelling had gone down, leaving sickly yellow bruises behind. Several cuts had scabbed over, and one above his eye had required stitches. The black threads looked like an unruly extension of his eyebrow.

"McCabe, what are you doing here?" Herschel glanced around the trailer, taking in the changes with narrowed eyes. He licked his lips, and his fingers tapped against his thigh.

"Working, sir. The developer asked me to continue in your absence. Everything is on schedule."

"Good, good," he said, hobbling over to the table and running a shaking hand over the papers, but not really looking at anything specific. He licked his lips again, and beads of sweat dotted his receding hairline. That's when Daniel smelled it. Fear. No matter what species, it was an unmistakable stench of old sweat, sickening sweet endorphins, and ammonia. Daniel's lip curled up in response.

"Looks like you have everything in order."

"We have a good crew. Drew's cousin came on board, and Patty sent another laborer over, so we're up to eight now. They're all hard workers." Daniel set his pen down and leaned back, watching the nervous man in front of him with interest.

"It's a damn shame I have to shut it down," Herschel said, wandering away to peer out the narrow window that was over the small kitchen sink.

"What?" Daniel leaped to his feet. "Why?"

"I need to leave town . . . indefinitely. Circumstances being as they are, I won't be able to operate this business anymore. I'll be liquidating everything. Right now."

"You can't do that! The men—their jobs. The building needs to be finished." Daniel struggled to keep his anger in check. The coward had clearly screwed with someone, and the beating was a warning. Now he was going to run from his problems without any regard for anyone else. "How much do you owe? That's it, isn't it? You owe someone money?"

"Much worse than that." The color drained from Herschel's face, making his bruises stand out even more. "When you make a deal with the devil and he comes to collect . . ." He trailed off when there was a loud bang outside, causing him to spasm, and the smell of fear grew, filling the room. Daniel recognized the sound of the dumpster lid behind Burger Bar slamming shut.

"Give me the chance to buy you out. I'm committed to this job, this crew." Daniel spoke before thinking it through. He had a little bit of money saved up, but he doubted it was enough to buy a business.

He had to try, though, and he knew if given the opportunity, he'd succeed.

Herschel approached the table and reached for the ledger, opening it up to the current balance of $6,457.86. He snatched up a pen and piece of scratch paper, then started writing down a figure. He included the amount in the bank account, the excavator, trailer, and an additional two thousand dollars on top for tools and other supplies. In total, in order to acquire a fully operational and established construction business in a town ripe for development, Daniel needed to come up with $19,657.86.

Fiddling with the edge of the paper, he thought through his options. He could ask his mom for a loan. She had her father's life insurance money. It might delay her buying a house, but he could build her one.

"Can I have until Monday to get this?" he asked.

Herschel licked his lips and ran a shaky hand over his balding head. "Yes, but no later than ten a.m. I need to be gone before noon."

"Deal." They shook hands, and Herschel quickly left the trailer.

For someone who wanted to disappear, running around town in broad daylight wasn't the best strategy, unless those looking for him operated under the cover of darkness. Herschel's comment about making a deal with the devil made Daniel shiver. If he came up with the money to buy Herschel out, he'd make the sure the notice of sale didn't have any hidden clauses.

After Herschel left, Daniel closed up the trailer and walked over to PPP Agency to pick up his paycheck. The arrangement Herschel had in place was that they managed all things personnel, from hiring to payroll. It was probably a good thing, as he probably would have screwed that up, too.

Patty Parker was sitting at her desk, and she greeted him with a big smile. "Daniel! How is everything going?"

"Good, except . . ." He spent the next few minutes filling Patty in on Herschel's visit. It was only fair to apprise her of the situation, in case Herschel disappeared and left the agency in a bind.

"Oh dear, that isn't good. Thank you for telling me. So, do you think you're able to buy him out?"

"I hope so. I want to."

"Well, I'm sure something can be worked out. Hold that thought." She stared off into the distance with a blank expression. Daniel looked over his shoulder and out the window to see if there was anything happening on the street outside, but there wasn't anything of interest. Seconds later, Patty smiled and came back to earth. "Have a seat, Daniel. Elsmed will be here momentarily."

"What?"

She tapped her temple and grinned. "He's telepathic. I just projected my thoughts to him, and he responded. Sure beats the telephone sometimes."

Stunned at this revelation, Daniel did take a seat. Moments later, Elsmed Fairchild entered the agency. He was almost as tall as the doorway, and instead of wearing a tailored three-piece suit like the first time they met, he was decked out in hiking gear like he was going on a safari. His long blond hair was pulled back in a ponytail, and he carried a walking stick carved out of some sort of red wood in one hand.

"Let's go for a walk," he said to Daniel.

They walked down Main Street and past the high school. Once they reached Blackstone Road, Elsmed turned right, and they stayed on the shoulder of the road. To the right was the high school and elementary school, but the other side of the road, to the west, was undeveloped. Acres of relatively flat land lay out before him, with the mountains looming in the background.

"My sister had a vision of the future," Elsmed suddenly spoke, his first words to Daniel since they left the agency. "She saw a world taken over by technology. Cameras on every street corner, portable phones that people can make their own films with and take pictures. There is no privacy in the future. With that, it will become more difficult for the supernatural population to remain hidden." Elsmed paused, and he was suddenly speaking directly into Daniel's head. A tickling sensation, like fingers stroking his brain, sent shivers down his spine. *Your father's fears are rooted in truth. Humans, corporations, and governments will seek to either control or destroy us. They will fear us. You don't want to know what experiments they're conducting on aliens they have in custody.*

Just as quickly as Elsmed entered his thoughts and probed his innermost secrets, he was gone and picking up the conversation out loud. "My sister said more supernaturals will seek out Havenwood Falls. They will be drawn by the magic and will stay for protection from the threats of the outside world. We already have a housing shortage, and more homes will need to be built."

"There definitely is a need for more homes now. Did Patty tell you about Herschel?"

"She did, which is why I'm here. I have a proposal for you." From one of the large pockets on his tan field jacket, Elsmed withdrew a scroll. He unfurled it and presented the fibrous paper to Daniel. In flowing cursive, written in what appeared to be gold ink, was a proposal to enter a business agreement. Elsmed would be an investor in the construction business, just a silent partner. There were a few clauses. The Court occasionally had construction needs, and they preferred a supernatural to do the work.

"Explaining to a contractor why a building can't have any iron or needs secret underground passages can risk exposure. You'll be able to accommodate these special requests."

Daniel scratched the back of his head as he read the rest of the proposal. It all seemed straightforward.

"Good," Elsmed said, either picking up the thought directly or seeing it on Daniel's face. "Now, back to the housing shortage. I own all this property, and I've been reading up on these developments called subdivisions that are built around a golf course. I want one of those built here."

"A golf course?"

"Yes. Oddly enough, I've quite the affinity for the game."

"Okay, but if we're building a subdivision, I want to utilize the natural environment, conserve the local ecology as much as possible."

Elsmed beamed at him. It was an off-putting smile, more

predatory than friendly, and his piercing blue eyes flared brighter. "What a marvelous idea! Being fae, I believe taking care of nature is a priority. I think we're going to get along famously."

"Now, there's another matter I want to discuss with you," Elsmed said as they started walking back toward town. His walking stick made a rhythmic *thunk-thunk* sound on the asphalt. "The Court likes each species to have a leader or representative for their kind. Someone who helps enforce the rules and such. Sheriff Kasun's wife is alpha of the Kasun wolf pack, and there's the Blaekthorn alpha. Each coven has their own leaders."

"And Jerome is the alpha of the mountain lions, right? That's why you sent him to welcome me to town."

"Well . . ." Elsmed paused with his hands crossed over the top of his walking stick and looked Daniel straight in the eyes. "He's not— not officially anyway. We approached him, and he declined. None of the other mountain lions are interested either. Your kind tend to keep to themselves."

"Why me? I'm an outsider, and young."

"Ah, you've made quite an impression in your first two weeks here. You're a natural leader, and I've been told youth will lead us to progress where some, myself included, are resistant to change."

"Natural leader? How do you know?"

Elsmed grinned again and started walking. "People talk and people watch. I listen and pay attention."

"Well. Let me think about that—one step at a time." Daniel's thoughts went to Colleen. She was his next step. He'd consider the leadership role later.

"Ah yes, your mate." Elsmed nodded, picking up on Daniel's thoughts—an unnerving ability Daniel probably would never get used to. *Don't think anything crazy around Elsmed.* At this, the fae laughed. *Crap, he heard that too.* "Don't worry about Miss Campbell. She's your mate, and while she's human, her subconscious recognizes you as such. When the time comes, approach the Court, and we'll assist with the reveal. There's a protocol in place for letting humans know about our existence."

Everything was falling into place. It almost seemed too easy, but after a lifetime spent moving, he was done, and he wasn't willing to turn down the opportunity to establish roots.

Since it was well past the end of the lunch break, Daniel brought Elsmed by the Miller's Plaza jobsite. His crew was already back to work, but they all came to a sudden stop when they saw him approach with Elsmed. Not all of them knew the fae's true nature or his role in town. He was seen as an eccentric man of wealth. He was a Fairchild, and the Fairchilds were one of the founding families.

"Hey, guys, I have something to run by you," Daniel called out, gesturing for the crew to join them. They gathered in a loose semicircle formation around him. "Herschel stopped by while you were at lunch," Daniel began and then filled them in on the opportunity to buy out the business and the proposal Elsmed had made. When he pulled the scroll from his back pocket, he almost dropped it, because it was no longer a scroll but rolled up regular paper, and the gold ink was now typewritten in black. He glanced over at Elsmed, and the fae winked at him, his blue eyes twinkling.

"I want to sign, but want your opinion first, since this is your livelihood, too."

"Do it, daddy-o!" Mickey shouted out, and the rest of the guys cheered in agreement.

"I know at least three other guys looking for work. They didn't want to work for Herschel, but they'll work for you, as they know you treat us well," Drew added.

"All right, I'll sign with you all as witnesses." Daniel took a deep breath and grabbed the pen from the breast pocket of his shirt. "I need someone's back."

Mickey volunteered and bent over so his back was straight. With a shaking hand, Daniel signed the contract and then handed the pen to Elsmed, who signed on the line next to Daniel's signature.

"It is done, Daniel McCabe. Now, let's go to the bank so we can finish this transaction."

After going around and shaking the hands of his crew, he and Elsmed left. Dizzy with excitement, Daniel barely remembered the walk to Havenwood Falls Savings and Loan. He registered the cool air from the air conditioning and the lemony scent of wood polish, right before Elsmed withdrew twenty thousand dollars and handed him the cash in large bills.

I'm glad you decided to stay in Havenwood Falls, Elsmed said directly into Daniel's mind. *Don't forget to get your tattoo upgraded to permanent resident status, and your mother needs one too.*

"I'm going to rename the business to McCabe Construction. Is that okay with you?" Daniel asked, out loud.

"Of course. It makes sense. Besides, I'm the silent investor. Do what you want."

That afternoon, Daniel tracked down Herschel, who was discreetly hiding out at the bottom of a bottle of whiskey in the Haven Saloon. Patty Parker had assisted Daniel in drafting the paperwork to buy the business off of Herschel, incorporating all the line items Herschel had listed out on the slip of scratch paper.

Daniel showed up at the saloon with the purchase agreement, notice of sale, and the cash. With the bartender as a witness, Herschel signed his business over without bothering to read anything, his eyes focused on the stack of cash. Before the ink was even dry, Herschel grabbed the money and bolted out the door.

"Hey! Are you going to pay your tab?" the bartender shouted after him, but Herschel was gone.

"Here." Daniel slapped a twenty-dollar bill down on the sticky bar. "Thanks for witnessing."

"Guess we won't be seeing old Hersch around anymore. Congratulations on your new business." The bartender poured them each a glass of Warded Whiskey, and he raised his shot glass for a toast.

"Just this one. I have a date tonight with a special gal," Daniel said when he reached for his glass.

"We'll make this a special toast then. To new beginnings."

"To new beginnings," Daniel repeated and tipped the glass back.

*A*pproaching the front door, Daniel held a bouquet of flowers in one hand. He had handpicked the colorful array of wildflowers from the meadow behind his cabin, and his mom had tied a pale blue ribbon around the stems. Clearing his throat, he ran his free hand through his hair before knocking. Taking a step back, he waited for someone to answer, hoping it would be Colleen and that her parents had changed their minds about meeting him.

No such luck. Her father opened the door. He was shorter than Daniel, and he adjusted his glasses when he looked up. His brown hair was graying at the temples and thinning on top, and he wore khaki pants, a white button-down shirt, and a green tie. He took a few moments to examine Daniel as if sizing him up, his eyes pausing on the bouquet that was already beginning to wilt.

"Callum Campbell."

"Daniel McCabe." He shook the offered hand. Callum didn't invite Daniel in right away, but stood in the doorway, barring entrance.

"What are your intentions with my daughter?"

"Daddy!" Colleen admonished from somewhere behind her father.

"Callum, let the man in," said another woman's voice.

314

Callum Campbell stepped aside so Daniel could enter. Colleen rushed forward and grabbed his hand. He swallowed hard when he saw her. She was a vision in curve-hugging black pedal pushers and a pale blue sleeveless top. A gold pendent sparkled around her long neck. Colleen tucked her arm through his and led him into the living room where the rest of Colleen's family waited.

The living room looked like the heart of the home and not one of those for decoration only. An oak coffee table had a bottom shelf covered with magazines. He recognized the recent cover of *Good Housekeeping*, as his mom had the same magazine at the cabin. Two low-sitting, deep purple chairs were positioned on one side of the coffee table, while a floral sofa with purple accent pillows was positioned on the other side, against the wall underneath the front picture window. Sheer ivory drapes covered both windows in the room, allowing for plenty of natural light. There were two matching end tables, and each had a lamp and one had a telephone.

A boy possessing the lanky limbs of adolescence sat in one of the chairs, and he regarded Daniel with cool blue eyes, sizing him up just like Colleen's father had. Two petite blondes, one an older version of Colleen and the other a younger version, sat on the sofa. Well, the younger one perched on the edge and grinned at Daniel. A giant family portrait hung above the fireplace mantle caught Daniel's eye.

"Colleen was seventeen when that was taken," the woman, who Daniel assumed was Colleen's mother, said when she stood up from where she was sitting on the sofa. She wore a pale-yellow dress with a full skirt that flared out the waist. A string of pearls decorated her neck.

"Daniel, this is my mom, Ellen."

"Pleased to meet you, Mrs. Campbell," he said and shook her hand.

"Colleen, why don't you put those flowers in some water? There's a vase in the hutch in the dining room." Ellen handed the bouquet to her daughter before turning her attention back on Daniel. "Please, sit down."

She directed him to the chair next to where Colleen's brother sat.

Callum followed them and continued on to sit down beside his wife on the sofa.

"Hello, I'm Daniel and you must be David?" he asked, extending his hand.

"Yeah, that's me." David shook his hand and at the same time snapped his gum. The loud crack sounded like a firecracker.

"I'm Kelly," Colleen's sister said with a giggle and waved from where she was sitting. "Do you have a younger brother?" she asked, eyeing him up and down.

"Kelly Marie!" Ellen scolded and shook her head. "Sorry Daniel, she's a little boy-crazy."

"A little?" David teased. "Try a lot crazy."

"Who's crazy?" Colleen asked, walking into the room. She set the flowers down in the middle of the coffee table before coming to stand beside Daniel. She placed her hand on his shoulder, and he felt himself lean into her touch. Her father noticed and scowled.

"Your sister is—never mind." Callum looked at Daniel. "So, what are your intentions with Colleen?" he asked again, crossing his arms over his chest.

"Daddy, cut it out," Colleen pleaded.

"It's okay, I get it," he told her. "I'll probably behave the same way when it's our daughter." As soon as he said it, Daniel realized his mistake, because the room went dead quiet with the exception of a surprised gasp from Colleen, and her hand tightened on his shoulder. "Er, I mean when I have a daughter."

An awkward silence filled the room, and Callum narrowed his eyes at Daniel. Ellen cleared her throat and changed the subject. "Colleen said you're taking her to dinner?"

Grateful for the change, he told them they were going to Burger Bar, and after, hopefully Colleen could show him around town a bit, since he was new to town. A few minutes later, the inquisition was over.

After closing the passenger door behind Colleen, Daniel walked around the front of his truck and slid into the driver's seat.

"Well, that was . . . terrible," he said, shaking his head and starting the engine.

Colleen threw her head back and laughed. "That was the most awkward . . . my poor father . . . the look on his face when you said 'our daughter.' Oh, my word." She paused and caught her breath, wiping a tear from the corner of her eye. "You certainly know how to make a first impression."

She dissolved into another bout of laughter, which was so infectious that Daniel joined in. Yeah, that was one heck of an impression. He hoped that was the only rough patch for the night. Unfortunately, it wasn't.

CHAPTER 14

While the date wasn't off to an auspicious start, the moment they were alone, things started to improve. Daniel drove them to Burger Bar, which was the place to go in town on a Friday night, if you were under thirty. Colleen was relieved he didn't take her to the Fallview Tavern & Grille, as it was kind of stuffy and the more refined, older crowd dined there. He parked off to the side and walked around to help her down. She placed her hand in his and stepped down onto the parking lot. Expecting him to let go once she was on her two feet, she was pleasantly surprised when he kept holding her hand. His touch was calming, and any concern she had been feeling about how it went with Daniel meeting her parents faded away.

Outside Burger Bar, all of the parking spots were taken where waitresses on roller skates came to take orders and brought trays of food right to the cars. She and Daniel walked past the rows of cars, and Daniel released her hand so he could open the door. He ushered her through, his hand on the small of her back, which sent a whole other feeling into her body that was the opposite of calm.

Inside, it was crowded and loud, and the delicious greasy smell of fresh French fries hung in the air. Music from the jukebox competed with the chatter of excited voices. Colleen noticed her friends, Peggy and Sally, sitting in one of the booths. She headed in that direction, with Daniel at her back. Peggy was facing them, and she grinned when she saw Colleen.

"I didn't know you girls were going to be here. What a nice surprise," Colleen said after introducing Daniel.

"Peggy needs help deciding on a china pattern, and decisions like those should be made over milkshakes," Sally said, taking a long suck on the straw sticking out of her chocolate shake. She looked Daniel up and down in the process.

"Oh, did you pick one?" Colleen asked Peggy.

"No. I like them all. This isn't an easy decision." She spun the catalogue that was open in the middle of the table toward Colleen. "Which one do you like?"

Colleen looked over the various patterns and descriptions in the catalogue. "I'm partial to the Noritake Edgewood pattern. The floral design that decorates the edge along with the silver trim is elegant and not too flashy."

With her input provided, Colleen and Daniel moved on to an empty table tucked in the corner.

"Your friends seem nice," Daniel said after they sat down.

"They are. We grew up together. How about you, do you have close friends?"

Daniel shrugged. "Not really. We moved around so much, it made making friends hard. Although since I've arrived in Havenwood Falls, Mickey Ahusaka has taken me under his wing."

"Mickey? He's a good guy. He was in the market this past weekend. I hope his brother is feeling better."

"What do you mean?"

Colleen filled Daniel in on Mickey's visit to the market, but how she saw his brother at Movies in the Park, seemingly fine.

"I'm sure he'd say something if his brother was ill." Daniel took a sip of his chocolate milkshake, and Colleen popped a French fry in her mouth. Just then "Whole Lotta Shakin' Going On" by Jerry Lee Lewis started playing on the jukebox, and people began to move into the middle of the makeshift dance area. Daniel suddenly stood up and held his hand out toward her.

"Come on, let's dance!"

"You dance?" she asked, raising her eyebrows in surprise, and placed her hand in his.

Daniel tugged gently on her arm, pulling her to her feet. They crossed the diner to the dance floor, and he surprised her when he spun around and effectively twirled her so they were in motion at the same time and perfectly in sync. He whirled her away from his body and then reeled her back in until they were face to face, their hands joined. They kicked their legs out and moved in unison, like they had rehearsed the dance for countless hours before. Daniel was graceful and moved so effortlessly that it took Colleen's breath away. She was grinning from ear to ear when he shimmied his hips like Elvis. The crowd surrounding the dance floor roared with approval, and she was laughing with sheer joy when he reeled her in again, causing her to land against his muscular chest. He lifted her and swung so her legs went to one side of his body, and he repeated this on the other side before dipping her low—so low she thought her hair was going to brush against the floor. The song ended, and Daniel slowly brought her back up to standing. She was panting slightly and couldn't take her eyes off of him.

The beginning notes of a ballad began to play, and they moved closer to each other. Daniel's arm slipped around her waist, his hand on her lower back, dangerously near her backside. Colleen looped her arms around his neck, relishing the press of her breasts against his chest. Elvis Presley's unmistakable croon filled the room. "I want you, I need you, I love you," Daniel mouthed the words along with the song, looking deep into her eyes the entire time. Their blue reminded her of the sky right after a storm moved through. Together they swayed in place, Daniel's hands burning through her clothes, setting her skin on fire. She imagined what it would feel like to be naked and flush against him. Her dreams involving Daniel had been vivid enough it wasn't difficult to imagine, especially with him so close to her now. He smelled incredible, earthy and spicy, natural . . . and familiar. Colleen leaned in and rested her head against his chest, letting out a contented sigh. She wanted to stay like this forever.

"Come on, I want to show you something," Daniel whispered in her ear. His lips brushed against the sensitive lobe, and she shivered in his arms.

"Is this where you turn from Mr. Wonderful to a cad?" she teased, winking at him, which caused him to throw his head back and laugh. It was a delightful, rich sound that sent vibrations through her body. She noticed the early traces of reddish brown stubble on the underside of his chin. Holding her hand, Daniel led her back to their table. She grabbed her purse, and he left more than enough money on the table to cover their bill. She waved goodbye to Sally and Peggy when they passed their table. Both girls were grinning like loons at her.

Once outside, Daniel led her in the opposite direction of his truck and around the back of the restaurant. Unlike the other night with Viktor, Colleen didn't hesitate. Something about Daniel made her feel safe. Dirt scraped under her heels, and she stumbled slightly. Daniel steadied her and moved so his hand was on the small of her back. They only had the distant glow of the lights from Burger Bar and moonlight to guide them, but Daniel moved with confidence, as if the darkness didn't exist.

They stopped in front of the door to the Airstream trailer, and Colleen briefly wondered if he *was* going to turn into a cad, recalling the sofa inside. She wasn't that kind of girl, no matter how badly she desired him.

Suddenly, there was movement behind them, and Colleen spun around to peer into the dark. A scrape of a flint followed by a flare illuminated a face before the Zippo lighter snapped closed, extinguishing the flame. The smoldering red dot of a cigarette gave the man's location away.

"Well, well, well, what do we have here?" A gravelly voice spoke, and a second man appeared, as if forming out of the shadows. Daniel moved in front of Colleen and stepped back, forcing her to be sandwiched between his body and the cool side of the trailer.

"Who are you?" Daniel asked, and she felt the tension coursing through him. He was practically vibrating with it.

"Depends. I could be your worst nightmare or your pal. It all hinges on information." The man with the gravelly voice moved closer, enabling Colleen to see his face clearer. Half of it was melted, disfigured by a horrific burn. The scars disappeared below the collar of his shirt, which stretched across his chest. He was a large man, his shoulders broad and square like he was carved out of granite. The man behind him, smoking, was even bigger, and he made an effective barrier blocking anyone's view of the trailer from Burger Bar.

"What kind of information?" Daniel asked, and Colleen noticed his hands had curled into fists. She sucked in a breath, bracing for a confrontation.

"I'm looking for Herschel."

Daniel's fists unfurled, and Colleen exhaled, slumping against the trailer, letting it support her weight, as her knees had turned to Jell-O.

"He's in the wind. He sold me his business and skipped town. Claimed the devil was after him."

Gravel man laughed, and it was a horrible sound, like boulders being ground against each other.

"That's not the answer I'm looking for." He moved closer. "What about you, sweetheart, do you know where Herschel is?"

The moment the man spoke to her, Daniel tensed up again. She placed a hand against his back, a silent plea for him to stay where he was. Menace choked the air, and Daniel was her shield. She didn't like the way the man's dark eyes glittered when they focused on her. He licked his lips and smiled, but only half of his mouth worked, the side that hadn't melted like wax. The lopsided leer left her more unsettled. While Daniel was muscular and in shape, the two men were giants in comparison. She didn't want to answer him, to open up a conversation, but she didn't want to anger him by not responding either, so she shook her head.

"That's a damn shame," he said to Daniel. "You see, Herschel owes me money. A lot of money. He wagered his business in a poker game. I came to collect. Only now the business is yours," He paused and ran a hand over his ruined face. "A pretty little morsel like your girl will be a decent consolation prize, though."

Without warning, a giant fist was heading toward Daniel's face. Colleen flinched, preparing for the impact, but before she could blink, Daniel had spun out of the way, moving Colleen with him and out of harm's way. He roared, an animalistic sound that reverberated down her spine, and then he was leaping through the air. Convinced it was a trick of the poor lighting, Colleen dismissed what she thought she saw because it looked like Daniel's hands had turned into paws tipped with sharp, pointy claws. The man cried out and toppled backward underneath Daniel's weight. Daniel raised his head and hissed, actually hissed at the smoking man, who tossed his cigarette to the side and began to advance. Another animalistic growl came from behind the smoking man, causing him to turn around and look.

Colleen recognized DJ Brewster standing at the edge of Burger Bar's parking lot. She hadn't seen much of him since they graduated high school. He stood in a fighter's pose, but his eyes captured her attention. They seemed to glow.

A piercing cry joined the other sounds around her, and she looked up to see a hawk circling overhead before it flew off with an incredible burst of speed. Soon Daniel and DJ were engaged in an all-out rumble with the two strangers. Every time a fist landed on Daniel's body, she flinched. He took a particularly hard hit and went down. He wasn't moving, and Colleen ran forward, not caring about the fight going on around her. Before she could reach Daniel, the man with the melted face had her upper arm in a vise-like grip. She struggled to free herself, but it only made him laugh.

"Feisty little bird, aren't you?" He started dragging her away from Daniel. One of her shoes slipped off, and the gravel tore at the skin on her foot.

"Stop! You're hurting me!" she cried out.

Something flashed in her peripheral vision, and she turned to see Daniel getting up into a crouch. Then, before her eyes, he transformed. His body bent and folded in the most unnatural manner, accompanied by loud cracking and popping sounds. With a triumphant howl, a mountain lion stood among bits of shredded clothing, in Daniel's place. She was vaguely aware of her arm being released, and she heard the man back away, but her eyes were fixated on the familiar, magnificent cat before her. She recognized him. This was the mountain lion she had seen in her backyard.

He was a blur of golden fur as he ran past and gave chase, pursuing the man who had threatened her. Within seconds, the man was down on the ground, pinned with a mouthful of fangs attached to his throat. DJ had taken control of the other man and had him pressed face-first into the dirt. This was how Sheriff Kasun found them when he arrived a few minutes later. His truck came to a stop, and he leapt out. Colleen was surprised to see Mickey get out from the passenger side. He was wearing jeans that were a little too big on him, and that was it—no shoes or shirt. Mickey's muscles rippled with movement, and he caught her looking. Embarrassed, she turned away just in time to watch Daniel transform back into his human form.

She had never seen a man completely naked before, and her pulse accelerated, her mouth went dry, and her lower extremities began to tingle when she took in Daniel's body. She was frozen in place and couldn't stop staring.

Sheriff Kasun snapped handcuffs on the melted-faced man and hauled him to his feet. The sheriff manhandled him like the man weighed less than one hundred pounds. Mickey joined Daniel and handed him an Army green blanket, which he wrapped around his waist. Their eyes locked, and in an instant, Daniel was there. He cupped her face, his hands warm against her cheeks, and he drew her in, crushing his lips against hers. With a moan, she reciprocated, feeding off of his urgency.

When they separated, there was still a wildness about him. His nostrils flared slightly, and his thick hair, usually smoothed back, stuck up in all directions.

"Are you okay?" he asked, his hands exploring her arm that the man had gripped. His nostrils flared again as his eyes zeroed in on her bleeding foot. The scrapes were minor, but not to Daniel. Heedless of the blanket loosely knotted around his waist, he scooped her up in his arms.

"Daniel, put me down!" she protested.

"No. You're hurt. Let me take care of you." His voice was rough. "I'll always take care of you."

He carried her over to the sheriff's truck and set her down on the hood. After examining her foot, he gently brushed the dirt off. He wedged himself between her legs, facing her, eyeing her.

"What?" she asked.

"You're not in hysterics or running away screaming. Aren't you afraid of me? You shouldn't have seen that."

Colleen took a few minutes to assess and gather her thoughts, since the shock was beginning to wear off. Was she surprised? Yes, but not scared. Daniel protected her. With him, she was safe.

"Would you have ever told me what you are?"

"Eventually. My kind haven't had it easy. It would have been difficult for me to disclose, but if we got serious, I wouldn't keep it from you."

"Your kind. So, there are more of you?" He nodded. "That's an awful lot of woulds and ifs," she said, tracing a finger along his chest, enjoying the silky feel of his skin and the way his muscles jumped under her touch.

"Do you want for there to be an us?" Daniel asked, cocking an eyebrow. He moved in closer, his hands resting on top of her thighs.

"Will you tell me everything?"

"Yes. Whatever you want. I am yours."

They followed Sheriff Kasun back to the station. Both men were handcuffed and secure in the back of his truck. Mickey and DJ followed behind in DJ's car. All of them were required to give their statements. Miraculously, for being so close to Burger Bar, a crowd hadn't gathered, and there weren't other witnesses to the fight. Colleen thought for sure her cries had been heard.

It didn't take long for her father to rush into the station. He wore a pajama top and a wrinkled pair of khaki pants. He had the bleary eyes of someone who had been rudely woken from a deep sleep.

"Pumpkin! Are you okay? Sheriff Kasun said you were involved in an altercation."

"I'm fine, Daddy. Daniel protected me."

"Oh, thank goodness." He sunk down in the chair next to her. "Where is Daniel?"

"Giving his statement. Apparently, those are the same men who beat up Mr. Ross."

"Anyone we know?"

Colleen shook her head. "Never saw them before, and their faces aren't ones I'd forget." She shuddered, remembering the lopsided leer.

The front door to the station opened again, and they both looked to see who had come in.

"I wonder what Elsmed Fairchild is doing here this late at night?" Callum asked.

"Daniel called him. He told me that Mr. Fairchild is his silent partner. Daniel bought Ross Builders."

"Well, I'll be. Guess he's going to be sticking around then, huh?" He gave her a knowing look. She just blushed and grinned in response.

CHAPTER 15

*E*lsmed entered the small room where Daniel sat across from Sheriff Kasun. Now that the two gangsters who had followed Herschel back from Grand Junction were locked up in the holding cell, Daniel had to face the consequences of his actions. He had shifted in front of a human.

"Colleen is my mate. When she was threatened, I lost control."

"You're lucky Mickey found me just in time. Had we arrived ten seconds later, you would be facing a murder charge. I know how close you were to ripping that man's throat out."

Daniel hung his head, acknowledging it was true. His fangs had punctured skin, and when the blood welled against his tongue, the killing instinct kicked in. How easy and satisfying it would have been to rip that man's throat out. To punish him for hurting his mate. *His mate.* "What's going to happen to Colleen, now that she knows?"

Elsmed fielded this question. "It's up to her. I'll give her the option of wiping her memory. She'll forget tonight's events ever happened. I can even make her forget you. You haven't fully consummated the mating bond, so the symptoms for her will lessen in time."

Daniel's palms grew sweaty at the idea of Colleen forgetting him. Now that he'd met his mate—had forged a connection with her—his inner mountain lion would slowly go feral. The longer he denied himself the mating bond, the deeper the descent into madness. The ache in his chest he felt when he was away from Colleen would become an unbearable pain. He'd heard of other shifters ending their lives to end the suffering.

"It's her choice, though. What if she refuses and doesn't want to have her memories altered?"

"Then you're a lucky man," the sheriff answered. "I'll go bring her into my office," he said to Elsmed.

Moments later, Daniel was alone in the room with his thoughts. Panic threatened to take control. What if she decided he wasn't worth it? What if she didn't feel the same way about him? He fought the urge to burst into the sheriff's office and abscond with Colleen—force her to accept him as her mate.

The door opened, and he looked up, hoping to see the petite blonde, but saw Mickey instead. He was followed into the room by DJ Brewster, whom he hadn't met before that night.

"Thanks for your help," he said to DJ. "I owe you one."

"My grandfather owed you, so we can call us even."

"Grandfather?" Daniel looked at the other mountain lion shifter, and he did seem familiar. There was something about his straight nose and thick, dark eyebrows, even his scent. "Wait a minute, is Jerome your grandfather?"

"He is, and he told me about our family's history. Guess I might not be here if not for your grandfather. When you're ready, I'll introduce you to the other mountain lion shifters. They're anxious to meet you."

"Yeah, well, I might be feral soon," Daniel said, rubbing the tightness in his chest. It had been growing worse the longer he sat in the confined space. The longer he was away from his mate.

"Have some faith, daddy-o." Mickey clapped him on the shoulder as he sat down next to him. "I hope to be so lucky someday to have a woman look at me like Colleen looks at you. Even from twenty-five feet in the air, I could see it."

"I hope you're right."

EPILOGUE

THREE YEARS LATER—SEPTEMBER 1960

"So, what do you think, Mrs. McCabe?" Daniel asked, nuzzling his wife's neck right above the faint scar from his mark. He loved the reaction this elicited. It never failed that goose bumps erupted over her entire body when he brushed against the sensitive area. He stood behind her, his arms wrapped around her waist and his hands cradling her belly that was just beginning to swell. They were standing at the entrance to the recently completed Creekwood Estates Country Club, which was built at the top of a small hill. Green grass, wildflowers, and trees stretched out before them on one of the most natural golf courses in the country. No chemicals were used to maintain the greens. A herd of antelope grazed by the ninth hole. Daniel tracked their movement, his inner cat's interest piqued. Streets dotted with new homes had been built around the natural landscape, some with dramatic curves around existing boulders. Phase One of Creekwood Estates was complete. The grand opening for the country club was scheduled for the following day.

"Oh, Daniel. It's beautiful," Colleen replied and leaned back against him, placing her hands on top of his and giving them a squeeze. "I see you used my idea of utilizing the natural springs for irrigation."

"I sure did, and it saved at least ten thousand dollars off the estimate from the landscape architect. Thanks to my brilliant mate." He kissed the top of her head. "Come on, are you ready to see the house?"

He stepped away and held out his hand. She entwined her fingers through his, and they walked hand in hand across the giant flagstone patio to the wide French doors that led to the club.

Inside it was all dark wood and rich tapestries in shades of green, brown, and gold. Vaulted ceilings with exposed beams loomed overhead. They crossed a dance floor, the parquet floors so brand new, they weren't marked by a single scratch. Then they walked through the dining room, which consisted of twenty tables, all with high-backed upholstered chairs. An enormous gold chandelier was suspended from the ceiling. A large stone fireplace took up one wall. A brown leather sofa and two green velvet lounge chairs were positioned in front. Along the other wall the bar was set up—a stone base with a long top made out of a red oak tree that had been uprooted during a blizzard the year before. Shelves built into the wall behind the bar were stocked with only top-shelf liquor. At the front of the club, there was the membership office, a banquet room, and the pro shop. When they stepped out front, twelve brand new golf carts were parked in a row along the curb of the curved driveway.

Their house was less than a block away, and soon they were walking up the driveway to their new split-level home. A large mottled-gray stone chimney jutted up from the center, and the bottom level of the house was built out of the same stone, where the second level had wood siding. Wide windows spanned the front of the house. Daniel and Colleen both wanted the view of the mountains to be unrestricted. Upon entering, a wide flight of stairs led them up to the second level and another set of stairs led to the first floor. They went upstairs, where several of the mountain lion shifters were moving furniture in the living room. A fireplace took up the center of this floor and would provide heat for the entire level. DJ, Daniel's beta, grinned when they entered the kitchen. All of the appliances were top-of-the-line General Electric and a butterscotch brown that blended in with the stained pine cabinets.

"Is it ready?" Daniel asked, and DJ nodded.

"What's ready?" Colleen peered up at him.

"You'll see." He leaned down and kissed the tip of her nose.

Leading Colleen down the carpeted hallway where the bedrooms were located, he pulled her into the smallest one at the end, and it was like stepping into a bowl of sunshine.

"Oh, Danny!" she gasped and twirled around in the center of the room, taking everything in. The walls were painted a daffodil yellow, and the trim was white. A natural wood crib sat against the wall underneath a bay of windows. A matching wood dresser was against the wall to the right, in between the door and closet. A rocking chair was placed next to the crib with a blanket knitted by Colleen's mom draped over the back. Pink, blue, yellow, and green yarn had been used to make it, since they wouldn't know the sex of their first child until he or she was born. A mobile extended over the crib, each item an animal: lion, tiger, bear, monkey, horse, pig, cow, and a special-order item Daniel requested—a mountain lion. Several pillows and stuffed animals were propped up along the sides of the crib. A mural of Winnie the Pooh sitting with his paw in a jar of honey had been painted on the wall to the left.

"It's perfect!" she announced and walked into his arms.

She slid her hands into the back pockets of his Levi's and hummed with contentment. The new fullness of her breasts pressed against his chest, and his hands slid down her sides, coming to a stop on her fuller hips. He loved her new curves and that she carried their child. He nuzzled her neck again, moving her hair aside with his nose so he could gain access to bare skin. Lilac and sunshine filled his nose, and he inhaled deeply before placing soft kisses along her neck. Sucking gently on her mark made her moan and shift closer, squeezing his ass through the thick denim. It never got old, how quickly they responded to each other.

Since the first night they truly bonded and he claimed her completely, they had been in sync. One of his favorite things to do was to listen to their heartbeats. They beat as one.

"Honey, we're in a house full of people and in our child's nursery. We'll get frisky later, when we're alone," Colleen murmured against his chest.

"You're right. We're definitely finishing this later," he whispered in her ear and felt her body quiver against his, her scent becoming muskier with desire.

"You're bad," she scolded breathlessly and swatted his chest when she backed away. "Let's go look at the rest of the house."

They finished exploring, and as they walked back to the country club, where their truck was parked, they started their debate on baby names. Since Colleen first found out she was pregnant, she had been obsessing over names. With four months left until their baby was due, she was feeling the pressure to pick out a name.

"How about Petunia if we have a girl?" Daniel suggested, and Colleen scowled.

"That's an awful name."

"Okay, what about boys' names? I've always been partial to Michael."

Colleen stopped in the middle of the newly paved street and tilted her head to the side, something he had learned early on in their relationship meant she was thinking the idea over, weighing the pros and the cons.

"Michael McCabe. I like it." She rubbed her belly, which was just beginning to test the confines of her shirt.

Looping her arm through his, they continued walking. The streets of Creekwood Estates were quiet now, but all of the homes of Phase One had already sold out, and planning for Phase Two was in the beginning stages. Daniel looked around at the life he was building for himself, for others, and for his growing family. His children would grow up playing on these streets, safe and unafraid of being singled out for being different. Looking down at his beautiful bride, glowing with pregnancy, Daniel was so glad he chose to accept her, that he chose love over hate.

~

We hope you enjoyed this story in the Legends of Havenwood Falls series featuring a variety of supernatural creatures. Books in the historical Legends of Havenwood Falls series:

Lost in Time by Tish Thawer
Dawn of the Witch Hunters by Morgan Wylie
Redemption's End by Eric R. Asher
Trapped Within a Wish by Brynn Myers
Blood and Damnation by Belinda Boring
Fated Beginnings by E.J. Fechenda
Emeline by Katie M. John
Released From a Curse by Brynn Myers
A Pack of Lies by Kallie Ross
Kiss the Ashes by Desiree Lafawn
Hidden Truths by Colleen Nye
Wrath and Retribution by Belinda Boring
Changing Fate by Char Webster

Also try the signature series, Havenwood Falls, and the YA series, Havenwood Falls High
Stay up to date at www.HavenwoodFalls.com

Subscribe to our reader group and receive free stories and more!

ABOUT THE AUTHOR

E.J. Fechenda has lived in Philadelphia and Phoenix, and now calls Portland, Maine, home. She is the Amazon bestselling author of the New Mafia Trilogy and in addition to working on the Ghost Stories Trilogy, she's a contributing author for the Havenwood Falls series. She has a degree in Journalism from Temple University, and her short stories have been published in *Suspense Magazine* and several anthologies. E.J. is a member of the Maine Writers and Publishers Alliance.

You can find her on the internet here:
Facebook: https://www.facebook.com/EJFechendaAuthor
Twitter @ebusjaneus (https://twitter.com/ebusjaneus)
Tumblr: http://ejfechenda.tumblr.com/

ACKNOWLEDGMENTS

A year has passed since my journey with Havenwood Falls began, and what an epic adventure it has been. I've met so many incredible authors and readers. We support each other, are silly together, and have built an amazing world together. My heart is full of love for you all. Kristie, I don't know how you keep everything straight and keep us authors on task. You are truly brilliant with a little bit of evil mastermind thrown into the mix. Thank you for taking a chance on me.

Every time I work on a new project, I lose myself a bit and withdraw to the "writing cave." My social life is impacted as most weekend nights are spent writing. To my family, especially the hubs, and friends who tolerate this and understand, I appreciate you more than you know and we will make up for lost time—promise!

AN EXCERPT

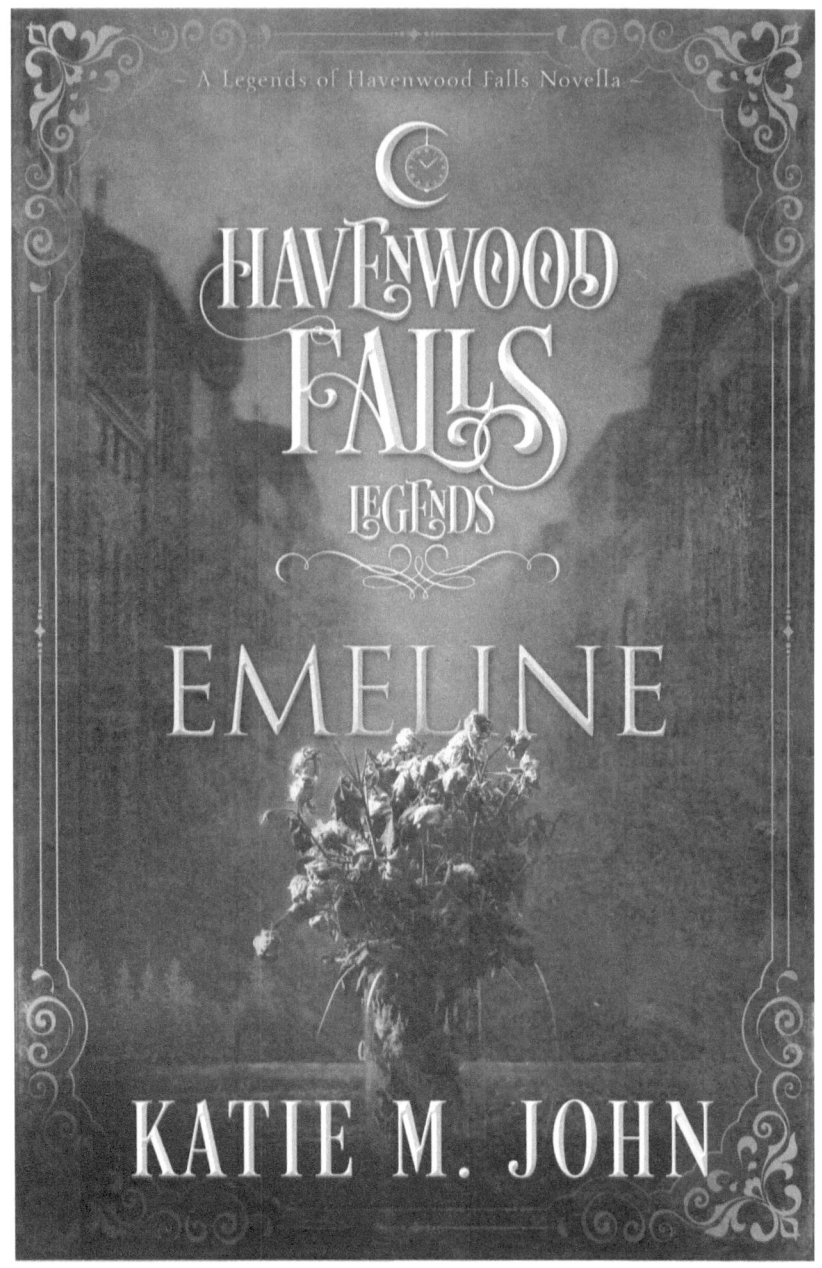

A Legends of Havenwood Falls Novella

HAVENWOOD FALLS LEGENDS

EMELINE

KATIE M. JOHN

Emeline (A Legends of Havenwood Falls Novella) by Katie M. John

Emeline Fairchild couldn't imagine a more perfect match for herself than Dragan Bishop. Her real-life Prince Charming, a powerful mage, freed her from a curse, awakening her to a new world in a new century. She finds herself in 1913, in a beautiful town in the Colorado mountains, with Dragan by her side. With such an enchanted beginning, their union would be nothing short of magical. Their love is full of fire and passion—some might say obsession. But as the much anticipated wedding approaches, Emeline soon finds the magic turning dark.

When tragedy comes to their burgeoning little town, Emeline is forced to ask what lengths Dragan went to in order to break her curse. Emotions and trust unravel, but Emeline's new art master shows her that light is a far greater power than the dark. Is her light enough to defeat the darkness of a jealous and insane mind? Or is it too late to save the true love of her life?

EMELINE

BY KATIE M. JOHN

SPRING 1913

It's spring, and I'm sitting in the garden with the man I'm going to marry. He's perhaps not the first man you'd think I'd be marrying. We're almost entirely different in every way. He's tall and straight, with dark brooding blue eyes that can read your soul for all its desires, and I'm petite, with snow-blond hair and green eyes that dream of meadows and woodlands and home.

He is witch, and I am fae, and our magic is real, but not entirely compatible. I am the early summer day, and he the storm that follows it. He has the power to destroy me, and I have the power to redeem him. Our love is a battle between the two, and it is fierce and full of passion in a time when passion is a secret activity, executed in brief moments, of crushed velvets and satins against library cases, in smoldering looks in the candlelight, in the touch of leather gloves against my skin. Stolen pleasures. Divine moments.

We are to be married in two months, on the night of a full moon, by the great falls. The ritual will be conducted by a member of the Court of the Sun and the Moon. Then we will be left in the woods as children of Nature, and when we return, we will be man and wife under the eyes of all the gods and goddesses; of Father Sun and Mother Moon, of Holy Creator, and all other universal energies.

We will be married in the humans' church on the following Sunday, for the sake of appearance; me dressed in pure cottons and carrying summer flowers. The town of Havenwood Falls will be there to witness the joining of our two powerful bloodlines. Founding families. The folks from the big houses. Mr. and Mrs. Bishop.

~

"Tell me our story again," I say, resting my head on Dragan's burgundy-velvet-covered shoulder.

He stretches out his legs and crosses them at the ankle, luxuriating in the weak spring sunshine. His smile could melt the sun. His dark blue eyes dance with secrets and promises. They are eyes that threaten to take me to dark places I've only just begun to imagine.

"You really want to hear it again?" he asks, cocking his brow.

I thread my arm through his and push myself closer to him. He smells of rich spices and faraway lands. It is through his stories I have come to love him. Stories of his home, of his magic, of the ravages of war and the terrors of the Ottoman invasions; of his Serbian mother, Anika, who was burned at the stake for being a witch, and his father's return to his native England, where he established a coven in Glastonbury, who worshipped at Stonehenge. And then, the family's flight across the big ocean to the New World on the promise of gold, mountains, and freedom—only the dream fast became a nightmare when the New World started burning their witches like the Old World had.

"I want to hear it all—right from the minute you stepped off the boat," I say, knowing Dragan will not spare the details like my parents do when I ask them about those times.

He's still looking at me with eyes so intense I can almost read him, but not quite. Dragan is dark waters.

"Okay, all of it, but in chapters, and not all today as I have to be somewhere in an hour," he says, taking a deep breath and checking his pocket watch. "Also, maybe a few little omissions." He smirks, making a gesture with his thumb and finger, and in a flash, I see the boy he once was and all the potential for delightful wickedness he holds.

"Yes, perhaps you should leave out the saloon fights and the brothels," I say, trying to shock him with my worldliness. He doesn't rise to the bait. His eyes have already filmed over and he's traveled into the past; a place that I both inhabited and didn't. A time I was both alive and dead, but more on that later.

"We had arrived in New England and made our way a little south, not yet sure where we would settle, for the land was far less hospitable than we had thought it would be. Everything seemed set to push us back out of the country, and we were seriously thinking about returning home to continue our father's coven in England.

"But just as we were about to give up, Rodavan had a vision while scrying that sent us south. We'd find a group of travelers who would lead us to home. I thought the idea was absurd, to go traipsing halfway across the nation on the basis of a vision, but Rodavan was adamant it was our destiny, and when Rodavan gets an idea in his head, there's no shaking it. To be honest, I was more than happy to leave.

"We had made a reasonable amount of money peddling potions and lotions and cure-alls, which in a land of new diseases and poisonous animals, made for rich pickings. We continued to make our way south, me riding our wagon with all of our worldly possessions and Rodavan following with our trade wagon. It made for slow progress, and the sound of rattling bottles soon became maddening.

"By the late 1840s, we had made it as far as Mississippi and were heading toward St. Louis, having heard rumor of other powerful witches and medicine men practicing a form of magic not too dissimilar to our own. It had been a hard journey, but we were used to a life of hardship despite our wealth and privilege. The war back home in Serbia during our childhood had not discriminated, and no amount of money could protect us entirely from the bloodshed.

"Nevertheless, Mississippi was unlike anything we had seen, and it certainly wasn't what we had hoped for when we had traveled to the New World with the hope of making a life in a new land without prejudice.

"When we traveled the banks of the Mississippi, we saw many a rich white man, 'civilized' and finely dressed, whipping his slaves, or placing them in shackles as if they were no more than animals. We were haunted by the songs of African slaves, their magic speaking to our own; their persecution and subjugation a song all too familiar to us—so that although we were different, we were the same.

"The horrors we witnessed in the cotton plantations flanking the river bank were enough to blanch even our hardened souls. Rodavan and I quickly came to the understanding we had swapped one ethnic cleansing horror for another. We were again wondering if we should return to England and see if we could find sanctuary there, when a caravan of wagons approached us.

"There was nothing novel about this. We had seen a great many caravans on our travels. The whole nation was in a flux of settlement and motion, but what was unique about this caravan of wagons was the powerful magic surrounding it. Whoever was coming, they weren't human—and they weren't just witches either."

Dragan pauses with the flair of a practiced storyteller.

"The Old Families?" I ask, knowing this part of the story well. "My mother and father?"

He nods.

"They told us how they had originally come south, with some hopeless hope of freeing some slaves, but the scale of the situation was beyond even their wildest nightmares. The overwhelm, even with their combined magical powers, had been too much. They had done everything they could along the way, petitioning and campaigning anyone who would even half listen, but in doing so, they had made many powerful enemies, who were only too keen to spread vicious rumors that they were a band of Satan-worshipping criminals and outlaws. They had been forced to flee and were now traveling, looking for a place they could finally call their home.

"The hardship of our circumstances meant friendships were made fast and firm with the group. My brother and I were keen to travel to a place where we could settle and make a world of our own, one based on freedom and possibility, one where we could practice our magic and our beliefs without fear. It was a notion that bonded us all deeply."

Dragan stops his narrative, and I look up to see Harriet, our maid, walking toward us with a tray of lemonade and plate of scones in one hand and a collapsible tray table in the other. Dragan removes my hand from his arm, and we straighten up into respectability.

"Your mother thought you might be in need of some refreshment," Harriet explains, putting up the table with a skilled flick of the wrist.

"Thank you, Harriet," I say, smiling.

I see the way she glances at Dragan from under her eyelashes and the blush on her cheek, and I know exactly what she thinks about when she's laying in her bed at night, because they are my thoughts, too.

"Your mother says not to be too much longer," she says. "She needs you to go over some of the menus for the wedding breakfast so we can start planning."

I nod and tell Harriet to assure my mother I'll be in within the hour, but to my disappointment, Dragan has already drunk half a glass of lemonade and is standing.

"Actually, I'm afraid I need to go," he says, checking his pocket watch. I have some business to attend to in town."

"Oh," I say, unable to hide my disappointment.

He sees my smile fall, but doesn't offer any kind of promise or apology. I stand up too and walk him back toward the house, leaving a disgruntled Harriet to gather up the lemonade and tray.

Purchase *Emeline* wherever books are sold.